# THE AUTOBIOGRAPHY OF A
## CHAMPION
# PETER SCUDAMORE

# SCU

## THE AUTOBIOGRAPHY OF A
## CHAMPION

# PETER SCUDAMORE

HEADLINE

*To Maz, Michael and Thomas*

First published in 1993 by
HEADLINE BOOK PUBLISHING

10  9  8  7  6  5  4  3  2  1

British Library Cataloguing in Publication Data

Scudamore, Peter
    Scu: Autobiography of a Champion
    I. Title
    798.4

    ISBN 0 7472 0917 0 (Hardback)

    ISBN 0 7472 7852 0 (Softback)

Book Interior by Design/Section
Illustration reproduction by Koford, Singapore
Printed and bound in Great Britain by
Butler and Tanner Limited, Frome

HEADLINE BOOK PUBLISHING
A division of Hodder Headline PLC
Headline House
79 Great Titchfield Street
London W1P 7FN

# Contents

# *Acknowledgements*

I would like to thank all the many people who helped
and encouraged me in writing this book, in particular my
mother and father, Maz, my secretary Fe Moore,
Monty Court, Sean Magee who compiled the records
pages and Gillian Bromley for her sensitive editing.

# COMING TO THE LAST

————▶◀————

The alarm goes off at six, but as I am riding out at home today there is no need to get up until half-past. After a wash and a shave I wake the boys, Thomas and Michael, who normally leave for school at half-past seven. Michael leaps out of bed and is downstairs a minute later, swearing he has washed and cleaned his teeth and eagerly awaiting his breakfast. Thomas, with luck, will make it down by 7.29, after several calls from Marilyn, by now also angrily up and dressed. They are both hopeless in the mornings.

It's a Wednesday, so I ring Nigel's wife Cathy, who does the riding-out list, to see whether I am riding at the top or the bottom yard, as they are a minute's bicycle ride apart. I then leave Michael alone in the kitchen to his breakfast and drive the mile down to the village shop to collect the morning papers. The back page of the *Daily Telegraph* leads with the story: 'Scudamore: I Quit Today'. After thirteen years of riding as a professional National Hunt jockey, this is to be my last day.

When I got back to the cottage, the kitchen contained two arguing boys; Michael was wearing Thomas's sweater. The phone rang: the voice on the other end said it was Jimmy Tarbuck. I thought it was Alfie Buller with one of his funny phone calls, but no – it was Jimmy Tarbuck, comedian and golf fanatic and somebody I had never met: Congratulations, he said, on a great career; and well done for getting out at the top.

I was flattered – and it dawned on me that today I was going to go through a routine that I had taken for granted all my working life, for the last time. And from then on the phone just went on ringing, with the BBC, ITV, Sky and other stations all wanting interviews. This was the last time that they would want to talk to 'Peter Scudamore, the jockey'. I'll make the most of it, I thought, and enjoy my last day of glory.

Thomas didn't want to go to school; he wanted to watch my last day's racing. Michael wasn't so sure – he doesn't like racing – but after a few minutes' thought he decided that even racing was preferable to school. As for me, I never got to ride out: with three telephones ringing, the house phone and two mobiles, a message was passed to the yard that Marilyn would be riding out without me that morning. Before long I had managed to book myself to do several interviews at the same time and had to ask Fe, my secretary, to come in and sort out the chaos. She wasn't very amused at my choosing this day to retire, when she was trying to shake off the flu: but she rose to the occasion and soon had my schedule sorted out.

The calls from well-wishers kept on coming, with Jack Joseph, Emlyn Hughes and many other owners and friends sending their best wishes for the future. Then it was my turn – the last time I would make the routine call to Martin to discuss the day's runners. Today it was two at Ascot, Grand Hawk and Dagobertin; the discussion was shorter than usual as there was no planning for tomorrow . . .

The next call was to Nigel, and we chatted about the yard's runners for that day: six of them, five at Ascot, where the ground had been made softer by the overnight rain, with the going over hurdles now officially heavy. Sweet Duke, who hadn't been quite level the morning before and had only been passed fit by the vet a few minutes before declaration time, had a burden of twelve stone to carry; but the ground would suit him. Nigel and I discussed the riding plan and decided that with that weight and the going, we would not employ the usual tactics of making all the running.

I always underestimate the time it takes to get from home to Ascot, and this morning, with the constant ringing of the phone, I was late setting off. All the time I was riding, I hated having any distractions from my routine that made me tense before racing. Driving to Ascot this morning I remembered how cross and irritable I had been on an earlier important occasion, heading for Warwick with the aim of breaking Jonjo O'Neill's record total of 149 winners in a season. On that day I had had both my parents, Marilyn and the journalist Dudley Doust in the car with me, surrounding me with small talk while I was trying to focus on the task ahead – racing. At such times, all the problems that affected the running of the household lay a lifetime away on the other side of the immediate business of an afternoon's racing, and my answers to the questions from Marilyn and the boys – 'What time will you be back?', 'What time are you leaving tomorrow?', 'Can you play cricket/rugby/football tonight?' – were very often rude and unsympathetic. To make things worse, Thomas, who studies the racing papers, had also acquired the annoying habit of discussing my chances – and to make matters worse he was often right.

At the jockeys' car park at Ascot the attendant, always so friendly and helpful in the past, signalled for me to park in my lucky spot. This has been a lucky course for me; I have ridden trebles here as well as some prestigious winners, and it was here too that I broke John Francome's career record to score the all-time highest total of any National Hunt jockey.

Today, on top of a barrage of journalists and cameramen wanting photographs and interviews, there were TV crews out to get pieces for the lunchtime news bulletins. The family had been invited by the racecourse to have lunch with Colonel Sir Piers Bengough, the Queen's Representative at Ascot – much to the disgust of Michael, who is never impressed by the constraints of ceremony – so I left them and headed for the weighing room, underneath the main stand. Many of the other jockeys were already changed and weighed out, handing their saddles to the trainers for their mounts in the first race. As I quickly changed, all my mates were wishing me luck, ribbing me for having kept my sudden decision to retire so quiet. The more riding gear I pulled on, the more the reality of the day's racing came home to me. It might be my last day; but I still had responsibilities to Martin and Nigel for my last three rides.

After passing the scales it was back to business as usual, discussing tactics with Jimmy Frost for the first race, a two-and-a-half-mile hurdle. We were both riding front-runners – he had ridden my mount, Grand Hawk, before and knew that he tended to hesitate at the start – and decided that it was pointless for us to slit our own throats by taking each other on too fast in the early part of the race. Then the doorman called for the jockeys to have their silks tied: I stood up, tucked my colours in my breeches, and walked over to Shane, assistant to the valet John Buckingham, who knotted the silk on to my skull cap. There was just time for a trip to the washroom to clean my goggles and check that I looked presentable – and then the final call came for us to go to the paddock.

There were nineteen jockeys for this race, and I set off in front for the 300 yard walk along the front of the stands to the paddock – but with photographers and camera crews out in force, each shouting for me to look his or her way so they could get individual photographs for their papers, plus a stream of requests for autographs, I was soon tailed off. I jogged across the paddock to Martin and touched my hat to Grand Hawk's owners, who were with him, and we finalized riding plans. 'Get a good start,' Martin insisted. The bell rang for jockeys to mount: Grand Hawk was at the other end of the paddock and we struggled to find him in the confusion. When we got to the horse, Martin's travelling head lad had already removed the paddock sheet. I checked my reins and leathers – they are intertwined while the horse is being led round, and you would feel pretty stupid if you fell off in the paddock because they had not been separated. When you are a jockey you soon learn to check for the little things that might go wrong; Sir Gordon Richards' career was ended by a horse rearing over on him in the paddock. On my instructions the horse was walked forward as Martin gave me a leg up, then walked on my off-side, repeating, as he often did, 'You don't need me to tell you your job – but get a good start.'

Grand Hawk followed other horses along the walk to the course. He can be a difficult horse at home; there is nothing nasty about him, but he likes to stop and look around him. Today he lunged on to the course and I had to pull on the right rein with all my strength to prevent him colliding with the rails opposite the exit. He was a bit edgy as we cantered to post; I liked to keep horses settled on the way to the start, and well away from other horses whenever possible, so that they didn't think they were already racing and waste energy.

We showed our mounts the first hurdle. Grand Hawk stared at the high Ascot stand before reluctantly continuing to the start down in Swinley Bottom. We cantered past the other horses already circling at post and stood until Mark Burrows, Grand Hawk's lad, came to lead us up to the start, where the Starter's assistant, former jockey Brian Reilly, checked the girths. Then we were called into line by the Starter, Captain Keith Brown, whose first day's racing this was since the Grand National débâcle. In previous races on Grand Hawk I had got round his tendency to linger at the start by managing to be walking forward when the gate went up; this time it didn't work as the field started to move forwards too early and had to halt again at the tape. I circled Grand Hawk in an attempt to get him moving forward, but when the tape went up he hesitated and I lost precious ground as Jimmy Frost took Cabochon to the front.

Grand Hawk, like Desert Orchid, tends to jump to the right, and as Ascot is a right-handed course I took him down the inside. Although I had missed the break none of the other jockeys had been particularly keen to make the running and we were soon tracking Jimmy, who took us a good gallop until approaching the fifth flight; here he began to ease down the pace and I saw my opportunity to move to the front on the run downhill back into Swinley Bottom. Grand Hawk is a bit of a lazy horse and I had been squeezing him along throughout the race; as we led into the straight with two furlongs to run I asked him to quicken again. Over the second last Richard Dunwoody on Hebridean moved smoothly up to Grand Hawk's quarters; as we made our final effort to the last Richard made a mistake and victory seemed possible – but Grand Hawk didn't jump well and we weakened on the run – in to finish fourth.

The next two races went to the Grange Hill partnership, Indian Tonic and Grange Brake both winning for Nigel, causing me to think that at least the future looked rosy. My second ride of the day was on Dagobertin, a French horse on whom I had finished fourth at Auteuil before winning a novice steeplechase; today he was reverting to hurdling. He had been working particularly well at home and I thought he was my best chance of a winner today but after travelling well to two out he faded and finished seventh.

I weighed out for the last time trying not to show any emotion, trying to think of it as just another race. This became increasingly difficult. Shane wouldn't tie my silk this time as my first two rides had ended in defeat; Andy, another assistant valet, did it instead in an attempt to change the luck. The call to the paddock came, and after a quick check on my appearance I led the jockeys out for the last time, picking my way through the photographers and autograph-hunters again. The applause that greeted my arrival in the paddock brought a lump to my throat. Veronica, who looks after my mount in this race, Sweet Duke, was close to tears. She said the clapping and cheering was for Sweetie. I'm still not sure which of us she meant.

There was more applause from the grandstand as we came out

on to the track to canter to post; I turned in front of the final hurdle and cantered to the start, where I was joined by the rest of the field. The usual discussion took place about who was likely to make the running in this three-mile handicap hurdle; it seemed certain that Jamie Osborne on Prime Display would go on. I lined up on the inside to follow him, determined to ride my last

*Going out for my final ride at Ascot on 7 April 1993, with six fellow jockeys determined to thwart the perfect ending: left to right, Peter Niven, Carl Llewellyn, Mick Fitzgerald, myself, Jamie Osborne, Declan Murphy and Richard Davis (GERRY CRANHAM)*
*(Right) The last flight of all – Sweet Duke with the Alpine Meadow Handicap Hurdle in his grasp (GERRY CRANHAM)*

race as I wanted to be remembered, going round the inside; I also felt as it was my last race I might get a little light.

Sure enough, Jamie and Prime Display led until we came out of Swinley Bottom the second time, and although Sweet Duke raced off the bridle for much of the way I felt he was travelling well, and he was jumping fluently off the heavy ground. When Prime Display faltered at the eighth hurdle I saw my clear run on the inside, and approaching three out we were in front. As we turned into the straight the little horse began to idle and to prick his ears, a sure sign that he was thinking of what was going on around him rather than the race. So I drove at the second last hurdle, not concentrating too much on my stride and realizing as we came to it that he was going to have to stand off a long way or shorten. I sat still to allow him to shorten, but he picked up off a

long stride – which surprised me, but also told me that he had more energy left than I'd thought. We hurtled towards the last, with me trying not to think of the importance of this moment: he got close to it, but flicked over quickly and stayed on dourly to the winning post.

All my other achievements seemed insignificant at that moment. They say you are only as good as your last ride, and it was a marvellous feeling to end on a winner. Brave little Sweet

*(Top) Sweet Duke goes clear... (GEORGE SELWYN)*
*(Above)... and passes the post (GERRY CRANHAM)*

*(Top) After it's all over at Ascot, with Maz, Thomas and Michael, Dad, Mum and Martin Pipe...* (GERRY CRANHAM)
*(Above)... and with the new champion Richard Dunwoody* (GEORGE SELWYN)

Duke and I returned to a tearful Veronica, a welcome from his owner Andy Mavrou and a tremendous reception from the crowd.

Having weighed in for the last time I went back to the winner's enclosure, accompanied by my fellow jockeys, to receive a presentation from Colonel Sir Piers Bengough and Ascot racecourse. After what seemed an age of talking to the press and signing autographs I finally returned to the weighing room to shower and change in time to watch Grange Hill's fifth winner of the afternoon – four here at Ascot and one at Ludlow. Nigel was very cross that I was retiring that day as it meant his achievement hardly got a mention in the papers.

Then home with the family: two sad ones and Michael, who was delighted that he wouldn't have to go racing so often from now on. While Thomas and Marilyn were asking me how much I would miss race-riding, Michael had the last word: 'Daddy, you might look back one day and think that those thirteen years were a waste of time.'

*Chapter One*

# LIKE FATHER . . .

————▶◀————

The accident that put an end to my father's race-riding career, and indirectly set me on the road to mine, happened in a hurdle race at Wolverhampton on 1 November 1966. I can still remember the day. I was standing at the bus stop, waiting to go home from school, when my mother and uncle came to pick me up and told me the news. A horse called Snakestone, which my father was riding for Fred Rimell, had slipped up on the flat on a bend: a horse in front of it had moved off a straight line and he clipped its heels. My father came out of the mêlée with a punctured lung, a broken jaw and cheekbone, a cracked skull and, which was what really put paid to his prospects of racing again, impaired vision in his left eye. He would never pass a medical test to ride in National Hunt races again.

By this time, Dad had been a jockey for sixteen years without breaking a limb. He finished second to Fred Winter in the jockeys' championship in 1954–5; in the 1956–7 season he won the King George VI Chase on Rose Park for Peter Cazalet and the Cheltenham Gold Cup on Linwell for Charlie Mallon, and in 1959 took the Grand National on Oxo, trained by Willie Stephenson. It was ironic that this illustrious career should come to an end on the flat, on a 20–1 outsider in a £340 handicap hurdle; certainly I grew up with no illusions about the unpredictability of a jump jockey's life.

Three weeks later father finally came home from hospital – scarred from the stitching the doctors had done and crowned in plaster of Paris, with his broken jaw and cheekbone supported by wire scaffolding. My sister Nichola, then aged seven, and I, aged nine, were frightened to speak to this Martian-like figure sitting in father's chair in the living room. He was to spend the next three months on liquidized food, because he could not open his mouth; and to top his misery he also later got toothache which could not be attended to.

17

The fall meant major changes not only for him but for the whole family. The atmosphere at home was dominated by the urgent need for father to regain his health and reorganize his life. Now he could no longer make a living as a jockey, he decided to set about building a new career as a trainer – a profession he had

*Racing was in my blood: my father Michael with Oxo, on whom he won the Grand National in 1959*

never considered while riding. As he recuperated, the old dairy farm was gradually transformed into a racing yard: stables were built and gallops laid. As for me, far from putting me off a jockey's life, the accident spurred me on to become a jockey myself; having my father at home with a yard full of racehorses fed my obsession with riding just as it was taking off.

I had learned to ride almost as soon as I could walk. Horses were an integral part of life in the farming community of south Herefordshire where I was brought up. My mother Mary, like my father, had been born and bred in Herefordshire; her father was a director of D. H. Sunderland, a firm of auctioneers and valuers who held livestock sales at many local markets, including Talgarth and Hereford. She had ridden show ponies and hunted as a child, though I can only remember her riding on odd occasions. My home from the day I was born was Prothither, a black-and-white Elizabethan farmhouse set in ninety acres of hilly Herefordshire countryside. The nearest village was Hoarwithy, on the banks of the river Wye between Hereford and Ross. Herefordshire and the bordering counties, an area of countryside both lush and tough, were home to many great families of horsemen and women: the Broomes, Sir Harry Llewellyn and Richard Meade in Monmouth; the Tates and Rimells in Worcestershire; Edward Hide in Shropshire; John Dunlop from South Hereford and the Biddlecombes from Gloucestershire.

My grandfather, Geoffrey Scudamore, was a great character who epitomized the resilience and individuality of the country people two generations ago. He was born and brought up on a farm on the outskirts of Hoarwithy, and passed down many tales of working with the old carthorses. One which always sticks in my mind tells of how one of the farm workers got caught out by a horse. One day the farmer (my grandfather's father) set out to take a day's milking to the local railway station. This task was usually done by a labourer on the farm, who for some reason couldn't do it that day. The carthorses knew their routine so well that they only needed pointing in the right direction and they would do the rest. This was the farm worker's undoing, for on the way home the horse that was pulling the cart turned straight into the yard of the local pub – as he had become used to doing with the labourer, who would call in for a swift half of cider before returning to the farm.

When he was seventeen, my grandfather left home to work in Canada as a logger in Newfoundland. He brought back some marvellous old photographs of Indians and prewar logging machinery that fascinated me as a child. He also became a good card player. Spending three weeks at a time in camp, there was nothing to do at nights except play cards, and so he got plenty of practice.

Back in England, grandfather began to ride in point-to-points. One of the trainers for whom he rode many horses was Wilfred Tate, whose son Martin I was later to ride for. Among the best horses he rode was Sawfish, who was at one time sold for five pounds; the vendor, who thought the horse was unrideable, gave the new owner ten shillings 'luck money'. Sawfish went on to win the Becher Chase at Liverpool and was favourite for the National: unfortunately, that year's race was cancelled because of the war. Grandfather joined the RAF and flew in Halifax bombers until he was shot down and captured. Released from prisoner-of-war camp by the Russians, he then had to escape from them to get back to Western lines. Even in the midst of the fighting, the racing connection persisted: Johnny Bullock, who was to win the 1951 Grand National for Jack O'Donoghue, passed through the same prisoner-of-war camp after being one of the few to survive the battle of Arnhem. The jockeys of that era – Arthur Thompson, who won the 1952 National on Teal when my father was second on Dorothy Paget's Legal Joy, Bryan Marshall (who some say was the best that ever rode), Johnny Bullock – must have been made of stern stuff, returning to racing after the war had taken the best years of their lives.

I spent many happy hours as a child on my grandfather's farm; although I already wanted to be a jockey, it was here that I conceived an alternative ambition. I saw a bulldozer working on the farm one day and decided I would be a bulldozer driver instead. This goal lasted until lunchtime on the same day, when my grandparents told me that to be strong enough to drive a bulldozer I would have to eat the broad beans that my grandmother had cooked. I decided to be a jockey after all.

Mum and Dad would shut me in the back yard on my pony and we would walk about in the enclosed space. Then there were the donkeys that we kept for a while – and it was on a donkey that I earned my first riding fee. After the gymkhanas at the local shows there would be donkey races, and at one of these I was asked to ride one of the best donkeys for a friend of the family, Christine Harding (née Williams). Soon after the start I fell off. I vaulted straight back on, only to land over the other side. Scrambling quickly to my feet, I chased round the circuit in vain pursuit as the donkey beat me to the line. For this performance I won ten shillings.

One of the donkeys, plus twenty pounds, was swapped by my father for a grey pony, Bobby, whom I rode for a time. I had no control over him: I remember many times cantering up a hill away from home and then a minute later hurtling back down towards the gate. Sometimes we would go out with the racehorses on to the gallops. On one such occasion, having cantered to the top with no trouble, I decided to canter back down. Bobby was soon running away with me and I pulled him into the cornfield alongside. There was a ledge between the gallop and the corn, and as it was early June the corn was quite high: the ledge tripped Bobby up and the next moment we were both lying in the corn looking at each other. He never ran away with me again.

It was Bobby's recalcitrance in the show-jumping ring that led to my acquiring my next pony. We were at the Ross Harriers Hunt Show for my first show-jumping competition off the leading rein, and as I entered the ring the commentator introduced me as the son of the great Michael Scudamore, winner of the Grand National and the Gold Cup. We set off for the first fence, where Bobby proceeded to refuse three times. This disaster persuaded my father to buy a pony for me from Terry Biddlecombe's father Walter. Black Opal, named after a good horse Dad trained in Norway, was a wonderful pony for a child to have, as he would jump huge fences in comparison to his size. That sealed my fate. I started to enjoy riding more and yearned to be a jump jockey.

There was a lot more to 'Black' than riding, however: first you had to find him. He would jump out of a stable if the top door was not shut, even if the lower door was so high that he had to put his neck at full stretch to look out; he had a little piece of his bottom lip missing where he had once landed on his head while escaping. Or you would go out to his field in the morning and he would not be there, having moved himself to another field. Often as we lay in bed at night we would hear the sound of his hooves as he took himself down the garden to the vegetable patch in pursuit of carrots. Sometimes he would disappear off the farm for as long as three or four days; eventually, however, he would come back. Having found him, the next problem was catching him; it could take most of the yard staff to round him up, plus vehicles parked in front of the gates to stop him jumping into the road and away.

He was worth the effort, though. We had a lot of fun show-jumping and in hunter trials, but he was really in his element out hunting. There were two local packs, the Ross Harriers and the South Herefordshire Foxhounds. In the 1966–7 season, after his accident, my father hunted the Harriers for a short time and Black and I went with him. This was the time of the foot-and-mouth disease epidemic, and hunting was restricted, along with all other movement of livestock, but despite the reduced number of days we had a great time; the Harriers were a fun pack, followed by country people enjoying themselves, and a young horse-mad lad like myself with a good pony couldn't have wished for a better time.

One of the most memorable of the local hunting characters was Robert Oakell, a solicitor in Ross-on-Wye. In his formal, Edwardian office Robert would sit behind the oak table that served as his desk, dressed immaculately in formal, Edwardian stiff collar and tie – except that on a Tuesday or a Friday, the days on which the Harriers met, if you looked under the table you would see his lower half kitted out in breeches and boots. Robert was a short man, with round arms, legs, stomach, face and glasses and, out hunting, a round bowler hat. He rode a roan cob with a hogged mane that always seemed to go through hedges rather than over them. To get to the meet he drove an old black Rover towing a trailer; all in all he was more akin to Jorrocks than any other man I have ever met.

They tell me that I wasn't a real hunting man because I hunted to ride, whereas Robert rode to hunt. 'Black' was the best conveyance a boy could have across country. He adored his days out hunting and would charge along as fast as his little legs would carry him. He hated waiting at gates, and as soon as some kind person had opened one he would be first through ahead of the field. Fortunately for me, with the relaxed atmosphere of this country pack and my father hunting the hounds, etiquette was not as strict as it might have been, and I was allowed to jump hedges in front of the Master. Father's advice to me as I set off used to be 'Don't jump anything you can't see over.' I remember once ignoring this wise principle only to sail over a hedge and collapse on the other side because of the drop.

I also hunted with the South Herefordshire Foxhounds. The Master was Harold Thompson, a great friend of the family who had grown up with my father and his brother, my Uncle Handley. As well as a hunting man, he was an accomplished amateur jockey, winning the National Hunt Chase at the Cheltenham Festival in 1960. Harold was always very kind to me out hunting, and at times would ask Black and me to give him a lead over a hedge his horse had stopped at. His father, Ray Thompson, was Master of the Wye Valley Otter Hounds and

Ross Harriers, and had kept the pack going during the war, buoying up the spirit of the south Herefordshire farming community when many of the young men had gone away to fight. The days hunting with Ray were legendary among the older generation.

My childhood was not spent entirely in the hunting field, however. The rural and equestrian paradise of south Herefordshire was regularly interrupted by school. My mother is a Roman Catholic and so I was given a Catholic education, first at a prep school near Monmouth, Llanarth Court, then at Belmont Abbey, a Benedictine monastery at Hereford. Both were boarding schools. I have no horror stories to tell about either of them, being as happy as I could expect to be anywhere away from the farm and the horses. I had many friends and played most sports to a reasonable level; but I always wanted to be riding, and ultimately to be riding races. When I was asked to write an essay on what I would be doing in fifteen years' time, I started it: 'I have been Champion Jockey for the last five years.' Outside, I would pick up a stone and aim it at a pillar or post, saying: 'If I hit that I will win the National/the Champion Hurdle.' With hindsight, I am grateful for my education, even though I chafed against it at the time; it was certainly a great help in my career.

One teacher in particular at prep school was a help in getting through termtime away from the racing business. This was Mr Ray Reardon, a Yorkshireman then in his mid-fifties: short, with a well lived-in face, short, pushed back grey hair and sharp, twinkling eyes that gave away his sense of humour. He would give me the racing results some afternoons, and I would try to give him some tips. He coached the rugby first fifteen and although a heavy smoker was a fit-looking man. He was also very strict, but although we all went in considerable awe of him he was very well liked and respected. For some reason, he was given the nickname 'Daphne'.

The school was in an old mansion, supposed to be haunted. The classrooms were in the converted stables, and in front of these was a concrete path, on which, between classes, Daphne would pause to roll a cigarette. Having taken the last precious drags on the roll-up, he would then put it out by throwing it onto the path and shuffling his feet on it. At this sound his next class would stand in silence awaiting his entrance. A joker among us could make a whole class rise to its feet in silence simply by shuffling his feet outside the door.

'Daphne' taught us French, Latin and maths, the three subjects I hated most. He would stand on the desk and stamp his foot to the beat as we chanted Latin or French verbs; he used to keep a piece of chalk in his mouth as a substitute cigarette, and if you weren't concentrating it would be sent winging at your head. He ruled his class with the aid of his 'tickler', a metre-long ruler with which he would beat us on the hands if our work was wrong or slipshod. Sometimes the whole class would be lined up for this treatment, which was at least leavened by his sense of humour: one day, when six boys had been pulled out of the class for misbehaviour or bad work, he hit the first three but sent the fourth, who was just recovering from measles, to sit down, saying, 'I don't want to infect my tickling stick.' He then continued with his 'tickler' on the last two boys.

Sometimes that sense of humour saved us all. One afternoon, after rugby practice, we had Latin followed by maths and French – 'triple Daphne'. We were milling around the desks when one boy, coming in late, said loudly: 'Oh my God, not triple Daphne!' What none of us realized was that for once Daphne had come in without shuffling, somehow materializing at the blackboard with his back to us. There was a horrified silence, then Daphne said: 'That name is *strictly* for the angels.'

*Chapter Two*

# 'THE AMATEUR IN THE HOUSE'

————▸◄————

With the cattle sheds and pigsties of the old farm transformed into stables, Prothither was now a thriving racing yard, humming with the activity of horses and lads, owners visiting, father keeping it all together – and, in school holidays, me, running round getting under everyone's feet but fatally bitten by the racing bug.

Since my father's accident and his change of career we had naturally seen much more of each other. I wasn't taken racing very often when he was riding, but now when he had runners at the races I would often go with him. From humble beginnings the standard of inmates rose steadily over the years, and with the horses came the results: the Grand Annual Steeplechase at Cheltenham with Fortina's Palace in 1970, and in 1974 the Mackeson Gold Cup with Bruslee and third place in the Grand National with Charles Dickens. Some of our horses also won renown for exploits other than winning races: Shore Captain, running at Worcester, fell in the race and then galloped into the river which runs right beside the course, from where he was eventually rescued.

Perhaps the greatest character we had in the yard then was a wilful old horse called O'Krieve. Like my pony Black Opal, he was a bit difficult to keep in his stable; if the lad forgot to fasten the bottom bolt on the door, he would undo the top one with his teeth and wander off outside to pick grass. He was also quite headstrong: I used to ride him at exercise on the roads, and it would take all my strength to keep him under control. Once we had turned for home he would be jogging impatiently, and not all the pulling in the world from me made the slightest difference.

O'Krieve had manners when he chose to show them, however. One day he was taken out by mistake by a visiting lady owner whose horse Waveney, another chestnut trained by my father, looked similar to O'Krieve. Mrs Taylor was in the habit of coming to ride her horse side-saddle in the summer breaks; arriving one day for a hack without telling anyone in the yard, she tacked up the wrong chestnut. O'Krieve looked after her impeccably and Mrs Taylor never knew her mistake.

We had a good bunch of lads at Prothither. Many of them were learning to ride and most of them wanted to be jockeys, but they didn't always want to take the good advice they were given by my father and the more experienced staff. In particular, some would ride with their leathers far too short for safety, and one of these, Jock, was always getting into trouble with father for this reason. He was eventually cured of his bravado by an accident. We used to stand the horses in the river after exercise as the running water was good for their legs, and one day while we were doing this the horse Jock was on unexpectedly stepped sideways to steady himself against the current. Jock, with his knees somewhere near his chin as usual, lost his balance; he hung on for fear of falling into the water, but what with the current of the river and his rider hanging over sideways, the horse lost his balance and fell over, and as it scrambled up it trod on Jock. He was very close to being drowned, but he let his leathers down after that.

Sometimes it was their cars, not their horses, that got the lads into trouble. Like stable lads everywhere, they were always hard up, and some of them would turn up in the most extraordinary vehicles. Andrew Younghusband came to work for us at one time, driving an old red postman's van. In his afternoon break he went shopping in Hereford, leaving the van parked on a double yellow line in the High Street. Unfortunately, when he went to start the van again, it wouldn't go, and he had to get a lift back to the yard for evening stables, thinking he would somehow collect the van later on. When he went back for it later that night, however, he found the street cordoned off by the police, who suspected his old van contained a bomb.

Though I worked in the yard in my school holidays I was never very interested in getting involved in the training set-up: what I wanted to do was ride, and for all the marvellous times I had with Black Opal and the other ponies, I couldn't wait to get on the racehorses. Thoroughbreds, with all their scope and power, are very different from even the boldest ponies, and the change took more getting used to than I was initially prepared to

admit. The first horse on which I rode a canter was called
Birchwood, the most docile of racehorses; I was convinced that I
would have no trouble holding him. I was put at the back of the
string and instructed where to go and where to pull up, with a
warning to be careful of a pale slab of rock in the hedge where
the canter came to an end, which sometimes spooked the horses.

Before I had gone a furlong Birchwood had overtaken most of
the other horses. I managed to pull up in one piece; then father,
who always rode out with the string, came up behind me and his
horse shied at the stone in the hedge, tipping him off to howls of
laughter from me. I had a lot to learn, not only about riding
racehorses, but about diplomacy, charm and good manners –
qualities that at times are just as necessary to a successful jockey
as the ability to hold a puller.

Not all the diplomacy in the world would have persuaded my
mother that I should become a jockey. Despite having been a
capable horsewoman herself and being married to a top jump
jockey, she was always against the idea; while she had trusted my
father to know what he was doing, she felt that I was too reckless
and likely to come to grief. So while father, who said that if he
had his time again he would still be a jockey, was quite happy for
me to decide for myself and to help me if I decided I did want to
make race-riding my career, mother lost no opportunity to try to
point me in other directions. From the time I started riding out
on father's racehorses at the age of thirteen she was very nervous,
and as I was determined not to be deflected from my chosen path
we had frequent arguments. I didn't consider race-riding more
than remotely dangerous, and used to find these battles
increasingly frustrating; at one stage I was even on the point of
leaving home before my father calmed me down.

In 1975, after five years of riding out and schooling at home
during the holidays, I finally persuaded my parents to get me a
ride in a Flat race. My mount was to be Stellemon, a filly they
had bred themselves, in a seven-furlong race at Leicester on 18
August. (Ironically, while Mum worried about my getting hurt
on the racecourse, Stellemon did me far more harm on the
ground: she was a real little madam, and kicked me while I was
grooming her at home. I have been very wary of horses being
free with their legs in the stable ever since.) A race over seven
furlongs takes no time at all and, complete novice that I was,
everything happened far too fast for my brain to take account of

any riding instructions; all the advice that my father had given me beforehand was forgotten until I was past the finishing post. My legs fared no better than my brain: when I dismounted in the enclosure for the 'also-rans' they were so tired that I nearly fell over.

However undistinguished that first outing, it whetted my appetite for race-riding, and it was only half-heartedly that I returned to Belmont Abbey in September to work for my 'A' levels in Medieval History and British Constitution. Why I chose two such obscure subjects still baffles me. There was no question of my leaving early, however; my mother was still not reconciled to my riding ambitions and both my parents were determined that I should complete my education so that I would be equipped to earn a living outside racing if I needed to. On reflection, however grudging about it I was at the time, it did me good to stay at school for those two last years. Apart from the benefits later in my career of a good education, and the discipline it instilled in me, this period gave me time to mature – particularly necessary in my case as up to now I had no experience of working away from home. I would not have been ready to go into an outside racing yard.

The school, in fact, was very sympathetic towards my passion for riding. My next aim was to get some rides in the local point-to-points, and the headmaster, Father Mark Jabalé, who was also the British rowing coach, and was particularly supportive of my ambitions, came to watch my first point-to-point ride, at Belmont, in view of the Abbey grounds, on Saturday 10 April 1976, during the spring term of my last year at school. Mine was the Members' Race, and Milford Boy was the unfortunate beast that had the dubious pleasure of looking after me. I was already a legend in my own mind, something of a cross between Fred Winter and Lester Piggott, with no time for my father's good advice about sitting still, not picking up my stick, and not riding too short.

I had good company in the race; among the other jockeys were three local friends, Ivor Johnston, a local farmer, John Chinn, whom I knew from the Pony Club, and John Williams, who rode out at home and is now Clerk of the Course at Hereford. They all looked after me on the way round, shouting hints across at me, but jumping the second last I was getting too excited to listen, and rode at the last fence as if it wasn't there. John cruised by with a last vain adjuration to sit still, I went one, two, three, up, the horse went four, and I was deposited on the floor right in front of the friends, family and headmaster who had turned out to watch my debut over fences. They left the races convinced that they had seen a young man who would *not* be following in his father's footsteps.

My mother hadn't watched any of this; she had 'gone for a smoke' (she doesn't smoke) in the ladies' loo, a habit she did not realize at the time she was going to have to get used to. She would say in later years that she worried about me riding far more than about my father, as she felt that he knew what he was doing. I was certainly very impetuous at this time and wanted to run before I could walk, but the dreadful beginning to my jump racing career made even me realize that I wasn't as good as I thought I was. When I asked my father how he thought I had done, he said: 'If you had been riding for a major yard, you would probably never be given another ride.'

Perseverance was the answer. I rode under National Hunt Rules for the first time nine days after the Belmont disaster, on 19 April at Chepstow on a horse called Jack de Lilo, trained by my father for Derrick Crossman, a friend of the family whom I had known since early childhood. This time the partnership finished intact, and in fourth place. Things were looking up.

In my own view, they were looking up even more when I finished school and, with my two peculiar 'A' levels under my belt, began work in the stables at home in earnest. Now, I

*At Belmont Abbey, looking as fashionable as was allowed at school, with headmaster Father Mark Jabalé*

thought, I would be a fully fledged jockey in no time. Father was in a difficult position: he wanted to give me a few rides, but quite understandably not many of his owners wanted to waste the training fees they were paying by having a novice like me put up on their horses. It is the same for all jockeys starting out: nobody wants to give you rides when you have no experience, and you can't get the experience without the rides. Still, there were always the point-to-points, where I was beginning to get a ride or two, gaining valuable practice over fences and learning the ropes of jump racing out of the limelight. Point-to-pointing, with its large fields and variety of abilities in both jockeys and horses, can be more dangerous than riding under National Hunt Rules, but father saw to it that the rides I did have were safe. I didn't really appreciate this at the time, but he was quite right: all you get from poor horses is hurt, and bad habits. Later on, as I got to ride more of my father's horses, he put me up on some very good schoolmasters, such as Steady Gaze – horses from which a young jockey could learn a lot about riding steeplechases. The power of racehorses enables them to stand off from their fences much further than you first imagine, and it took me several rides to adapt to riding over regulation fences.

As the point-to-pointing season went on, I decided I had to give up my rugby. I had played in the school team with some success and was now playing for my local town, Ross-on-Wye, and thoroughly enjoying it, but apart from the problem of clashing fixture dates, there was the risk of getting injured and not being able to ride.

Among my point-to-pointing contemporaries was Nigel Twiston-Davies, a friend from Pony Club days – I remember him coming racing with father and me when I was in my teens – and later my business partner and a successful trainer in the Cotswolds. Nigel still reminds me that he 'stuck me in for' my first spare point-to-point ride, and as he was usually to be seen during the season walking round in plaster, with teeth missing and black eyes acquired when running into wire or riding a horse that had 'never seen a fence before', I must have been a very brave man to take one of his cast-offs.

We had both been a bit wild in the Pony Club: our first encounter was just after a mid-morning break at camp when we decided to race our ponies back to our riding instructor. We were severely reprimanded by the District Commissioner and were very lucky not to be packed off home. Perhaps the fact that the camp was taking place on Nigel's father's farm had something to do with our getting off relatively lightly.

This farm, the Mynde, which bordered on my grandfather's land, had been built up by Nigel's father into one of the most efficient agricultural set-ups in the area, with a mixture of arable and stock. The main house is an impressive building, reached at the end of a two-mile private drive up which Nigel and I learned to drive in his old and much-loved Austin A40. I have no mechanical sense, whereas Nigel prides himself on his understanding of machines. Our friendship was severely stretched in its early days when on one occasion I put the gear stick into reverse from third while still moving forward, and the gear stick snapped off in my hand. Still, Nigel had some trouble himself with cars on this drive: one day, while driving a vehicle recently acquired by his sister Penelope over a cattle grid, he bounced the engine out of the chassis. He also had to learn to drive the Land Rover and trailer in which the ponies were taken around to hunter trials and Pony Club events, because his mother, who ferried him and Penelope around while they were young, could not reverse the trailer and if they met oncoming traffic in a narrow lane she had to ask the approaching driver to do it for her.

By the time I got going in point-to-points Nigel was already riding winners under Rules: one of his successful rides was Emperor's Gift, later to become the dam of the great Mrs Muck. At last, on 30 April 1977, I won my first point-to-point on Monty's Reward, owned by Herbie Sharpe, at Mucklestone in Staffordshire. I have an old newspaper cutting about the race, which says, 'in the Men's Open 18-year-old Peter Scudamore had his first ever winner, and although his task was made easier by Entertainment's mistake two fences out, it was a creditable performance to hold off John Docker's renewed challenge'.

After the point-to-point season was over, I continued my racing education by going to work for Willie Stephenson. This was to be a kind of trial period; so far I had not worked for anyone other than my father and he sensibly thought that a spell in another yard might sort out whether I was really serious about a racing career – and also show whether I was likely to have the ability.

Going to Willie Stephenson was jumping in at the deep end.

*My first taste of riding winners. Monty's Reward wins the Men's Open at the Meynell Point-to-Point in Staffordshire on 30 April 1977*

Not only had he trained Oxo, on whom my father won the Grand National in 1959, he had also trained a Derby winner – Arctic Prince in 1951, ridden by Charlie Spares. Vincent O'Brien was the only other man living to have trained a winner of both races. Willie was also a director of Doncaster Bloodstock Sales and owned Gibson, the Newmarket saddlers, as well as farming and training in Royston, Hertfordshire. My father used to tell me that he was a great man to ride for and would always stand by him in front of owners if a dispute arose. But he was also a hard man, and along with most other people I was petrified of him. It's just as well that his bark was worse than his bite, because he could certainly bark. He used to speak with a slight stutter and at a fairly high pitch: it sounds comical, but in fact it was simply frightening.

I had heard reams of stories about Willie, but none of them prepared me for the experience of working for him. By this time he was an old man, so I had it soft compared with those who went before me. Whatever Willie ordered, you did, no questions: but this wasn't always easy, as he tended to speak in riddles. He would say that the worms were playing him up, which meant that he was hungry; or that he was going for a swim, which meant taking a bath. One evening he told me that there were three white pheasants in the garden and that I was to get his gun and shoot them. Now, I knew that there were no white pheasants anywhere in the garden, but you didn't argue with Willie. Off I went with the gun in pursuit of three phantoms.

I lived in the house, along with Willie's wife and two of his five daughters; we all got on very well, and it was certainly more comfortable than the lads' digs, but I didn't get any more peace as a result. Willie was perpetual motion itself, and some of the lads were less than helpful to 'the amateur living in the governor's house'. However, Dennis Ryan, who was head lad when I arrived, was very good to me and helped me all he could; and Sean Keightley, one of the yard's apprentices, has been a friend of mine ever since. Sean was very brave, even in those days before he started riding in races. On one occasion, while he and I were riding out third lot on two-year-olds, he took his horse into a field past which we were walking and schooled him over a small box hedge.

Yet however tough it was, I learnt more in my six months with Willie than in all my years at school. Many good jockeys had been through the mill with Willie and benefited from his expertise and experience: Bruce Raymond and Dennis Ryan, both his sons-in-law, were apprenticed at Royston, as was Des Cullen, who used to ride work on Oxo. When I arrived Willie Ryan, the governor's grandson and now a successful Flat jockey, was just starting to ride out.

I used to go to the yard at six every morning to muck out. I had three horses to look after, one of which, Crazy Harvest, was a really sour old horse, always trying to kick and bite, and his legs had to be bandaged for exercise. One morning I must have been too busy avoiding his teeth and heels to tie the bandages properly as one came off; luckily only Dennis saw, and I was able to put it back on before Willie arrived.

I learnt from the older staff of the yard as well as from Willie and Dennis. One useful tip given to me by an old stager was how to stay secure on a horse that was liable to whip round with you suddenly: namely, not to fight it, but to drop your hands on to its neck, holding a piece of mane or the neckstrap. Apart from being more likely to settle the horse than wrestling with it with your hands in the air, this trick kept your centre of balance low and thus made it much easier for you to stay in the plate.

Willie owned a farm as well as a training yard, and some of

our afternoons were spent rounding up cattle, either to de-horn them or administer injections, or to load them into the lorry to go to market. The loading bay had a pond next to it and some of the lads spent more time trying to get at least one of the beasts in the pond than getting the lorry loaded. Then later in the afternoon it was back to the horses for evening stables. This was the most relaxed time of day (apart from my efforts to escape the effects of Crazy Harvest's ill-temper); all the horses were brushed down, checked over, watered and given their hay before the evening feeds went round. The yard had a great history, and although by this time it was in its twilight years, there was still a shared sense of pride attached to working in the establishment where Oxo, Arctic Prince and Sir Ken, three times winner of the Champion Hurdle, had been trained.

My evenings were generally spent either driving Willie to meet someone, or chopping logs. Many times I would fall asleep sitting on the log-pile; but there was no chance of sleep in the car. I never worked out which was worse, driving Willie around or being driven by him. If I drove, he would forever be telling me 'G-g-go on, we haven't got all day,' and 'G-g-go on, overtake, there's a g-g-gap,' or, if I failed to go for a slender gap between oncoming vehicles, 'You'll never make a jockey!' When he drove, it was if anything more nerve-racking. He never used first gear; you could feel the strain on the clutch every time he moved off. Once on the road, everybody else was in the wrong. Turning right into the yard one day, he pulled across in front of an on-coming car, which screeched to a halt, the driver hurling obscenities at him. Willie wound the window down, remonstrating: 'What's the matter with you, I've got my arrows out, haven't I?' He obviously believed that having indicated, he was quite in order to claim right of way to cut across the road. The other driver subsided, driving off with a face as white as mine in the passenger seat.

Willie's driving may have been erratic, but on racing and jockeyship he was a mine of wisdom. He had been a Flat race jockey himself until breaking his leg; after recovering he tried jump riding but had no taste for it. I learnt a huge amount from listening to him telling me about the great jockeys of the past and their qualities and skills – about Tim Molony, Bryan Marshall and my own father. He gave me advice about riding style and tactics, about use of the whip, about changing hands. He told me, too, about training Arctic Prince to win the Derby, and how he had backed Joe McGrath's horse after one of the favourites for that year's race, another Irish colt, had come over to work on the Royston gallops with Arctic Prince; Joe McGrath's horse came out so much the better that Willie knew they were in with a chance. Like many racing men, he could be superstitious; he thought (as does Martin Pipe) that green was an unlucky colour – and yet he won both the Derby and the National with horses carrying green colours.

It was not until later in my career that I rode winners for Willie, but during the six months I spent at Royston in 1977-8 he gave me two rides. On one of these I had to do nine stone seven, way below my normal riding weight now; but with the work and the anxiety my weight had dropped to nine stone one pound, the lowest I can ever remember it being as an adult, so this was not a problem. The second outing was on Cara's Trump at Market Rasen, and this time I really should have won; but I held up the horse for too long and the winner got away, leaving us running on in second place. Sean Keightley never tires of reminding me that he won on the horse a few days later.

Willie came to the conclusion that I wasn't tough enough to make a jockey, that what I should be aiming at was making good money, and that estate agency was a fairly easy way to do this. Willie at full steam was an irresistible force, and before I knew what was happening, he had introduced me to Michael Haydon, a senior partner in Bernard Thorpe's estate agency, and arranged for me to go and work for him in Stow-in-the-Wold the next autumn. This seemed quite a good idea at the time, especially as I thought it would make me rich; but though I could see the advantage in having a job to fall back on if I needed to, Willie's assessment of my character hadn't put me off and I still intended to become a professional jockey as soon as I could.

My last piece of work for this great man was escorting a batch of horses to the Doncaster Sales, a trip combined on the way home with a ride for my father at Catterick. Father had a filly running in an amateurs' race which he thought she should win, as it looked a pretty moderate affair on paper. Tony Dickinson won the race with a horse that had never tackled hurdles before: it was called Silver Buck, and went on to win the 1982 Cheltenham Gold Cup.

Back home I set about getting as many rides as I could in point-to-points and hunter chases. I had a lot of help from Lionel Ensten, whose horse Greektown, trained by Willie, won the Cotswold Chase at Cheltenham (now the Arkle) first time over fences. This horse had a reputation for standing a long way off his fences – father thought because he was frightened of them. Having the benefit of my father's judgement and past experience was a great asset to me when I was riding, as thinking about what he had to say about horses helped me to work them out for myself. Lionel Ensten kept his point-to-pointers up in Leicestershire, where they got good hunting and preparation and were always very fit and well trained for the races. Through Lionel I got to ride at some very good point-to-point tracks, such as Lincoln, Cottenham and Garthorpe. It was at Cottenham that Toby Balding first noticed me riding, something that was to have a very important impact on my racing career.

I was also beginning to ride father's horses more often. One Bank Holiday at Hereford I had a ride on Steady Gaze in the same race as Peter Duggins, who often rode for Dad and was booked for several races that afternoon. During the race in which we were both riding, Peter's horse slipped up on a bend and he came off, hitting his head on a concrete post. Luckily he was not seriously hurt, but the incident put an end to his rides that afternoon. Father had taken another group of runners elsewhere, so my mother was in charge of the yard's contingent at Hereford: the rest of the programme passed in turmoil, with me trying to get on as many of father's runners as possible and mother trying to persuade their owners to put up another jockey.

I had a great time point-to-pointing; along with hunting it is both a lot of fun and very good experience for a would-be steeplechase jockey. Altogether I rode five winners in point-to-points – one of them, it is true, resulting from the disqualification of the horse first past the post: jockeys are allowed to weigh in a pound lighter than they weigh out, and the connections had intended to take one pound of lead out of the weight-cloth, but accidentally took two out, giving me the race. In racing you have to get used to benefiting from other people's misfortune . . .

## Chapter Three

# GATHERING PACE

In September 1978 I became an estate agent. Needing a base near my new job in the office of Bernard Thorpe and Partners in Stow-on-the-Wold, I moved into Maugersbury Manor – or, more exactly, a room in it. My new home had no telephone, a shared bath and a hole in the window through which the snow came in during the winter; it didn't seem that the 'easy life' that Willie had envisaged me having as an estate agent was going to materialize straight away. I wasn't too bothered: my sights were still firmly set on racing. At least Richard Hurley, the head of the office, could understand my ambitions: he was a farmer who kept point-to-pointers as well as a partner in the firm, and was married to the sister of racing trainer Willie Musson. But although this might seem a sensible way to combine a lucrative career with a lively interest in racing, I could never see myself as the kind of amateur jockey who rides for fun while having a 'proper job' to pay the bills. I thought it might be useful to have some kind of other work experience to fall back on if racing didn't work out, but that was as far as it went.

It's probably just as well that I never had to make a career of estate agency as I don't think I had much flair for it. Most of my duties were fairly humdrum: licking stamps, making coffee and taking For Sale signs down (or, more often, forgetting to). My most responsible task was keeping the petty cash box in order. I wasn't let loose on clients very often and on one occasion when I was I nearly caused havoc. I had been showing a man round a cottage in the nearby village of Lower Slaughter, and quoted him a lower rental than was advertised; when he discovered the true amount he looked like having to spend Christmas with his family on the streets. I never did find out what happened to him.

The best thing about Stow, as it turned out, was its proximity to Condicote, where David Nicholson trained. My father, who was an old friend of 'the Duke' – I had been page boy at his wedding – had arranged for me to go and ride out there, and throughout the 1978–9 season I would make the ten-minute drive out to Condicote every day before work. To me, that was the real business of the day: back in the office at Stow, I was just filling in time between getting off one horse and getting on another.

David Nicholson and my father had ridden together many times, and I had watched him frequently over the years; I had been at Hereford races when he had his last ride on Lord Vestey's What A Buck. However, I used to try to avoid meeting him on the racecourse; while I must have been presentable enough on our earliest acquaintance, in my teens he was always telling me to get a haircut. Looking at old photos of myself in seventies-style floppy hair, flared trousers and platform soles, I think he might have had a point. My father certainly thought so.

David was known as a disciplinarian of the old school, a reputation in part inherited from his father, the legendary Frenchie Nicholson. Frenchie, for whom my father rode Irish Lizard into third place in the 1954 Grand National, produced some of the greatest jockeys of the modern age from his Cheltenham yard, including among others Pat Eddery, Paul Cook and Walter Swinburn. Similarly, young jockeys who spent time with David Nicholson could learn a great deal that would stand them in good stead in their careers – Graham McCourt, Peter Niven and David Bridgwater are among those many good National Hunt jockeys who started at Condicote before moving on to other yards. What is more, you didn't just learn how to ride racehorses: you learnt how to conduct yourself according to the old-fashioned code of the profession.

Mindful of these matters, and mindful too of the fact – which I had learned for myself at Willie Stephenson's – that an amateur, and worse still an amateur with ambitions, was not likely to be the most welcome arrival in any yard, I made sure I arrived at the Duke's in good order, with neatly cut hair and clean jodhpur boots, and on time – a principle I would stick to throughout my career.

In fact, though I met with a certain amount of hostility from some of the younger lads, who felt I was taking their opportunities to ride, the more senior riders were very good to me. John Suthern, Robin Dickin, Roy Mangan, Paul Carvill and Allen Webb were regulars at the yard then and Jeff King was the retained jockey. Allan Haycock, inevitably nicknamed Strawballs, who at first dismissed me as a useless amateur who prevented him from getting rides, mellowed later and we became good friends – he would even sometimes ask my advice about his point-to-point rides. In any case, there was no point in anyone being standoffish for long; after all, you need to have a few laughs and a bit of fellow feeling to be able to cope with the constant misfortunes of a jump jockey's life.

Take a wet winter's afternoon at Leicester, for example, with the never-ending stream of moderate novice chasers to ride that such meetings always seem to throw up – about as close to sheer hard work as steeplechase riding can get. It was on one such day that Suthern, Dicko, Webby and I shared a lift to the course. Dicko had a spare ride on a fourteen-year-old in the novice chase: 'Surely,' he said hopefully, knowing nothing about the horse, 'he must have a little bit of sense at fourteen?' 'You're thirty, and you haven't,' was the helpful reply. Poor Dicko had a dreadful fall in that race and ended up in hospital – where I followed him for an X-ray on a cracked wrist after being brought down on the flat. We both returned to the racecourse to find John Suthern moaning that he had missed two winners on rides he could have had at the day's other meeting. This left Webby the only one of us in any sort of good mood, and this was soon quenched when Suthern sat down on a towel containing his false teeth. They cost eighty pounds to be repaired.

Apart from the top few, jockeys are always skint, and as a poorly paid office junior and amateur rider I was no exception. This makes another good reason for getting on with the others around you: you are constantly needing to share lifts to the races. Indeed, one of the advantages of being in a yard with quite a few jockeys is that there are more lifts to be had. My conveyance was a rusty maroon Hillman Avenger, in which on one occasion it was my turn to ferry Allen Webb, Richard Evans and John Suthern to Fontwell races, a drive of about two and a half hours from base. We had only got as far as Wantage when the car conked out because of worn points. Fortunately, we had ground to a halt quite near a garage, and although they couldn't mend the car on the spot, they did offer to hire us another one – until they found out we were jockeys on the way to the races. The insurance, it seemed, would not cover us. Now at last my official profession came into its own: I managed to convince the garage owner that I was not a jockey but an estate agent, and moreover that I would drive very slowly there and back. (That garage owner, incidentally, is now Richard Dunwoody's father-in-law.) Once out of sight I drove flat out – but still failed to get to Fontwell in time for John's ride in the first. That apart, the day went safely, all of us and the car arrived back in Wantage intact, and I collected my old Avenger, now in perfect running order, for the drive home.

To make things up to John Suthern for his missed ride, I said I would drive him to Taunton the next day. Some good turn this was! About a mile from the motorway the old car let me down again, but after some fiddling with the points we managed to get as far as Taunton town centre – where we broke down once more. We had with us in the car Nigel Wakley, a local trainer who had begged a lift to the same meeting, and he kindly organized for a garage to get us to the course, at the same time wisely arranging another lift home for himself. John and I got to the races in good time and both rode winners – which was just as well, because we needed all the good humour we could get to see us through the ten times we broke down on the way home. I did not belong to the AA or the RAC, and I had no spanners, torch or any instrument that could be the slightest use to us; despite the kindness of horsebox drivers, members of the public and even the AA as we limped on to the hard shoulder of the motorway, the car eventually gave up for good in the middle of Cheltenham at midnight. Allen Webb came to our rescue.

Never mind getting to the races, even getting to the yard to ride out in the morning could be an obstacle course. One morning I tried to bump start the car by running it down the nearest hill. This failed, so I left it there and hitched a lift to Condicote. Later that morning my father had a phone call from Stow police to say that a car registered in his name had been stolen and left at the bottom of Stow hill.

Condicote was run on well-established traditional lines. In that early autumn of 1978 when I arrived, the horses were doing their road work: for three weeks after they came in at the end of their summer break they were walked and trotted around the Cotswold hills, to clear their wind and start gradually building their muscles up before the faster work began. First lot pulled out of the yard at half-past seven, when the whole string would parade round a large roundabout, known as the 'pound', in front of the house. Here each horse and jockey was inspected by the Duke before being sent off to its work. David rode out every morning, usually on the now retired What A Buck, from whose back he would deliver his orders. There were three roads leading off the pound, each of which took the horses off on a different exercise. I dreaded being in front, as I never knew where I was going and when orders were given to go round 'Dartnell's' or 'Scott's' I was always afraid I would go down the wrong path. After their work, whenever the weather allowed, the horses were unsaddled and led out for a pick of grass in a paddock near the stables. They would then be sent in one by one. This time I was always hoping to be called in first, as I was always pushed for time to get to the office.

Once the horses had done their stint on the roads they were ready to start cantering. For this we used a four-furlong all-weather strip along the side of one of the grass gallops. Here the horses did steady canters until the autumn rains had softened the ground, when we would begin to move on to the grass for faster work. There were four grass gallops; two of them were circular, each about a mile round, but the best was Arkle's Bank, opposite Donnington's Brewery − a two-furlong uphill climb which was used in preparing horses for the more important races.

What impressed me most about David Nicholson's was the schooling arrangements. There was a special jumping paddock equipped with baby logs, telegraph poles and tree trunks − small, unintimidating obstacles over which the horses learnt their trade. When they were ready they moved up on to the top bank where the proper schooling fences were set out: flights of hurdles and three sets of fences in pairs. Sundays and Thursdays were schooling mornings; on Sunday a young jockey trying to get a ride could turn up and, if he was lucky, get to school a horse over a fence or two. Thursdays in mid-season were a much more hectic affair, with a string of twenty or so horses circling beside the obstacles with various jockeys hopping on and off to school them.

Now my assiduity in the point-to-pointing field paid off. When Toby Balding had runners in amateur races he usually got Jim Wilson, the leading amateur of the day, to ride them. However, on 31 August 1978 Jim was already booked, and on the previous day Toby's secretary rang David's yard in search of a substitute to ride Rolyat in the three-mile-one-furlong handicap hurdle at

Devon and Exeter. Toby had seen me ride at Cottenham and thought I would do.

Richard Hurley was happy to allow me time off to ride the horse, and I drove down to the West Country track feeling very excited to be riding for such a prominent trainer. Toby, a tall, thick-set man with glasses who never seems to be without his *Sporting Life* on the racecourse, cuts an imposing figure, and when I entered the paddock he gave me very precise instructions on how to ride the race. Referring to his paper for details of the main dangers, he told me to ride up with the pace and kick for home a mile out. At first it looked as if I had blown it: I lined up on the inside, but as the tape went up Rolyat spun round and by the time I set off in earnest I was already several lengths adrift of the field. Fortunately the leaders did not go very fast, and I was soon able to recover a good position. Down the back straight Rolyat went into a clear lead and despite clouting the last hurdle won by twenty-five lengths.

Rolyat went on to win for me again in the Horse and Hound Handicap Hurdle at Newton Abbot, but that first winner under Rules was more exhilarating than anything I could remember. For the first time in my life I felt that I had turned a dream into reality.

Suddenly I was in demand to ride in amateur races, and later that autumn I chalked up my first winning ride over fences on Majestic Touch for John Yardley at Ludlow. The Duke himself started to give me rides; my first winner for him was at Worcester on a little horse called Jacko, a real character and a favourite in the yard. He had his quirks: you had to hold him up for a late run otherwise he pulled himself up. Riding him at Newbury, I hit the front too soon and he tried to refuse with me going to the last: I was headed by Fred Winter's seventeen-year-old stalwart Sonny Somers, but Jacko came back gamely to get home by a neck in our second victory together.

As the winter wore on, I was getting plenty of rides, with support from David and also from John Yardley, Martin Tate and others, but the real tests were still to come, with the high point of the National Hunt season approaching: the Cheltenham Festival.

The first trainer who engaged me to ride at the Festival was Ray Peacock, who trained at Tarporley in Cheshire. He asked me to go and school a horse at his stables one Sunday morning after riding out at Condicote – and here my hopelessness with cars enters the picture again. Geography not being my strong point, I did not realize how far it was from home to Peacock's yard, and though I got there punctually I didn't have time to fill up for the journey home, or indeed any money to buy the petrol. On my return journey, after creeping down the motorway with the petrol gauge on empty, I just got off on to the Stow road before the car drifted to a halt. Abandoning it (again) I hitched a lift into Stow, raided petty cash at Bernard Thorpe's and bought some petrol which I carried back to the car. It took some creative organizing of the books to buy me the time to raise the money and return it.

But the journey brought its reward: I got the ride on Ray Peacock's High Prospect on the Wednesday of the 1979 Cheltenham Festival. On the Tuesday I had my first ride at the premier meeting on David Nicholson's Westberry Lodge in the four-mile amateur riders' novice chase: I fell two fences from home coming down the hill, and brought down Lizandon, the Duke's other runner, ridden by Major 'Crasher' Cramsie. Both jockeys reported to the Duke that they would have won . . .

On Thursday, Gold Cup day, I had no ride, and was left holding the fort at work. Stow comes to a halt during the afternoons of Cheltenham week and I could not believe that anyone would want to buy a house while the Gold Cup was being run, so I locked the office and ran up to the local hotel to watch the race, which was won by Alverton in a snowstorm. Returning to mind the shop for the remainder of the afternoon, I was sitting at the front desk with my feet on it, reading the paper, when I was startled by the entrance of a very well-dressed gentleman whom I quickly recognized as Mr Bernard Thorpe, senior partner of the firm. I quickly composed myself into a more professional attitude, but he quite rightly pointed out that my heart did not seem to be in the job and that it would be to the benefit of both parties if we went our separate ways at the end of May. He sweetened this tactful dismissal by saying that he was going to have runners at the hunter chase meeting at Folkestone and that perhaps I would like to ride them.

After Cheltenham the National Hunt fraternity looks towards Aintree, and this year I rode in the Topham Trophy over half the Grand National course. Five of David Nicholson's jockeys took part in this event – myself on Majestic Touch, John Suthern, Allen Webb, Paul Carvill and Nigel Hesketh – and not one of us completed the course. Paul, who was quickly gaining a reputation as the fastest jockey riding because he always made the running, stole the headlines with a fall at the third fence, the Chair, in which he did a complete somersault, earning himself two for effort and ten for artistic impression. My race ended less flamboyantly at Valentine's.

While at Aintree, I had the pleasant surprise of a phone call from Michael Sampson, the father of an old schoolfriend, Christine, inviting me to come and stay at his house while the racing was on. Being skint as usual, this kind offer was particularly welcome, and from then on he had the dubious pleasure of hosting me for the Grand National meeting every year.

Aintree in 1979 gave me my first encounter with the denizens of the northern racing circuit, including the valets who looked after the jockeys and cheered them on from the weighing room. This meeting also gave me my first winner of any real importance in the race after Rubstic's National. Mac's Chariot was a very decent horse: he had won the Waterford Crystal Novice Hurdle at the Cheltenham Festival for Mick O'Toole in 1977, but he had been erratic over fences and had broken Jeff King's leg when falling at Wetherby earlier this season. At Aintree, however, he gave me the most exhilarating ride to beat the New Zealand horse Royal Mail a comfortable eight lengths.

That was to be my penultimate winner of the season. At Ascot the following Wednesday a fall off Regal Command going down the hill gave me my first experience of concussion: I remember lying in the weighing room trying to work out where I was and what day of the week it was. An X-ray later that evening in Cheltenham hospital revealed that I had also cracked a bone in my arm, and I was told by the nurse to come back to the hospital the next morning to have it plastered. Naturally I did not, and continued riding until the Saturday, when, coming to the last at the same meeting on Westberry Lodge, I felt the bone in my arm move. I ended up in plaster for three weeks. I did, however, get back before the end of the season to ride one more winner, bringing my total for my first season as an amateur under Rules to nine.

*Chapter Four*

# DECISION TIME

———————◆►◆———— —

At the end of the 1978–9 season David Nicholson asked me to go back in the autumn as his assistant trainer, an offer I naturally accepted with alacrity. Before embarking on that new challenge, however, I had another job in prospect: working in Ireland over the summer for Jim Bolger at Clonsilla.

Among the closest of the numerous friends my father had made in Ireland during his riding career were the Taaffes and the Hartys. (Pat Taaffe, Arkle's jockey, was my godfather.) Eddie Harty had ridden many winners in England, his most notable victory being on Highland Wedding in the 1969 Grand National; he is now a successful trainer in Ireland and has also provided Toby Balding and Fred Winter with some of their very best horses. His brother John was both a qualified solicitor and a consummate horseman: he had represented Ireland in the Olympic Three Day Event team as well as riding Jim Bolger's few jumpers. It was through John that my job at Clonsilla had been arranged.

Nothing seemed to worry John: in his book, the man who made time made plenty, and his expansive attitude to life made him a lovely person to be around. However, when this relaxed outlook extended, as it invariably did, to timekeeping it made for some fairly hair-raising journeys to the races. He would tell me to be at his house at ten, say, but we never left on time – I used to wonder why he bothered mentioning a time at all – and he made up for the delay with fast and furious driving. He would never sit in a traffic queue, driving instead up the side of the waiting cars trying to drop in. 'The worst that can happen,' he would say, 'is that we'll end up where we started from.'

Jim Bolger is now, of course, among Europe's foremost trainers, but in 1979 he had not long since started. His yard, on the outskirts of Dublin, was a few miles from Phoenix Park racecourse – now, sadly, defunct. Despite his reputation as a hard man, I got on very well with Jim, and found working for him a truly enlightening experience. A self-taught and brilliant trainer and a very industrious man – on both counts like Martin Pipe, another trainer for whom I was to gain a huge admiration later in my career – he knew his horses inside out. He timed their preparation to perfection, and when at peak fitness a Bolger horse would often win a sequence of races in quick succession.

The horses here would built up fitness with lots of long, steady cantering on the circular gallop, about a mile and a half

*My first and only winner on the Flat – Pigeon's Nest for Jim Bolger in the John Player Amateur Handicap at Galway on 31 July 1979 (LIAM HEALY)*

round, to the rear of the yard. For fast work, they would sometimes go on the racecourse, either at Phoenix Park or at The Curragh, where Jim often let me ride. As I weighed under ten stone I got plenty of opportunities to ride work on the Flat horses, which was excellent experience. I also learnt a lot from the stable jockey Declan Gillespie, a very professional and stylish rider. He now trains on The Curragh, but some of the lads who were working with Jim that summer when I was there are still with him now: Kevin Manning, Jim's son-in-law, was apprenticed to the yard then and now rides many of the stable's horses when first jockey Christy Roche is not available. There was also a coloured lad called Sam, who was very impressed with the American style of riding and copied his heroes avidly. Poor Sam came to grief one day when riding a hard-pulling filly called Galliano (on whom I later got beaten in a Flat race). For some reason, when tacking her up he had got the stirrup leathers and irons the wrong side of the surcingle, the strap which goes over the saddle and round the girth to hold the saddle in place, and consequently once mounted he had no mobility in his legs. When riding a puller you need to be able to use your legs to set your weight against the horse, so of course Sam was in trouble. This was one of the mornings when we were doing long, steady canters round the circular track; Galliano pulled harder and harder as we went on and eventually pulled Sam out of the saddle over her neck.

With the assistance and support of John Harty I got rides at many of Ireland's delightful racecourses. There was Bellewstown, a unique track in an outstanding location just to the north of Dublin, which is host to a three-day carnival meeting every July; here the scales in the weighing room were the old balance type, and the course itself was railed only on the inside, apart from the home straight where the lined-up horseboxes formed an outer barrier. The informality of these arrangements had its perils; Declan Gillespie found himself arriving at the start rather faster than he had intended on a two-year-old wearing blinkers for the first time when a football being kicked around by some young boys having a spontaneous game by the side of the track landed on the horse's quarters as they were cantering to post; and in a bumper one of the horses ran out to the horseboxes, no doubt preferring to go home rather than finish the race. Sometimes the interference came from on the track rather than off it: after one bumper at Sligo I was taken on one side and privately reprimanded by a stipendiary steward for taking 'a snake-like course up the straight', a warning that I thought was rather unfair as I had been forced to dodge about during the race to avoid various enthusiastic but erratic amateurs.

The first winner I rode for Jim was a filly called Tishoo, who had appeared at times to be less than genuine. She tended to carry her head very high and in her races she didn't always seem to carry her effort through to the line. Jim, with his typical application, had given this filly a lot of individual attention, riding her himself some afternoons to try to get her to drop her head. I was given the ride on her at Gowran Park, where on the advice of John Harty I jumped her off in front and made all – and she stayed on to win. That same afternoon I was associated with another winner when I led in John's own victorious ride in a steeplechase – the only time I can recall being the winning horse's lad.

The Galway Festival at the end of July is one of the highlights of the Irish racing calendar, a week-long bonanza of mixed Flat and jump racing in the west of the country, centring on the two

*My last win as an amateur, on Oakprime (no. 3) at Warwick on 17 November 1979 (PADDOCK STUDIOS)*

big races of the Galway Hurdle and the Galway Plate steeplechase. This year I stayed for the Festival with John Harty and his family in a house on an island in the middle of the lake – about an hour's drive and a short journey in a rowing boat from the course. It was at Galway that I won the most prestigious race of my stay when taking the Amateur Riders' Handicap on Pigeon's Nest – my first and only winner on the Flat. Jim Bolger had intended to ride the filly himself, but had had to go to saddle a runner at Goodwood, thus letting me in for the ride.

Ironically, it was this win that led to my departure from Ireland a little earlier than I had intended. After the race we discovered that I had claimed a seven-pound allowance whereas I was only entitled to five pounds, because of the number of winners I had now ridden. I had been going to stay another week in the hope of riding in a bumper on a horse called Daletta, which had been working exceptionally well at home; however, after this mistake with my allowance it was thought better that I slipped away to England and got myself out of sight and out of mind until it was too late for the authorities to disqualify me. In the event Daletta did not win his bumper – and I would probably not have been on him anyway, as Jim also wanted to ride the horse. Daletta did, however, go on to win the 1980 Irish National with John Harty aboard.

So for me it was back to England, to take up the proffered post at Condicote. It wasn't that I wanted to be a trainer, but now that my brush with estate agency was over I needed to earn my living somehow, and a paid stable lad cannot ride as an amateur jockey. As David's assistant trainer, I could earn a wage without affecting my amateur status. The next big question, of course, was whether to keep that status.

There were plenty of people to advise me against taking the plunge and going professional, from Willie Stephenson, who had thought I lacked the toughness necessary to earn a living race-riding, to Richard Evans, a talented jockey with whom I often now travelled to the races. Richard's view was that I could earn a better living outside of racing and still enjoy riding as an amateur. There was also the risk of failure to be considered. Riding as an amateur, however much you want – as I did – to ride as many winners as possible, the pressure on you is less; people don't expect you to ride as well as the professionals, and in the back of your mind you have the thought that as you aren't trying to make your living from race-riding, you couldn't be deemed a failure if you turned your back on the sport to pursue a career elsewhere. Many amateurs, after all, give up when they find their other commitments no longer give them time for race-riding. In my own case, fear of failure was sharpened by thoughts of my father's success. Yet I was now getting a good number of rides and the question of turning professional was going to have to be confronted.

A horse called Oakprime played a significant part in my eventual decision. This horse, trained by David Nicholson, had been beaten on his previous runs, but I won with him on 3 November at Worcester and then again at Warwick on 17

November, bringing me level on winners with last season's leading amateur Geordie Dunn, who rode for Arthur Stephenson and was again now at the head of the amateurs' list.

Oakprime was my last winner as an amateur. After the win at Warwick, David Nicholson and my parents discussed with me the timing of turning professional, and we decided that if I was going to do it at all, I should do it now. I was having a good run of winners, but still had ten more to clock up before I would lose my claim. This weight allowance is very important to a young rider trying to establish himself, as it acts as an incentive for trainers to put you on their horses. The aim must be to get a name as a decent jockey before you lose that temporary advantage.

My father had taken seventy-six rides to achieve his first winner as a professional, so I shouldn't have had extravagant expectations; but in the event my debut could not have gone better. At Worcester on 21 November, riding for the first time as plain P. Scudamore, without the amateur's prefix 'Mr', I won by twenty lengths on Sea Lane, and later the same afternoon was back in the winner's enclosure with Birshell, trained by Toby Balding.

*Flitgrove (second from left) on his way to a hard fought victory at Nottingham in December 1979. I got him up in the last stride to beat John Suthern and Eastern Citizen by a head, with Maytide a neck away in third. Flitgrove, a grand servant to David Nicholson, is now in retirement with Raymond and Jenny Mould, down the road from Mucky Cottage (WALLIS PHOTOGRAPHERS)*

The next three weeks went really well, and by the end of them I had ridden the ten winners I needed to become a fully fledged jockey. This was the crunch: now that I could no longer claim a weight allowance trainers had no artificial incentive to give me rides, which I would have to earn by ability alone. This moment is an anxious one for many young jockeys. Trainers who were using you because of the weight advantage tend to forget about you until you have established a reputation in your own right; to do that you need the rides, and it can be very difficult to get that essential experience in competition with the more senior riders. Again I was fortunate: in my case losing the allowance had a good rather than a bad effect, as I was now no longer looked upon as a novice, and the rides continued to flow.

Turning professional wasn't the only big event for me that season. Back in 1978, I had been riding in a point-to-point for John Kington, whose daughter Marilyn led the horse up. It was a wet, muddy day and my first words to her were to the effect that I hoped the horse moved better than she did on the ground. You probably wouldn't have predicted from this unpromising start that a couple of years later we would be married.

By 1980 I was sharing a cottage with fellow jockey Allen Webb, a few miles from the Condicote yard, and Marilyn, who was a schoolteacher in Newbury, would sometimes come and stay at the weekend. One Sunday morning when I got back from schooling she told me that an old man, sounding like a farmer, had been on the phone wanting me to ride a horse for him. Later that evening the 'old man like a farmer' rang back: it was Fred Rimell, offering me the opportunity to replace Colin and Nigel Tinkler as his stable jockey. No one had made a greater impact than Fred on National Hunt racing since the war: he had trained four Grand National winners and a host of other stars, including horses such as Comedy of Errors and Gay Trip. Marilyn was going to have to be more perceptive if my budding professional career was to thrive.

To be asked to ride for such a successful yard so early in my career was a great opportunity, but obviously I had to discuss the situation with David, as by now I was sharing the majority of his yard's rides with John Suthern. I also talked to my father, who had ridden many horses for Fred Rimell over the years – including Snakestone, the horse whose fall put an end to his race-riding – and his advice was invaluable in helping me decide what

I should do. He made me see that it would be a huge responsibility for someone with so little experience to be committed to one such prominent yard, and that perhaps it would be better if I tried to ride for both yards until the end of that season. This way I could benefit from the chance of riding some of the high-class horses in Fred's yard as well as putting myself in a good position from which to negotiate a post as first jockey to a major stable for the following season.

My first ride for the Rimell team was at Ascot on 11 January 1980, when I won on a horse called Swashbuckling. However, my relative lack of experience took its toll later in the afternoon, when I was riding Western Rose, a good horse over hurdles but a strong puller. My instructions were not to go to the front until late in the race. At the start it became obvious that no one wanted to make the running, and when the tape rose none of the jockeys moved until Andy Turnell and Beacon Light took the field out. I was so worried about riding to my orders that I never really challenged them and they went on to win.

The new riding arrangement gave my fledgling career a great boost, and despite a couple of setbacks, including a week's enforced rest after a fall from Royal Gaye at the Cheltenham January meeting, by Wednesday 6 February 1980 I had ridden thirty-four winners. That day, while being driven up to Haydock by my father, I was enjoying the contemplation of some exciting rides at the Cheltenham Festival in March, and even the prospect of a placing in the jockeys' championship. Instead I had one of those experiences that make racing people superstitious.

I had just bought a new pair of boots and was keen to try them out. Tom Buckingham, who with his brother John made up the team of valets who looked after me at the races, advised me against wearing them on this occasion, but I ignored him. My first ride of the day was a horse called Brian's Venture in a novice hurdle. We finished fourth; and then, as we pulled up past the winning post, another horse and jockey cannoned into me. I knew instantly what had happened: my right lower leg was broken. Somehow I had to get off the horse and into the ambulance, a process I managed with the aid of my father and the ambulance staff, who carried me to the doctor. Tom Buckingham was standing over me as the nurse cut the new boot off my injured leg. I've never thought of myself as superstitious, but from then on I hated new boots.

*My first winner of the 1980–1 season – returning to unsaddle after landing a three-year-old hurdle at Worcester on Critical Times in August 1980* (BERNARD PARKIN)

My leg was put in plaster in a local hospital in Liverpool, after which my father drove me, laid out on the back seat of the car, back home to Herefordshire. Once again his experience stood me in good stead; I had learnt from him that in cases of injury, when your livelihood is involved, it is worth getting the best medical attention you can afford. On his advice I now went to Bill Tucker, a surgeon in Park Street, London W1, who had contrived to get many sportsmen, including my father and several other

jockeys, back in action sooner than they expected. In this instance
it turned out that my leg had not been set properly, and I had to
have it reset in an operation in London.

I had aimed to make my comeback for the Grand National in
April, but it soon became clear that this was sheer fantasy. At
least I had some company and moral support, for two of my
mates at Nicholson's, Allen Webb and Roy Mangan, had both
been injured around this time. Also, while the break from racing
was obviously a bitter blow, it did give me time to reflect on
whether I should go to Fred Rimell as first jockey the next season
or stay with David Nicholson. The decision would have to be
made one way or the other: it was obvious that the two yards'
horses were going to clash, and I couldn't ride them all.
Eventually, I decided to stay at Nicholson's, and Sam Morshead
took the job at Rimell's. My riding career had taken off very
quickly, and although I really hated missing so many good rides,
there was  the consoling knowledge that I had a good platform
from which to relaunch myself after the summer.

One thing the accident didn't manage to stop was the wedding.
Marilyn and I were married on 29 May at Belmont Abbey. My
best man was Nigel Twiston-Davies, who on the stag night at
Billersley Manor near Stratford won the dubious accolade of
being described by the proprietor as the only person he had ever
seen leaving a stag party better dressed than when he arrived.
Nigel had been thrown in the swimming pool three times and
each time he had replaced his wet clothes with clean ones from a
suitcase in his car. Fortunately he didn't have to go so far as to
wear his wedding outfit.

Marilyn and I had a two-month honeymoon in Norway –
which for me was a working holiday, as I was determined to get
back to race fitness as quickly as possible. This I did by riding in
as many races as I could, and in the process I notched up six
winners. We returned to England in August to a new house in
Lower Swell, rented from Captain Macdonald-Buchanan, a
racehorse owner and member of the Jockey Club. Just to round
things off nicely, a sponsorship by Warners Garages in
Tewkesbury put paid to my car troubles with a brand new
Peugeot to start the new season.

*Chapter Five*

# THE DUEL FOR THE TITLE

There is something of a north/south divide among National Hunt jockeys, each group sticking to its respective circuit and being attended by its own valets. The midland tracks of Leicester, Nottingham, Market Rasen and Uttoxeter, and the two major Festival meetings of Cheltenham and Aintree, are the only places where northerners and southerners meet regularly, and when the jumping season begins in the first week of August, each group has its own early fixtures. For the southern jockeys things get going at Newton Abbot, but with the sun still shining and the ground hard there are not often many runners and it can be a difficult time to get rides; those best placed are the ones who have a small West Country yard to ride for that campaigns its horses early. For the northern jockeys these first weeks are even more difficult as there is very little racing – after the opening day at Bangor-on-Dee there is only the Market Rasen meeting three times in a fortnight.

Many jockeys and trainers treat the first week in the south as a kind of holiday, staying down at the Palace Hotel in Torquay. This was particularly so before the M5 was built, when horses, jockeys and trainers alike had to lodge in the area if they were to get to the races at all. When my father was riding he used either to take the family down to stay at Salcombe, about an hour's drive from Newton Abbot, or else drive down very early in the morning before the holiday traffic was on the roads and then go to the Turkish baths in Torquay for a sweat and a sleep.

Anyone who knows the West Country will be familiar with the traffic hold-ups, even on today's motorways. I learnt a valuable lesson on the very first day of the 1980–1 season, when I nearly missed a ride on one of David Nicholson's horses because of the jammed roads: I never took the chance again, but like my father either went down the night before or left very early in the morning.

At the beginning of this season Jonjo O'Neill was odds-on to retain the National Hunt jockeys' championship that he had taken the previous season with 115 winners. No one else had a chance – least of all me, who didn't even figure in the betting. But I was determined to make a good start none the less: I needed to re-establish myself in my own and other people's eyes after the prolonged absence from the saddle in England that had followed my accident the previous February. The week after Newton Abbot, I rode a double at Worcester for Willie Stephenson and straight away found myself in demand from several trainers; even though I had no thoughts of the title, I never really lost touch with the leading contender – who turned out not to be Jonjo after all. He had a terrible fall at Bangor in October, and by the New Year it was obvious that only John Francome and I were in with a realistic chance of the championship.

John and Jonjo were two of the greatest jockeys ever to ride. I can remember following their careers while I was still at school, and I found it rather awe-inspiring now to find myself up with these olympians as a live contender for the title. Nevertheless, I didn't feel under any pressure to fight for the crown this year. I remember Ron Barry, himself a former champion, telling me that I had no chance; and I knew that as I chased rides all over the country from Exeter to Kelso I was not after the title for its own sake, just trying to ride as many winners as possible on a day-to-day basis. But I also now had the germ of the idea in my mind that I might be good enough to be at the head of the table one day.

Such hopes as I did have were boosted by the fact that David Nicholson was having his best season ever; however, John seemed to be supplied with a never-ending stream of winners by his number one trainer, Fred Winter, who had been champion jockey himself and by now seven times champion trainer as well; and he also had the support of other powerful yards, such as those of Les Kennard and Richard Head.

John, whose sense of humour is legendary in racing circles, gave the impression of being very laid-back, but he worked very hard for his success. While I was content just to be riding, and not expecting rides, especially in the big races, John hated to sit in the weighing room looking at the card advertising a large purse for a major event in which he was not taking part. 'I should have a ride in this,' he would say. I learnt a great deal from him; he

was always prepared to talk, and always had a kind word to say,
whereas I was completely ignorant of the art of conversation.

The first good horse that I rode was Broadsword, a big, imposing
bay owned by Lord Northampton. He was by an American sire
called Ack Ack and had been bought out of John Dunlop's yard
at Arundel. This reflected a change of policy on David's part.
Previously the yard's novices were big, backward store horses,
bred for National Hunt racing and not fully broken until four:
now David was buying in a number of three-year-olds off the
Flat. I had schooled Broadsword at home, but a great deal of the
groundwork had been done by Roy Mangan, now retired from
race-riding. The horse had his first run over hurdles at Kempton
on 18 October, and lived up to the promise of his excellence at
home by winning. He and I then went on to win five of our next
six races.

The one we didn't win was at Sandown, a fortnight after the
Kempton debut, and this led to an unfortunate argument after
the race. We were beaten by a horse called Lir who had finished
a long way behind us at Kempton. David was livid, and had
heated words with Lir's owner, Ken Higson, about the horse's
improved form. I think the argument soured the pleasure of
victory for Ken, which was a great shame; he has for years been
one of racing's most loyal and dependable owners, keeping horses
first with Charlie Moore and then with Charlie's son Gary.

In fact what had happened that day was that I had held
Broadsword up too long – in accordance, as David told the press,
with his instructions. In those days, before Michael Dickinson
and Martin Pipe brought front-running back into fashion, many
jumping trainers did not like to see their horses in front for too
long. Very often David would say to me of the chief opposition,
'You'll beat him for speed,' and he liked to see his horses
'dropped in fourth or fifth'.

Rides continued to come my way, not only at the small tracks
but at the bigger meetings as well. The first major race I rode in
with a realistic chance was the Hennessy Gold Cup at Newbury
in November 1980, in which I had got a spare ride on Silent
Valley for the Newcastle trainer Ian Jordan. Spare mounts can be
a bit dodgy, but this horse gave me one of the most exhilarating
rides I have ever had. We went at a very good gallop and Silent
Valley jumped faultlessly from fence to fence, finishing second to

the Irish-trained Bright Highway.

The best horses are often not the easiest to handle, either on the racecourse or off it. One good chaser I rode this season was Sugarally, a big brown horse trained by George Fairbairn. Before I ever rode him I had watched him unseat Sam Morshead at an Ascot ditch, and I realized that he had to be driven into his fences or he hesitated and that was when he made mistakes. We had chalked up one win together in a race at Newbury before I rode him in the Tote Pattern Handicap Chase (now the Racing Post Chase) at Kempton. In this race we were always prominent, and I pushed him into his fences, trying to instil as much confidence into him as possible and keep him jumping boldly. Horses like this can jump impeccably and then suddenly make a horrendous blunder: his came that day at the third last when I asked him to stand off and he literally banked the fence, shooting me into the air. Luckily he was still underneath me when I came down and we went on to win the race.

As for off-course behaviour, a typical eccentric was Great Developer, a favourite of mine at Condicote. He was a very hard puller, so I often got the chance to ride him out. On some mornings he would decide he didn't want to be tacked up and would turn his backside on me; when I tried to go to his head he would turn again, pinning me into the corner where I would have to climb on to the manger to avoid his flying legs. Perhaps he never actually meant to make contact, or perhaps he just couldn't reach that high. It may have been just a game to him, but it was quite frightening to be on the receiving end. In the end I took to going into the stable with a broom, and thus armed he never took me on.

Toondra, one of Lord Vestey's horses, was an individual of whom a lot was expected, but he turned out to be rather disappointing. Horses like this have a way of getting you into trouble; when a trainer has an expensive horse, or one from a major owner on which high hopes are pinned, he often becomes blind to reality and will look everywhere for reasons why the horse gets beaten – except at the truth that it isn't up to it. So it proved in this case, with the Duke and I having cross words when he had a go at me for getting beaten on Toondra at Nottingham. I had followed John Francome on the favourite Franciscus, and David accused me of playing cat and mouse with my rival jockey instead of concentrating on winning the race; but

I knew that the horse was simply no good.

The Cheltenham Festival of 1981 was going to be my first chance to ride there as a professional – my last visit having been on crutches. These three days in March dominate the National Hunt season: from the very first day at Newton Abbot or Bangor-on-Dee everyone is hoping that their horses will run well enough to warrant participation in a race at the Festival, all of which are considered to be championship standard. I had some good rides lined up this year: Slaney Idol for my first attempt at the Champion Hurdle; Broadsword, ante-post favourite for the Triumph Hurdle despite his defeat at Sandown; and Chinrullah, trained by Mick O'Toole, for both the Queen Mother Champion Chase and the Gold Cup.

Throughout my riding career I tried to cultivate tunnel vision as far as racing was concerned. I didn't want to be distracted, either by pressures at home or on the course, or by expectations from the press. Brough Scott once wrote an article about a 'purple patch', as he put it, that I was enjoying; but I tried never to think about good or bad runs. I wanted always to be consistent, to ride each race for itself, and never to be affected by what was going on around me.

Yet in March, with the Festival inexorably approaching, it was very difficult not to share in the general increase of tension and anticipation – especially as I lived so close to the racecourse, in an area invaded at this time every year by racing people from all over the world and buzzing with talk of the sport to come. The routine in the yard would change, too, with horses being taken off to work on different gallops in their final preparation for the meeting. I knew how much the build-up was affecting me when I realized how pleased I was on the Saturday evening before the meeting that racing was over, giving me Sunday and Monday to prepare myself for the three big days ahead. On Monday I walked the course; the ground was heavy, and my tension continued to mount. Early on the Tuesday morning I went down to the racecourse to give Slaney Idol a canter. Because of the traffic congestion there would be later as the cars flooded into the course, I left my car down there and walked into town for a cup of coffee before returning to face the most hectic three days of the year.

None of the horses I rode on the first or second days was

*Post mortem. On the Members' Lawn at Cheltenham in March 1981, I explain to David Nicholson just how I was unseated from Highway Patt in the Ritz Club National Hunt Chase. Somehow I don't think the Duke is too impressed by my analysis* (BERNARD PARKIN)

placed; when Fred Rimell's Gaye Chance won the Sun Alliance Novices' Hurdle on the Wednesday I couldn't help thinking 'if only . . .'. So all my hopes for a Festival winner came to rest on Broadsword in Thursday's Triumph Hurdle. I had a long chat about the race with Tommy Carmody, who had much more experience of Cheltenham than I did, and he told me about the problems I would face: that the field goes very fast and that it can be a very rough race. He told me how he had been at the back of the field the year before on Starfen before taking up the running approaching the last – and then falling.

Taking into account this advice, the experience of the previous two days' racing and my riding orders from the Duke, I was beginning to piece together how I would ride Broadsword. It is very difficult to get a clear run on the inside at Cheltenham in a large field, as there are a number of places on the left-handed track where horses on the outside can lean over and impede those inside them. So I settled Broadsword behind the leading bunch, racing towards the centre of the track. With a clear run to the second last, I began to assess my chances and those of the others around me. There were three Irish horses in front of me whose form I was not sure of; I didn't want to allow them first run on me, so I tracked them until we straightened up for the last hurdle. I then moved to the stands side so as to have the opportunity of following the rail up the run-in, and hit the front approaching the last. It was all going so well, until we were outstayed up that notorious Cheltenham hill and beaten to the line by a 66–1 outsider, Baron Blakeney. What was to have been my first major success was instead a landmark for Baron Blakeney's trainer – Martin Pipe. I was dreadfully disappointed, but I felt that we had no excuses on the day. A fortnight later Broadsword reversed the form on the easier track at Aintree.

That left only the Gold Cup on Chinrullah, who had already been beaten in the Queen Mother Champion Chase. We pulled up two fences from home when a long way behind Little Owl – so far, in fact, that although I was still trying to watch the race, I couldn't see who had won.

I was now looking for my first ride in the Grand National. I found it on Cheers, trained by John Edwards, after winning on the horse at Wolverhampton a few weeks before the National meeting. My father, who had ridden in sixteen consecutive Grand Nationals, walked the course with me, explaining the route he

*The style was still in need of some refinement: Bridge Ash at Chepstow in April 1981* (GEORGE SELWYN)

used to take. The drop behind Becher's was much bigger on the inside and many riders would jump it on the outer, as he had done when riding Oxo to win in 1959. You then need to move leftwards as the course bears left, to avoid swinging too wide at the right-angled Canal Turn. Despite this careful planning, I finished last – but I was pleased to have completed the course.

There is always celebration in the weighing room after the National, with friends swapping good and bad experiences of the race. This year, with Bob Champion's tremendous achievement of having brought himself back to win after recovering from cancer, the atmosphere was very emotional, and there was a lot of champagne flowing. I had a glass or two before going out to ride my old friend Great Developer in the last. I walked out to the paddock with Richard Linley, telling him how much I liked the horse and what a good jumper he was – only to fall at the first.

With Cheltenham and the National over, the focus was on the championship, now a contest between myself and John Francome. This season I had been picking up some very good spare rides in addition to the Condicote runners, and winning also on horses that appeared from the betting to have no chance: Arthur Stephenson's 33–1 shot Spring Chancellor, for instance, and Doug Francis's China God, whom I dropped out last at Ludlow before making rapid headway to win at 20–1. My occasional over-enthusiasm with the whip was already getting me into trouble: after winning on Passing Parade at Chepstow, Mick O'Toole asked me to ride him at Punchestown, where I was warned over my use of the stick by the Irish stewards.

Come the beginning of May I had ridden ninety winners to John's ninety-six; with five weeks of the season still to go, I had every chance of making the top of the table. Then came an evening meeting at Taunton, a course John used to describe as 'the wall of death' because of its sharp turns and the consequent tendency for horses to slip up on the bends after a shower of rain. I was happy to ride anywhere, lacking the foresight to realize that some tracks were far more dangerous than others. This evening I had the mount on a horse from David's yard called Salad. He was a complicated ride, and had formerly caused problems for John Suthern, who was blamed for the horse not running as expected. One of the problems with Salad was that unless you were travelling well on him he would put in an extra stride before an obstacle and fall. Having frightened himself (and me) over fences in this way he was returned to hurdles.

I was coming to the first hurdle down the back straight when Salad put down on me and slid into the obstacle on his back legs before crumpling to the ground. The fall itself was not a particularly bad one, but a horse behind us galloped over me, kicking me on the back of the head. Although I didn't lose consciousness I knew I had been hurt, and when I put my hand up to my ear I felt blood. X-rays later revealed that I had cracked my skull and perforated an eardrum, and I spent the following four days in Taunton hospital. Here I had a visit from Martin Pipe, which as I had then never met him I thought a very kind gesture. I appreciated it particularly as I was sick with disappointment – not least because I missed out on two winners at Worcester the day after Taunton. Looking back, I was lucky to escape so lightly: my helmet was badly cracked from the impact of the horse's shoe, but at the time I wasn't in the mood to feel grateful. I returned after three weeks to ride one more winner for my father, a horse called Rapallo: he brought my total to ninety-one, but my chance of the championship was gone.

Before the next season had begun, I was back in circulation, riding out at Condicote and renewing my acquaintance with various trainers who might help me in my quest for winners. One of those for whom I rode out was Neville Callaghan. Like most yards in Newmarket, he mainly trained for the Flat, but had a few dual-purpose horses which were schooled on a rotovated dirt strip on the Links, one of the training grounds. It was a two-and-a-half-hour drive from my Cotswold base to Newmarket, but the travelling paid dividends when Can-Do-More won for me at the Market Rasen evening meeting on the first day of the season.

My connection with Callaghan also got me the mount on two good hurdlers: a very high-class horse called Royal Vulcan and a good early season type called Arnaldo. One of Arnaldo's victories was at Worcester, considered by many to be one of the best of the smaller courses with its level, left-handed track and well-sited obstacles. The only drawback from a jockey's point of view is that because a lot of trainers like it, there tend to be a lot of runners in the novice chases, which makes the prospect of falling more dangerous. On this occasion I took Arnaldo down to post away from the other horses, to try to keep him relaxed. I showed him the first hurdle; he backed off it a little, indicating to me that he had some respect for what he was going to do. Some horses will stand on the base of the jump when you take them to look at it, suggesting an ignorance of what it means that might carry over into their attitude in the race.

When the tapes went up I set off in front. With a horse like this it is best not to get head to head with something else; if you can avoid being taken on, you can put your hands on the horse's neck and leave his mouth alone, encouraging him to settle. In fact, I find that horses that have run on the Flat tend to concentrate on the obstacles when racing over hurdles, and this also helps them to settle. Arnaldo really stood off the first two hurdles, clearing them in a fast and accurate style. Controlling that speed, with the element of danger involved, is an exhilarating feeling. When you are travelling well within yourself the stride pattern approaching the hurdles becomes very easy to see, enabling a smooth and fluent performance. I can't have been concentrating fully during this race, because knowing that my parents were present I remember thinking what my poor mother must have been going through watching the horse and me as we apparently toyed with the hurdles. Although I knew that Arnaldo had only limited ability, racing against far inferior opposition he

*A nasty tumble – from Sugarally at Cheltenham in November 1981*
(BERNARD PARKIN)

gave me the same adrenalin kick that I got from riding top-class horses.

This sensation is one of the reasons why National Hunt jockeys go on risking life and limb day after day, year after year. The real high would not be there without the element of danger; it is a feeling no money can buy and with it you know you are a member of an elite club open only to very few.

Because of the nature of the risks and rewards of jump racing, the compulsion to win and the physical dangers, there is a very strong camaraderie among jockeys and an equally strong rivalry, sometimes manifested in quite violent ways. At this time my main adversaries in the weighing room, apart from John Francome, were Richard Rowe, Hywel Davies and Graham McCourt. We were all much of an age and all still trying to establish ourselves, and the competition sometimes got rough in the races as we sorted out our pecking order and how far we could push ourselves and each other. Hywel, Graham and I once rode in a three-horse race at Huntingdon, where we continually hampered each other before Graham, getting his own back, trapped the other two of us against the rail. I think we all realized then that we had to show each other a little more respect, and rarely poked up one another's inside again.

Taking the inside rail is important; it is the plum position and no one wants to be considered a pushover. But there is an etiquette of when and when not to give way on the inner, and earlier in my career when I didn't have the experience to understand the difference I had quite wrongly 'murdered' Peter Haynes on a horse at Stratford by stopping his move on my inside after my own chance in the race had gone. The reprimand I got taught me a lesson: it is only senior jockeys that can educate younger riders in what can and cannot be done. For example, before the closing stages of a race, light on the inside will be given to someone in trouble; however, once the business end of the race is under way no quarter should be expected from a rider still in contention. A jockey does well to remember that the day will come when he wants a little help himself, and to give a helping hand when his own chance has gone.

By now I believed that I had the ability to be champion jockey. On top of the confidence engendered by the previous season's successes I now had the boost of a really good start to this campaign – David's horses were once again running consistently well – and I had even headed John at one point after a win on Arnaldo at Fontwell on 20 October. He soon pushed me back into second place, but by 20 November I was snapping at his heels again with a deficit of only two. A treble at Ascot had helped me, with Leney Dual's victory in the H&T Walker Marie Elisabeth Chase a typical demonstration of how the Condicote horses were running as he fought like a tiger to hold off Bob Champion on Approaching.

John and I continued our battle for supremacy without Jonjo, whose recovery from his broken leg had been prolonged by his attempt to return to riding too soon the previous season, thus adding serious complications to the original injury. It is a truism of the game that jockeys benefit from each other's misfortunes, and I am sure that I picked up many spare rides as a result of Jonjo's absence. Bob Davies's retirement this season also gave me the opportunity to ride some good horses from David Morley's stable.

In December both of us – and everyone else – had to mark time while the coldest winter I had ever known descended. For three weeks before Christmas, snow and ice prevented racing taking place anywhere in England. One night the thermometer in the yard showed −25 degrees, which made getting water to the horses a major problem. Taps and pipes were frozen solid and had to be thawed every few hours, as did the horses' water buckets.

However bad the weather, the horses still had to be exercised. Riding out in these conditions was very unpleasant. For the first few days of snow we could still get out on the roads, but soon the snow ploughs and cars created a lethally icy surface. The horses were taken out in three lots for trotting and slow cantering around a field, each being exercised for about an hour a day. By the time they came in they looked uncanny, fringed in white where the frost had formed on their manes, ears, eyebrows and whiskers.

Three lots to ride out made keeping warm an overriding priority. The places where the blood circulation is thinnest – the tips of your ears, fingers and toes – are always the hardest to keep warm in the winter, let alone in cold as severe as this. My survival uniform consisted of a pair of boots that were too big for me, warmed up on the kitchen stove, lined with a big pair of woolly socks that I put on over a pair of woollen tights, all covered by a pair of cavalry twill jodhpurs; and on my top half a thermal vest, shirt, jumper, warm jacket and scarf. On my hands I wore mittens, so that I could keep the tips of my fingers warm on the horse's coat, and over the top of my helmet I pulled a balaclava. And I was still cold!

The hiatus didn't seem to do any harm. Horses and jockeys alike work hard during the season and sometimes appreciate a short midwinter break. The Nicholson horses had been running really well all autumn and they continued to do so when the thaw came, enabling me to stick fairly close to John's rising total of winners as 1982 got under way. On 2 March a double at Plumpton for David Morley brought me to eighty-two: just four behind my arch-rival. By this stage John was feeling the pressure more than I; everything I was achieving was a bonus, whereas he had the burden of expectations to carry.

At Newbury on 5 March an incident occurred which substantially boosted my chance of becoming champion. Celtic Rambler, trained by Mercy Rimell who had taken over her husband's licence when Fred died in the summer of 1981, fell with Sam Morshead, bringing down John Francome's horse. John was not badly hurt, but Sam suffered a punctured lung and when it was clear he would not ride again that season I replaced him on the Rimell horses. Naturally, no trainer likes a jockey on whom he relies to take bad rides from outside the stable, thus risking injuries that might prevent him riding his main yard's horses, but this was an opportunity to ride good-class horses and David, knowing how keen I was to challenge for the title, was very supportive in my quest for winners. I had a great run on Mercy's horses that shot me clear in the championship race.

As the Cheltenham Festival drew closer again, my main hope of a winner rested once more with Broadsword. We hadn't got off to a very good start this season: he was beaten at Newbury first time out, and I missed his winning run at Cheltenham on 13 November 1981 on account of a crunching fall from Sugarally earlier in the afternoon. The eleventh fence on the chase course was a ditch, very badly sited on the bend in front of the stands, and horses tended to ignore it. Sugarally put down in the ditch, falling and bringing two others down with him. I was out of action for the rest of the day and Broadsword went on to win under Steve Smith Eccles. Though the horse did not strike form again until the Cheltenham January meeting, an impressive win at Nottingham in the City Trial Hurdle further confirmed him as a live prospect for the Champion Hurdle.

My first serious chance of a Festival win was Sailor's Return in the Arkle Trophy Challenge Chase. This horse had taken well to jumping fences, and had won for me in an extraordinary race at Ascot. I had come to the last upsides Steve Knight (who won the 1987 Grand National on Maori Venture and is now head lad to Richard Hannon) on Run Hard and John Francome on Fifty Dollars More. At the fence they both fell independently, an event which escaped my notice, and I rode up the run-in as if all the hounds of hell were after me! I was mercilessly teased about this in the weighing room afterwards. John said he would have won, and although I didn't agree, his opinion was borne out when Fifty Dollars More finished in front of Sailor's Return in the Arkle. However, though I didn't win I benefited indirectly from this race, because John had turned down Fifty Dollars More in favour of Sea Image in the race, and in so doing lost the rides on Sheikh Ali Abu Khamsin's horses from then on to Richard Linley.

Later that afternoon in the Champion Hurdle Broadsword started second favourite to Daring Run, whom I was lucky to avoid when he slipped up on the bend at the top of the hill. Broadsword dived at the third last and landed flat-footed, and we lost ground on the final turn when hampered by Ekbalco and For Auction, the 40–1 outsider who won the race. We managed second place, seven lengths away.

Chinrullah again ran twice at the meeting, this time in the Queen Mother Champion Chase and the Cathcart, and came second in both. Three seconds; but still no Festival winner.

Aintree at least brought me a victory on an old favourite, Silent Valley, making a comeback after cracking a bone in his foot. In the National I rode Tragus for Lord Hartington, trained by David Morley. This was a good-class horse and I felt I had a realistic chance. Unfortunately, after recovering from a bad mistake at the first, we could finish no better than sixth. This year the usual weighing-room banter after the race revolved around Hywel Davies pulling up Tiepolino in front of Becher's and baulking Rough and Tumble, who refused, depositing John Francome in the ditch on the other side of the fence. I suspect this is what happened to Captain Becher all those years ago when the fence got its name!

On Monday 12 April, twelve winners ahead of John, I went to Chepstow for what turned out to be one of those glorious days that redeem all the wet winter afternoons at Leicester. Chepstow, an undulating left-handed course just under two miles round, with a five-furlong home straight, set in picturesque Welsh countryside near the Severn Bridge, is one of my favourite courses. I had six booked rides, four of them favourites and three of them for Mercy Rimell. Celtic Isle, formerly a good-class long-distance hurdler, was a comfortable winner of the opener, a novice chase, and Gaye Brief – full brother to Gaye Chance, on whom I had won the Keith Prowse Long Distance Hurdle five days earlier and whom I was intending to ride in the three-mile French Champion Hurdle – won the Panama Cigar Hurdle in good style from Ryeman, who had been an unlucky loser at the Cheltenham Festival.

Then came what I consider to have been one of the great races of my career, with John on the favourite Our Bara Boy, Jonjo on Rogairio and myself on Great Developer all fighting it out to the line. John led from the ninth hurdle until a mistake at the last allowed me to take the lead for a few strides up the run-in, when Jonjo in turn headed me until the last stride, at which point John at his brilliant best forced Our Bara Boy past to a neck victory. Was this handicap hurdle a contest to show who was the best jockey of the era? I would like to think I was only a neck behind Jonjo or John.

In the following race, the Welsh Champion Hurdle, Broadsword failed to redeem himself after his defeat at Cheltenham and a subsequent fall at the last when in contention at Aintree, finishing third to Jonjo and Ekbalco. But I won the next two on Eastern Line and Midnight Song; I was now fifteen winners ahead of John and felt that with any luck at all the championship would be mine.

And the winners continued to flow: three more for Mercy at the Cheltenham Spring Meeting on 21 and 22 April and two more the following day at Market Rasen, one for my father and the other for Willie Musson, brother-in-law of my ex-boss at Bernard Thorpe's. I was now twenty winners ahead of John.

Getting to Market Rasen for that meeting proved just about as exciting as riding at it, which is saying something for a jockey. David Nicholson and I were at a dinner in London the night before, and he had arranged for me to get a lift to the races with the owner of Tinker's Trip, a horse I was to ride there. I had only met Alfred Buller once before, when he walked down David's yard with his father, Bill, after inspecting their horse. Tinker's Trip had on occasion run off the end of the gallop, and was later to run away with Paul Carvill at Hereford racecourse, jumping a high wire fence into a children's playground. After my lift to Market Rasen, I could see that owner and horse had a lot in common. We were due to leave London at 9.00 a.m. At 9.55 I was still pacing up and down on the pavement outside my hotel while the Duke made frantic phone calls to see where Alfie had got to. At 10.05 his BMW screeched round the corner, I jumped in and we headed north. Nothing looked like overtaking us until a policeman stopped us for speeding near Lincoln. 'Which one of you two was driving?' he said, 'because the driver was leant so far over into the passenger seat I couldn't tell.' Alfie showed his Ulster driving licence and we were waved on without a charge.

We were getting on like a house on fire long before we got to Market Rasen. Alfie was a very successful Northern Irish property dealer, with a business based in London. He was the same age as me, loved horses and when working commitments allowed he rode in point-to-points and horse trials at home. We have been good friends ever since that hair-raising journey. Tinker's Trip, unfortunately, did not on this occasion run as fast as his owner's car, and finished seventh. He was to be my last completed ride in England that season.

On the Saturday I didn't ride – I was now well ahead, after all – but went to Aarau in Switzerland on the Sunday to ride over fences for Peter Piller (who became champion owner in England with the horses he had in training with Arthur Stephenson). In this race, which I won, I jumped the biggest fence I have ever negotiated: a very tall and wide bullfinch. It rode much better than it looked, as horses who knew what they were doing jumped through the finch rather than trying to clear it. On the same day I saw John Reid ride in the Swiss Derby, which to my eye looked far more dangerous than any steeplechase I had ever seen. Starting from stalls just in front of the first bend, he had a good break, but by the time all the other riders had crowded in to go round the turn he had no room, and his horse's legs hardly touched the ground as he was carried into the back straight.

On Monday 26 April I had a ride on Prairie Master at Southwell. I didn't need it: in the last eight weeks I had ridden forty-two winners to John's fourteen, had already notched up more rides in a season than anyone before me, and had half an eye on Jonjo's seasonal record of 149 winners. But it was my policy of chasing rides all over the country that had taken me to the top of the table, and I suppose it was that same impulse that took me up to Southwell.

When Prairie Master fell I broke my left arm in two places and was knocked out. Coming round in the tin shack they called the 'ambulance room' I bleated out to Steve Smith Eccles, who had come to see how I was, that I was not to be sent to fight in the Falklands War – I must have been worried that I was being conscripted into the army! With my arm in a plastic splint I was driven to hospital in Nottingham. While I was sitting in the

*John Francome's gesture in hanging up his boots once he had drawn level with me in the race for the 1981–2 championship following my injury was a great example of his sportsmanship. In December 1983, we both rode for Lord Vestey at Newbury. We look happy enough beforehand but were both beaten in the race!* (BERNARD PARKIN)

waiting room with my X-rays, waiting for a doctor to attend to me, John Webb, whom I had never met before, saw me still in my breeches and boots and came over to ask if he could help in any way. He explained that he was a surgeon, based at Queen's Hospital in Nottingham, and that if I could stand the journey he would take me across the city and operate straight away. This he did, putting a metal plate in my arm. When I came round from the anaesthetic, he told me to rotate my forearm slowly to keep it mobile and to speed the healing process. I was never put in plaster, and within a few days I was out of hospital.

John Francome rang me at home and offered his sympathy; then he told me that if he could draw level with my total of winners he would stop riding so that we could share the championship. The last time the jockeys' title had been shared was in 1969, when Terry Biddlecombe and Bob Davies each rode seventy-seven winners; this year I had amassed 120, and John, true to his word, pursued this total and, having matched it, stopped. It was a gesture that made the last month of the season bearable, and I am eternally grateful to him for it. The championship was what mattered to me; whether I won it outright or shared it was of infinitely lesser importance. And now I was champion jockey.

*Chapter Six*

# THE TRIALS OF JOCKEYSHIP

—▶◀—

I returned to riding that summer in Ireland, taking part in a challenge between Irish and English jockeys at Limerick racecourse. The English team, consisting of Hywel Davies, Ron Barry, Jonjo O'Neill, Steve Smith Eccles, John Francome and myself, stayed at the Dunraven Arms in Ardare, a picture-postcard village with thatched cottages lining the streets and the naked ruins of an abbey in the background. Despite the idyllic setting, however, getting the event under way proved to be something of a scramble.

We were riding on the Monday evening, and that morning Hywel had decided to go to Dublin, a considerable distance away, to see a diet specialist, Dr Dara. He was going to come back by train with John, who had been delayed in getting over. First of all, when the doctor took a blood sample, Hywel passed out; then, when he and John eventually got to the train, it broke down about an hour from the racecourse. By this time the rest of us had already ridden in one race and it began to look as if the other two would miss the whole competition, which would have been a dreadful shame for the racecourse executive, who had put so much into organizing the event, and the paying public who had turned up to see us all. But they did arrive – without a second to spare – and to cap it all John at his brilliant best gave a sparkling display of horsemanship to ride a winner. That display, however, was nothing compared to the exhibition the jockeys made of themselves at the party in the hotel afterwards.

After this light-hearted interlude it was unfortunately down to earth again with a thump. The shadows of the previous season gathered round me on my return to England, where I had not only to ride wearing a hard plastic arm protector but also to face a Jockey Club inquiry into the running of the Schweppes Handicap Hurdle at Newbury in February.

John Francome, Steve Smith Eccles and I all had rides in the

1982 Schweppes, John for Paul Kelleway on Donegal Prince, and Steve and I both for Nicky Henderson, he on Mount Harvard and I on The Tsarevich. The morning of the race, John, Steve and I were sitting in the sauna trying to get down to our respective race weights of ten stone four pounds, ten stone two pounds and ten stone when John asked us if we would like to divide the prize money of the Schweppes if any of us won it. As the winning jockey stood to get £600, this meant that if any of us won, we would give the other two £200 each. This seemed a good idea to me – the Schweppes is a notoriously open race – so by the time John, who never sweated if he could help it, announced that the sauna was too hot and left, saying he would rather put up overweight (which he did – four pounds) than sit there all morning, we had decided that if one of us won, he would split the purse with the other two.

I didn't give the deal much more thought until realizing, as John and I were upsides coming into the straight two out, that both of us looked beaten. I said to John, 'Your two hundred isn't looking too good,' and then I was swallowed up by the pack. John, however, pulled one of his great riding feats out of the bag, conjuring a great run from Donegal Prince to win, with Steve and Mount Harvard coming in third. Being a man of his word, John gave Steve and me each a cheque for £200 before he left the course; and the following Monday, he recounted the tale in the column he wrote for the Sun.

Three months later, I had a phone call from a representative of Racecourse Security Services, informing me that they were investigating a case of betting in a race between jockeys, and would be coming to interview me. I told my 'interviewer' that the arrangement was not a bet at all, simply an agreement between three riders in a race to pool their potential winnings – a deal of the kind that is always being informally made among participants in a host of sports. The idea being put forward seemed bizarre. No one, surely, could seriously consider that any jockey, however corrupt – which none of us was – would alter the finishing position of his horse for £200, or even that any remotely competent jockey would consider it possible to dictate the result of a twenty-seven runner handicap hurdle? Nevertheless, the three of us were charged with receiving money for a race other than from the owners of the horses we were riding. The technical infraction of the Rules of Racing involved was serious enough for us to hire a solicitor to represent us before a Jockey Club disciplinary committee, as it dawned on us that if this charge were pressed we risked losing our licences to ride.

The committee hearing was set for after our return from Ireland. John, Steve and I had a meeting with our solicitor, Matthew McCloy, over a cup of tea in a hotel in Portman Square, a few yards away from the Jockey Club headquarters, then dutifully trooped up to present ourselves to the panel of Stewards. We sat on one side of a large oak table; they sat on the other. Mr McCloy presented our case, explaining that what we had done was in essence not dissimilar from the common practice of the winning jockey in a big race buying champagne for the rest of the weighing room – a well-established gesture that has on occasion certainly cost me more than £400. But the Stewards, who seemed to know remarkably little about the established practices within racing, were unmoved by the comparison and the inquiry dragged on, with their solicitor expanding at considerable length on the whole question of payments to jockeys. John, who had been taking piano lessons, started to try out some chords on the table-top to pass the time. One of the 'cabbage-patch dolls', as he referred to them, barked at him: 'Francome, what are you doing?' 'Practising my piano,' he replied.

We were suspended from riding for a week under Rule 62c, according to which 'It should be a breach of the Rules of Racing for a Jockey to receive presents in connection with a race, wherever run, from persons other than the Owner of the horses he rides in that race.' While the comparative leniency of the punishment indicates that the Stewards must have realized the essential harmlessness of what we had done – if that Rule were applied literally, there wouldn't be a jockey riding – it seemed ludicrous to me that disciplinary proceedings had been brought at all, and even more curious that it had taken the Jockey Club three months to start an investigation. It all suggested a witch-hunt against either one of us in particular or all three of us, by someone involved in the race or within the racing authorities.

I did, however, learn that the Stewards must read page three of the *Sun*, otherwise they would not have read John's story of the account in the first place . . .

Eventually we were able to put this distasteful episode behind us and concentrate on the important things again. My work and home life had by now become to an extent interlinked. David had been very keen that I should find somewhere to live near his yard, and Marilyn and I were now living just a couple of hundred yards away in a house that we had bought from Mary Lycett-Green. In spring 1982 Marilyn, then expecting our first child, had given up her teaching job; as David's secretary had left to go abroad, she had been helping out in the office, and after Thomas was born she took on the job. It made a lot of sense for her to become more closely involved with racing, and the arrangement worked very well for all of us.

Despite these developing links with Condicote, I was continuing to broaden my riding base; this year John Thorne, who trained at Bridgwater in Somerset, asked me if I would like to share his stable's rides with John Francome. I was obviously delighted to have a good West Country yard to ride for and went down there to ride work and school along with John and Richard Linley, who still rode all Sheikh Ali Abu Khamsin's horses.

John's training facilities included a three-furlong wood-chip all-weather strip, bordered on the left-hand side with pig-netting and on the right with a six-foot drop into a ditch. We galloped the horses up this track and cantered back down again; some of the young horses were also schooled over obstacles here, with small branches threaded through the pig-netting to make a sort of wing to the jump. One horse I rode took a dislike to the leaves on the 'wing' and jumped the ditch in preference to the hurdle. We then moved on to the turf. Richard set off for the sequence of three hurdles on his mount, a big, ignorant horse that he was trying to give its first experience of jumping. Richard was riding with the full length of leather and found he didn't have as much control as he would have liked: having run out at all three hurdles, the horse went trotting and cantering off over the undulating ground, impervious to all Richard's attempts to pull it up, and eventually the pair of them disappeared over the brow of the hill. Some time later, Richard came back to find John and me still in hysterics.

One of the good horses I came to ride through this connection was Artifice, trained by John Thorne for Paul Barber, one of the most sporting owners in racing. The horse was already twelve when I came to ride him, but had his best ever season, winning five races including the two-mile chase at Liverpool at the Grand National meeting and finishing second in both the Mackeson

Gold Cup and the Queen Mother Champion Chase at the Cheltenham Festival. He wasn't very big, but made up for lack of inches with abounding enthusiasm, and for a small horse he had a lot of scope. He was a very easy ride and thoroughly genuine: I used to grab a piece of mane and leave his head alone as much as possible so as not to interfere with him.

And there were winners and promising young horses back 'home' at Condicote; but as so often in racing, the high hopes and early successes were all too frequently followed by disappointment and frustration. Connaught River, a former inmate of Michael Stoute's, won three races over hurdles before becoming temperamental and running out on the top bend at Sandown, depositing me on the floor in the process. Two horses about whom the yard was particularly excited, Gambir and Charter Party, also started off well. After winning his only start in a bumper in Ireland, Gambir had gone on to win his first two races over hurdles for us, only to be soundly beaten by Very Promising in the Panama Cigar Hurdle Final at Chepstow. Charter Party, owned by the partnership of Colin and Claire Smith and Raymond and Jenny Mould, took a great deal of schooling to get him to jump properly but also went on to win over hurdles at Haydock. And then, when in front in the final of the Haig Whisky Novice Hurdle at Newcastle, he unseated me at the last. We had all flown up for the race and it was a miserable flight back home.

But there are always compensations, and as well as the home winners I had many good mounts outside the yard this season, among them Royal Vulcan, on whom I won the Scottish Champion Hurdle by a head from Ekbalco. In the Grand National I rode Fortina's Express for Arthur Stephenson, but had to pull up while Corbiere went on to take his place in history. Kathies Lad, having won a good handicap at Newbury, was made second favourite for the Arkle Chase at Cheltenham, but unfortunately went lame early in the race.

The highlight of Cheltenham this year, and indeed of the whole season, was Michael Dickinson's herculean feat of training the first five home in the 1983 Gold Cup: Bregawn and Silver Buck, the runner-up and winner the previous year, plus Captain John, Wayward Lad and Ashley House. Michael, a former jockey who had taken over the training licence of the Harewood yard from his father Tony, had come to dominate the National Hunt scene over the past two seasons. It was difficult to ride against his horses: they were very fit and often made all the running. If you rode up with them you were accused of making too much use of your horse; if you dropped in behind you were accused of giving your horse too much to do. Consequently there was a psychological as well as a physical challenge in competing against the Dickinson horses.

Sadly, Michael's success aroused a great deal of jealousy among the ranks of the other trainers, and unfounded rumours of drug abuse and blood doping were being spread. I was to see this churlish type of reaction to the success born of talent and hard work once again when the meteoric rise of Martin Pipe in the late 1980s ruffled a lot of established feathers. For myself, I had a great deal of respect for the way Michael worked, and knew that if I wanted to be a great jockey I needed to ride for someone like him: it was my great good fortune that in striking up a partnership with the Pipe team I was able to.

But those days were still some way off; 1982–3 was as close as I got to John's total of winners in a full season's racing, and in 1983–4, with Jonjo back to his best as well, I rode only ninety-eight winners to his 103 and John's personal highest total of 131.

The autumn of 1983 came in dry, and the fields were correspondingly small, especially at the bigger meetings. It is under these conditions that two-runner races most often arise; these can be really strange events to ride in, especially if one or both of the horses does not want to be in front for too long. The pace is often false and some odd results are thrown up. At Ascot this year I rode Artifice in a two-horse race against Sam Morshead on Western Rose. Trying to play the situation down, I commented to Sam that we could not wish to have two safer horses to ride in such a contest – and then promptly fell at the third fence. Later, at Cheltenham, in another two-horse race the boot was on the other foot when my opponent fell at the first, leaving St Alezan and me to complete the course in eerie solitude. It is a very curious feeling: on the one hand you are trying to canter round carefully without falling yourself, but on the other you are constantly worried that you have got it wrong and that your opponent is going to appear suddenly at your shoulder and sweep past to beat you. And if you do make it, unsaddling alone in the winner's enclosure is weird, too.

One of the main worries for a jockey when the ground is fast is that a shower of rain on firm ground can make the going slippery. Craig Smith, who shared the rides at Martin Tate's with me, had broken his leg when Scot Lane slipped up on the bend at Nottingham, and Artifice came down in just the same way on the bend at Sandown. This incident is an example of another problem that jockeys have to face from time to time: whether to remount after a fall. On this occasion, out of the four runners two of us had slipped up and Paul Barber, Artifice's owner, came down the track and asked me to get back up and jump the last three fences for third prize money. I declined because I felt that the horse might have hurt himself, and indeed it turned out that he had pulled some muscles in his back. On the other hand, there are cases where it is worth getting on again, despite the old saying that 'there are fools, damn fools, and those that remount in a steeplechase': years later at Chepstow I came off Capability Brown in a nine-runner novice chase and knowing that neither of us was hurt was able to remount him to win with no harm done. It is always a difficult decision to have to make, and highlights the fact that a good jockey needs a level head as well as nerve and ability. I do not believe that the Jockey Club should legislate on the question: most horsemen know what to do when the circumstances arise.

For all the problems attached to these conditions, there are horses who love the top of the ground and really come into their own in a dry winter: St Alezan was one such, a magnificent jumper of fences when the going suited him, and during the 1983–4 season he won four steeplechases for me before being beaten a neck in the Mackeson Gold Cup by Pounentes and Neale Doughty. Martin Tate, who trained St Alezan, gave me a lot of support; the Chaddesley Corbett point-to-point course was on his farm and I used to school his horses over some of the fences.

Another horse who blossomed this year was Tom's Little Al, trained by Billy Williams in the West Country. This was an incredibly tough little grey that had been beaten when being held up in his earlier races. On my first ride on him, no one wanted to go on, so I made the running and he won! From then on we always ran him up with the pace.

Judging pace and racing tactics are essential talents for a successful jockey; not only must you know your horse and take account of your riding instructions, but you also have to learn how to read between the lines of the conversations among jockeys that take place in the weighing room and while walking round at the start. This is where riders discuss how they are going to tackle the race, whether or not they are going off in front, and so on. It is not collusion, or attempting to rig the race in any way: simply a group of people trying to find out what sort of pace the field is likely to go and how the race is likely to develop. And because each one of them wants to win, you also need to know when to take what others say with a pinch of salt.

There is an old adage in racing: 'You can give weight, but you can't give start.' In large fields, especially in the big races such as those at the Cheltenham Festival, it can be difficult to find room at the starting gate to line up, as many are eager to be up with the pace. In less competitive races it is necessary to know how fast the field is likely to set off: if two or three horses are going on you will probably get a good pace, but if only one horse wants to be in front its jockey may be able to dictate the race as he wants. And this is where the pinch of salt can be useful. Sometimes a jockey will say: 'I'll go off at a good gallop, but don't worry, I'll come back' – in other words, once the horse has settled he will be unable to keep up the good gallop. To know whether to believe a statement like this, you need to know the form book. Through experience of racing against various horses and studying their form, you become able to make a judgement that is not based solely on what the jockeys say. You also come to know the form of the jockeys as much as that of the horses: certain jockeys ride similar races time after time, very often under the influence of the trainers they ride for, and this too helps you to assess how the race is likely to be run.

I would study the form for two reasons: to identify the bad jumpers, and to assess the ability of the opposition and pick out the likely main dangers. The bad jumpers are obviously not ones to track because of the risk of being brought down; in fact, experienced jockeys will very often take horses like this round towards the outside, out of the way of the others, and it used to irritate me when some idiot said: 'Don't follow me, I am going down the middle/round the inside,' as he was bound to have most of the field following him.

As a professional jockey, albeit a former amateur myself, I disliked riding against inexperienced riders, whether they were amateurs, women or other professionals, both because they increased the dangers of the race and because they did not usually understand the etiquette prevailing among the regular jockeys that enabled them to survive. I remember riding on the Mildmay course at Aintree in a two-mile handicap chase on the day of the Grand National. The Mildmay is a very fast track running on the inside of the National course, and on the top bend the horses would have to turn sharp left to stay on the

*I know my place – giving the lead to HRH the Princess Royal on David Nicholson's gallops as she prepares Against the Grain for a charity race at Epsom in 1985 (BERNARD PARKIN)*

course, because if they went straight on they would go over the Melling Road where two JCBs would be pulling cinders over the tarmac surface so that the National runners could cross it on their way to the first fence.

The quickest horses of the day – Badsworth Boy, Drumgora and Western Rose – were taking part, and it was obvious that we were going to go a very fast gallop. Among the jockeys for this race was Norman Babbage, an amateur riding a horse called

Spinning Saint. I was worrying about where he was going to go during the race, and when I enquired he told me he would be unable to hold the horse! Being rather wound up at the time, I gave him a mouthful about how anybody would be able to hold any horse in the likely pace of this race. We set off and Norman, pushing his horse along, was in front after the second, taking the field along at a frantic pelt. On the top bend he went straight through between the two JCBs and fell at the first fence on the National course, allowing the remainder of the field to continue on the correct course at a much more sensible gallop.

All the same, there are good amateurs and bad amateurs just as there are good and not so good professional jockeys, and having myself experienced the kind of reception amateurs sometimes get in racing yards I had a degree of sympathy for them and tried to help whenever possible. Of course, evident ability helps to deflect open derision or hostility – as does being a member of the royal family; and Princess Anne had both advantages when she came to ride out at David Nicholson's in the 1985–6 season in preparation for some rides in amateur races on the flat. I thought her coming into the yard would change the atmosphere, but I was quite wrong: once things had settled down and we had got used to the paparazzi lying in the hedges with their cameras everything went on as normal.

All of us at the yard were concerned about using the proper mode of address when talking to the Princess; we learnt that 'Ma'am' was the correct term, but my son Thomas, then four years old, didn't quite get the hang of it. The Princess would arrive in the mornings with her detective and leave her car outside the office, where Marilyn worked as David's secretary, while going to ride out. One morning around nine, as she came back to the car to leave, everyone was saying 'Goodbye ma'am' when Thomas, standing with Marilyn, piped up 'Goodbye mum!' The Princess replied, 'Thomas, I think you have ideas above your station.'

The Princess was an excellent horsewoman, as I should have known: I had forgotten that she had been European Three Day Event Champion. She soon adapted her style to racing and had a very good eye for a horse. Long Engagement was one she particularly liked, even when he was running badly over hurdles, and his later successful steeplechasing career proved her right. She quickly commanded the respect of all of us and was soon riding work; she went on to school over fences and in future seasons was to ride in steeplechases. There too the same respect was shown to her without altering the atmosphere of the race; she may have ridden as an amateur but had a resolutely professional demeanour. We would all discuss riding plans at the start as usual, the only difference being that Steve Smith Eccles tempered his language a bit – but I would expect that from him in front of any lady!

One of the horses that the Princess regularly rode out at the Duke's, a colt called Solar Cloud, unseated her one morning. The reason I remember this incident is that, knowing only too well how undignified it feels to chase a loose horse up the gallops on foot, I got off my horse and gave it to her to canter up to the top, where Solar Cloud was by then standing with the Duke. I think this is the most noble thing I have ever done in my life; however, the news cannot ever have reached the Palace as I am not now Sir Peter.

It was through the Princess's kindness that I fulfilled a non-racing ambition: to fly in Concorde. I was trying to ride at Wincanton on the Thursday, in Nashville on the Friday, and back in England again on the Saturday. Concorde would get me to New York, but I then had a problem getting a connection to Nashville. As the Princess was also riding there, her office took care of the arrangements for the whole party. I was told to be at the Duke's on Friday morning to get a lift with him and his wife Dinah to Heathrow, where we would meet the Princess to fly to New York. Arriving in the VIP lounge to await the royal party, we put our luggage down in the middle of the room; soon the Princess appeared, shortly followed by the Deputy Chairman of British Airways, who picked up my bags and carried them on to Concorde. When we got to Kennedy Airport in New York, the mayor of the city was there to greet us and plain-clothes detectives again materialized to collect all the luggage and take it to the private jet that had been laid on by the racecourse to fly us down to Tennessee.

On arriving at Nashville we were met by yet more detectives, this time in three-piece suits with pistols in ill-concealed holsters bulging within their jackets. This time I had to carry my own bags as I clambered into the jeep at the back of the eight-vehicle cavalcade that was to escort the Princess's limousine to the track. Overhearing the radio conversations opened my eyes to the kind of organization needed simply to get this convoy along a ten-mile stretch of road to the racecourse without its breaking up at traffic lights and road junctions.

The Princess won her race, after which I slummed it back to England on an ordinary flight in time to get beaten for the second time in twenty-four hours.

One of the best horses I rode during the 1983–4 season was Charter Party, who had now progressed to steeplechasing. Despite a lot of careful schooling at home he still found the business of jumping very difficult, and his first few runs over fences were a matter of survival for both of us. However, he got his act together to win at Worcester on 15 February 1984 before putting up a good performance to take the Betterton Chase at Newbury a distance ahead of the second horse.

Our best novice chaser this season was Voice of Progress, on whom Niall Madden, now second jockey to me at David Nicholson's, had done most of the schooling. He was a very free-running horse and, like Charter Party, did not look entirely happy over fences to begin with, but with Niall's tuition he began to show real promise. And then one of the recurrent dilemmas of a jockey's life intervened. The day before I was due to ride him at Newbury, I had a fall at Hereford on a grey filly of my father's. The fall itself was not a bad one, but as I wrapped myself in a ball to protect myself from damage by the following horses, I got kicked on the index finger of my right hand and broke it.

I knew that if I went to hospital to get it seen to they would put it in a splint, which would mean no riding at Newbury the following day. And if I didn't ride Voice of Progress at Newbury, and Niall did and won on him, I risked losing future rides on him. On the other hand, the horse could not be considered a safe conveyance on his first time out over fences, and the last thing a jockey necds is further falls making existing injuries worse. I decided to put my potential future partnership with a promising young horse above the prospect of worse damage and rode Voice of Progress the next day. We won; when I look at my bent finger now I wonder if it was worth it!

At the 1984 Cheltenham Festival I finished second in the Champion Hurdle on Cima, three-quarters of a length behind the great Dawn Run and Jonjo. On reflection, brilliant though she was, Dawn Run was lucky to win that day. There was no Stewards' Inquiry after the race, but in getting to the line in front she had undoubtedly drifted right-handed across the track, taking Cima with her, and when you add to that the fact that this was the first season in which mares in National Hunt races were given a five-pound allowance over horses and geldings it's easy to start thinking that perhaps Cima should have got there.

The third horse in that race, Very Promising, was one of a pair (the other being Eastern Line) that after Cheltenham were taken away from Mercy Rimell's yard and sent to David Nicholson, specifically to ensure that I would be able to ride them. This decision by the owners caused some bad feeling between Mercy and David, as well as between Mercy and myself, and for the time being brought my association with the Rimell yard to an end. Another, much earlier, connection was revitalized to good effect: while at school at Belmont Abbey I was friendly with Kieran Ennis, and it was for his father Jim that I came to ride Rushmoor to victory twice at the end of the season, once at Ascot and once in my second successive victory in the Scottish Champion Hurdle at Ayr.

I had a less pleasant end-of-season experience after winning the Tia Maria Hurdle at Haydock on Bajan Sunshine. I had been second on this very good hurdler to Fealty in the Sun Alliance Novices' Hurdle at Cheltenham and knew his ability. For my efforts to achieve this victory, however, I was fined for excessive use of the whip. Not for the last time, I found the censure hard to accept. Peter O'Sullevan wrote in his book *Calling the Horses* that it was one of the worst examples he had seen; Timeform's *Chasers and Hurdlers* for that year contained the following passage:

> With Scudamore riding at his strongest Bajan Sunshine battled on gamely, and had a head to spare over Secret Ballot. It was an exciting race but surely Scudamore didn't deserve to be fined for improper use of the whip. Bajan Sunshine, who needs strong handling, responded each time he was asked for an extra effort. Scudamore along with many other jockeys now uses a padded whip. The veterinary officer who examined Bajan Sunshine twice could find no marks on him.

I honestly feel that I would not have won that race without

riding as I did. I can remember my thoughts as I battled up the run-in that afternoon; I was determined not to be beaten, and I knew my horse could win. In the same way as a good horseman knows when and when not to remount after a fall, so he knows when the whip can encourage a horse and when it will simply hurt and discourage him. The question of the whip was not going to go away and its use was a dilemma that we jockeys were going to face more often.

# Chapter Seven

# CHAMPION OUTRIGHT

———▶◀———

The next season was numerically the worst of my professional career. In 1984-5 I rode only fifty winners; John Francome was again champion jockey with 101. David Nicholson's yard produced just seventeen wins.

The reason for the stable's bad showing was the virus. This is easy enough to state with hindsight, but at the time it was not immediately obvious, and the general anxiety about the yard's performance caused a lot of aggravation. When horses are wrong, for whatever reason, one of the first symptoms on the racecourse is that their jumping becomes sloppy under pressure; they begin to make mistakes and falls become more frequent. As stable jockey, I was blamed for the horses' failure to produce results, and this in its turn feeds back into a lack of confidence: you tend to start coming second a lot when you should be winning, because you lose faith in the ability of the horse to run on to the line.

All this becomes much clearer in retrospect than it is at the time; when you are going through lean times you just carry on trying harder, knowing that if you concentrate and persevere things will improve in due course. And in fact my own season started well enough: at Chepstow in early October, the first televised meeting of the season and, for me, the start of the better-class National Hunt racing, I rode a double on Statesmanship for Richard Hannon and Broadheath for the Duke.

There was some fun in the autumn too, with a jockeys' competition between England, Ireland and France, organized by the writer and racing enthusiast Alan Lee, with one heat to take place in each of the three countries. The first leg was at Galway, where I rode a winner. The 'English' leg – held at Chepstow in Wales – was won by the French jockey Dennis Bailliez, and I failed to make the French leg at all owing to a fall from Charter Party on the day we were due to leave, but while I was recovering from concussion John Francome rode a winner for the English team at Auteuil. Competing against the French jockeys was good experience, and gave us the chance to appreciate their riding style. In general they were smaller than us as the weights are lower in French jump races; they rode very short and sat stiller at the obstacles. All in all they were very stylish and good jockeys.

Back at home, the signs that all was not well were beginning to mount up. Gambir, whose prospects had excited us all the previous season, was one of the first horses that ran badly, finishing last in a good chase at Wincanton. At the time we thought the horse had been doped; it is only when you look back that you see the real problem developing. Very Promising, too, was disappointing early in the season, being beaten on one occasion by Gaye Brief in a needle match against his old trainer, Mercy Rimell. We had another sort of problem with Very Promising that related to his jumping. After a spate of disappointing runs, the Duke and I discussed switching him from hurdles to fences. David was worried that the horse was too small to do himself justice over the stiffer obstacles, but schooling sessions at home convinced us that he had talent, being able to stand off his fences or get in close.

Riding horses over fences early in their careers is always difficult; no matter how much they have been schooled, their reaction to the fences on the racetrack can be totally different. A horse who is 'popping' his fences nicely at home might really take them on when racing. In schooling, I liked to give a young horse time to warm to his task and not rush him into the jumps, quickening him up as he gains experience. It is important that he learns both to stand off and to fiddle a jump; otherwise, when you start asking the horse to go flat out in a race you are asking him questions that he has not faced before and this is when he is likely to make a mistake. Very often after a fall I would wish I had chosen a different stride; however, at the time you have to make an instant decision between safety and speed, and only by taking calculated risks can you continue to win.

Very Promising had done such good work at home that we gave him his first run over fences at Haydock. This course houses the biggest and most intimidating fences in the country, and many trainers would not see it as an ideal venue for a horse's first steeplechase. However, I have always considered it among the best chasing tracks in the country. The fences are fair and well sited, and the fact that they are so big tends to frighten away

*Returning to unsaddle after winning a novice chase at Ludlow on An-Go-Look for my father (right) in May 1985*

much of the opposition, keeping the fields relatively small. This may be unfortunate for the racccourse executive but it is good news for jockeys as fewer runners mean more room at the fences and usually a slower pace, both factors that enable you to give a younger horse a good ride. It is racing as I imagine it to have been in my father's day, when fences had to be treated with much more respect because they were stiffer. The real horsemen among jockeys, like Mark Dwyer and Neale Doughty, do particularly well at Haydock.

Very Promising vindicated our choice by winning his race. His next run was at Newbury, where he was disputing the lead when he fell at the third last, the open ditch. It was an extraordinary fall: I asked him to stand a long way off the fence so he had to make a tremendous effort to clear it and in bravely doing so sprawled on landing; as he struggled to remain upright he catapulted me off into the air, and I ended up running by his side. We were then beaten in the Arkle Chase at the Cheltenham Festival by Boreen Prince and Buck House; he was chopped for speed coming down the hill, and though he always ran with distinction at Prestbury Park I felt that he did himself more justice on tracks like Ascot and Newbury.

John Francome had a nasty fall off The Reject in the Arkle that may have brought to a head his thoughts about retirement from race-riding. By now he was beginning to realize that he could earn a good living off the course, and the sport no longer had the same appeal for him. John had always been known as carefree and a great joker – in the weighing room our valet, John Buckingham, kept to the quaint tradition of hanging our riding clothes on the pegs in order of seniority, with John first, Steve Smith Eccles second, and me third; John and Steve were great mates and there was never a dull moment changing next to them – but when he returned from his fall that afternoon he was clearly shaken, and instead of characteristically laughing about the mishap he gave up to Steve his ride on See You Then in the Champion Hurdle, thus establishing a partnership that went on to win the race three times. John went on riding for a few weeks, but retired on 9 April after another fall from The Reject at Chepstow.

Earlier in the spring, in the middle of all the frustrations of a yard off form, there had been a good omen for the future, though I didn't realize it at the time. On 2 March there had been two spare rides in a race at Haydock. I tried to secure the mount on Horn of Plenty for John Edwards, but discovering that John Francome had been engaged for it took the other, a horse called Hieronymous trained by Martin Pipe. To quote the form book: 'Hieronymous, 4, 10.7, P. Scudamore. Looked well, made all, soon clear, hit 7th and 3 out stayed on.' He won by fifteen lengths and after the race I told Martin Pipe that he was the fittest horse I had ridden all season.

The highlight of this otherwise rather unsatisfactory period was my ride on Corbiere in the 1985 Grand National, which I acquired after his regular jockey, Ben de Haan, got kicked in the unsaddling enclosure at Wolverhampton. I had won on the horse in his final preparatory race at Chepstow, and Jenny Pitman phoned to book me for Aintree while I was sitting in the sauna at home.

'How much do you want for riding him?' she asked.

I replied that I would ride the horse for nothing but £200 would be very helpful.

'I've got you £300,' she said, 'so you can give me the rest.'

As soon as I had put the phone down it rang again. This time it was Gordon Richards, whose stable jockey, Neale Doughty, had dislocated his shoulder and would not be fit to ride Hallo Dandy in the race: would I like the mount? In the space of a few minutes I had been offered the ride on the last two years' National winners.

The three-day Grand National meeting at Aintree, good as it is, never quite matches the importance or the atmosphere of Cheltenham a few weeks earlier, though the National itself is of course unique. For me it meant something of a change from the normal routine, with two nights and three days away from home. I always liked to get a ride on the Thursday in the Topham Trophy, which is one of the three races at the meeting run over the National fences, to get my eye in for the big race. My mount in the Topham this year was Burnt Oak, whom I had ridden in the National in 1984; he had led for a circuit, at one stage of which he was so far clear that I couldn't hear any of the other runners behind me and was worried that I had taken the wrong course. As he had gone so well in the first part of that race we decided to run him over the shorter distance of the Topham. Again he led – until the ninth fence, the one before Becher's, where he gave me a crashing fall, breaking my nose and severely bruising the calf muscle of my left leg.

My first thought was that this was the end of my Grand National ride on Corbiere. However, Dr Allen, the Jockey Club's Chief Medical Officer, was very encouraging and told me to get some treatment and go back to see him the next day. He was well aware that if you missed a ride through injury it could cost you future rides on the horse, and was always helpful to jockeys wanting to be passed as fit, so long as they were not putting themselves at risk of permanent damage. Jenny Pitman, obviously, was also concerned, and told me that she did not want me riding Corbiere unless I could prove my fitness by riding on the Friday. On Friday morning I couldn't even walk at first; but after treatment from a physiotherapist and with my leg heavily strapped I was able to walk on to the racecourse to be passed by the doctor as fit to ride that afternoon. Then there was the problem of getting my breeches and boots on over the strapping: I solved this by wearing a pair of boots that would normally have been too wide in the leg, and waterproof breeches that are designed to fit over the top of the boot.

I did however cry off a couple of rides that afternoon; I was still in some pain and could not afford the risk of another fall. I could not tell the trainers the real reason, that I was not really fit, and they therefore assumed either that I was frightened of the horse I was asked to ride or, worse, that I thought it was no good. A day like that taxes your diplomatic skills to the limit.

One of the most pleasant aspects of the National is going to the course early on the Saturday morning and riding a canter on your mount in the race. You can feel the history of the place and the spirit of all the great horses and riders that have competed in the event since 1839. I always have a lot of respect for a horse that has been brave enough to get round in the National. Corbiere, of course, had not only got round but had won it, and it was a good feeling to be on him. After a cup of coffee I then walked – or limped – the course with Jenny Pitman while she pointed out to me how she wanted the horse ridden. I always found that the riding instructions she gave were very clear and to the point; and also, unlike some trainers, she was realistic about the ability of her horses.

It is always good to have a ride on the Saturday before the National to release some of the tension and make you focus on the business in hand, and on this day I had the bonus of winning the opening hurdle race on my old friend Bajan Sunshine. Riding in the earlier races also relieves you of some of the inevitable hanging around: most jockeys get to the course early because of the traffic congestion later on, and this means a lot of waiting about that plays on the nerves. The jockeys' changing rooms at Aintree are behind the covered winner's enclosure, in a large, white building that also houses the Stewards' room. The parquet floor and the austere wooden boxes in which we put our belongings are a reminder of the history of the place, of all the National riders who have been in and out of here over the years. However, the antiquity of the environment has practical disadvantages: there was no sauna, which made it harder than ever for the jockeys at the bottom of the handicap to do their light weights.

The jockeys' pre-race banter avoids the usual subject of hopes and aspirations in the day's big race; perhaps it is felt to be unlucky, or perhaps everyone is just too wound up. Instead it tends to focus on some of the previous night's exploits – like the time Steve Smith Eccles went to sleep in the back of his car

covered in coats and rugs, woke up to find the car belting down
the M57 and wondered who was going to get the biggest shock,
him or the man who had stolen the car. Others will just sit
quietly and read the racing papers, or watch the BBC's build-up
to the event on the two televisions in the room. There is also the
inevitable stream of calls to the weighing-room door to deal with
enquiries from trainers and journalists.

The large number of runners and the pre-race parade mean
that jockeys need to leave for the paddock early. Usually the
more experienced ones wait until about forty-five minutes before
race time before changing into their riding clothes; many,
nervous and wanting to be doing something, will have changed
earlier and be checking their weight on the trial scales. After
passing the scales proper in front of the Clerk, you hand your
saddle to the waiting trainer and return to the sanctuary of the
weighing room for the final touches: having your cap silk tied on
by the valet, pulling on clean goggles. Then comes the doorman's
call and everyone files out, exchanging comments – 'Good luck,'
'Safe journey,' 'If I don't win I hope you do' – as we make our
way through the human corridor between the crowds towards the
paddock. You notice a cameraman walking backwards while
filming you; then you are briefly held up as someone asks for
your autograph. In the paddock itself, brimming with horses and
their connections, you struggle to find the owner and trainer you
are riding for, to receive your final instructions before you are
thrown up on to the horse. On mounting Corbiere I was alarmed
to be reminded how short his neck was in front of me; he was a
stocky horse, but did not immediately give you the feel of being
as safe a jumper as in fact he was.

Walking out on to the track along the pathway, you can hear
the chatter among the crowds pressing against the ropes.
Liverpool humour looms large: David Nicholson once told a
Scouser to get out of the way when walking beside me on my exit
on to the course, and when he told the crowd to 'mind their
backs' as we went out for the next race a voice came back –
'Look, there's God there.'

Once on the course itself the runners circle to get into
racecard order for the parade. As Corbiere is top weight he leads
the string of horses past the crammed stands to shouts of
encouragement before turning to canter back up to the first
fence. Then we turn to go back to the start, being careful to

avoid those later in the parade who are still cantering down to look at the fence.

At the starting gate we all circle round while final adjustments are made to the tack. The Starter moves towards his rostrum and the watching crowds fall silent. My orders on Corbiere are to take a prominent position down the inside, so I line up on the left-hand side of the track. I have a good look round to see who my neighbours are: in the National you break from the gate faster than in ordinary races and there are certain horses you don't want to be behind. With the long run to the first, there is a tendency for horses to go too fast and consequently to overjump and fall.

In race-riding you very rarely hear the crowd or the commentator, but you do notice the roar as you start and pick up little bits of the commentary from the loudspeakers that line the track. Landing safely over the first, I hear ' . . . and Hallo Dandy is a faller.' Coming to the third, I see in front of me and just to my left a horse that I don't want to track, so I pull away from it to make room for Corbiere to jump the ditch. The way in which the Aintree ditches are built allows you to run a horse into the bottom of the fence, and given the width of the ditches this is the

*My best ride in the Grand National – jumping the last on Corbiere to finish third behind Last Suspect and Mr Snugfit in 1985*

best way to tackle them. Corbiere, however, doesn't seem to be relishing the prospect of dragging himself over these yawning gullies and makes a mistake. I have to wake him up with a slap down the shoulder; if he does that again we could fall.

The sixth fence is Becher's; you recognize it because it is set at an angle and there is a small path running across the track about 100 yards in front of it. To compensate for the angle, riders tend to drift to their right before running back down left-handed. The real hazard of Becher's is the drop, which is more severe on the inside where we are, so I quicken Corbiere, asking him to jump out over the drop, and he makes a superb leap. With the track now bearing left and the sharp corner of the Canal Turn approaching, I become aware of the danger of horses taking my ground. I have to keep a neck up on a horse to my outer to prevent him coming across me. Corbiere makes the turn well, saving precious ground which allows me not to rush him into Valentine's Brook, which is the next fence. Then we are heading back to the racecourse proper and after jumping the fences that will be the second last and last next time round we come to the Chair, in front of the grandstand. This fence, an open ditch, is much narrower than the preceding ones, with correspondingly less room for the horses to spread out along it. Having safely negotiated this and the water jump, we set out on the second circuit.

Approaching Becher's for the second time I notice Richard Dunwoody going easily on West Tip, and think, 'I'm not going to beat him.' Then, as we land, out of the corner of my eye I see him fall. There is no time for emotion, for feeling pleased that another competitor is out of the race or sorry that a good horse is down: I am concentrating on every fence as I come to it and on producing Corbiere at the right time. Again he lands well over the Canal Turn and goes to the front. The line of four fences that follows rides well, encouraging horse and rider to stand off them as you fight for every length you can take off the pursuing pack. As we turn for home with two fences to jump John Burke, who pulled Lucky Vane up lame on the first circuit, is standing by the rail; he shouts, 'Keep going, Scu, you'll win!'

'—,' I think, 'I'm going to win the National. Bloody well concentrate.' As I come round the bend to the second last I feel a horse coming upsides me; surely it must be a loose horse? Then Phil Tuck and Mr Snugfit shatter that hope, and I find myself battling to get back past him. Corbiere is staying on, but then Hywel Davies appears, conjuring a run out of Last Suspect to beat us both.

We hadn't won: but everything had gone right, and I was delighted. On the day, with the weight we were carrying, we were just not quite good enough, but it is very touching to be associated with a horse of such courage.

Despite the thrill of Aintree and Corbiere, I was glad to see the back of a troubled season. The poor performance of the Condicote yard had been creating friction between David Nicholson and myself, and I began to feel that the days of our partnership might be numbered. There are always plenty of people ready to put you down when you are not having a good run, and I started the 1985–6 season in real need to re-establish myself.

Now that John Francome wasn't riding any more, my main rival for this year's championship was going to be Simon Sherwood, a natural horseman and a jockey whom I would rate as among the most talented of all those I rode against, as well as the nearest in style to John. My one advantage over him was that he was a wealthy young man in his own right whereas I was hungry – though on reflection it seems less of an advantage. Certainly in the first part of the season it looked like being rather an unequal contest. Simon had the backing of John Jenkins, whose early season horses got him off to a good start while I was really struggling to get going at all: it was not until the end of August that I got off the mark at Newton Abbot, and with the firm ground continuing well into October there were very few rides coming my way. Even those I did have failed to produce results, and if you lose races you tend to lose rides; after getting easily beaten on Ace of Spies by Nebris at the October Chepstow meeting, the owner gave me the sack, which did nothing for my morale.

Finally the luck changed, and on 2 November I rode four winners for the Duke – Very Promising, Tickite Boo, French Union and Cottage Run – to bring me within ten of Simon's tally. Very Promising was by now turning into a top-class chaser, and gave the yard a real boost after the doldrums of the previous season when winning the H&T Walker Handicap Chase at Ascot on 16 November, coming home eight lengths in front of Buck House.

*Coming into the unsaddling enclosure for the last time having won on Sweet Duke at Ascot on 7 April 1993 (GERRY CRANHAM)*

*The first really good horse I rode: Broadsword winning at Chepstow,
December 1980 (BERNARD PARKIN)*

*Pearlyman (on the near side) holds on in a thrilling finish to win the
1987 Queen Mother Champion Chase by a neck from Very Promising
(GEORGE SELWYN)*

*My first Champion Hurdle win is a few hundred yards away as Celtic Shot lands over the last just ahead of Classical Charm (Kevin Morgan) at Cheltenham in March 1988 (GERRY CRANHAM)*

*The common Grand National story of 'What might have been.' Strands of Gold tips me off at second Becher's when leading in 1988 (GERRY CRANHAM)*

*The team. Mrs Muck – with jockey explaining just how he pulled it off – returns after winning the Postlip Novices' Chase at Cheltenham in October 1987, with stable lass Maz and Nigel and Cathy Twiston-Davies. This was the only time Mucky won a chase, though she was successful in six hurdles and three bumpers and was instrumental in putting Nigel on the map*

*Bajan Sunshine was a funny old character with whom I had plenty of ups and downs. Here, in one of his more cooperative moods, he's getting on terms with the Queen Mother's Sun Rising at Ascot in October 1988 – and he won by a short head (TREVOR JONES)*

*Falls – an occupational hazard. My tumble from Lulav at Worcester in October 1984 was used by Ransome's to advertise the effectiveness of their backpads, and you can see why (BERNARD PARKIN)*

*Arden gives me the record 1,139th winner in the Kennel Gate Novices' Hurdle at Ascot on 18 November 1989 (TREVOR JONES)*

*Pondering the race ahead in the paddock at Cheltenham (*DAVID HASTINGS*)*

*Sabin du Loir was a marvellous horse and we won thirteen races together. Here he's about to take the Thunder and Lightning Novices' Chase at Ascot in January 1989. He's now enjoying retirement in a paddock beside Mucky Cottage (GEORGE SELWYN)*

*With Martin Pipe, for whom I rode 792 winners. At least I have an excuse for the shape of my nose! (DAVID HASTINGS)*

*Rolling Ball winning the Sun Alliance Novices' Chase at Cheltenham, March 1991 (BERNARD PARKIN)*

*Carvill's Hill in the Welsh National at Chepstow in December 1991. The press called his performance 'awesome' but for me it was just a characteristic display from this relentless galloper (GERRY CRANHAM)*

*One of my first big winners – Run And Skip, a marvellous little horse, leads Kumbi (Steve Smith Eccles) on his way to victory in the 1985 Welsh National. Kumbi finished third (BERNARD PARKIN)*

The Hennessy Gold Cup at Newbury proved to be a significant race this year. I remember sitting in the sauna before racing with the other jockeys, talking about the likely prospects of our various mounts – except for Mark Dwyer, who remained silent as the rest of us made fools of ourselves trying to pick the winner. During the race itself I heard him shout across to Mick Williams on Mount Oliver: 'Look at this!' I looked across too, and saw Mark on Galway Blaze absolutely cantering as they approached the cross fence five from home. A little horse in front called Run And Skip was running the race of his life, and as Charter Party and I vainly pursued him and Galway Blaze, we slipped and fell at the eighteenth. Galway Blaze went on to win easily.

Sam Morshead, who rode Run And Skip that day, had a horrible fall at Warwick on 28 November. He suffered severe concussion, from which he never recovered sufficiently to ride in another race. Sam was one of the great characters of the weighing room (his underpants were legendary) and was greatly missed;

happily he is now the very successful Clerk of the Course at Perth and Ayr. Again the merry-go-round of racing turned, and it was through Sam's misfortune that I took over the ride on Run And Skip. I rode him first at the Cheltenham December meeting, where we won a handicap chase. He was a real fighter, and we seemed to get on well. John Spearing, who did a marvellous job of training him, could not school the horse because he would not jump at home; but on the racecourse it was a different story. He was a front-runner and a superb jumper, and as with Artifice I used to hold on to a small piece of mane and leave his head alone. He didn't need me to interfere with his stride; if he was wrong at a fence he would shift slightly right-handed to correct himself.

After the Cheltenham win Run And Skip was aimed for the Welsh National at Chepstow, and here I was faced with a bit of a dilemma. As well as riding out for the Duke I would occasionally school for Jenny Pitman, and she now asked me if I wanted to ride Smith's Man for her in the race. It is a difficult position for a jockey to be in, and however many times it happens it doesn't get any easier: you can only ride one horse at a time, and yet if you pick the wrong one when you have a choice you not only lose out financially at the time but probably upset the connections of both horses and lose future rides to boot.

In this case I stuck to Run And Skip and he repaid me generously with a brilliant performance, setting off in front and coming home in front. We went out once more that season in the Anthony Mildmay, Peter Cazalet Memorial Chase, and again this marvellous little horse made all to win.

After the King George VI Chase at Kempton on Boxing Day the merry-go-round took another turn: because of the horse's poor showing that day Phil Tuck lost the ride on Burrough Hill Lad, whom he had ridden to victory in the 1984 Gold Cup, and I replaced him. I felt very sorry for him, and rang him to say so, but all the same was glad to take up the offer of the ride. It happens all the time: I had lost Ace of Spies to Brendan Powell earlier in the season and though I didn't wish them any luck I certainly didn't begrudge Brendan his chance. To survive as a jockey you have to take your opportunities when they come, and we all know that.

On the Flat, jockeys were employing agents to book their rides for them, and some National Hunt riders were beginning to follow suit; I preferred to book my rides myself, but to make sure

I didn't lose out by not being at the end of a phone when a chance came up I did invest in a mobile telephone as soon as they were affordable. The investment was repaid on the way to Doncaster for my first ride over fences on Burrough Hill Lad. I set off northward bound knowing that the meeting was in some doubt because of the previous night's hard frost, and in fact rather hoping that the meeting would be called off: Doncaster is a very fast track where the ground is often firm, and I felt all this would count against me. I didn't want to get the sack from the horse's owner as soon as I'd got the ride. So when I called the course from my mobile phone while still about an hour away, I was very pleased to hear that the meeting had indeed been cancelled, and was in time to contact Rod Simpson to tell him that I was now available to ride Tangognat for him at Cheltenham later that afternoon. This horse was one of the ante-post favourites for the Triumph Hurdle and having won on him at Cheltenham earlier in the month I was very keen to ride him at the Festival. Tangognat duly obliged, making my rather circuitous route to Cheltenham well worth while.

In the end I first rode Burrough Hill Lad over fences at Sandown on 1 February; and I had to turn down the ride on Run And Skip, the 11–4 favourite, to do so. This was a nerve-racking afternoon, and I knew that there were a lot of people who would have liked to see us fail. Jenny as usual gave me her precise and well thought out riding instructions, telling me to give the horse plenty of room, going wide if necessary. I had put a lot of thought into preparing for this race, going down to Lambourn the previous morning to school the horse, and also consulting John Francome, who had won on him. John told me not to let go of his head, because that was when he made mistakes. Even when he met a fence wrong, if you just sat still and kept hold of his head he would sort himself out and keep jumping. This was the key to the horse, and meant that I needed to ride him in exactly the opposite way to how I rode Run And Skip. I remembered that when I had ridden him over hurdles he had a reputation for falling at the last, and I suspect that this was because he was no longer being held together. I had come across the same trait in a horse called Broadheath that eventually won the Hennessy for David Barons: he could jump superbly, but if you let his head go in front of a fence he lost confidence and put down on you at the last minute, often falling as a result.

I practised my technique on Burrough Hill Lad when schooling and carried it out again at Sandown. I squeezed and lengthened him up to a fence sooner than I would with most horses, thus being able to keep my hands closed on the reins and ease him back on to his hocks to jump. He jumped well, apart from one fence at which he was a bit slow; Run And Skip went his usual gallop with my replacement, Graham Bradley, until slipping on landing over the seventeenth. He recovered, but could not make up the lost ground and we eventually stayed on to win by ten lengths from Rainbow Warrior, with Run And Skip a further four lengths back in third. Burrough Hill Lad was immediately made favourite for the 1986 Gold Cup.

Back home in the Cotswolds, my old friend Nigel Twiston-Davies was making strides. He had bought a farm at Naunton, by coincidence just five miles away from where I was then living, and asked me if I wanted to buy two cottages on his land. At the time I declined, but more was to come of the idea later. After leaving home, Nigel had spent time with Richard Head, Fred Rimell and Kim Bailey, taking with him a mare owned by his father called Emperor's Gift. She was a good racehorse, winning eight times for Nigel despite occasionally putting herself on the floor, and eventually did him an even better turn in 1981 when she produced her first foal, a filly by Air Trooper. Nigel named her Mrs Muck; I told him that she would never win with a name like that. How wrong I was.

I first rode Mrs Muck at Cheltenham in January 1986, by which time she had run in three bumpers and won two of them. I wasn't counting too much on this background; in my experience horses learnt very little about racing in English bumpers – in fact, some picked up bad habits that then had to be eradicated, or just got wound up and became more difficult to settle. The Irish system is different and in my view much better. There are more bumpers (in England a horse may run in no more than three) and horses are allowed to run in hurdles and then return to a bumper. The Irish also have schooling races with no betting and therefore nothing hanging on the result, in which older horses can be given a gallop and younger ones taught their job.

So although Mrs Muck had run in her third bumper at Sandown earlier this season, I felt that when it came to introducing her to hurdles she would probably need nursing round a bit. When racing a horse over hurdles for the first time I often tried to give it some room at the obstacles, taking it wide or down the middle, so that it had a chance to learn its business without too much trauma. This was not preventing the horses running on their merits, just teaching them to cope with racing and jumping without getting them knocked about too much. Nigel, however, had told me that Mrs Muck was absolutely brilliant over her hurdles, so I decided to abandon my usual plan and take her down the inside. We were prominent going to the first but when I kicked her into the hurdle she flattened it, losing a few places. I thought to myself, 'That must have been my fault. I'll have to be really definite at the next.' But again she made a mistake, and at the third she jumped really slowly and I completely lost my place. At this stage I was seriously thinking of pulling up – and also that it was never a good idea to do business with friends. Then I moved her to the outside and she absolutely flew: making up all the lost ground over the top of the hill, she came down it hard on the bridle, took the lead approaching the last and scooted away to win by twelve lengths.

Thus began the jumping career of one of the most remarkable and likeable horses I ever rode. 'Mucky' wasn't very big – she was one of only eight foals to survive a virus that swept through the stud where she was born, and Nigel attributes her diminutive stature to this illness in youth, as her close relations are much taller – but she shared with many of them the toughness and fighting spirit that made her such a marvellous racehorse. When Marilyn and I did eventually move to Naunton, we named our cottage after her.

Now the championship was beginning to come alive, and any luck that was going seemed to be coming my way rather than Simon's. I drew level with him on forty-nine winners apiece after scoring a double on Young Nicholas and Memberson at Windsor on 29 January. I was lucky to be on either. Simon would in fact have been riding Memberson that day had it not been for the severe weather that prevailed throughout much of the winter: I had been booked for the horse subject to availability, but had a prior engagement to ride at Hereford. When the snow put paid to that I was able to claim the ride on Memberson – who himself arrived only just in time as the horsebox had to be towed three-quarters of a mile from Pat Dufosee's yard to the main road. In their hurry to be away the connections left behind the colours and the bridle, so they borrowed the latter from Les Kennard, another trainer, and used a different set of colours. The ride on Young Nicholas was another stroke of good fortune: Steve Smith Eccles had been down to ride him but was feeling rather under the weather after a bad fall in the novice chase and, thinking the horse didn't have much of a chance, gave up the ride, which I took when it became spare. As none of the connections fancied the horse either, I was under no pressure and was able to ride a very confident race: he was not a particularly good jumper but responded to being given time to jump and won as a result. People in the stands – even those who should know better – are very quick to criticize jockeys for being 'windy' or not giving a horse a ride; sometimes I just found it easier to ride a horse to please the connections because if you did get beaten it was bound to be your fault however you rode! There were many among the trainers I rode for who neither knew the capabilities of their horses nor understood race-riding.

So while the country endured these Siberian winter months I was glowing in a run of successes. At last everything was going according to plan. I had another double at Ascot, winning on Tickite Boo and Very Promising by a head and a short head respectively – the former in a triple photo finish, having been apparently nowhere near going to the last. Back at Ascot in early February I had a win on Bolands Cross, whom I was riding for Sheikh Ali Abu Khamsin because Richard Linley had been put out of action by a car crash earlier in the season.

The flip side of this, of course, was that the pressure began to mount, especially as the Cheltenham Festival approached. I was now leading jockey, and consequently the focus of media attention; and the first question every interviewer seemed to ask was: Why haven't you ridden a winner at the Festival yet? In this respect at least the Duke and I were in the same boat, as he hadn't yet trained one. Both of us felt the pressure and had hopes for this year; the horses were certainly running better, and a new gallop recently added to the training facilities at Condicote had seemed to play a role in the improvement.

Solar Cloud was to be my ride in the Triumph Hurdle, but I didn't feel too optimistic about our chances. He had won two races before the Festival, the latter being at Kempton, where he had hung so badly left when going to the front after the sixth that he nearly threw the race away, hanging on to win by only a head;

and after passing the winning post he galloped through the tape that functioned as a temporary rail on the outside of the course. I didn't think he had either the temperament or the ability to win at Cheltenham.

On the first day of the Festival meeting the only piece of luck that came my way was second place to See You Then, who was

*My first winner at the Cheltenham Festival – Solar Cloud in the 1986 Daily Express Triumph Hurdle. Solar Cloud started at 40–1, the longest priced winner I've ever ridden (GERRY CRANHAM)*

repeating his previous year's success in the Champion Hurdle. In the last race of the afternoon I made the mistake of staying loyal to John Thorne's County Stone instead of riding Pearlyman, the 14–1 outsider and a novice running in a handicap. On the second day I was on Bolands Cross in the Sun Alliance Novices' Chase; the horse was 5–2 favourite and I couldn't see him being beaten. However, the race itself, with a field consisting of thirty novice chasers including several bad jumpers and many social runners whose connections wanted to see a bold showing early in the race, was one of those occasions when only humour will displace fear. The horses were being lined up on the tape as if the first fence were the winning post, and it took the Starter several attempts to get us off. Remembering the jockeys' comments still makes me smile: 'Why the bloody hell did I take the ride on this?', 'This has no chance of getting round,' and 'Surely I don't need the money this badly?' were some of the repeatable ones.

Out of this massive field twenty fell, seven of them, including me, at the open ditch. (There would have probably been more fallers here, but there wasn't any room.) I was terribly disappointed. I hadn't been going that well and would not have won even if we'd stayed on our feet, but I was beginning to feel that I would never have a winner at the Festival and my morale was approaching rock bottom. I was rescued by Hywel Davies dragging my attention back to the funny side of the day: I was after all in one piece and there were so many jockeys trying to get lifts from the fences to the weighing room that helpers were having to run a shuttle service to get everyone back in time for the next race.

By the time the third and final day's racing got under way I had given up hopes of a winner this year. Solar Cloud was 40–1 for the Triumph; I had wanted to ride Tangognat, but Graham McCourt now had the ride. I had been told by the Duke to hold the colt up until the last possible minute, which didn't strike me as likely to be a problem as I thought he would not be good enough to get to the front. However, we had a dream of a run. The start was not the usual scrimmage and at the top of the hill I found myself in front; as I was there I kicked for home, getting first run on the others, and although Solar Cloud wandered a bit up the run-in he held on to win by a diminishing three-quarters of a length. Tommy Carmody, who was a short head away in third, called 'I've won' as he passed me just after the winning post: I thought for a minute that I must have mistaken the position of the line, but no – I had at last ridden my first Festival winner, and at the same time given the Duke his.

I didn't have a ride in the Gold Cup as Burrough Hill Lad was lame, so I was able to watch Jonjo and Dawn Run put up the greatest performance I have ever seen in a steeplechase. The whole of Ireland was willing them to win, and the reception they received on coming in after the race was a fitting tribute to this great mare and equally great jockey.

I was back on board for the Ritz Club National Hunt Chase, in which Charter Party completed my double in a course record time, thus winning me the Ritz Trophy for the leading jockey at the meeting. He jumped superbly to beat Richard Rowe and Catch Phrase, trained by Josh Gifford, leaving them to take over from David and me as jockey-trainer partnership still to achieve a Festival victory.

The battle with Simon for the championship was gathering pace; my campaign received a great boost on the Saturday after Cheltenham when I rode four winners, but then Simon responded with an equal number at the Newton Abbot Easter meeting. I had drawn a blank at Wincanton that weekend, and though I was still in front I was going to have to fight to hold on to the lead. In my pursuit of the title I was riding for a large number of trainers. I rode a few times for Martin Pipe this season, his stable jockey Paul Leach having broken his wrist in the Champion Hurdle, but the bulk of his rides were still going to the other jockeys with established connections to the yard, Jonathon Lower and Mark Pitman. David Elsworth gave me several rides when his jockey, Colin Brown, was not available; and both Simon and (occasionally) I picked up spare rides from Fred Winter, where the succession to John Francome was still uncertain. Jimmy Duggan and Ben de Haan had taken over as stable jockeys, but the season had not been going well for the yard and some of the owners wanted other jockeys put up.

Meanwhile, the Duke's yard was having a much better season than last year, with Very Promising and the two Festival winners its best advertisements. However, the organization of the business was changing: shareholders were being brought in and the yard, henceforth to be run as David Nicholson Racing Ltd, would no longer be under David's sole authority. This was not good news for me: if one of the new shareholders took a dislike to my riding I could find myself out of a job. David and I had had a great run together during the seven years of our association, but the strains between us had been mounting and even though the winners at Cheltenham and elsewhere had taken some of the pressure off, we were beginning to lose that mutual respect on which any successful partnership between jockey and trainer depends. So, although I had already turned down approaches from other trainers, when Fred Winter rang me at the beginning of April to offer me the job of riding his horses it seemed too good an opportunity to miss. I drove down to Lambourn to discuss the proposal with Fred and the next morning went to see the Duke and told him of my decision. He did not take it particularly well at the time, considering my departure disloyal, but I knew that I had made the right decision for both of us. It also meant the end of Marilyn's job at Condicote, although she had always got on very well with David, and after helping her replacement learn the ropes she left. This replacement, in fact, was Fiona Moore, who is now my secretary at Naunton.

I was still just in front of Simon in the winners table, and the press were beginning to assume that I would be champion jockey this season; I found this very annoying, knowing that with the backing Simon had he could very easily overtake me again – or I might be injured. However hard you try to hide your emotions, it can be very hard to remain impassive when the screws tighten, and though Simon and I were great mates both on and off the course, the rivalry did begin to get to me. At Folkestone on 29 April he rode two winners to my none; as we had travelled down together from Lambourn I had not only to sit in the car after my solitary and unsuccessful ride listening to the commentator calling Simon home on both his victorious mounts but also to try to endure with equanimity his mickey-taking on the way home. It wasn't easy.

The day that clinched it was 17 May. I had gone to Newcastle to ride Mrs Muck, despite meetings at Bangor and, in the evening, Warwick, where I could have had rides. Simon had ridden Mucky to victory in her last race at Cheltenham, where I had forfeited the ride in order to be on a horse of Mercy Rimell's in the same race; she was now beginning to offer me some rides again and I needed her support for my championship bid. However, Simon didn't want to go up to Newcastle to ride the mare, so I went and he took some of the rides I could have had at the other meetings. I flew up to Tyneside while Nigel drove Mucky up with Tracy Bailey, Kim's wife, as travelling head girl, and stayed with her parents who lived a few miles from the track. On arriving at the course I feared that the ground would be too fast for Mucky, but she put up her usual game performance and won. I then picked up a spare ride on Silent Valley, now thirteen years old, and he won too; while all the horses I would have been on at Bangor and Warwick were beaten. Nigel and I retired to the sponsors' tent and emerged feeling very dizzy . . .

On 26 May I rode a treble at Hereford, and the title was mine; to be champion jockey outright at last, after two hard and at times discouraging seasons, felt very sweet. And there was a bonus: two of those winners at Hereford were trained by Martin Pipe, who rang me shortly thereafter to ask if I would ride some of his lower-weighted horses next season which Paul Leach would not be light enough for. At the time it seemed unlikely that Fred's and Martin's horses would clash, and I readily agreed. From this base I was in a position to retain the championship that I had just won.

# Chapter Eight

# SUMMERTIME

To celebrate my first outright championship at the end of the 1985–6 season, Marilyn had organized a surprise party for me in Stow-on-the-Wold. It was great fun, but even then I couldn't allow myself to eat or drink too much as I had to go to Australia at the beginning of June fit to ride in the English jockeys' team challenge against the Australians.

For many jockeys it is hard enough to make a living through the ten months of the National Hunt season in Britain, let alone to survive through the two-month summer break of June and July with no money coming in. Even worse, no riding can mean a gain in weight and a loss of fitness that affect your chances of getting rides when the next season starts. I was fortunate enough to be able to solve both problems by spending most summers of my riding career racing abroad, and over the years I had a lot of fun and gained valuable and varied experience as well. Whenever I was riding in Europe the family joined me for a holiday, and even though my younger son Michael doesn't think much of racing, we all had some very good times.

What was to become an established pattern of summering overseas that took me to Ireland, the European continent, America, Australia and New Zealand began in 1977 when I took a working holiday in Norway. My father had ridden and trained there in the summers of 1965 and 1966, taking some of Willie Stephenson's horses over with the idea of boosting steeplechasing in Norway – where the most popular equestrian sport is trotting races – and it was through these connections that my visit was arranged.

I worked for Dennis Holmberg and his girlfriend, Marianne, who trained twenty horses in a yard about thirty minutes' hack from Norway's one and only racecourse – Øvrevoll, near the capital, Oslo. In layout the track is similar to Fontwell: there is a left-handed Flat racecourse on which portable hurdles are placed for the hurdle races, and in the middle of this is a very tight figure-of-eight steeplechase course. Most racehorses are stabled in American-style barns at the racecourse and exercised on a dirt track just on the inside of the turf track. I have always found that horses trained in these conditions – as in America, for example – pull a great deal harder than those worked on gallops away from the course.

Most of Dennis's horses were dual-purpose, that is to say they ran on the Flat and over jumps. The first jockey for the jumpers was the champion jockey, a lady rider called Scarlet Bather. She was a very capable jockey and the horses went very well for her; she did not, as many British women riders do, try to ride as strongly as a man, but had a good technique and looked very neat and tidy on a horse. The stable jockey for the Flat horses was Jamos Tandari, a Hungarian who had twice defected from the communist regime in his homeland. The first time he was caught, taken back to Hungary and forbidden to travel abroad with horses; however, he worked his way back into the confidence of the authorities and when some horses were being transported across to the West he seized his chance and escaped for good. He was a very good rider, a natural lightweight and very strong – and always immaculately turned out, whether riding out at home or at the races. He now trains in Sweden.

This was the land of the midnight sun and in the long daylight hours of the summer months work would start at five in the morning. The horses were mucked out and brushed over before being tacked up for riding out. They were not groomed in the evening as is customary in English stables – there was hardly time as each member of staff looked after eight horses. Most days we exercised the horses on the racecourse, but once or twice a week we would hack out on the rough tracks in the forests above Øvrevoll. Sometimes we would meet elk up here, beasts that terrified the horses; but the thirty-minute hack to the course was even more nerve-racking as it meant riding down roads with container lorries thundering past, driven with scant regard for the horses. Luckily I never saw a horse or rider seriously hurt, though I know that there were accidents. The Norwegians as a nation did not have an equestrian tradition like our own, and drivers found it tiresome and unreasonable to be expected to slow down for horses on the roads.

Riding work on the track could also be exciting in unexpected ways. I don't know what it is in the make-up of trainers, but there is something that makes many of them insular and oblivious to the problems of others. In the small training community of Øvrevoll, all concentrated on the one racecourse, this was a recipe for disaster: most of the trainers disliked one another and were forever at odds. Once I witnessed a brawl between two of them that arose as a result of their respective strings of horses working on the dirt track at the same time. One horse working down the home straight ducked out at an exit on the inside of the course, unshipping his rider and galloping along the path across the centre of the track that led to the stables at the side of the racecourse. Unfortunately, a rival trainer's string was galloping past the exit directly opposite, and the loose horse collided with them, depositing one rider on the floor. Both loose horses and their jockeys were fine, but one of the trainers ended up in hospital as a result of the ensuing scuffle.

Despite the pugnacity of men like these, in Norway it is against the law to hit a child, or an animal, with a stick; in racing you may carry a whip but may not take your hands off the reins to hit the horse. I felt that this law led to more rather than less hardship for the horses: many tended to become lazy and not run up to their best, and in the attempt to counteract this they were wound up more at home. It also led to some unusual riding styles; in a finish jockeys tended to ride with a sideways movement of their hands so that they could repeatedly hit the horse down the shoulder with the stick, rather than adopting the correct pushing movement with the hands favoured in most other racing countries. I felt that on the whole the British horses were better off.

There were some great characters riding in Norway, one of the most notable of whom was Albert Klimscha, a highly accomplished jockey whose father trained in France. Legend has it that when he was apprenticed to a stable in Newmarket he first lived in digs run by a very strict landlady, along with several other apprentices. After the evening meal all the boys had to stand and say, 'Thank you very much for the meal, may I leave the table?' Albert could not yet speak English and the others had the task of teaching him to say thank you for the meal. Poor Albert duly learnt to say: 'Thank you, you silly old cow, for the awful meal.'

Albert rode mainly on the Flat, even though he had to waste

very hard to make the weights; occasionally he would ride over hurdles, keeping his leathers very short. He had the reputation of being something of an eccentric, and also a rooted dislike of the Stewards, whom he blamed (quite wrongly) for the rule about the use of the whip. Both these characteristics were in evidence on the only occasion I rode against him. Having been sitting in the sauna drinking champagne, he was so late in the changing room that he was still putting on his colours when the rest of us were leaving for the paddock. He came on to the track rolling over his horse like a drunk, then while we were inspecting the practice hurdle (in European races you jump an obstacle on your way to the start) he galloped down between us and leapt it. During the race itself he stood bolt upright, shouting and hollering, yet still came to the last with a chance. Instead of riding for the line, however, he picked up his stick and threw it at the Stewards' box, then finished the race hitting the horse down the shoulder with his elbow.

There were some very good (and less unconventional) English jockeys riding in Scandinavia at this time, among them Walter Buick, Ken Stott and Joe Youds – men who had served their apprenticeships in Newmarket but had not been given the opportunities to ride in England. I admired them for their hard work and the rewards they reaped from their industry. Their racing circuit comprised the twice-weekly meetings in Norway and Sweden, plus weekly meetings in Denmark and occasional visits to Germany, and by working the rounds of these few courses they earnt themselves a high standard of living.

I raced in both Norway and Sweden that summer, but didn't manage to ride a winner. My first mount in Norway was a horse called Da Gol, bred, like many of the Scandinavian racehorses, in Poland. Unfortunately, though he had bags of enthusiasm this was not matched by jumping ability, and we duly fell. As I was regaining my senses an obnoxious woman came up to me and said, 'On the continent we do not ride like that; we do not kick our horses into the obstacles.' I thought, 'What the heck do you know?' but in fact she was right; the continental obstacles are softer through the top, and the jockeys in general ride much shorter than we do, and sit stiller.

I was back in Norway in 1981, this time to ride for Terje Dahl. For many years one of Norway's most successful steeplechase jockeys, riding winners in England as well as in

Scandinavia and elsewhere on the continent, Terje was now Norway's leading trainer. I rode eight winners for him that summer, and also rode at one of Scandinavia's more unusual racecourses – Stromsholm, in Sweden, where the Swedish National and Champion Hurdle are run in early June. The racecourse follows the paths through a wood, with some sharp bends; when I walked the course there was very little grass on the track, and rain early that morning on ground hardened by the early summer sun made for very slippery ground. There was pony racing that day as well as the Thoroughbred racing, and even the ponies were slipping over.

Hywel Davies was riding out there and we were both competing in the Swedish Champion hurdle on Terje's horses. I was brought down on a bend when a horse in front of me slipped up; Hywel went on to lead going into the last, where the same horse that had brought me down appeared out of another track in the woods and carried Hywel and his horse round the wing of the hurdle. Two of Terje's runners being taken out by the same horse, ridden for a rival trainer, seemed a bit suspicious, and arguments about sabotage raged after the race.

The jockeys competing in the Swedish National, again including Hywel and me, were taken to the paddock in a stagecoach pulled by a team of four horses driven by two men dressed as cowboys – a term that could be applied to some of the opposing riders in the race, who weaved all over the place. I was knocked off my horse when one of the French-trained runners fell heavily in front of me, bringing my horse screeching to a halt and firing me into the air. I was very pleased to leave Stromsholm in one piece.

Two years later, in 1983, my summer 'holiday' took me all over the continent, and I was able to appreciate how different European jump racing is from the English and Irish model. For a start the courses are much more adaptable: many are not the circular or oval shapes that we are used to, but are designed in figures of eight or even more complex layouts, with turns to both left and right and obstacles that can be jumped from either side – even in a single race – so you need to have a good memory for course plans and keep your wits about you. At Auteuil in France I very nearly hit the headlines for going the wrong way: I had studied what I thought was the course, but had memorized the wrong one and was only saved from going down the wrong channel when a French jockey cut across me and took me the correct way.

There is also a wider variety of obstacles: you are likely to have to jump oxers (a fence with a rail in front), stone walls and bullfinches (tall hedge-type fences with a top the horse has to brush through) as well as plain fences, open ditches and water jumps. However, the fences tend to be more forgiving than English and Irish steeplechase fences: as long as you clear the body of the fence, marked by a horizontal white-painted pole, the horse can safely flick through the top part. Try that at Haydock Park and you end up on the floor.

Some courses have their own particular idiosyncrasies. Hamburg, for example, which I would rank with Baden-Baden and Hanover among the best of several excellent racecourses in Germany, runs a famous steeplechase for amateurs which involves swimming through a lake. The jockeys have to approach with caution, to avoid their horses slamming on the brakes at the edge and depositing them in the water, then swim through and once across complete the course – then empty their boots of water before weighing in! And Ostend in Belgium, a good galloping course with a fairly typical mixture of continental fences, has no racecourse commentator, which makes for a rather eerie atmosphere.

There are also more meetings where Flat and jump racing is mixed – sometimes also intermingled with trotting races, where horses pull very light, fast vehicles called sulkies, a very popular sport on the continent. In August, Baden-Baden – my favourite of all the German tracks – hosts a week-long festival, with horses from England and France taking part in Group races on the Flat as well as some good jump racing. In Britain, apart from a few charity occasions and the Whitbread meeting at Sandown in the spring, the Flat jockeys and the 'jumping boys' tend not to mix much, and the German festival was one of the rare occasions on which we would bump into the likes of Steve Cauthen, Lester Piggott and Walter Swinburn.

Sometimes the glamour and wealth attached to the top international Flat jockeys can be a bit hard to stomach for jump jockeys who haven't reached those dizzy heights, but behind the private jets and luxurious lifestyles I found many of them to be very pleasant people. In 1983 John Francome and I were both riding in the Baden-Baden festival, he for Nick Gaselee and I for Dennis Holmberg, my Norwegian friend. As we sat in the weighing room, in walked Gary Moore, then champion jockey of Hong Kong and riding for the French trainer Criquette Head – immaculately dressed and carrying his riding gear in a smart bag with Gucci written all over it. To John and me this was like a red rag to a bull, and we were muttering to each other, pulling the poor man to bits, as he crossed the room. Then he looked up and saw us, and came over with hand outstretched. 'Pleased to meet you,' he said. 'I get the *Sporting Life* at home and follow you two.' After a short chat he left to get changed and we both agreed what a nice man he was.

It was in Germany that I had some success with a Polish-bred horse called Bas. This little bay gelding was trained in Norway but had limited opportunities for winning over there; he was a quick and accurate jumper and did well in Germany – even over some of the oddest obstacles. At the Baden-Baden Festival in 1983 our race included a bank about 100 metres long: we had to gallop up it and along the top before racing back down a steep slope on to the main course. Bas coped with his usual aplomb and went on to win comfortably.

However much these summer expeditions took on the flavour of holiday as well as work – and we did have a lot of fun – it's impossible to put ambition and competitiveness aside altogether. Indeed, the trainers for whom we rode would have been justifiably cross if we hadn't taken the sport as seriously as on our home turf. I couldn't help noticing, therefore, that while I had had winners in Norway, Sweden, Germany and Belgium, I didn't seem to be able to win a race in France. In 1985, at the end of a very disappointing season at home, I went to Auteuil to ride Bajan Sunshine and the hopefully named Out Of The Gloom over hurdles; both ran below form and were well beaten. Then there was 1986, when I had the ride on Gaye Brief in the French Champion Hurdle. This year I had taken the family over with me to Chantilly, with its magnificent Chateau les Grands Écuries - built by the Prince de Condé, who was convinced that he would return in a subsequent life as a horse, and constructed this equestrian palace as a result – and while all around me were enjoying the French cuisine, I was wasting to get down to ten stone one pound, practically my lowest riding weight.

Gaye Brief had gone well in his schooling session before the race, but the race itself was a disaster. In France, as elsewhere in Europe, you jump a practice hurdle on a sand track on the way to the start; as Gaye Brief landed the surface gave way and we fell. None the worse, apart from a covering of sand, we were reunited and continued to post. I should have stayed where I was; after one circuit I had a crashing fall, the horse doing a complete somersault and landing on the back of my legs. I was lucky they weren't broken. However, all this was nothing compared to what happened to poor Dawn Run, who in the same race fell with her French jockey, M. Chirol, and broke her neck.

After this race I drove to Brussels with Richard Dunwoody, who was also in the English team due to ride against the Belgians the next day. It was a scorching hot afternoon and I was suffering not only from the soreness resulting from the fall, but from dehydration on top of the effects of wasting. Richard was in somewhat better spirits than I, having finished second in the Auteuil race on the American horse Flatterer. In Belgium we were hoping to repeat our team's victory in the previous year's competition, when I had ridden a winner on Prince Epi; but despite improving the state of my legs with some physiotherapy, my luck was still out. The Belgian jockeys were great fun and looked after us well, but not all of them could speak English and I could not speak a word of Flemish. Consequently, when one jockey babbled something at me while we were circling at the start I had no way of knowing that he was telling me that his horse was a terrible jumper and not to track him – and sure enough he fell at the first fence, bringing me down. Neither horse went far; he caught his and remounted, signalling for me to do likewise; but I had long since learnt that there are fools, damned fools and those who remount when they can't win, and let him go off alone. He was still out on the course when I arrived back at the weighing room, and the last time I saw him that afternoon he and his horse were stranded across a fence . . .

Finally, in 1991, my ambition to ride a winner in France was at last realized – not at Auteuil but at a small provincial course in the Mayenne region. Martin Pipe usually had one or two people from France working at his yard, and one of these, a very capable amateur rider called Florent Monnier, organized an invitation for me to go to ride at Senonnes-Pouanc that summer.

Senonnes racecourse, an hour's drive from Nantes airport, is situated next to a large training centre with excellent facilities, including a schooling ground with typical French fences – well-built privet hedges, ditches and a small stone wall – positioned along a five-furlong sand gallop. I rode for the main trainer in the centre, Etienne Lennders, who handled over 100 horses – as many as you would find in the largest jumping yards in England – and ran them at courses all over the north-west of France. The course itself, where racing takes place only three times a year, is rather like an upmarket point-to-point, with a strong local flavour: the townspeople are very proud of the festive atmosphere of race-days. The setting is beautiful, dominated by the small castle which presides over the town and top end of the course; scattered around the public area were tents and agricultural stone buildings where food and drink were sold, and the changing room and weighing room reinforced the point-to-point atmosphere. These immaculate stone buildings still contained agricultural machinery from the days when farms were worked with horses, and in the middle of our changing room a huge cartwheel with the rim removed, held up by an old log, served as a saddle-rack.

The organizers' hospitality lived up to the surroundings. On my arrival their welcome included a pressing invitation to lunch with Le Comité de Senonnes; I was worried about my weight but didn't want to offend them by refusing, so I sat and pushed some food around my plate, keenly aware that my preoccupation was completely alien to the hedonistic mood of the day. After a small glass of wine I slipped away to walk the course. The programme for the day was typically eclectic, including Flat races, trotting and a cross-country race over natural obstacles all round the middle of the main track as well as the hurdling that I was there for. I had a look at the large French hurdles: they were as tall as those at Auteuil, possibly softer through the top and not so wide, but still quite large enough for my three-year-old mount. I thought to myself that not many English three-year-olds would jump them.

Despite the lavish welcome I passed the scales and went out for my first ride at Senonnes on a horse called Cupids Halary. I just managed to understand my riding orders from Etienne, whose English was not much better than my French, but had a problem not knowing the French for 'false start': the fifteen-runner field was keen to get away, and some of the horses set off before the Starter brought his flag down. Just to be safe, I only pulled up when the others around me did, which was after we had jumped the first. Second time around we had a clean break, and I had a good run – with a stroke of luck when, choosing to come wide into the straight, I missed being hampered by a faller on my inside. (One of the hazards of riding abroad is that you don't know the form and so have less idea of which horses to track and which to avoid in a race.) From there the horse galloped on well and we scored a comfortable win.

Now at last I could celebrate, and spent the warm evening with Le Comité and the other jockeys learning about racing in the French provinces and enjoying the French cuisine and hospitality in a less strait-laced fashion. In fact, the more wine I drank the better my French became; I'm sure if I'd had a glass or two in my French lessons at school my exam results would have been better.

From Senonnes I continued my pre-season fitness campaign in Ireland, with a visit to the Galway Festival. Martin Pipe and I had just the one winner here, Tri Folene, but as ever had a wonderful time. Even the disaster at Auteuil in 1986 had been in part compensated for by the subsequent trip to Ireland: on that occasion, again racing at Galway, I had stayed at Ashford Castle, a magnificent building in the style of a French chateau in the breathtaking surroundings of the shores of Lough Comb, an environment to soothe the most wounded spirit. And my spirits were further boosted by an easy win in the Galway Hurdle on Jim Ennis's Rushmoor.

Racing on the European continent has its differences from the home variety, but the real culture shock comes with crossing the Atlantic. After the close of the 1988–9 season in England I was invited to go to America to ride a horse for Jonathan Shepard, America's leading jump trainer, at Belmont Park in the Temple Gwathmey Chase, one of the very few jump races at the New York track. Although by then I had ridden in the USA several times, this trip to one of the biggest of America's racing centres still threw up some surprises.

I was collected from the airport by the Firestones' private Flat trainer, Bill Mott, at whose house I was to stay my first night. It seemed curious to me that the New York trainers were city-dwellers: their horses were stabled in barns on the huge Belmont complex, so they did not live alongside them in the way that English trainers do.

Early next morning I went down with Bill Mott to his barn. One of the first people to see the horses in the morning is the vet who comes to administer drugs to those horses that are under medication: the rules about running while under medication are very different in America, and given the severity of the 'dirt'

*After my first victory in the USA – the Temple Gwathmey Chase at Belmont Park, New York, on Jimmy Lorenzo in June 1989*

surface on which the horses train and race, many of them have leg problems that can only be kept under control with substances such as the anti-inflammatory drug 'bute' that would not be permitted on British courses. This morning the surface of the track was particularly unfavourable because of the unseasonably wet weather. It had been raining hard for the last two or three days and the dirt had become sloppy, like a thick grey soup; these conditions meant even more strain on the horses' legs and feet, because their hooves would penetrate the surface material and strike the hard membrane below.

Because of the number of horses all working on the racecourse, there is a strict convention about where and how the work is done. Those nearest to the inside rail are doing fast work, and as you move out from the centre the pace decreases, so that those on the outer rail would only be trotting. The track was not overcrowded and the system seemed to work well. There were quite a few journalists and TV crews about, most of them following Sunday Silence and Easy Goer, the two main contenders for the next day's Belmont Stakes. Bill Mott reckoned that Easy Goer would win because of the rain, which would make the surface faster – another surprise for me, as this is of course the opposite effect to that of rain on turf.

After riding out, I spent the rest of the morning trying to obtain my licence to ride. In most countries you can ride on your British licence, but in New York, because of the state gambling laws, you have to have a New York licence; to my disgust this cost $100, and the bureaucracy involved had to be experienced to be believed. After filling out endless documents concerning my parentage, drug intake and felony record and having photographs and fingerprints taken, I was ushered along for my medical test, in the course of which a very pretty nurse held my testicles while telling me to cough – the only bit of luck I had in the whole trip. When they went on to ask me about broken bones, eyesight and hearing I began to worry that I might fail, but eventually got through.

Because jump racing at Belmont is such a rare phenomenon, we 'tall' jump jockeys are something of a novelty among the tiny Flat riders. Many of the American jockeys come from the southern continent and Spanish is much spoken. The weighing room, situated in the basement of the gigantic stands which line the length of the home stretch of the racetrack, has a very different feel about it from any British equivalent. The jockeys are based at one track for long periods of time rather than being in perpetual motion as we are, and the changing rooms and personalized cubicles reflect this, with crucifixes (many of the South Americans being Roman Catholics) and photos of wives, girlfriends and children pinned on the walls. The valet service, too, was much more personal, with pretty much one valet to every jockey – compared with one to as many as fifteen sometimes in England. Slippers, towelling robe and towels were hung ready on the peg, so that you could go to the sauna or steam room or have a massage. If you didn't want to do any of these you could play pool or ride the mechanical horse in the cafeteria at the end of the room.

My valet guided me through the pre-race procedures and got me changed and weighed out in time for him to take the saddle and help the trainer get the horse prepared. Soon it was time for me to join the trainer and get on my mount, Jimmy Lorenzo — not in the paddock, but in the saddling stalls, so that you go into the parade ring already mounted. From here we were led on to the track, where the 'outriders' on ponies each take one horse and escort it to the start.

There were fifteen runners in our race, and my instructions were to hold Jimmy Lorenzo up until we came off the last bend, with one fence between us and the line. (The fences are based on a metal frame, filled with plastic birch and fronted with a green foam roll. In size they are somewhere between a hurdle and an English steeplechase fence.) We had a good run up to that last bend, and I was confident that we could win if only I was not blocked or hampered. The jockeys on my outer were doing all they could to hinder me, but I was able to nudge Jimmy Lorenzo's shoulder against one of their horses; not only did this get him away from me, but he then became unbalanced and ended up impeding the horses on his outside rather than me. This gave me the gap I needed to challenge for the lead, and Jimmy Lorenzo went on to give me my first victory in the United States.

Even winning was different! In accordance with the established procedure, I waved my stick at the judge to attract his attention; when he signalled permission I dismounted, there on the line in front of the stands. Still in the same area I got on the scales, and my saddle was taken back to the weighing room by the valet. When I got back to the basement I learnt that one of the other jockeys was objecting; instead of having to go to the Stewards' room I had to give my evidence down the phone, using one of the instruments that lined the wall behind the Clerk of the Scales' desk. I denied all knowledge of bumping and boring on the bend, and the result stood. I had a flight back to England booked for the same night, and was looking forward to getting back.

Earlier in the 1980s I had been to America with John Francome, Steve Smith Eccles and Jonjo O'Neill to ride against a group of American jump jockeys in a team challenge organized by Alan Lee, the *Times* cricket correspondent and an ardent racing fan. These races took place at Fairhill racecourse in Maryland, which, although it had its own training centre with barns and exercise track adjacent to the course, felt more like a point-to-point course than like the huge urban centres of Belmont and Pimlico. On our first team trip we had no one to explain all the procedural differences to us, with the result that we caused pandemonium before the first race. Unaware that the saddles were taken down to the barns by the valets, we were all waiting for the trainers to come and collect the saddles from the weighing room as they do in England, and consequently all the horses were late getting tacked up.

In the racing itself, two things in particular took me by surprise. The first was the actual start. All the runners walked round in numerical order behind a three-string elastic barrier; then, keeping in the same order, we were all called in quickly and the barrier raised. In England you choose your own order and it is up to the Starter to make sure everyone is ready to go; in the States you stay in numbered order and it's up to you to be ready.

*Down Under. Steve Smith Eccles (right) and me in action at Moonee Valley racecourse, Melbourne, in June 1985*

121

The second surprise concerned the route taken by the jockeys at the last obstacle down the back stretch before the turn for home: it was like being at the Canal Turn in the National, with all the jockeys running down the fence to save ground at the approaching bend, and innocent Englishmen were liable to get cut up on the inside. Despite our unfamiliarity with these various aspects of the business, we managed to win the team event, with Steve riding two winners.

Quite apart from the racing, we were entertained superbly. We lodged with various families: I stayed with the Wintersteins, keen followers of racing, on whose farm Janet Elliot had a successful training establishment. During the week we were there we paid a visit to the former jump jockey Tommy Skiffington, who now runs a stud and training establishment. The walls of his house were hung with some wonderful paintings, including some outstanding studies by Sir Alfred Munnings of Romany gypsies in the early years of the century. There were racing scenes too: the one I liked best was a sketch of a barrier start at Newmarket, obviously done for a friend of the artist, for it had with it a letter describing it as 'an autumn start at Newmarket, too good for the ordinary ass to appreciate'. Many of the houses we visited contained paintings and drawings of English sporting scenes: they appreciated country sports and the country way of life – sometimes, it seemed to me, more than many English people do.

The area around Fairhill is home to many jumping trainers and owners: Jonathan Shepard, whose horse I rode at Belmont in 1989, lives here, as does Burly Cox, for whom my father rode in the late 1950s. The leading jumping owner in America, Mrs Miles Valentine, was based in the area; she kept horses with Fred Winter in England and Mouse Morris in Ireland. Also nearby was Mrs Harry Duffy, who was to win the Grand National in 1990 with Mr Frisk. American jump racing has a long and happy association with the National; two of their amateur riders, Charlie Fenwick and Tommy Smith, won the race.

These team trips were great fun. We did all the childish things that any group of sportsmen will do when let loose on holiday, with the added element of relaxation that came from riding on the same side rather than in competition with one another as we did at home. In the normal course of things I didn't socialize all that much with other jockeys, and it was on this trip that I got to know Jonjo O'Neill better. Up to then I hadn't spent much time with him outside the weighing room, where I and many other jockeys looked up to him as a role model. While in America we had time to talk more and I came to understand how much hard work he put into becoming a jockey; he told me of how he got going, how he worked for Gordon Richards and then for Peter Easterby, and of the great horses he rode, such as Alverton and Sea Pigeon. I was glad I had this chance, as he did not come with us the next year; and as John Francome had retired by then, our touring team looked a bit different.

The group that set off for three weeks in June 1985 consisted of Steve Smith Eccles, Hywel Davies, Graham Bradley and myself, with Richard Dunwoody as reserve. This year we were not only going to America, but after that were heading for Australia and New Zealand. It was a memorable tour, the hardest part of which turned out to be the dieting: eventually the struggle with weight became too much for Brad, who after riding two winners at Fairhill couldn't find a horse with a weight he could do, so he swapped places with Richard to be reserve. Hywel, who always works hard at keeping his weight down, spent an hour or so in the sauna most days, and went very pale as a result. One morning at Jonathan Shepard's when he and I were waiting for our horses, the coloured lad who brought them out of the barn took one look at Hywel and said, 'Man, that's the whitest white man I've ever seen. Ain't you got no sun in England?'

After our four races against the Americans we flew down under, where we were to ride at three Australian courses: Moonee Valley and Flemington, both in Melbourne, and the country track of Seymour. Here again we had to adjust to the local conditions. We noticed that the first track, Moonee Valley, was very sharp, and the Australians said that they raced much tighter than we did in England. Also, all the hurdle races were started from stalls. The hurdles themselves were similar to ours but were portable and based on a spring mechanism, so that if you knocked one over it slowly came back up again. The chase fences consisted of rails piled up on top of each other and set at an angle, with a foot of birch on top loose enough to brush through. The standard of stewarding here was much higher than at home, and we were given a briefing by the Stewards at which they told us what was expected of us, covering use of the whip and interference at all stages of the race, rather than only from the second last, as in England.

The first two races were won by Steve, whose confident approach and skilful riding impressed the Australian media. According to one paper: 'Smith Eccles oozed confidence before the steeplechase and the trainer told the rider that he thought the gelding was good enough to win. "Well, I'm good enough," he replied as he mounted the favourite.' He was also complimented on his superb timing in bringing his horse to the front approaching the last. But the journalists didn't know the true story. As we went out on the last circuit Steve turned to me and said,

'Why are all these Aussies in such a hurry? We've got another circuit to go.'

'No we haven't,' I said.

'Bloody hell!' said Steve, and set off in pursuit of the leader.

We went on to ride at Flemington and Seymour, where Richard and I won a race apiece, bringing the team's total of victories since we left England to seven – every race we had contested. Our buoyant mood didn't survive the journey on to New Zealand, however. We had spruced ourselves up for our arrival, remembering that when we had landed in Melbourne we had been met, scruffy and unshaven as we were, by the assembled television and newspaper crews, but when we got to Auckland – nothing. Not even a single person to meet us. By now we were all pretty tired and Steve was all for booking a flight home. Eventually we were collected by Andrew Denson, now a trainer in Epsom but then, having like me been an amateur with David Nicholson, on a working holiday with Kenny Brown, a New Zealand trainer and one of the organizers of the event. Torrential rain made the drive to the hotel not only hazardous but long, as Andrew got lost.

It was still raining in the morning, when we made our way to the racecourse and introduced ourselves to the officials.

'We're the British team,' we said.

'What British team?' they said.

They were completely unprepared for us. By now this was really getting us down and all any of us wanted to do was go home. However, as that day's racing was cancelled because of flooding, our event was rescheduled for two days later and we hung on.

Eventually the rain stopped and we went to look at the course, at which point we got another jolt. It would not have passed a safety inspection in this country. Both the inside rail and the hurdle wings were made of metal piping, while the hurdles themselves, made of thick wooden slates, looked like British hurdles but could not be knocked over. We considered not riding, but as we had travelled halfway round the world to get there we thought we'd better be diplomatic.

In the hurdle race, which started out of open-topped stalls, I was drawn on the inside. As this meant jumping next to the metal piping I did not cling to the rail as I would at home but kept two or three horse's widths off it. When one of the New Zealand jockeys tried to come up my inside along the back stretch I leant over and stopped him; then, as we turned into the straight and Steve kicked for home another of the home team moved up on my inside, so I pushed him into the rails.

On returning to the weighing room I was summoned before the Stewards, who found me guilty of 'foul riding and elbowing another jockey' in the first incident and suspended me for six days. I was halfway out of the room, thanking my lucky stars that they didn't seem to have seen the second incident, when they called me back and banned me for a further three days for 'careless riding on the bend' . They could not, however, put the ban into effect while I was in New Zealand or there would have been no British team to compete at Ellerslie later in the week (our reserve, Graham Bradley, being over the weight). So my suspension was scheduled for 27 June to 8 July – during my holidays.

Hywel was tremendously amused by my being hauled before the Stewards; however, I had the last laugh, as he was called in too, and fined for coming in overweight.

The second race we rode in that afternoon, the steeplechase, was a complete farce. There were obviously not enough horses as the mounts we were given were quite clearly not fit; we had to pull up after a mile.

After this things took a turn for the better. Ellerslie, approached up an avenue lined with palm trees, was one of the finest racecourses I have ever visited: a big, right-handed, galloping course with several tracks on good turf and splendid large grandstands. Safety standards were very high here and the fences were well constructed. The batten hurdles were stiffer than English ones and had to be treated with much more respect; the steeplechase fences, on the contrary, were more of the continental type, with soft tops that the horses brushed through. I had an excellent ride in the hurdle race on a horse that jumped the obstacles well; Hywel, who having won the Grand National that spring was getting most attention from the New Zealand media, had a less happy time in the steeplechase because he was not used to horses jumping through the fence. Coming to the first he prepared to tackle the whole jump and was not ready when his horse, who knew all about these obstacles, dived through the top half, sending him flying out over the back.

There were more unfamiliar jumps to get used to before we left the country. We were invited out fox-hunting on a deer farm, and were startled to learn that the horses were used to jumping wire. You had to aim for a spot marked with white horizontal pegs, placed so the horses could see them and jump safely. Hywel and I shared a horse, a common old mare who wore a bitless bridle and had a mouth so hard that neither of us could hold one side of her. When it was my turn for the ride Hywel spent the rest of the afternoon photographing the proceedings – until he got an electric shock from one of the high strands of wire used to keep the deer from escaping.

Hywel, Steve and I were back down under in 1986, this time with Simon Sherwood to make up the team and no reserve. Once again we started off well: I rode a 66–1 winner, Top Music, in a steeplechase at Flemington, coming from the rear to overhaul the runner-up after making up six lengths approaching the last; and Steve rode a determined and forceful race to win the International Hurdle at our next port of call, a country track called Moe. After that it was on to Warrnambool, an hour's flight away from Melbourne. This is a course steeped in tradition: the first Grand Annual Steeplechase was run here in 1872 and that race, over 5,500 metres, is still the highlight of the three-day carnival held every May. The course is a demanding one, including post-and-rail fences and fallen logs as well as such specialities as the Tozer Road Double, where you jump into a road and out again a few strides later, and the Man Trap, which consists of sloping rails over a wide ditch. In an eventful steeplechase here Simon broke his collarbone at the second and by the time we came to the second road double three of the Australians had fallen too.

Our record in the country had not gone unnoticed, and Hywel

Davies's win in that race prompted an article in an Australian newspaper before the final event at Sandown, headlined: IT IS TIME TO NOBBLE POMMIES. It read:

> What about these Pommie riders, eh? I reckon we're going to have to do something about it in the steeple today. Last year they won all the races in the jumps series and so far this time they've knocked them all off, bar one. I reckon it's time for a bit of rough stuff. No eye gouging, or ankle tapping, mind you. If you want to see that you'll have to go to Waverley, not Sandown Park. But a bit of leg grabbing and stuff wouldn't go astray, don't you reckon? And if that doesn't work and they're in front over the last fence, then they could close the gap on to the course proper and make them go around again. If Hughie sends down a bucketful of rain this morning, then we won't have to do anything to stop them, because Magic Paul will win by as far as you can kick your hat and he's being ridden by an Aussie.

As it happened the Aussies had no need to nobble us. Simon was already out with his broken collarbone, Steve fell at the first, I fell at the second and Hywel could only manage fourth – and Magic Paul did indeed win.

I was pleased to read the summary of the tour in the *Racing Age* –

> One wag during the week suggested that the world's best jockeys were riding the world's worst horses, but the English riders impressed with their demeanour, professionalism and courtesy. Memories include Scudamore's feat in picking up rank outsider, Top Music, when he seemed beaten when winning the Novice Steeplechase; Steve Smith Eccles's vigour and never-say-die ride to win at Moe; and Davies's quick adaptation to Warrnambool to win on Prince Pura.

– but all I can say about the social side of the trip is that it was a good job for some members of the team that the Australian press were not writing such detailed reports about us off the track.

As a less strenuous interlude, I was invited out to Sri Lanka in late July 1992 with Marilyn and the boys to visit some betting shops and a racecourse at Nuwar-Eliya. Our hosts, the Sumathipala brothers, ran one of the main bookmaking firms on the island, and gave us a fascinating insight into this extraordinary place. Most of the population of 17 million live in the capital, Colombo, where betting shops are plentiful; curiously, English racing is very popular and many of them are open in the evenings so that people coming home from work can go and have a bet. Some of the betting parlours were very luxurious, with huge television screens, but others in the poorer parts of the city were very grim, and the crush of people inside could be quite frightening. Betting in Sri Lanka is not consistently legal or illegal; from time to time the government forbids it and closes the betting shops down, but racing is so popular that it cannot enforce the law.

The racecourse was a day's drive away in the cooler climate of the mountains, where the famous tea plantations can be found and where in former times the British colonists, who built the racecourse for their entertainment, spent their summers away from the humidity of the city. Now the colonial period is long past and the Sumathipala brothers are among the wealthiest and most powerful businesspeople on the island. Through them we were escorted around the Sri Lankan parliament, had tea with the Speaker and visited the house of the former President. We also visited a temple in the town of Kandy where a sacred relic of the Buddha is kept – a tooth which once a year is paraded through the streets on an elephant adorned with fine cloth, silver and jewels. The centrepiece of the display is a silver casket, donated by the Sumathipala brothers, in which the tooth is carried.

It was all a very far cry from riding strange horses over strange obstacles on unfamiliar courses; but the excited crowds in the bookies' shops in downtown Colombo were not so very different from punters at Flemington, Hamburg or Belmont Park. Horse racing exerts its fascination the world over.

*Chapter Nine*

# UPLANDS

———▶◀———

In autumn 1986, for the first time starting a season as sole defending champion jockey, I went to ride for a man whose career put all that I had so far achieved sharply into perspective. Fred Winter, four times champion jockey and eight times champion trainer, was one of the all-time greats of National Hunt racing and it was not just a privilege but a great responsibility to be stable jockey to the yard that had produced horses such as Pendil, Lanzarote and Crisp.

Before the campaign got under way I drove down to Uplands to talk to Fred about the coming season, and asked him among other things how often he wanted me to school.

'There's no need for you to come in at all if you don't want to,' he said. 'When I was riding for Ryan Price I never went and schooled, all I did was go and see the horses at the beginning of the season. I hated schooling.' This would make life much easier in terms of travelling – the new arrangement would be rather different from nipping down the road to Condicote in the morning – but I decided that I would go to ride out at least twice a week or when there was racing in that direction.

I hardly ever had to ride work for Fred, which was something of a relief; just as when I started at Condicote I hated having to lead the string in case I went up the wrong track, so now I could never work out the different routes up the gallops the Uplands horses used and dreaded taking the wrong one. Fred's short, sharp comments to work riders and jockeys when things went awry were famous: Jimmy Duggan told me how, on an occasion when a horse had refused with him, depositing him on the other side of the hurdle, Fred had come up to him and said, 'You never stop improving, do you?' before walking away. Neither Jimmy nor Ben de Haan, who had been the stable's jockeys before I was brought in, showed any bitterness or jealousy towards me: in fact, they both stayed around for quite a while and were very helpful in getting me used to the new routine.

The Winters' head lad, Brian Delaney, had spent three years in the King's Troop and ran the yard with military precision. The string pulled out at 7.45, and Fred had told me that it was pointless for me to arrive before then; I used to stand with Brian and watch the horses walk by as he legged the pilots up. I would then go up to the schooling grounds in the car with Fred and wait for the lads to bring up the horses at ten-minute intervals. Jimmy, Ben and I would then take the horses, usually in pairs, over a set of three obstacles, hurdles or fences as appropriate.

Fred let me school each horse as I thought best. It is important to start horses off slowly, without rushing them into the fences, so that they learn to jump correctly before you quicken them up and start to ask them to stand off. I used to dread hearing an inexperienced trainer tell me as I joined him in the paddock before a race that 'this one jumps brilliantly', because it usually meant that it could stand off a fence but the moment it met one wrong and had to shorten you were in trouble – and there are very few horses that are good enough to jump round a steeplechase course without getting close to at least one fence.

Fred was never a man for small talk; but though he did not say much, what he did say about riding races was always worth listening to. He would never dismiss questions or gloss things over: if I asked him for a piece of advice about riding he would give it to me, and if he had a view on something he would let me know. For instance, we discussed the use of the stick and he told me he did not like me to ride over the last one-handed unless it was absolutely necessary; and he was a mine of information on how to ride certain racecourses. 'At Lingfield,' he said, 'you have to be near the pace at the bottom of the hill to come up otherwise those horses in front get first run on you, and they don't come back to you.'

By this time, Fred knew everything there was to know about National Hunt racing and had seen it all. Whereas I had it all to do and would rush round the country in search of winners, he was only really interested in the good horses, or ones with a lot of potential. All the inmates of his yard were real steeplechasing types, a very distinctive stamp of horse. The first winner I rode for our new partnership was Tamino at Warwick on 20 September 1986 – for Fred, a good sixtieth birthday present, and for me like the first run in a cricket match, after which some of the anxiety and tension ebbs away and you can settle down to get on with the job.

Now that I wasn't tied to the same yard every morning of the week I was able to fit in more schooling sessions for other trainers, which in turn led to more rides in races. I regularly rode out for Nick Gaselee, who was providing me with some useful winners, and later on that same afternoon at Warwick I rode the 600th winner of my career for him on Prasina Matia. I also occasionally went to ride work or school at Kingsclere, one of the best private training establishments in the country, where royal trainer Ian Balding, who loves National Hunt racing, kept a few jumpers. The facilities here were magnificent, with the all-weather gallops and schooling ground to the rear of the yard and, fifteen minutes' hack away, the outstanding turf gallops of Watership Down. Mill Reef's owner Paul Mellon had a couple of jumpers with Ian, both of whom I won on: Buckwheat Cake, out of a sister to Mill Reef; and Ivor Anthony, for whom Ian had a soft spot despite very possibly being the slowest horse he ever trained. As with Fred Winter, Ian's horses jumped well because they were very well schooled; Ivor Anthony won his race with me purely through jumping skill.

When there was racing in the West Country I would go and school for Martin Pipe. Ironically, in view of later successes, our partnership got off to a rather shaky start. He still had Paul Leach, Jonathon Lower and occasionally Mark Pitman riding for him, and when I did get rides I was tending to get beaten on horses that might have won. London Contact, for example, lost his race at Devon and Exeter only because he wandered coming up the run-in. This is, however, a course that puts an emphasis on stamina: it is excellent to ride around, but the gradual climb from halfway along the back straight can tire a horse before it gets to the last jump. Several times horses fell with me there due to fatigue. None the less, it is winners that make a jockey's reputation and I wasn't winning on Martin's horses.

Then, also at Devon and Exeter, I rode Martin's first winner of the season, Melendez, on 20 August; and subsequently won for him on Adamstown at Ludlow, having taken over the ride from Mark Pitman after they had made a bad mistake when leading at the last at Stratford. These two victories were vitally important in building up my status with the Pipe yard and so proved to be landmarks in my career. When you are struggling for winners for a particular yard and morale is low, so much hangs on every race: each ride is a winner gained or a winner lost and may decide your future. If you push yourself too hard, constantly ringing the trainer for rides, he knows you are desperate for the mounts and can use you as and when it suits him; if you don't show an interest, you are unlikely to get the rides and may miss the winning chances. The only way to be in demand is to ride winners; and luckily for me Fred Winter's horses were running well.

With the change of ground in the late autumn the better horses came out – and so did the usual weather hazards. I won the Rehearsal Chase at Chepstow on Cybrandian in fog so thick that the remainder of the meeting had to be abandoned. Riding in dense fog is a very strange sensation: you lose all sense of distance, and markers, fences or hurdles loom up at you suddenly when you and the horse are least expecting them. The fog also dampens sound so that you are racing in an eerie silence. Some horses jump badly in these conditions, but the chief danger is posed by loose horses as collisions are that much harder to avoid.

A very good hurdler that I rode at this time was Nohalmdun, trained by Peter Easterby. This was a horse that ran best when fresh, but had little respect for his hurdles; he had been Jonjo's final ride when unseating him at Ayr the previous season. None the less, we won together at Ascot and then took the Christmas Hurdle at Kempton – possibly a slightly fortunate win as Colin Brown fell on Floyd at the last, leaving the race open to us.

My main challenger for the jockeys' championship this year was Mark Dwyer. Jimmy FitzGerald, for whom Mark was retained to ride, had taken odds of 100–1 about Mark winning the title, and for much of the season he was snapping at my heels: by 22 December I was just four ahead, with fifty-eight winners to his fifty-four. Once again I was scanning the papers anxiously to see what my rival was riding, and equally anxiously listening for the results.

As Mark rode mainly on the northern tracks and I in the south, our paths did not cross that often. We did, however, quite often meet at Haydock, where in December 1986 I rode at a meeting that stands out in my mind as significant for several reasons. First of all, I rode a double, on Mou-Dafa for Martin Pipe in the seller and Tarqogan's Best for Ray Peacock in the novice chase – the latter a double victory of a different kind as Mark and the 15–8 on favourite Comeragh King fell when clear two out. Second, on the next day I had one of the most exhilarating rides of my career on Corbiere in the three-and-a-half-mile handicap chase. As we did not go a great gallop Corbiere was able to show the full range of his jumping ability, standing off or popping the fences as he met them. It was the kind of ride, and the kind of horse, that remind you what steeplechasing is all about. Third, Martin Pipe was cross with me because later that afternoon Jonathon Lower won on High Knowl and I wasn't there to see it, having taken a lift home with some other jockeys. It was this that made me realize that he must want me to become more involved with the yard – at the time, after all, I was sharing the rides with several other jockeys and had not been doing that brilliantly, and it hadn't dawned on me that he saw me as in some way committed to him.

Despite the early start – Nicholashayne, in Somerset, was an hour and a half's drive from my Cotswold home – I enjoyed going down to ride out for Martin. The atmosphere was progressive and refreshing, with the constant stimulus of new ideas to be discussed and tried out. Martin, as is by now well known, did not come from a traditional training background, but had completed the Horse Husbandry course at Worcester College as well as reading widely on equine subjects, and his knowledge of horses was far superior to mine and to that of many so-called 'experts'. Even the timetable of the yard was not bound by tradition. In contrast to the conventional pattern, in which the stable staff work from 7.30 through to 12.30, have the afternoon off and return for evening stables from 4.00 to 6.00, at Nicholashayne the lads would start work at 7.30 and work right through until 5.30. The first two lots pulled out at eight and ten, with a coffee break in between; third lot would go out straight after second lot, then there would be an hour's break for lunch. Horses that needed extra work or schooling would be exercised during the afternoon. Typically for Martin, the routine was dictated not by what was usual but by what he wanted to achieve with his horses.

Martin used to start schooling his jumpers in an indoor sand ring over straw bales and telegraph poles before venturing outside to take them over the schooling obstacles on the all-weather gallop. These were small, solid frames covered with synthetic grass-like material, but were not high enough to make horses that were not natural jumpers come back on their hocks and spring. The two schooling fences, on the contrary, were quite intimidating: one was narrow and approached up a steep rise; the second was a large open ditch that frightened me, let alone the horses. In those days when we were schooling chasers, of which there weren't many in the yard, it wasn't unusual to have a refusal or a rider unseated. However, training methods and their effects were constantly reviewed under Martin's ever-watchful eye, and as the establishment gained in experience and success over the years so the facilities were developed until now they are second to none – as the results suggest.

Not only does Martin himself have an unconventional background for a trainer, so does his assistant. Chester Barnes, the ebullient Cockney and former national table tennis champion, is widely seen as some kind of court jester, but Martin's instincts in his choice of partner were as usual unerring. Chester, now perfectly at home saddling the yard's runners despite his complete lack of experience with horses prior to teaming up with Martin, is an invaluable part of the business and a good foil to Martin's quieter and less forthcoming demeanour towards the outside world.

As I got more involved with the team at Nicholashayne I heard all the stories of Chester and Martin: of the game of table tennis when Martin, fancying his chances at the table, won his bet in beating Chester; of the coup with Carrie Ann at Haydock, when they were so excited about winning that the pair of them and the stable lad all forgot to hold on to the horse in the winner's enclosure; of the coup that went wrong at Market Rasen, after which they made the jockey Rod Millman drive home and woke up in the middle of Birmingham where Rod had got lost; of Martin and the head lad, Dennis Dummett, trying to deal with a stable full of unmanageable horses, with Martin regularly falling off. A particular gem was the tale of a horse running away with Martin, jumping a hedge and dumping him in the road; as the horse galloped up the road Martin, in hot pursuit, realized that his watch had come off and as the watch was worth £2,500 and the horse only £500 he ran back to find the watch – only to find it had just been squashed by a passing car.

One of the factors that has taken Martin from these somewhat haphazard beginnings to the very peak of professional success has been his relentless competitiveness. No stone is left unturned in the never-ending quest for more winners, and inevitably this stress takes its toll. Early in 1987 Martin's wife, Carol, persuaded him that he could not survive the season without a short break and whisked him off to Tenerife – an only partly successful stratagem, as the phone calls home cost more than the actual holiday. While he was away Martin's father, David Pipe, took charge of the yard as he did in any of his son's absences, and it was Mr Pipe senior who was at Wincanton with the stable's runners when I rode Travel Mystery on her not very successful debut over hurdles. She didn't jump well and we were nearly on the floor three out, before coming home a fast-finishing fourth. To the Stewards this looked less than convincing and I was summoned to explain her running, along with Mr Pipe as the trainer's representative.

Had David Pipe not gone into bookmaking, he would have been a brilliant lawyer: the Wincanton Stewards stood no chance against him. As for me, the wrath of the racecourse officials was as nothing compared with that of Mr Pipe, who thinks all jockeys are idiots to start with, and considered me the worst of the lot that day. It was fortunate for my lowered morale that I had ridden a double for David Elsworth earlier in the afternoon.

But there was worse to come that week. On the Friday at Kempton I was well clear in the novice chase on Alkepa when we fell at the last – a fall that was my fault as I had driven the horse at the fence too hard. Once more, the luck was balanced by a winner, again for David Elsworth; and then, on the following day, I made one of the biggest blunders of my career when getting beaten on High Knowl at the same meeting. Well clear going to the last, I eased down and made a mistake at the fence, allowing Dermot Browne on Framlington Court to get up and beat me three-quarters of a length. Amazingly, there was no Stewards' Inquiry. Equally amazingly, I was not flung out of the Pipe establishment on my ear.

It wasn't only the Pipes who had to put up with my mistakes. Earlier that month I had gone over to Ireland to ride for Eddie Harty in the Irish Champion Hurdle at Leopardstown. The day was a disaster. I fell at the first on Eddie's horse; then in the next race, riding Lastofthebrownies for Mouse Morris, I took the wrong route, going on the inside of a doll, and was suspended and fined. On the return journey, Eddie tried to cheer me up by telling me how he had ridden a premature finish in the Scottish Grand National: on passing the winning post he stood up in his stirrups and waved to the crowd – until the remainder of the field galloped past him for the last circuit. He said that I had gone wrong in the Stewards' room at Leopardstown: when he was hauled in to give an account of himself to the Ayr Stewards he had explained at such length that in the end they were too pleased to see him leave to punish him.

On the Monday morning after my return from Ireland my misfortunes were headline news in the racing papers. I was riding out at Uplands before going on to Fontwell to ride a few for Martin, and was dreading what Fred would have to say about my exploits. After schooling he still hadn't mentioned the incident and, thinking that he had not yet seen the papers, I thought I would slip away without going into the kitchen for my usual cup of coffee. As I left he walked over to the car and said: 'You won't do that again, will you?'

At Fontwell that afternoon, Chester was in charge of the Pipe runners. As I walked into the paddock for my first ride and touched my cap to the owners, he handed me a map of the course.

Riding for Martin and for Fred was a very good combination for me. I was learning from each and benefiting from their different approaches: Fred was by now concentrating on high-class horses and the top races, whereas Martin wanted to win with every horse he sent out on any course, be it Cheltenham or Fakenham. Martin had a great deal of respect for Fred, and for his part Fred was very helpful to me as I combined riding for both yards in my pursuit of another championship.

On one occasion that February Fred had runners on the same day at Ascot and Ludlow, and on looking at the declarations the evening before I decided that I would have a better chance of riding a winner at the Shropshire track. I rang Fred to ask whether he would mind if I swopped meetings; he was perfectly happy for me to do so, even though I was down to ride at Ascot in several evening papers. During the middle of the night the telephone rang and a voice told me that if I won on Dewspry Boy I would be shot! I went back to bed laughing, and sympathizing with Jimmy Duggan, who had now taken the ride on the Ascot runner. In the event my switch to Ludlow didn't do me much good; I was cantering on Wollow Will three out when he fell. That third last fence at Ludlow I found one of the most difficult to ride anywhere on the southern circuit. It is positioned just off a long bend and horses tend not to have re-established their balance when they come to it – and judging by the number of falls that happen there I am not alone in finding it tricky.

From the beginning of March all the jockeys are trying to sort out their rides for the Cheltenham Festival. It is never easy,

*Perhaps the best two-mile chaser I ever rode, Pearlyman leads Very Promising at the last in the Queen Mother Champion Chase at the Cheltenham Festival in March 1987 (MARK CRANHAM)*

particularly not when you are in the throes of a tight race for the championship – and on 2 March Mark was just twelve winners behind me. Again, Fred could not have been more accommodating, telling me that I was not obliged to ride his horses in either of the two novice hurdle races. I therefore booked myself to ride Jenny Pitman's Smith's Gamble in the two-mile Waterford Crystal Supreme Novices' Hurdle, and the ride on Celtic Shot went to Jimmy Duggan, who had won on him first time out at Leicester in December. In the two-and-a-half-mile novice hurdle I opted for Midsummer Gamble, the 4–1 favourite trained by Dermot Weld. Despite all the planning, however, both my mounts were well beaten – the only perverse consolation being that Celtic Shot didn't win either, falling at the first in the two-mile event.

Mrs Muck had given me a fabulous ride at Newbury in the Tote Gold Trophy to finish second behind Toby Balding's Neblin, to whom she was trying to give ten pounds, and I had hoped to ride her in the Champion Hurdle; but I was claimed by Corporal Clinger's owner, Steph Stephano, who rang me to say that in the absence of the horse's usual jockey, Paul Leach (Paul had hurt himself in a fall at Sandown) he felt that I had an obligation to ride his horse as Martin was now giving me a lot of rides. I couldn't argue with that, and a win at Fontwell made me hope that I had a chance in the Festival race; but when it came the horse ran disappointingly, finishing well behind See You Then and Steve Smith Eccles, clocking up their third Champion Hurdle together.

This year the Queen Mother Champion Chase, in which Pearlyman was taking on Desert Orchid, was being billed as the race of the meeting. I had got the ride on Pearlyman earlier in the spring when John Edwards's stable jockey, Paul 'Dick' (Special Agent) Barton, had retired, and I had rung the trainer to ask if I could ride his horse at Newbury in the Game Spirit Chase, an acknowledged trial for the Cheltenham event. Pearlyman, who had been a bit sticky over his fences, jumped well and won comfortably, and my ride for the Festival race was secure.

There were eight runners; Desert Orchid took the field along at a good gallop in his characteristic style and I was able to drop Pearlyman in at the rear of the field. He was another horse that jumped better if you could keep the contact with his mouth, and coming round the top bend still on the bridle I took a prominent position to come down the hill to the two fences before the home straight. Riding these downhill fences at Cheltenham you needed to set your horse alight at the top of the hill and then get it back on the bridle so that it would take you into the fence with the choice of going for a long one or coming in short. If you got in too close to the bottom, the momentum and the incline of the hill could mean your brushing the top and tipping over, but if you over-jumped you risked stumbling on the slope away and losing ground, if not a fall.

Pearlyman took the first of the pair well, but going to the second last he got in close and lost ground, allowing Richard Dunwoody to come at me on my old partner Very Promising. I waved my stick at Pearlyman: his response was immediate and we quickened away towards the last, where again he fiddled it while a superb jump by Very Promising put Richard back in contention. But Pearlyman would not be denied and fought back up the run-in to win by a neck.

In the last race of the day I rode Malya Mal, a horse usually ridden by Richard Linley. Poor Leg Lock Linley – so called because of the position he sometimes got himself into when landing over a fence – had not had much luck recently. Having recovered from injuries sustained in a car crash to begin riding again in the New Year, he won the Arkle Chase on the opening day of the Festival for his patron, Sheikh Ali Abu Khamsin, but in the process dislocated his shoulder, and I replaced him on the Sheikh's other horses at the Festival.

Malya Mal was a horse that had to be held up, and I arrived at the last with every chance, but after the jump Mark Dwyer and Joint Sovereignty hung badly right, taking me with them across the run-in and putting paid to any chance of victory. In the end I finished second to Gee-A, ridden by Gee Armytage: a tremendous performance by a tough lady to achieve her second winner of the meeting.

Thursday, Gold Cup Day, saw High Knowl start favourite for the Triumph Hurdle despite my mistake on him at Kempton, but we could only finish fourth behind Steve Smith Eccles on Alone Success. Steve was having a good Cheltenham: having won his third Champion Hurdle with See You Then, he now took this race for Nicky Henderson for the second time in three years. In the Foxhunter Chase, the Winter yard had its first winner of the meeting with Observe, ridden by Fred's assistant, Charlie Brooks.

As I and the other jockeys went to the paddock for the Gold Cup itself, Cheltenham was suddenly hit by a snowstorm. By the time we reached the start there was a good covering on the ground and the Stewards recalled us. Back to the weighing room we went to wait for the snow to stop and for the Stewards to decide whether the race should go ahead. I always get nerves before a race, especially before a major event; once the tapes go

*Another National winner. Little Polveir on his way to an emphatic victory in the Scottish National at Ayr in April 1987 (GEORGE SELWYN)*

up the nerves disappear as you concentrate on the job at hand. This year I really thought my mount Bolands Cross had a good chance, which made the waiting even worse – and I felt especially sorry for Mark Dwyer on the favourite, Forgive 'N Forget.

One hour and twenty minutes later the race finally got under way. Bolands Cross unseated me when dropping his hind legs into the third ditch, but although we were in second place at the time he was not travelling particularly well, so the disappointment was not as bad as it could have been. Meanwhile The Thinker, trained by Arthur Stephenson and ridden by Ridley Lamb, went on to win after recovering from a bad mistake at the third last.

The rest of the card had to be hurried through in the gathering gloom before darkness fell. In the Ritz Club Chase which followed the Gold Cup the aptly named I Haventalight ran very poorly and Fred blamed me, I felt unfairly. In fact, he was livid. 'It is not a game out there, you know,' he said, 'it is war!' At least I managed to redeem myself by winning the last race in the lowering dusk with a length victory on Half Free – another ride for which I had the injured Richard Linley to thank – thus also snatching the Ritz Trophy for the leading rider at the Festival for the second year running.

Both my Cheltenham winners were spare rides, horses I could not have foreseen riding a couple of months earlier; which goes to show both that nothing is predictable in racing and that you have to be alert to opportunities when they come up – they won't wait around for you. Unpredictability hit Mark Dwyer with full force a few weeks later when, still very much in contention for the championship, he broke his wrist at Aintree on the second day of the Grand National meeting after falling at the first on Giolla Up. National Hunt racing is a hard game, and it would be dishonest to say I wasn't relieved, but I really felt for Mark; after all, I had been in just the same position twice when trying in successive years to take the crown from John Francome.

My single victory at the National meeting was Convinced, trained by Martin, who was now providing me with an increasing proportion of my winners. Pearlyman slipped back into his bad old ways in the two-mile chase and we parted company when still going well. At that time the Aintree chase track had a very difficult fence coming off the final turn that was both the first and the fourth last in the two-mile race; set at an angle at the point where the race begins in earnest on the second circuit, horses often met it unbalanced and would try to put in an extra stride. This is just what Pearlyman did and it cost us our chance of winning.

In the Grand National this year I rode Plundering, who finished well down the field behind Maori Venture, but I had a future prospect in another unsuccessful contender for this race: Little Polveir, an early casualty at Aintree, was to go to Ayr a week later for the Scottish National and I was booked to ride him. The real attraction for me at the Scottish meeting was Yabis, trained by John Edwards, in the Scottish Champion Hurdle, but in the event he was well beaten; and Mareth Line, whom I rode for Martin in a novice hurdle, tired badly and fell three fences from home. Again the unexpected winner came on a spare ride: Bally-Go for Jimmy FitzGerald, replacing the injured Mark Dwyer. Second to me in this race was a Mr J. Osborne, claiming seven pounds.

Little Polveir had ten stone for the big race, so my social life at the meeting was severely curtailed. I spent much of Friday

evening in the sauna at Ayr racecourse, after which I found a bed
for the night, along with a number of other jockeys, in a nearby
hotel. My host, a Scot with a large beard and kilt and also a keen
racing man, gave me a complimentary Scotch to help me sleep
and I went to bed, leaving the others to party. It was all worth it:
after another session in the sauna in the morning to shed the last
couple of pounds, Little Polveir romped home in the heavy
ground.

Using the sauna as a way of losing a lot of weight quickly –
some jockeys I knew would try to shed seven pounds before
racing – was not something I ever liked doing, as it is very
weakening and this can obviously affect your riding. The most
uncomfortable part of doing a light weight in the winter would
often be the cold, because you simply couldn't afford the extra
ounces of clothing to keep out the weather. I could ride at five
pounds above my body weight (some jockeys could do three
pounds above, and on the Flat, I believe, two pounds). This
meant two-and-a-half-pounds for the saddle and three-quarters of
a pound for boots, the rest being accounted for by colours and
breeches: there was nothing over for a sweater or tee-shirt. The
light saddle I never noticed once I was up and cantering, and it
was often far preferable to having a great deal of lead under the
saddle if you had to make up extra weight.

I did once try weighing out in 'cheating boots' – boots made
specifically for weighing out in, not for riding, with practically no
soles. I was caught by John Isherwood, Market Rasen's Clerk of
the Scales, and made to ride in them. I put some racecards inside
them to try to ease the pressure from the irons on the bottom of
my feet, but they were still very uncomfortable – and worse,
dangerous, because they had no heel and my foot could have
easily slipped through the iron in a fall, leaving me hung up. I
remember this happening to John Francome in one of his last
rides: when he fell his foot, still in the iron, got entangled in the
reins, but fortunately he got it free before any serious damage
was done. Others have been less lucky: in Australia I saw Grant
Ace being dragged between fences, luckily coming loose just
before the next jump; he broke his leg and never rode in another
race.

I compromised by having special light boots made which I
could ride in occasionally when the weight was really a problem.
They were made of very thin leather and if I had ridden in them

regularly they would have not have lasted long; moreover, the more they were used, the heavier they became with accumulations of polish and horses' sweat, which defeated the purpose. I insisted that all my boots had a decent heel; my father had early dinned into me the risk of a foot getting stuck in the iron if you rode without proper heels on your boots. If I ever saw anyone actually intending to ride in 'cheating' boots I would tell them off for their own good: it simply isn't worth risking serious injury, even death, for the sake of a few ounces.

As spring 1987 wore on, Martin was for the first time within reach of a seasonal total of 100 winners. The crunch was to come at the Spring Bank Holiday meeting at Cartmel, where I was sent to try to get the yard off the ninety-nine mark.

Cartmel, in Cumbria, must be one of the most inaccessible racecourses in the country, but it is well worth the journey – for spectators at least. On the approach to the course you drive through the stone village that prospered in the heyday of the wool trade, built up by the monks of the town's priory. Behind the town is the racecourse, unique among English courses and in many ways more akin to the character and atmosphere of Ireland. Spectators park in the middle of the course, which they share with the small stand and the fairground. The track, surrounded by stone walls, is a tight, left-handed circuit of just over a mile. Races over fences here have the longest run-in in the country: after jumping the final fence the horses travel round a final bend that takes them through a wood, out of sight of spectators (and Stewards), before turning up the finishing straight which bisects the course.

To avoid the holiday traffic jams I left home early and got to the course at about nine o'clock. I left my car there and wandered into the town for a bite to eat before returning for a snooze. Walking the course did nothing for my pre-race nerves: the six fences on the circuit looked even bigger than they were because they were narrow, and some of them were positioned on the top of a rise; the ground was firm and the camber of one of the bends was all wrong. All in all, this looked like a course where a horse might easily slip up.

Having got changed into my racing gear I stood and watched the first race; my morale was further depressed by discussion about a later race with an owner who told me I had absolutely no chance of beating his horse. With these rather dim prospects I set off on Nitida in the selling hurdle over two miles and seven furlongs. My fears about the camber on the bend were vindicated when one of the runners slipped up; on negotiating the turn for the second time I had to overcome not only the hazard of the ground but also that of a golden retriever that had left its owner to join in the race and was now standing in the middle of the track. It was infuriating to think that all Martin's hard work to reach his century could have been derailed by an unnecessary incident because someone couldn't take proper care of a dog – but it wasn't.

Martin was at home that day planning for more winners, so it was Carol and I who posed for the photographers and presentations afterwards in the winner's enclosure to celebrate her husband's admission into the select band of trainers who had produced 100 winners in a single season: Michael Dickinson, Gordon Richards, Arthur Stephenson. I felt that his achievement, happening as it did on one of the busiest racing days of the year, did not get the recognition it deserved; but perhaps the press may have had a premonition that they were going to be writing about even greater heights scaled by this man, and reserved their best efforts for later.

The afternoon went on as it had begun, with two more winners: Guymyson beat River Gambler, the horse whose owner had ridiculed my chances, by a head; and Mou-Dafa put in a faultless jumping round in the novice chase to give the yard a 100 per cent winning run on our first visit to Cartmel.

The season drew to a close, my championship secure with 123 winners (later adjusted to 124 after the disqualification of another horse). The figures for the yards with which I was associated spoke volumes for the future: Fred finished on a total of fifty-one winners (eleventh in the ranking according to prize money) and Martin on 106 (sixth in prize money terms). It was obvious that it was only a matter of time before the 'small West Country yard' clashed with the claims of my main employer.

## Chapter Ten

# A FOOT IN TWO CAMPS

————◆▸◀◆————

Paul Leach's riding career had been waning of late, and when he retired in 1987 I took over the rides in Martin's yard for the new season. Jonathon Lower remained as second jockey, as well as keeping the ride on a few horses of his own. Before racing began again we needed not only to ensure that the horses were fit to run as soon as suitable races became available, but to get them jumping fluently and confidently. For me, this meant daily riding and schooling at Nicholashayne, so for the last week of the close season and the first week of the new National Hunt term I took the family down to Devon, where we stayed in rented accommodation, so that they could have a bit of a holiday while I could be on hand to ride at Martin's and concentrate on the job without any of the inevitable distractions of being at home – and with the added benefit of peeling off the last couple of pounds and getting myself racing fit again. I never let my weight rise too much over the summer, and kept fit by jogging when I was not racing abroad, but there is always that extra element of fitness that can only be regained by regular riding and racing.

I would arrive at Pond House around 7.30 in the morning, driving down the short avenue of fir trees to the white farmhouse fronting on to the yard. The bottom floor of the house contained three offices: one for the three secretaries, headed by Gail 'Boycott' Harrison – so called because nothing gets past her – one for Carol and the accountant, and one for Martin himself. By the time I arrived Martin would be ensconced in his swivel chair behind a large desk, from which he presided over his office and yard with an efficiency and methodical logic learnt from his father's bookmaking business. On a board to his right were the magnetic strip markers bearing the names of horses matched against the names of the lads who were to ride them, with coloured dots of red, orange and blue indicating the stage of work each horse had reached. Near the entrance to the main office was another board on which the temperature of each horse was noted twice a day by its lad. All the horses' work was recorded in a file, and each horse had its own form card, telling the trainer at a glance details of all that horse's previous runs, with its weight and blood test results at the time. When a horse ran from Nicholashayne, there was never any doubt about the state of its fitness: its work record could be checked against its weight record and blood test results and the data were there in black and white (and red, orange and blue).

The former pig farm turned racing yard was growing and developing all the time, with new stables for the increasing number of inmates and new facilities added as soon as Martin was convinced of their usefulness. Better blood-testing equipment was introduced, and plans were under way for an indoor canter. One of the first training aids Martin had acquired was a swimming pool; as he pointed out to me, you can keep horses fit by swimming, which is a weightless, stressless exercise but very effective.

Martin and I would discuss which horses needed schooling that morning; while we were talking, Jonathon would be warming up some of them in the sand ring so that I could get on them when he had made them safe! At 8.15, when the rest of the yard had pulled out, Martin would take his *Sporting Life* (which nobody else was supposed to touch, mark or crease) and his mobile phone to the Range Rover and drive Chester and myself up to the schooling ground. By now we were schooling the hurdlers over small obstacles on a frame made by Eddie Fisher, the groundsman at Newton Abbot racecourse; the chasers would often be schooled with second lot. After this first session we would go back to the welcoming kitchen, where over a cup of tea provided by Carol we would discuss races and lay our plans in between the constant interruptions of two telephone lines. Then it was back to the office before second lot so that Martin could study the next day's declarations with the aid of the head lad's reports and the results of the blood tests indicating the horses' well-being.

One horse that was receiving special treatment during that last week of July was Rahiib, who was being prepared for the novice chase at Newton Abbot on 1 August; he duly became our first winner of the season. This was the first year in which we dominated the early jumping: by 14 August I had ridden thirteen winners. The good run continued all that month until on the thirty-first I had a crashing fall from Verbading. It was very often the case when I fell that I hurt my right shoulder or wrists, and on this occasion it was the right wrist that suffered. I won the following race on Parcelstown for David Gandolfo, but at Pond House that evening, where I was staying with the Pipes during the three-day Devon meeting, the wrist swelled up so far that I could not move it. They drove me to the local hospital for an X-ray and it was discovered that I had cracked a bone.

By now I knew from experience the value of my father's dictum that when your living depends on riding, you get the best medical care you can afford immediately, and the next day I went straight up to the National Rehabilitation Centre at Lilleshall, just north-west of Wolverhampton. It is here that many of the country's leading sportsmen and women train and recover from injury; the England cricket team is put through its paces at Lilleshall before going on tour, and many footballers whose injuries cannot be treated by their own clubs are sent here. The physiotherapy unit is quite superb and the staff are excellent. The first thing they did to my wrist was to pack it in crushed ice to reduce the swelling; the intense cold is a horrible feeling and my only consolation was that, to judge by the complaints filling the air in the treatment room, some of the footballers were being put through the same agonies. After two days of ice and laser treatment I was back riding.

Also in hospital at this time, and in a much more serious condition, was Fred Winter, critically ill after falling downstairs in his house. The accident had resulted in partial loss of movement down his right-hand side and some loss of speech; clearly it was going to be a long time before he could run Uplands again personally, if indeed he ever would. I visited him in hospital and again when he eventually returned home, but small talk was never a strong point with either of us and conversation was difficult.

That the yard continued to function so well was a tribute to Fred's organization as well as to his young assistant, Charlie Brooks, and the head lad, Brian Delaney – and, of course, to his wife Diana, who during this very distressing time remained a tower of strength to everyone around her. Once Charlie and Brian had taken over the management of the yard she maintained a keen interest but never interfered. With me she was as direct as ever; if she thought I had ridden a bad race she would tell me so and that would be an end of it. There was never any back-stabbing or nursing of grudges.

Charlie and I had a good working relationship already, and so with him continuing to run the yard on Fred's long-established lines, we could concentrate on the business of making sure that the horses ran well. The flagship of the yard this season was to be Celtic Shot, a horse that I had only ridden twice before. He had a habit of standing too far off his hurdles and sometimes landing on them: on the first occasion, at Wincanton, we fell when he picked up too early, taking his cue from horses in front of him, and crashed through the hurdle; on the second, at Uttoxeter, he was still picking up too far away at times so I concentrated on getting him round safely and we finished second; I wondered whether we should have won. On his first run this year he did win, by twenty lengths in a handicap hurdle at Sandown, despite reverting to his old habit and blundering at the last. He then went to the Cheltenham November meeting for a handicap hurdle on Mackeson Gold Cup day.

I had a good start to the meeting when winning a handicap chase on Pearlyman on the first day, giving lumps of weight away. Sadly, this was to be my last ride on him as he was henceforth to be ridden by Tom Morgan, John Edwards's new stable jockey. On the second day of the meeting the ground was not only soft but, as often happens after several races or on a well-used course, getting cut up on the inside. In these conditions it pays to look for the better ground, even if this means going wide. This is where judgement and experience pay off as you get to know your courses, and as a jockey it gives you great satisfaction when you get it right. On this occasion I took Celtic Shot round on the outside where the going was faster and, settling much more readily now with the experience of his early races behind him and so not tiring himself out by pulling too hard in the early stages, he won easily, ten lengths ahead of Nos Na Gaoithe. After the race Kevin Mooney, first jockey to Fulke Walwyn (and now assistant trainer to Barry Hills), a very shrewd judge of a horse, told me the horse would go close in the Champion Hurdle; very rarely, he said, did horses come up the Cheltenham hill so easily. I thought he was being a bit optimistic; I didn't think Celtic Shot was good enough to beat See You Then – although the triple winner of the Champion Hurdle was coming to be known as 'See You When' on account of his lack of racecourse appearances, and there were doubts about his soundness.

In fact there was another horse I was riding at this time who seemed to me to have better credentials as a Champion Hurdle prospect. This was Celtic Chief – another horse by the sire Celtic Cone – a big horse and a relentless galloper, though you did have to drive him into his hurdles as he wasn't very fast in the air over them. Celtic Chief was trained by Mercy Rimell, and it was for her that I had ridden the horse to victory in his first three hurdle races of the season, all at Newbury. In the first of these, in October, we beat High Knowl, ridden by Jonathon Lower who had won the Welsh Champion Hurdle on him; then followed a comfortable win over Jimmy FitzGerald's Special Vintage; and finally a hard-fought two-and-a-half-length victory over Osric and Hywel Davies. That, however, was to be my last ride on him as he was now going to take on Celtic Shot, who had a prior claim on my services.

Fred's yard also claimed me for the ride on Malya Mal in the Mackeson Gold Cup, which meant that I was unable to ride Beau Ranger for Martin Pipe. This horse, which had only recently come to Pond Farm, had formerly been trained very successfully by John Thorne; on his death in 1986 his daughter Jackie had taken over the yard but gradually the horse dropped a long way down the handicap and for the Mackeson he had only ten stone two pounds to carry. He won by fifteen lengths, ridden by Mark Perrett. Obviously I had regrets, but you can't always be on the winner, and obligations to a yard will inevitably mean missing other chances. I was lucky, after all, to have two such good stables wanting me on their horses, and if you spend too much time hankering after lost opportunities you miss the future ones.

However well things were going for me, I knew perfectly well that I would not be able to go on riding in races indefinitely. I had gone into racing for love of the sport, not for money, but there would eventually come a point when I could not earn my living riding, and I knew that it would be foolish not to make some provision for that time – however far off it seemed. I had been impressed by John Francome's clear-sighted attitude towards his future. He had a great affinity with horses and a great talent, but still saw racing as a means to an end. The older generation of jockeys told us that they had a more cavalier attitude to the sport, that they lived for the day and consequently got more fun out of it; but John had no intention of finishing up, as so many good jockeys have, with nothing to show for the good years and no capital on which to found another life. He made me aware that what we earnt as successful riders should be wisely invested if we were to be comfortably off past our mid-thirties when the rides dried up or we retired.

It was with all this in mind that I sold Eubury Ring, my house at Condicote, and bought fifty acres of arable land in Herefordshire, with the idea that I might move back there one day. However, I decided that from the point of view of my riding career it would be better to go on living in the Cotswold area, which was more convenient for travelling to Lambourn, Nicholashayne, and all the various racecourses in the south. So I took Nigel up on his offer of one of the cottages on the farm at Naunton, where he was still training as a permit-holder, and just before the 1988 Cheltenham Festival the family and I moved down the road – where we have been ever since.

We named the house Mucky Cottage after Mrs Muck, who this year had won her first run over fences at Cheltenham. After that she had been rather disappointing and had been switched back to hurdling, but that one win had earnt us a glowing write-up in the *Chaseform Notebook*, which said what an excellent ride I had given the mare. I discovered this comment while travelling up to Chepstow with Martin and Chester to ride Up Cooke in a novice chase. This filly was a real little madam who had unseated me at Devon and Exeter on our previous outing and had schooled very badly at home. Showing off to Chester, I produced the *Notebook* and read out what it had to say; he retorted, quite rightly: 'If you're so clever, do that on Up Cooke this afternoon!', which rather took the wind out of my sails. However, after giving the filly no ride at all I arrived at the last two lengths down from the leader and she ran on to win by three-quarters of a length. Chester was as sick as a pig. I never told him that I was a little bit lucky . . .

Nigel had another horse called Donald Davies (originally Donald Duck, to go with Mrs Muck, but Wetherbys would not accept Donald Duck as a name), whom he ran in a race at Worcester in which I rode a horse called Military Band that I thought had a better chance of winning. Simon Sherwood, also a great mate of Nigel's, took the ride on Donald and coming up the straight was on my inside travelling much better than I was; going to the last three fences I weaved about in front of him trying to stop him coming by and really hampered him at the last – and still he got up and beat me. When I'm telling everybody in Nigel's house what a good jockey I am he often threatens to show them the video of this race.

Worcester must bring out the worst in me, as it was here that I won a race on an objection in a way that doesn't make very comfortable telling. I had been beaten by Thomas Tate, Michael Dickinson's brother-in-law, in a novice hurdle, and as I went back into the changing room I saw him gathering all his riding equipment up together again to go back out to weigh in; he had forgotten to weigh in, so I objected and was given the race. It was not a very sporting gesture; there was a lot of fuss in the weighing room and I got a fair amount of barracking when I went out to ride in my next race. All the same, I did have an obligation to the owner I was riding for to make use of all the advantages I could and I had to think of that too. I remember thinking at the time that it would have been easier not to object, but on at least one view that was the coward's way out. As I left the weighing room at the end of the afternoon to go home, I saw a rough-looking bloke standing by my car and thought for a moment he was going to belt me for what I had done to Thomas; but as I came up to the vehicle he just asked for my autograph.

In fact, though there were arguments between jockeys all the time, some of them quite heated, there was hardly ever any actual physical violence in the changing room, which is perhaps surprising when you consider the competitiveness and stress of the sport. The nearest thing to a fight I ever saw blew up between Steve Smith Eccles and Billy Morris; John Buckingham, the valet, tried to cool things down by holding Steve's arms, but unfortunately this just gave Billy the chance to dive in and belt Steve, who ended up with a black eye.

Most of the arguments between jockeys were about one cutting up another in a race; I would often swear to myself that I would get even with another rider or never speak to someone again after he had ridden a race that did not suit me. In nearly all cases all these growlings blew over very quickly. Only once can I remember being properly stitched up, and that was by Mark Dwyer in the wood at Cartmel, where the Stewards can't see what goes on. There had been three of us in with a chance going into the wood: me, Mark in front and Kevin Ryan in third place. Mark left a good gap on his inside; like a dummy I went to go through and as I did so he stopped me by turning me sideways on to the rail. This manoeuvre cost him ground and let Kevin come up to beat both of us. At the time I was livid; but after about a month I spoke to him again and we laughed about the incident.

This year I came in for a bit of stick from the other jockeys after a race at Taunton in which my horse, Cat's Eyes, tried to refuse at the second fence when in front: the other horses coming up behind hit him up the tail and knocked him over the fence, after which his jumping improved no end and he won. However, in the commotion at the second he had knocked over three other runners, and understandably I was not a popular man when I returned to the weighing room. But I couldn't complain; I had after all won the race, and indeed won two more that afternoon to clock up a welcome treble.

The season was progressing nicely, with plenty of winners through the autumn. Celtic Shot continued to do quite well, winning the Mecca Hurdle at Sandown by eight lengths; but I still didn't think he justified his starting price of 6–4 or had much optimism about his chances in the Champion Hurdle. Nevertheless, he did go on to win a race that is considered a trial for the Cheltenham event, the New Year's Day Hurdle at Windsor.

Christmas can be a very frustrating time for a top jockey; there are so many meetings all on at once that you are bound to miss winners whatever you do – and this is exactly what happened to me at Christmas 1987. I did at least get the ride on Beau Ranger in the King George VI Chase at Kempton on Boxing Day, where I thought we had a chance; he had after all won the Mackeson, as well as the three-mile Edward Hanmer Memorial Handicap Chase at Haydock, making all in both cases. However, good as he was, he was not the only front runner on this occasion, and we were taken on by both Cybrandian and Desert Orchid. I was riding to get the best possible placing on Beau Ranger and was not concerned with impeding Colin Brown on Desert Orchid, as was suggested several years later; we kept up a genuine pace until the horse tired, but the three of us had gone off at a crazy gallop and in the end the French challenger Nupsala came past everything to win.

I have always considered Newbury one of the best jumping courses in the country – a flat, left-handed course a mile and three-quarters round, with stiff, wide, well-built fences that encourage horses to jump well. The only problem obstacle is the cross fence (and hurdle), approached on a downhill slope and positioned before the final turn into the straight, about five and a half furlongs from the winning post. It was a shame, then, that it was at Newbury that I had two wrangles with the Stewards in the 1987–8 season.

The first concerned the running of a horse called Arbitrage. I had gone to the races on 2 January 1988 intending to ride Tivian in the L'Oreal Handicap Hurdle as Graham McCourt, who had ridden Tivian earlier in the season, along with many other horses for his trainer Ian Matthews, had been claimed to ride another mount in the race. That other horse, however, did not run, and Graham was then booked to ride Arbitrage, a horse on which I had won for Graham Thorner two seasons previously. While Graham and I were sitting in the sauna before racing, he asked me if we could swop mounts as he had a better connection with Tivian than with Arbitrage. I agreed, subject to his obtaining permission from the respective connections, which he did.

The swap was a mistake: Tivian won and I pulled up Arbitrage, who simply failed to fire, before the last. I had ridden him round the outside, looking for the better ground, and we were tailed off from the fourth. The owner reported me to the Stewards, who having interviewed me fined me £300 under Rule 151(ii) for making 'insufficient effort to secure the best possible placing'. I thought this outrageous. When I had won on the horse in December 1985 I had ridden him in exactly the same way, as the form book records: 'In rear to fourth, good headway sixth, led approaching last, led near finish.' The only difference today was that the horse just did not respond; I later learnt from Graham Thorner that it had broken blood vessels when in training.

Arbitrage next ran at Kempton, drawing the following comment from John Oaksey in the *Sunday Telegraph*:

The Newbury Stewards who fined Peter Scudamore £300 under Rule 151(ii) the other day will no doubt take note of the fact that Scudamore's Newbury mount Arbitrage, ridden this time by leading conditional jockey Carl Llewellyn, raced as at

Newbury with the back-markers throughout. He finished with only one behind him.

What annoyed me most about the incident was not the fine or the stigma of an accusation of cheating but the Stewards' lack of understanding of race-riding. If I had jumped him off in front on the inside and lost the race they would have not said a word; but precisely because I *was* trying to obtain the best possible placing for the horse I rode him in a manner that suited his way of running, not a manner calculated to impress the uninformed. The Stewards did not know their form-book, and without that knowledge should not have been in a position of authority.

The second problem was somewhat more straightforward, and this time I really couldn't blame anyone else for either the incident or the punishment. I was riding a horse called Ghillie Hills for Nick Gaselee in a twenty-seven runner novice hurdle on 12 February. As the field approached that difficult cross hurdle, we were just behind the leaders on the inside. The inside rail on the bend coming out of the back straight stops some way short of the hurdle and Bruce Dowling thought that as there was no rail he could get up on my inside; I stopped him by squeezing him up against the hurdle wing, whereupon he fell on landing over the jump. The ironic part of the incident was that I was myself badly hampered on the next bend, which cost me my chance of the race, but the Stewards didn't see that. They sent both Bruce and me to Portman Square, from which we emerged with three weeks' compulsory holiday apiece. Fortunately for me, this both ended on the Saturday before the Cheltenham Festival and coincided with our move to the cottage at Naunton, so what with moving house and running and riding to keep fit I didn't have much time to indulge my annoyance or depression at being off the racecourse for three weeks. I returned with a bang on 12 March at Chepstow, with a double on Cat's Eyes for Martin Pipe and Ardesee for David Wintle – just the thing to tune me up for Cheltenham.

Back in February, Celtic Shot had been beaten eight lengths by Celtic Chief at Sandown. Two explanations were offered: first, that I had gone down the inside on the final turn, and second, that he did not like the heavy ground. Neither seemed convincing to me; he was just not good enough on the day, and this

154

*Driving for the line on Celtic Shot in the Champion Hurdle at Cheltenham in March 1988 (GEORGE SELWYN)*

disappointing performance crystallized all my doubts about his chances in the Champion Hurdle. I was now very keen that he should not run so that I could get back on Celtic Chief; however, it was not up to me. With Fred still ill, Celtic Shot's owner, David Horton, had a great deal of input into the decision whether to run the horse at Cheltenham, and one evening over supper during my suspension he told me he was convinced that the horse would win. There and then any lingering ideas I had of regaining the ride on Celtic Chief were gone.

Celtic Shot's preparation for the big race therefore continued, and I went to Lambourn on the Wednesday before the meeting to ride him in his final piece of work. At home he had become lazy, but on this particular morning he worked well over a mile and a half with two lead horses, one from the beginning and one jumping in at the halfway stage. Unfortunately the pleasure in this performance was all destroyed by an awful noise behind me when Drumlin Hill, a horse with a lot of potential, broke a hind leg while galloping.

The atmosphere in the jockeys' changing room at the Cheltenham Festival is much more intense than at ordinary meetings, and also more cosmopolitan, with jockeys from France and Ireland, as well as both the northern and southern English circuits, cheering on their local man as they watch the races they aren't riding in on the television screens. On the first day, as I didn't have a ride in the Arkle Chase, I was able to change early into Celtic Shot's colours, check my weight on the trial scales and grab a cup of tea

*This is the horse and these are the colours that won the 1988 Cheltenham Gold Cup with Richard Dunwoody in the saddle. I won eight races on Charter Party – including this one, the Golden Miller Chase at Cheltenham in April 1986 – and another old warrior is now a near neighbour at Raymond and Jenny Mould's stud* (BERNARD PARKIN)

to sip while the northern jockeys cheered on Mark Dwyer and Danish Flight to win. Then, having passed the Clerk of the Scales, I handed my saddle to the travelling head lad, Mick Cullen, who took it down to the saddling boxes where Charlie was waiting to saddle Celtic Shot.

After congratulating Mark on his Arkle win, and checking to see if some of the jockeys who fell were OK, I had a final glance through the form in the *Sporting Life* to remind myself of who the front runners were likely to be. High Knowl, Convinced and Juven Light were all bound to be up there; and what about the

French challenger Marly River? Would he handle the hurdles? If
he didn't, would he fall and bring me down? If he didn't, would
he beat me into second place? Just my bloody luck, I thought, to
be beaten by the first French challenger in the race for years.

It was difficult to get to the paddock through the crowds
outside the weighing room. To the right I caught sight of my
father's trilby and distinctive field-glasses; he wished me luck as
I entered the parade ring and headed for Charlie and the Horton
family, all eager to give me last pieces of advice on how to ride
the race. They were still full of confidence; privately, I couldn't
see my horse reversing form with Celtic Chief on this soft
ground, and I knew that the betting reflected the same view: 5–2
favourite Celtic Chief, 5–1 Cloughtaney, 13–2 Swingit Gunner,
7–1 Celtic Shot. At the very least I was going to have to go to the
front sooner, as the Sandown race had impressed on me that I
was not going to beat Celtic Chief for speed.

There is a parade for the race in numerical order, and I follow
Mercy's horse out of the paddock, through the corridor made by
the crowd and on to the course. The commentator is now
announcing the runners and their past form as we file past the
stands. There is no reigning champion here: See You Then has
had only one run this season and pulled up lame. Whatever wins
this year will be winning for the first time. Past the winning post,
we turn and one by one set off to canter to post. A look at the
first hurdle, then a walk to the starting gate. The chatting and
joking usual before an ordinary race are absent; the occasional
comment is passed on who is going to take up what position, but
most of us are deep in thought.

Aiming for a trouble-free run I line up towards the outside; as
the gates go up I urge my horse forward and he takes a good
hold to the first, standing off and clearing it well. They are going
a good gallop and already I can feel the pressure of the pace.
With Celtic Chief just to my inside and going well I judge that I
can't be too far off the correct pace. I have a good run round the
bend past the stands, although a little wide; as we enter the back
straight I am losing ground and there seems to be no chance of
winning. As the race unfolds my concentration sharpens and I
focus on every move as it comes up. Two more hurdles and the
horses in front are beginning to tire. Celtic Shot jumps the fourth
last well, allowing me to dominate my position on the outside,

and giving no help to those on my left. Now I can tighten up on those on my inside. Approaching the third last I move to the front, gradually galloping left-handed to jump the second last nearer the inside. The pack are still on my tail as we straighten up to the final hurdle and the hill; I am still in front but thinking of nothing but getting a good stride to that last hurdle. As we jump it a horse's head looms upsides me. It must be Celtic Chief and Richard Dunwoody: they are bound to beat me. With my stick in my right hand I drive the horse on to the line, and now I can see that it isn't Celtic Chief at all, it is Classical Charm, but he never heads me and as I pull my stick through to my left hand to keep my horse straight after the inner rail stops we draw four lengths clear to win Fred Winter's last Champion Hurdle.

Other jockeys come up to congratulate me as I make my way back down the course to be led in by a delighted David Horton. I jump off and after a few words with him and with Charlie I walk back to the weighing room, up the steps past a proud father who is there to pat me on the shoulder. And all the time I am telling myself: 'Don't forget to weigh in . . .'

Racing is a great leveller; after all the euphoria of this victory, after the trophy presentation and the television and newspaper interviews, I spent the evening sitting in the sauna to do ten stone the next day on a horse called Tarconey for Peter Cundell – and next day I found it was withdrawn. For me the rest of the Festival was places and might-have-beens: Pearlyman won his second Queen Mother Champion Chase on the Wednesday, this time ridden by Tom Morgan; on the Thursday I was third in the Triumph Hurdle on Chatam behind Kribensis, and third again in the Gold Cup on Beau Ranger behind Charter Party, both ridden by Richard Dunwoody. Charter Party, Pearlyman and Private Views, the winner of the Cathcart Chase with Brendan Powell, were all horses on whom I had won in the past and naturally I wished I could have won on them here; but I knew that in riding for two powerful stables I was going to miss other chances – and the more rides I was offered, the greater the chance of having to turn down a winner. It often seems cruel at the time, but in fact it is no bad thing; it keeps your feet on the ground and reminds you that you can't have everything.

And there are also pleasures to be had in others' successes. On the Thursday evening Charter Party's owners, Raymond and

Jenny Mould, held a celebration party at their magnificent Cotswold stone mansion, Guiting Grange, just a mile down the road from Mucky Cottage. I don't think Jenny could quite believe her luck; it seemed that evening still not to have sunk in that the store horse she had picked out at Doncaster Sales had just won the Blue Riband of National Hunt racing.

Anyone having trouble keeping their feet on the ground after Cheltenham can do no better than to go to the meeting that traditionally takes place on the following day at Wolverhampton. This soulless occasion, which along with the card at Lingfield has the unenviable task of taking up the thread of the calendar after the Festival, is in complete contrast to the buzz and hubbub of the previous three days. There are usually a few punters, those who either have no money and cannot get home or still have a few quid left to give to the bookmakers on their way, and they lend the only semblance of atmosphere to the proceedings.

It's true that I always had something of a personal grudge against the place where my father had the accident that ended his riding career, and although the track had actually been a lucky one for me, I would often find myself thinking of Dad's misfortune as I drove up there. But the facilities at Wolverhampton did nothing to endear the place to me. As you travel round the country courses you get to know the gatemen, the caterers and the tea-man or lady in the weighing room; and here these friendly faces were the only attractive aspect of the course. The changing room felt cold and damp, with two calor gas fires failing to take the chill off the air that felt a good two degrees cooler than it was outside. The toilet facilities were continually under water, the cheap, shiny, hard loo paper summing up the degree of welcome the place afforded. The three showers did not have taps, but economical push buttons, and it was an acquired skill to run a shower for long enough to get hot water out of it.

The lack of creature comforts and the thought of riding some of the lesser lights of the equine world brought out a particular brand of humour among jockeys condemned to earning their wages here. Seamus O'Neill, one of the less fashionable jockeys but a good rider all the same, was second to none in his stories of the horses he had had to ride and the trainers he had ridden them for. He told of a trainer who was leading him in a piece of work up the gallops one morning; halfway along he turned to shout to Seamus to move upsides him and as he shouted his false teeth fell out. Seamus was unable to carry out his instructions for laughing and spent the rest of the morning grovelling in the grass looking for teeth. And then there was the business of explaining the ability – or lack of it – of the horses to their owners. Having trailed in last on one occasion, he told the owner that the horse made a noise.

'What sort of noise?' asked the owner.

'Eehaw! Eehaw!' explained Seamus.

The track itself at Wolverhampton is a sharp left-handed course, with a severe bend in front of the stands. The final straight runs slightly downhill, encouraging horses to run on to their forehands, which increases the risk of falling. There is very little room around the steeplechase track, with the two-and-a-half-mile start particularly tight. One day Hywel Davies was riding an animal of no particular ability in a handicap chase here and after missing the break was blocked in on the inside. I wouldn't let him out and eventually he finished running on. The trainer was so cross with him that he reported Hywel to the Stewards; he ended up in London in front of a Jockey Club Disciplinary Committee and I had to go and give evidence on his behalf, thus losing a whole day's racing. I wished I'd let him out.

On this particular Friday the wet and cold were mitigated by a win in the first on Parlezvousfrancais, owned by John Fairbrother. John, whose horses ran under the name of Fairlord Wholesale Confectioners Ltd, provided Martin's yard with mints for the horses. A self-made man who drove a Roller in his racing colours of red and black and loved a tilt at the ring, he was among the most pleasant and loyal owners I ever had the pleasure of riding for – win or lose, he supported the jockey. I always rode with more confidence for owners such as he; knowing the owner will stand by you does make a difference.

Despite my long enforced 'holiday' before Cheltenham I had a clear lead in the championship – which was just as well, for the next few weeks were not particularly fruitful in terms of winners. Celtic Shot returned to the racecourse for the Welsh Champion Hurdle, for which he started 3–1 on, but fell. At Aintree I had a second to Celtic Chief on the nine-year-old Sabin Du Loir, whom Brian Kilpatrick had sent to Pond House in an attempt to revitalize his flagging career. We were to see more of each other.

The story of this year's Grand National begins on the day before the Aintree meeting, at Mucky Cottage. Having two growing sons forced me, at least some of the time, to take my mind off my own preoccupations with racing, thereby giving me much needed mental relaxation. They were both keen that I should do well, but for them their own problems and concerns were more urgent, and so they had to be for me too when I was with them. Today I was helping Thomas, now aged six, with his jumping on his pony, Flea, explaining to him that if he held on

*One of the great old campaigners with whom I was associated at Martin Pipe's was Beau Ranger. Mark Perrett rode the gelding to win the 1987 Mackeson, but here I'm partnering him to victory in the South Wales Showers Mira Trophy at Cheltenham in April 1988* (BERNARD PARKIN)

to a piece of mane he would not fall off. Three days later I was riding Strands Of Gold for Martin Pipe in the National; a game, solid little bay horse who started at 20–1 behind the favourite Sacred Path, trained by Oliver Sherwood. For the first circuit he gave me a great ride, jumping boldly over the daunting fences; moving effortlessly into the lead on the inside at the fence before second Becher's he popped it well and I quickened him up to jump out over the drop – but no stride came and we hit the fence very hard.

We were lucky the fall was no worse. It was suggested in the post-race analysis that I might not have fallen if I had gone towards the middle of the fence, but we hit it with such force that I think we would have gone even if it had just been an ordinary fence. Anyway, there I was, picking myself up off the floor, realizing that I had just handed the 1988 Grand National to Brendan Powell and Rhyme 'N' Reason. I was furious and threw my helmet and stick to the ground in temper. Turning round to hitch a lift back to base I caught sight of the billboard behind me: 'I bet he drinks Carling Black Label'!

Back at the weighing room, the race over, the jockeys were studying the replay on television, telling one another to watch their performances, swapping stories of good and bad luck. I was feeling too depressed to watch the race all over again and shuffled off to the antiquated showers. Washing the mud off I heard a voice address me, and as I wiped the shampoo from my eyes I saw the figure of Thomas, who had come up with Marilyn for the meeting. Thomas loves racing and jumped every fence with me from the stands; I didn't mind his being there if I had a fall because it helped him realize what jump racing is all about. On this occasion he hadn't come to see if I was all right, but to admonish me:

'Daddy, were you holding on to the mane? Because you should have been and then you wouldn't have fallen off.'

I couldn't help smiling. How could I go on feeling sorry for myself after that?

The Cheltenham Spring Meeting, the last major meeting of the season, produced two good winners: Ten Of Spades for Mercy Rimell and Beau Ranger for Martin. For the South Wales Showers Trophy Chase the ground was perfect for Beau Ranger, good to firm, and he was able to dominate the race. He was not good at fiddling his fences and tended to chest them; today I was able to ride him on the loose contact he preferred and he bowled along jumping fluently: all I had to do was to keep his momentum up coming into the fence and he would find his stride. Going to the second last Richard Rowe on Chief Ironside drew upsides, but a spectacular leap from Beau Ranger sealed the race for us.

It was this spring that the Jockey Club introduced guidelines on the use of the whip, under pressure from certain sections of the media and the RSPCA. At the time I was very much against these new regulations, but although they have proved difficult to enforce sensibly, they certainly made me more aware of how I used the whip and this ultimately made me a better rider.

By this time I had ridden in various parts of the world and had got to know different countries' practices and rules on the subject. In Australia, for example, where jockeys are much more vigorous in their use of the whip, the construction of the stick is regulated: the shaft length must be between 20 and 22 inches with a flap 3–4 inches long. When I was there as part of the touring jockeys' team the Australian Stewards told us that they would penalize excessive use of the whip and that no horse should ever be hit on the head or neck. In Sweden, the restriction stated that you could not hit a horse behind the saddle twice without replacing the stick in the forehand position between blows. In Norway you were not allowed to take your hands off the reins to hit the horse, which led to a rather peculiar sideways movement of the hands in jockeys riding a finish.

The 1988 Jockey Club guidelines covered both the construction of the whip and its use. It was to be of maximum length 76 cm, minimum width 8 mm, with a flap no longer than 10 cm. No jockey was allowed to strike a horse more than ten times between landing over the second last obstacle and passing the winning post. This latter rule did prove very unfair in operation, often penalizing good jockeys riding good finishes for the sake of stopping the cowboys who hit horses unnecessarily.

*With Maz at Richard Dunwoody's wedding, July 1988* (BERNARD PARKIN)

Moreover, local Stewards did not all interpret the rule identically, so as a jockey you never really knew what to expect.

The fundamental problem with the rule was that, in my view, it was introduced for the wrong reasons. In general the horse's welfare was not under threat from the whip; the rule was brought in to pacify a public that for the most part did not understand racing and horses, and consequently it proved very hard to apply consistently in practice. The vast majority of trainers I rode for would not tolerate ill-treatment of their horses, let alone outright cruelty. If I made a mistake in a race I expected to be reprimanded, if I made a serious mistake I did not expect to ride for that trainer or owner again, and exactly the same principle applied to the use of the whip. If the trainer or owner is unhappy with the way a jockey uses the stick, it is their prerogative to replace him. Brian Kilpatrick, the owner of Sabin Du Loir, was one of several owners who particularly asked me not to use the stick on this horse and to be sparing with it on his other horses. I followed his wishes because if I had not I would not have been able to continue riding for him.

I believe that by using the stick correctly you can make a horse go faster. With experience you instinctively know which horses to hit and how often; some were best ridden just with hands and heels, others really responded to a couple of smacks. I had a reputation, especially earlier in my career, for riding vigorously, and I did get into trouble for my use of the stick sometimes; later on, when I was able to ride effectively with or without it, depending on the horse and the circumstances of the race, I was a better jockey. But it was experience and advice, not riding by the rule-book, that made me so.

Often this year I had felt that it was I who was under the whip. Towards the end of the season I had been working extremely hard, often riding at two meetings a day and when time was very tight flying from the first to the second in Martin's helicopter. The rewards were there to see: I held on to my title with 132 winners – Chris Grant was runner-up with eighty – and Martin's total of winners came to 129. But I needed a break, and so this summer Marilyn, Thomas, Michael and I went out to Trinidad and Tobago with twelve other jockeys and their wives or girlfriends for three glorious weeks of sun, sand and rum – before we all plunged back into the routine of another season.

*Chapter Eleven*

# THE RECORDS START TO FALL

—————►◄—————

The West Indian holiday had its desired effect, and I returned to England refreshed to tackle the preparation for the new season. It was all the more important to start feeling fit and fresh as once work got under way again the pace was unrelenting – and because the pre-season preparation for the early campaign in the West Country meant that my summer holidays ended earlier than a lot of other jockeys'.

It had become apparent by now that Fred Winter was never going to recover fully from his tragic accident, and Charlie Brooks took over the trainer's licence at Uplands. We came to a slightly different arrangement about my riding commitments: as Martin's stable could no longer be regarded as a 'second string' in any sense, the Uplands horses would not have automatic first claim on me any more and I would split my rides between Charlie and Martin. Though for most of my career I rode mainly for one or two yards, I never took a retainer to bind me to one stable; by working instead on the basis of more informal commitments I could keep some flexibility in my riding arrangements.

The horse that chalked up the first win of what was to be a record-breaking season was Rahiib, who had opened the Pond House account the previous year and now won the first race of the season at Newton Abbot by a head. On the second day of the meeting, however, I was in trouble with the Stewards over the running of My Cup Of Tea in a handicap hurdle. This horse was a very hard puller and over hurdles was best ridden from behind; in this race he made some headway to the fifth but weakened after the third last, and finished sixteen lengths behind the winner. Once his chance was gone, there was no point in my being hard on him, but the Stewards thought that Martin and I had a case to answer. We explained that there was no response from the horse when the leaders quickened from the fifth, and were annoyed when the Stewards formally recorded our version of events – which was tantamount to saying they didn't really believe us.

Already, it seemed, we were becoming victims of our own success: having taken other trainers and riders by surprise with our front-running tactics on super-fit horses, we were now expected to follow the same pattern every time, and if we did not questions were asked. All this season – and beyond it – Martin

*My only win in the Mackeson Gold Cup – Pegwell Bay picked out against the Cheltenham sky in November 1988 (MARK CRANHAM)*

*(Right) Michael (left) and Thomas with the Mackeson Gold Cup after my victory on Pegwell Bay (BERNARD PARKIN)*

was to ride the roller-coaster of success upon success followed by suspicion, jealousy and resentment from competitors and observers who lacked understanding of the real foundations of his achievements.

The Stewards at Newton Abbot did have a point, however, because My Cup Of Tea went on to run over fences and won eight races that season . . .

The winners kept on coming, and by 25 October I found myself driving right across the country to the small Norfolk course of Fakenham in pursuit of the fastest fifty of all time. Martin had trained forty-three of the forty-nine I had so far amassed and today I was riding Wolfhangar, on whom I hoped to take the record. The previous best had been set by John Francome on 9 November 1984, and was a record that I was keen to take because at that stage I didn't think I would hold any others. In itself it was of no special significance, but it caught the attention of the racing press, who were by now beginning to divert their sights from the tail-end of the Flat season to the gathering momentum of the National Hunt programme.

From home to Fakenham is the longest trip I have on the southern circuit. It is a tight track of a mile round, one of the

sharpest in the country, which exacerbates one of the biggest
dangers to jockeys riding in the autumn, namely slippery going
caused by rain on hard ground. One horse had already slipped
over in a hurdle race that afternoon, and to add to my
apprehension Wolfhangar was a big, gangly creature and a free
runner, not the compact, handy type best suited to these
conditions.

Rather than pulling the horse about trying to settle him, I set

off in front and allowed him to take a slightly wider route on the
bends than I would normally, so that he could keep himself
balanced. After surviving two blunders and rounding the last
bend still in front I rode for the last fence well in control,
keeping him together to ensure a safe jump and the crucial
victory. However, we did run left-handed down the last, taking
the ground of Hywel Davies on Bigee, who fell. A Stewards'
Inquiry was called. I asked Hywel whether the incident had
made any difference to him; he said not really, and as he had
fallen, he couldn't be awarded the race anyway, so he would help
me in the Inquiry.

I should have known that Hywel's help can come in many
forms. We have been great mates for a long time – I am
godfather to his eldest son, James – and I know only too well his
talent for quite unintentionally dropping one in it. For example,
once when reassuring Marilyn about my conduct on a summer
jockeys' tour in Australia, he said of me, 'Oh yes, he was very

well behaved; on the dance floor he just had a kiss and a cuddle, nothing more.' This was the kind of help I got from him in front of the Fakenham Stewards.

'I don't think I would have fallen,' he explained; 'I only had a slight chance at the time. Yes, I did slip, but that may not have been the cause of my fall'.

I think the Stewards were ready to take the race away from me until, with equally unintentional good effect, Hywel gave them a fence-by-fence description of how the race had gone that left them so pleased to get rid of us that they let me keep it. Remembering Eddie Harty's tale of his discussion with the Ayr Stewards, I thought how entertaining it would be to see a confrontation between him and Hywel in the Stewards' room.

A week later at Ascot, my old friend Bajan Sunshine vied with Hywel for lack of diplomacy when beating the Queen Mother's Sun Rising a short head. Earlier in the season I had ridden my one and only winner for the Queen Mother on Insular, trained by Ian Balding; now I managed to snatch a race from her that I felt I had really earned by the time we reached the winning post. Bajan Sunshine did not always put his best foot forward and it took everything I had over all three miles of the race to coax this win out of him. I knew if I went for my stick too soon I would have played my last card and he would only run flat out for a very short time; so I pushed and shoved him most of the way round, squeezing and cajoling as we took advantage of Sun Rising's blunder at the last to grab the lead on the last stride. Typical of the old character to win when it would have been more discreet to turn it up and give the race to the most popular owner in the winter game.

Hywel was at this time the only one of the three jockeys used by Captain Tim Forster still in circulation, Luke Harvey and Carl Llewellyn both being temporarily sidelined through injury. When Hywel had to go to Hereford for the Captain, leaving rides elsewhere unclaimed, I rang to ask whether he wanted a jockey for Fiddlers Three at Devon and Exeter, where I had seen the horse win earlier in the season. It may seem slightly vulture-like to pounce on opportunities thrown up by the misfortunes of others in this way, but I had learnt from my father that there is an etiquette in these things: you don't ring to try to steal other people's rides from them, only when you think the trainer is looking for a jockey because his usual choice is out of the running

*My first Hennessy Gold Cup – on Strands of Gold at Newbury in*
*November 1988 (GERRY CRANHAM)*

for some reason. Injury attacks randomly, and everyone's chance
comes up.

Fiddlers Three won for me, and it was through this victory
that I secured the ride on Pegwell Bay, trained by the Captain,
for the Mackeson Gold Cup. His win in that race rounded off a
great day of three winners, the other two being Run And Skip
and Martin's latest early season superstar, Liadett, who was
winning his third race of the season – or rounded off the racing
day, at least, for that evening was the Champion National Hunt
Jockey's Ball. This event, traditionally held on the evening of
Mackeson Gold Cup day, is organized by the Directors of the
Steeplechase Company (Cheltenham) and the National Hunt
Committee to honour the previous season's champion rider. John
Francome, my predecessor in this role, had made some excellent
speeches on these occasions; lacking his talent as an after-dinner
speaker, I found it best to keep my remarks short. Some years
earlier Frenchie Nicholson, David's father, had told me that the
best thing to do was get up, say 'Thank you very much,' and sit

down again – and on this occasion I did just that, having been presented with a delicate porcelain figure of a jockey painted in Pearlyman's colours. I then went over to Martin Pipe's table, where, referring to Pearlyman's colours, I said, 'When are you going to get me a horse as good as that to ride?' and firmly plonked the figurine down in front of him, at which point it broke at the boots and toppled over on to the table, where the jockey's head fell off.

However bad I was at making speeches, my brief thanks to Cheltenham racecourse were heartfelt. The course's Managing Director, Edward Gillespie, and Clerk of the Course, Philip Arkwright, are both outstanding at their jobs, and along with Haydock (where Philip Arkwright is also Clerk of the Course) Cheltenham is the most helpful and welcoming to jockeys of all courses. I am always proud, too, to be able to show overseas visitors round Cheltenham, which in my view is simply the best course in the world, its beautifully maintained track, well-tended fences and excellent facilities making it equally inviting to participants and spectators alike.

Later that week I learnt a lesson: be careful whose advice you listen to about riding a horse. It was the Wednesday, at Kempton, and I was riding Penalty Double for Charlie Brooks, a horse I could not recall from schooling at Uplands. After receiving vague instructions from Charlie and being legged up to ride out of the paddock, I was making polite conversation with the lad leading up the horse. I always thought it was good manners to do this as the lads and girls are vital parts of the training teams and are often overlooked. This lad, whom I hadn't met before, told me that Penalty Double was lazy and to grab hold of him and give him a smack, which I did – to find myself struggling to pull him up after cantering half a mile further to the start than I had intended. This was the horse's first run on the course, and after settling him in at the back I was able to bring him through to win; but from then on I remained suspicious of what anybody told me about a horse until I had found out for myself.

At Haydock, which was becoming a happy hunting ground for the Pipe team, Beau Ranger won the Edward Hanmer Memorial Chase for the second year running as the third leg of a treble for me; and the second day brought a double. Unfortunately, it also

brought me a two-day suspension for my use of the stick on Run
And Skip, whom I had marked. It was a bitterly cold and frosty
day and the horse had just been clipped out, factors which I was
sure contributed as much to the marking as any force with which
I had used the stick.

From Haydock it was back south again to the two-day meeting
at Newbury. During the journey I had a call from David
Elsworth to say that Simon Sherwood had been injured and to
ask in his jocular way whether I would like to ride 'a decent
horse, instead of the rubbish you're used to!' The 'decent horse'
was Barnbrook Again, one of two winners I rode on the following
afternoon. On the second day of the meeting I was riding Strands
Of Gold in his first race of the season in the Hennessy Gold
Cup. Martin was renowned for sending his horses out fully fit for
their first run, but sometimes he was the hardest person to
convince that a horse *was* fit if its weight did not tally with that
on its previous season's best runs, and such was the case today
with Strands Of Gold.

'He can't win,' said Martin to me in the paddock. 'He's not fit
enough.' I knew that Martin's 'not fit enough' was still a lot
straighter than most other trainers'.

I said, 'He's been in as long as Beau Ranger, hasn't he? He's
done the same amount of work, and Beau Ranger won on
Wednesday. He can't be far off, he's got to be fit.'

And so it proved. Strands Of Gold, with me doing my
minimum weight of ten stone, won the Hennessy easily by six
lengths.

Sandown the following weekend was less fruitful, though
equally spectacular. Friday brought one winner, in a novice
hurdle, and two falls. The first of these, in the novice chase, was
straightforward enough; the second, however, appeared shortly
thereafter on BBC TV's *Question of Sport* in the 'What
Happened Next?' slot. It was my old mate Bajan Sunshine again.
This time, instead of taking off when in the lead at the last,
without warning he jinked left and refused, sending me flying
over his head – much to the amusement of the spectators in the
stands (except, presumably, those who had backed us) and the
jockeys in the weighing room. Even less amusing for me was the
next day when, serving the first day of the ban handed out at
Haydock, I had to sit fuming as two of 'my' horses won:
Corporal Clinger, ridden by Mark Perrett, and Baies, ridden by

Simon Sherwood – one from each of my main yards.

Celtic Shot had made a winning seasonal reappearance at Leicester, but I didn't think he did it in the manner of a Champion Hurdler. He started 6-1 on against moderate opposition and although he looked to have won comfortably enough I was not happy with him. In his next race, a Champion Hurdle trial at the Cheltenham December meeting, he again started a short-priced favourite, but was comprehensively beaten into fourth place by Jim Bolger's Condor Pan. The good ground was blamed, but to me this was no more than an excuse. I often thought that connections tended to blame too many variables for a poor running rather than confronting the possibility of a decline in the horse's enthusiasm or ability. That particular day failed to improve; I got beaten a length and a half on Beau Ranger in the A. F. Budge Gold Cup, giving a stone in weight to the horse I had ridden to victory in the Mackeson, Pegwell Bay. Even riding for Martin was no guarantee of winning.

Yet despite a couple of setbacks, the season was really flying, and Martin, Chester and I were all in good spirits as we headed back to Haydock in the Rolls on 14 December, at which point my tally of winners had reached ninety-four. Much as I loved riding at Haydock, I always treated the course with respect; the fences were big and I had, after all, broken my leg there once. Chester and Martin were very bullish before racing, never seeing the problems as I did. Chester in particular was hopeless. As a former sportsman himself you would think he'd have had some recollection of the ups and downs of sporting life, but he would allow his enthusiasms to run away with him – he was a great winner but a terrible loser.

On this occasion he drove while Martin and I read that day's *Sporting Life* and discussed the horses and tactics of the afternoon ahead. Both of us had mobile phones and our attempts at conversation were constantly interrupted as owners rang to enquire into the chances of their horses in today's and future races. Many of Martin's owners were also personal friends, such as Jack Joseph and John Fairbrother, and we would rib each other about the information we gave them. Chester would not be able to see any dangers, I would point out the likely problems of the race, and then the pair of us would be arguing about how little the other knew about racing.

What with all this going on I could never sleep in the car on the way to the races, but liked when I could to concentrate my mind on the day ahead, sitting quietly and going through my plan of campaign.

We won the first at Haydock that day with Sondrio – a great big horse that had won a Grade 1 race in Canada before coming over here to run, and not a very good jumper. My next mount was Rusch de Farges, who had been brought over from France; French horses often take a while to adapt to the stiffer English fences and Rusch de Farges had fallen on his first run over here. Today, after a horrendous mistake at the first and with the favourite Saffron Lord unseating Eamonn Murphy at the second, he went on to win by fifteen lengths at 16-1 – my longest-priced winner of the season.

While Martin and Chester started on the celebratory champagne, I spent forty-five minutes in the sauna before joining them for a small glass. Chester had left his jacket hung on the back of a chair, and out of the corner of my eye I saw someone swipe it; by the time I could tell Chester it was too late, jacket and predator were gone. I could barely contain my laughter as Chester told the story of his misfortune to anyone who would

*With Martin Pipe and my father after winning the Welsh National at Chepstow on Bonanza Boy in December 1988 (BERNARD PARKIN)*

listen – until, that is, we discovered that the car keys had been in the pocket and the car would have to be towed to a garage for safe keeping overnight while a replacement key was obtained. We spent the night in the Four Seasons Hotel, owned by Tim Kilroe, whose Forgive 'N Forget had won the 1985 Gold Cup. He was a good friend of Jim Ennis, owner of Rushmoor, and the two of them would often come and have a meal with us when we were staying up there.

Dealing with social occasions is always difficult when you are dieting to keep the weight down, but with Bryan Robson, the England football captain, making a special effort to dine with us that night it would have been extremely rude to absent myself. (Bryan kept horses with Martin, despite the latter's abysmal ignorance about football. As Chester never tired of repeating, he once remarked to Bryan, 'No wonder you're captain of England if your father Bobby is the manager.') I sat with a bowl of soup, a glass of champagne and a cigar while the others ate. In fact I never found not eating too difficult because I had a pressing incentive not to do so. Even Chester's frequent stops at service stations on our journeys to and from the races to stock up with chocolates and sweet drinks, followed by detailed descriptions for my benefit of the exquisite taste of the food he was eating, didn't much bother me.

By the next day I was on ninety-seven winners, with Jonjo's record of the fastest 100 in my sights – though I didn't really believe I would be able to break it at Haydock, despite having some good rides. I spent much of that morning in the sauna, quite an entertaining pastime in the north as the likes of Graham McCourt, Graham Bradley and Neale Doughty would often be there too. Brad was one of those who would rub himself all over with baby oil as he believed it helped him sweat more freely and lose weight better; for myself, I was happy with just a cup of tea to sip when my mouth got too dry.

The afternoon started off well, with my first two rides, Stepaside Lord and Voyage Sans Retour, both winning for Martin. All of a sudden I was faced with the prospect of riding my 100th winner of the season on Fu's Lady. This was a tall, long-backed mare who tended to jump very flat, so I didn't think Haydock's big, solid fences would suit her; but fortunately the race was a typical Haydock chase, with no one going too fast in the early stages, and I was able to dictate the pace and get her back on to her hocks to jump. Coming to the last with a fair bit in hand she was able to pop it and sprint up the run-in to become my 100th winner – or so I thought at the time. It later turned out that an earlier winner, Norman Invader, had failed a dope test taken after his race at Cheltenham on 5 October and been disqualified, so I was still one short. It was when I went out to win on Sayfar's Lad in a novice hurdle at Leicester five days later, in what I thought was just another race, that I officially achieved the century.

At the time, of course, we were blissfully ignorant of the hitch with Norman Invader, and our journey home from Haydock was as much fun as the trip up. We'd got the car back, along with a new set of keys, and with a jacketless Chester behind the wheel the mobiles were soon at full stretch again as we reported in to our loved ones, telling them when we'd be back, and gave Mr Pipe senior the run-down on the day's activities.

Christmas can be a miserable time for a jockey, as food and drink are such a large part of the festive atmosphere. The type of food around is the worst possible for anyone trying not to put on weight – puddings, pies and salty snacks that retain body fluid. This year I had to be especially careful as I was riding Bonanza Boy with ten stone in the Welsh National on 27 December. I tried to make an effort to join in the family celebrations until after lunch, but had to resort to the sauna for the evening.

The Christmas holiday racing made it all worthwhile. On Boxing Day I had forsaken the glories of Kempton for Newton Abbot, where I was to ride one of my favourite horses, Sabin Du Loir, over fences for the first time. This horse had been a high-class hurdler and was making the switch to fences at the comparatively late age of nine. Neither Martin nor the horse's owner, Brian Kilpatrick, was totally convinced that he should tackle the stiffer obstacles, but he was becoming complacent over hurdles and I believed it was high time that he faced the challenge of steeplechasing. He was not a big horse, but had been jumping fences superbly at home and I felt as confident as it is possible to be about a horse racing over fences for the first time.

Sabin won by thirty lengths, though after the race I had an argument with Richard Guest, who said that he would have beaten me if he had not fallen at the ninth. I told him he was talking rubbish, but as Beech Road went on to win the Champion

Hurdle four runs later he may have had a point.

Next day it was the Welsh National at Chepstow and Bonanza Boy. Stamina and jumping rather than speed were his real strengths, and in his prep race, a handicap chase at Newton Abbot, I had struggled to carry out my instructions to 'make all', but he won comfortably none the less, and Martin was very confident about his chance in the big race. Soft winter ground at Chepstow, a left-handed, undulating, galloping track, puts a great deal of emphasis on stamina and this, together with the weight of Chester's money, sent him off the 9-4 favourite.

I liked the fences at Chepstow, but as on many courses there is one particularly tricky one, the first of the five up the home straight. The fact that you meet it coming off the bend means that horses tend to run into the bottom of it and not get their landing gear out. Also, at this late stage of the race a horse can come off the bridle and put down on you in front of the fence; or it might overjump and then peck on landing, as the ground runs slightly away from the fence on the far side. Like many small horses, Bonanza Boy was very athletic, agile and supple in his jumping; he only found it difficult when I asked him to stand off too far, as his lack of scope meant that he would go higher in the air over the fence rather than stretching out for the other side. Jumping was a slight problem for him early on in this race as the pace was a bit quick and I was having to rush him; there was no time to choose strides carefully and at times we would come to a fence on too long a stride and he would have to reach for it. However, as the race developed and he took up the bridle more, he came into his own and by the time we turned into the home straight he was going easily. It was his fast, efficient, foot-perfect jumping that achieved his twelve-length victory, the highlight of my day's four-timer.

Two days later Martin achieved his own 100th winner of the season when I rode Mareth Line to win a novice chase at Taunton – appropriately, Martin's local track.

The success of Pond House was by this time starting to attract a lot of jealousy and resentment among the racing community. The after-dinner gossip was that the horses from Nicholashayne were being doped – 'How else could they win like they do?' – and that Martin was ringing up owners of horses in other yards and offering to train them for nothing. Martin was said to be sending all his staff out of the yard by five in the afternoon and then going round giving medication to the horses when even his employees couldn't see what he was doing so that no one could leak the information to the press; he was even supposed to be able to perform blood transfusions to improve horses' performance, and to have a false floor in his laboratory under which were hidden bags of blood to be pumped into the horses! One West Country trainer told me with a straight face, 'I know what he'd be doing; he'd be taking the blood out of the good ones and putting it in the bad ones.'

The rumours reached such a pitch that a national newspaper, the *Daily Star*, sent a reporter to join the yard. As the paper chose to put it, 'The reporter broke through the fortress-like security at this ten-million-pound yard to get a job as a £1,500 a year stable girl.' To be fair to the girl herself, the only derogatory comment she was able to make in her report was to quote one lad as saying, 'All we go for here are winners, nothing else. If we don't get one, there is a lot of disappointment.' How many racing yards *don't* care about getting winners?

As Martin's methods were obviously successful, some owners did decide to bring their horses to him from other yards, and it was no doubt the bad feeling so aroused that led to the accusations of 'poaching'. Once put about, such rumours are hard to quash, and even though, for example, George and Angie Maude, owners of Bonanza Boy and Fu's Lady, publicly denied the allegations that they were getting their horses trained for nothing, comments to the contrary were still made.

All this didn't affect me much personally as I was not the target. The hostility was directed at Martin by a number of other trainers for whom I did not often ride and who felt under threat by someone who was not 'one of them' and yet was very successful. All the same, I felt angry on Martin's behalf that he should be subjected to this treatment, and very disappointed that his achievements should be met with such carping, even malicious, reaction – though at the same time I suppose we were to an extent flattered that the yard's success had attracted so much publicity.

People in racing mistrusted Martin because his route to the top of his profession had been unconventional – a bookmaker's son and sometime bookmaker himself, at one point he had even been the manager of a country singer – though if he hadn't been successful they would no doubt not have cared what he did.

What they failed to appreciate was that the businesslike and methodical approach that he imported from his bookmaking background was the key to the efficiency with which his stable was run and therefore played a very large part in his achievements. In addition, Martin is by temperament a workaholic and a perfectionist, with very high expectations both of himself and of those around him. He works very long hours and is constantly alert, always looking for ways to improve his horses and their training. Those who fail to understand this devotion to the business fail to understand Martin.

In fact, the technology and modern facilities that set off some of the wilder rumours – particularly the blood-testing laboratory – are just parts of the larger jigsaw. The indoor canter, the swimming pool, the walking machine, the laboratory, are all supplements to carefully monitored work on the wide wood-chip all-weather gallop, laid by Mr Pipe senior, that rises up a hillside for four furlongs. Here the horses do a form of interval training, cantering in groups of three upsides until the whole string is at the top, then lobbing back down to do the whole thing twice more. The most striking aspect of the set-up is how calm and relaxed the horses are in their training. The routine and the care they receive, and the relaxed atmosphere of the Devon and Somerset countryside that surrounds them, keeps the horses at ease with themselves. These aspects of training, which are at the core of its success, are not newsworthy, nor can gossip be manufactured from them.

It seemed to me that for most of the time Martin was able to cope well with the personal attacks on him. He knew that his rapid rise to the top was inevitably going to attract some hostility; but he also knew that he could rely on the support of a trusted circle of owners and friends who knew him better. Chester and Carol were experts at responding to his moods, and knew when to talk to him and when to leave him alone. Carol is a remarkable lady. In the early days she had worked for Martin's father on the accounts side of the bookmaking business, and her accounting expertise was invaluable in the business aspects of Martin's yard. She also takes a keen interest in all the horses, and has an opinion on how they should be ridden in their races. I found her to be a solid ally, but also quite ready to tell me if she thought I had ridden a bad race – in this respect, in fact, she was not dissimilar to Mrs Winter. Yet at the height of the whispering campaign even

Carol was coming in for character assassination among leading members of the racing fraternity.

Perhaps it was just as well that Martin had the irrepressible Chester to fend off the worst intrusions – as well as to help lighten the atmosphere sometimes. For although we all took racing very seriously, and although the malice and idiocy of the rumour-mongering did get us all down sometimes, we also had a great deal of fun. Take the time when we were trying to school a reluctant Melendez over fences. The horse was in the habit of refusing, and Chester announced boldly that he would give 33-1 about my getting the horse up over the three newly erected schooling fences. There were several other horses being schooled in this session, and so I got Jonathon Lower – always a good ally to have in these situations – to trot in a circle at the bottom of these fences, with the other horses round me. I was not being very brave, but I knew Melendez could jump – and I had my twenty pounds on at 33-1. On my instruction Jonathon set off, with me tucked in behind, up over the fences without looking at them. The other horses were still covering me and Melendez flew the jumps as if he had been doing it all his life. I never got paid, though. Chester complained, 'You were meant to do it by yourself!' Funny how people change; he was always moaning about a particular bookmaker who wouldn't pay him out . . .

Martin would take infinite pains with his horses. He and Chester owned one called Patriot, a beautiful-looking creature that galloped well at home, but when I rode it it wouldn't jump the hurdles. When we schooled it, it would take off with its front legs, but would not lift its hind legs and thus pulled the hurdle over. They wouldn't give up; the horse was even schooled over fences, which it jumped quite well, but in races would not gallop on between the obstacles. I think Patriot was the only horse Martin never won a race with after many years of trying. He loved his little sellers: horses of limited ability but brave in their jumping, that he could place where he wanted. Many times I would school a horse and think, 'He'll never win with this,' only to be proved wrong – sometimes once, sometimes with a whole run of victories.

By New Year 1989 I had ridden 112 winners. It all sounds very easy – but like every National Hunt jockey I was aware that the total could only go on mounting so long as I avoided serious injury. The risk of falling or being brought down is just part of the job and something you can't do much about, but the risks associated with unsafe courses and equipment can be minimized, and safety standards in National Hunt racing have improved a lot over the years. In the Cleeve Hill Handicap Chase at Cheltenham on 3 January I had a fall which a few years earlier, before the introduction of the plastic rail, I would have been lucky to survive. The horse I was riding, Tarconey, was marginally in front going to the last when he cocked his jaw and ran out to the right. His sharp jink sent me hurtling into the wing of the fence, which he just missed. I got away with superficial cuts and was able to continue riding for the rest of the day; if the wing had been the old wooden type, or if there had been any concrete posts in the vicinity, as there were in my father's riding days, I would probably have been done for.

Another major step forward was the development of the body protector. When I started racing, some jockeys wore back protectors but most did not bother; in those days they were not very well made and tended to stick up and look unsightly, making the rider look amateurish. There was a feeling that even if you could not ride like a professional jockey you should try to look like one, and most riders took a pride in having correctly fitting breeches, boots and racing equipment. I could often tell an amateur from a professional by the elastic bands round the top of ill-fitting boots, or the heavy exercise saddle that no professional would dream of riding a race in.

On the other hand, looks don't save you from injury, and these back protectors were the only form of padding against a kick in the kidneys or back. John Suthern once fell in a steeplechase and got kicked in the back; a senior jockey asked him if he was all right and if he was wearing a back protector, and on being told 'no' on both counts, told him it served him right. John Francome was a pioneer in the development of a satisfactory body protector for National Hunt jockeys. His mother sewed polyester oblongs, three inches by one inch and half an inch thick, on to a light shirt for John to wear under his colours. This gave all-over body protection as well as the neatness and flexibility that the old back protectors were unable to provide. After a campaign by Monty Court, former editor of the *Sporting Life*, a more sophisticated manufactured version of the basic idea was made compulsory, and at the beginning of the 1988–9 season a one-pound allowance was given at the scales to allow for the extra weight. I thought these things were a marvellous innovation; they could make all the difference between a minor tumble and a fall that put you out of action.

This season Haydock Park racecourse, in an attempt to attract more steeplechasers, had offered a £25,000 bonus to any trainer who could achieve six wins out of a minimum of eighteen runners in steeplechases there. The winners were no problem for Martin, but assembling eighteen runners was more difficult. In the last race on 7 January – the final chase of the season at Haydock – he needed four more runners to achieve his target. He managed to get them, for a race which turned out to have only one other runner, but they were not big chasing types, and the four jockeys – myself, Rory MacNeice, Jonathon Lower and Lars Kelp – were somewhat nervous pilots. In the event Mareth Line jumped boldly and well to win thirty lengths from the outside runner, and Lars Kelp came in third. But Rory's horse refused at the third, an open ditch, hampering Jonathon, who ended up standing in the ditch with his horse, Celcius. The groundsman had to let them out through the gate on one end.

Mrs Muck continued her remarkable career, still trained by her owner and farming permit-holder Nigel Twiston-Davies, whose finances were often dependent on her success. Her journeys to the races were remarkable in themselves. In the horse box she would be accompanied by another horse as travelling companion, plus in front Nigel, his wife Cathy, my wife Marilyn, Simon Sherwood's wife Lucy, Stanley the collie, and the gin and tonic of which Nigel needed a constant supply to steady his nerves. This elixir was transported in bottles ready-mixed; on a memorable trip to Ascot on 13 January the girls gave Nigel a bottle containing only tonic, and he was so engrossed in the thought of the day's proceedings that he arrived at the races not realizing that he had been duped.

On this occasion I was riding Wollow Will for Charlie Brooks and so Simon had the pleasure of steering Mucky round one of her favourite hurdle courses to win a £9,000 bonus for the farm. On his return, Nigel made up for the G&T shortfall at the local shrine, the Black Horse at Naunton.

By the beginning of February my total of winners was on 147, just two short of Jonjo's record seasonal total of 149, and since my last win at Lingfield I had been followed around by journalists and photographers hovering to catch the win that would break the record. Four days then passed with no horse obliging. On the fifth I drove to Fontwell with the prospect of riding three favourites; two of them, Delkusha and Battalion, won, thus bringing me level with Jonjo's total. By this stage my diplomatic skills with the non-racing press, who clearly had little idea of the delights of being a National Hunt jockey, were running low, and on being asked whether I was disappointed in having ridden only two winners that day, I retorted that on the contrary, I was pleased to be in one piece and able to ride at Warwick tomorrow.

Throughout this season I had been accompanied about the country by a charming journalist, Dudley Doust, who was intending to write a book on my run-up to this year's Cheltenham Festival that would have as its climax – he hoped – a Champion Hurdle or Gold Cup winner. Dudley had written other sporting books, notably on Ian Botham and Mike Brearley, but knew very little about racing when he first got into the passenger seat to be driven round the National Hunt courses. What he did have was the inquiring journalistic mind; he liked to find a new angle from which to look at his subject, and would often centre a piece of writing on a particular quirk of the personality he was writing about. He was good company and we got on very well.

However, on the morning of my trip to Warwick in pursuit of the ride that would take me over Jonjo's record I was getting a bit tense – not so much about the occasion itself, more about all the fuss that was surrounding it and the consequent disruption of my routine. Dudley had arranged for my parents to come to Mucky Cottage so that they could travel up to the races with him, Marilyn and myself. I held to the belief that no one understood the problems I had to face (I'm sure there is a psychiatric explanation for this); and as the first of these was to get to the races on time I liked to leave ten minutes before I said I was going to leave. This of course made everyone coming with me ten minutes late and put me in a bad mood. The next problem on this particular morning was my mother, who will not be driven by me as she says I drive too fast. So we were chauffeured slowly up to the midlands by my father, with Dudley studying my parents and asking them deep and meaningful questions while I simmered resentfully in the back, wondering if I was going to be the first champion in sport to fail to break a record because he did not get to the event on bloody time!

All the panic was unnecessary; we got to the course with time to spare, Anti Matter won the first race comfortably – and Jonjo was there to present me with a memento of the occasion.

A week later I was trying to achieve the feat that gave me the most pleasure of all the record-breaking totals – that of joining John Francome and Stan Mellor as a winner of 1,000 races over a career. Other records will be broken, but this is an elite club. The non-racing press had not cottoned on to the significance of the day and I was able to follow a normal routine. Racing was at Newton Abbot, so I left home at six to school some horses at Martin's on my way down to the course. Arriving at the Pond House office at seven-thirty as usual, I discussed the day's plans with Martin and took Wingspan, a faller at the second last time out, for a school over fences. At ten I was in the sauna at the Forte Hotel in Exeter, where I often went while down in the West Country for meetings at the Devon tracks; when I had shed the necessary number of pounds I would drive on to the course, aiming to arrive in time to catch a few minutes' sleep before getting ready for the afternoon. Early mornings, dietings and saunas all together are very tiring.

The three winners I needed for my thousand were acquired with the minimum of fuss. Wingspan had benefited from his school in the morning and jumped well. Let Him By accounted for the second of my rides and Avionne took the novices' selling hurdle, in which I took a wide route to get the better going and won by three lengths to beat my father's horse Proud Soldier into second place – and he still congratulated me afterwards.

The greatest accolades I received from the racing press this winter were for riding Bonanza Boy to win the Racing Post Chase at Kempton on 25 February, when he stayed on gamely to win half a length. In fact I did not consider it a great riding performance as I was out at the back most of the way and flat to the boards, but luckily the other horses tired in the ground, enabling Bonanza's stamina to bring him through.

The real story of that win in fact goes back to a month earlier, to 28 January when Bonanza Boy was engaged in a moderate race at Cheltenham. We were checking the details of his work card and blood tests, to ensure that all was well for him to run, and Martin discovered that his blood wasn't quite right: there were too many white blood cells, indicating either the early stages of a virus or a small wound infection. We asked Donna, who looks after him, about his well-being, and she said he seemed fine; and an inspection revealed no little wound that had escaped notice. Martin therefore decided not to take the risk of running him, as putting a horse under stress lowers its ability to combat any virus. The judgement was correct; Bonanza did have a virus, and by not running him at Cheltenham Martin was able to bring him back to run at Ascot in a prep race for Kempton. He fell there when going well, but in the absence of Martin's eagle eye and fail-safe systems he most probably wouldn't have been anywhere near a racecourse.

The Saturday before Cheltenham 1989 meant one of those double shifts with the helicopter, as I was due to ride Fetcham Park and Battalion at Chepstow as well as Travel Mystery at Sandown. Flying was in fact a relatively safe method of travel, but I never took it for granted; and if I felt at all nervous I only had to look across at Chester to know that there was someone more worried than I. Chester had been involved in two minor accidents with the helicopter and could detect the slightest change in the tone of the engine. Once they had just taken off when the engine failed just below the critical point; they were only a few feet off the ground and the craft dropped down again safely. The more memorable occasion was when they took off from Cheltenham racecourse by flying forwards and got the wire of a starting gate caught on the landing skis.

Safely delivered to Sandown on this occasion, I rode Travel Mystery to victory in the Imperial Cup, and though she didn't jump particularly well this win made her ante-post favourite for the County Hurdle at Cheltenham the following week.

It was my worst ever Festival. In the first race of the meeting I got off Sondrio, who had been jumping really badly, to ride Elementary, owned by Paul Green, for Jim Bolger; but a visit to Charles Radcliffe's jumping academy in Oxfordshire had worked wonders for Martin's horse, who carried Jonathon Lower to a memorable victory. Then Sabin Du Loir, favourite for the Arkle, failed to show the form of his early season runs – as he was to do again in later years – and was beaten a length and a half by Waterloo Boy, having finished twenty lengths in front of David Nicholson's horse on their previous meeting at Ascot. Celtic Shot finished third in the Champion Hurdle, having been outpaced early on, and my one and only win on the Tuesday came in the last race on Pukka Major, trained by Tim Thomson Jones.

On Wednesday I again chose the wrong horse to kick off with, going for Pertemps Network instead of Martin's other runner, Sayfar's Lad, who won with Mark Perrett on board. This was a treble mistake on my part: first, I turned down the winning ride; second, the following season Pertemps Network's owners took the horse away from the yard; and third, they then appeared on television making unfair criticisms of Martin.

Desert Orchid, ante-post favourite for the Gold Cup, was supposed to like fast ground, so I was cheered up when I awoke on Thursday morning to see a covering of snow that would surely turn the going heavy to favour Bonanza Boy. Simon Sherwood was staying with Nigel in the farmhouse just up the lane from Mucky Cottage, and when I saw him for a cup of coffee he was very depressed about the chances of the horse running, let alone how he would handle the conditions underfoot if he did. He need not have worried, and I need not have been so cheerful; Simon, who got on so well with Desert Orchid, produced one of his finest riding performances and the great horse won.

The day failed to improve. Rusch de Farges, sent off 5-4 on favourite, ran disappointingly in the Cathcart Chase – mystifyingly so; horses run badly for many different reasons, but there was no apparent cause for this uncharacteristically lethargic run. It is easy in these circumstances to jump to the conclusion that the horse has been 'got at', but usually the real reason emerges later; however, in this case no explanation for his poor showing ever became apparent. In the County Hurdle Travel Mystery could only manage second; her jumping was not fluent enough to hold her position and I got into trouble on the bends.

If I had finished that season one short of a total of 200 winners I would have blamed Mrs Thatcher, as it was because of her that I missed the winning ride on a horse of Martin's called Bavard Ash at Wolverhampton. Martin and I had been invited to a reception at 10 Downing Street and in order to get there on time I had to miss the last race. (I was still late arriving because of a bomb scare in one of the approach roads.) We were introduced to the Prime Minister and I introduced myself to the Minister of Environment Nicholas Ridley, who lived in our village of

Naunton. He said: 'Oh, you're the jockey. I do not like racing.'

Back in 1986 when I had been riding for David Nicholson I had had a chance to appreciate the horsemanship of event riders when Princess Anne came to the yard. Now I was to see for myself why they need to be so good. Richard Pitman had organized a promotion for Seagram, the sponsors of the Grand National, in which a group of top jump jockeys would ride round Gatcombe Park cross-country course and a group of event riders would ride round Aintree a week later. We were used to being invited to ride at show-jumping events – the jockeys' show-jumping competition at Wembley was one of the best while it lasted – at which, wearing slippery nylon racing breeches on horses used to making sharp turns, we would often fall off. Steve Smith Eccles for a long time had the dubious distinction of never having completed a show-jumping course with the partnership intact. (He did complete at a jump jockeys' show-jumping event at Finmere once, only to fall off while showing off his skills at a large triple bar on his way out of the ring.) We had also been entertained at Gatcombe during the horse trials when the jockeys rode in a gymkhana competition against some Pony Club riders.

So we thought that this would just be a bit of fun over a small cross-country course – and got a very nasty shock when we walked the course to find that it was the Open Championship track, with only a couple of fence alterations. I had done my best to cry off already, but even my final excuse, that I had a Jockeys' Association meeting in Leicester that I could not miss, failed: they sent a helicopter to pick me up.

Gloomily looking at the obstacles on that cold March morning, and examining the soft ground, I thought: a man who is nearing 200 winners for the first time in a National Hunt season shouldn't be doing this. Richard Pitman, for some reason, had not turned up; judging by the reactions of the rest of us he was wise. Brendan Powell, Richard Dunwoody, Simon Sherwood and I had at least competed in hunter trials as children so had a minimal chance of survival; Eck and Graham McCourt had not, so their survival was even less certain. We had a disastrous practice before lunch in which Graham fell off over a drop fence.

Richard went first on Mark Phillips' former eventer Cartier, and they put up a superb clear round to give the rest of us some much-needed confidence. Simon went next on Robert Lemieux's After Dark and jumped round with just two refusals. The Eck,

*Towcester, 27 April 1989: Thomas and Michael offer their congratulations after my 200th winner on Gay Moore (*TONY EDENDEN*)*

full of bravado and whisky, set off on Rachel Hunt's Piglet, a very free-running horse at the best of times; approaching the drop fence at number four in record time they stood too far off and had a nasty tumble. Horse and rider got up and, reunited, continued on their way; afterwards Steve said he had concussion, but everybody else put it down to the drink. The combination of Powells, Brendan on Rodney's Pomeroy, then produced the fastest round, while Graham on Mark Todd's Mr Todd paid the price of trying to jump the quickest route over the angle of a 'V' too far from the corner and ending up in a heap. He too remounted to finish the course. Then it was my turn on Ian Stark's Mix 'n' Match. Mark Phillips said my round was the performance of a true craftsman; I'll have to take his word for it as I had my eyes shut most of the way and my hands firmly embedded in the horse's mane. In fact I had never ridden such a well-balanced and well-mannered horse, and the whole experience gave us jockeys a new understanding of and respect for the event riders. We trooped back to the Barbour/Seagram sponsors' tent to have a few drinks and bore the eventers stiff with our tales of heroism.

A week later we got our own back when they came to ride round Aintree – on their own horses. The night before we joined them for a well-supported dinner at which we found, in the course of several ridiculous party games, that they hold their drink much better than we do; and they rose even further in our estimation by turning up, admittedly looking awful (so I'm told – I didn't make it), to walk the National course a few hours later. I managed to get there in time for lunch and to see them tackle one circuit of the fences. They all completed, Robert finishing first, and we decided that the competition was an honourable draw.

Back on familiar ground, I won at Worcester on 29 March for Jim Wilson on Elvercone; but after that didn't have another winner for a fortnight. No injuries, no suspensions: just a frustrating run of twenty-four losers. It wasn't that I was riding badly, or getting beaten narrowly; the horses were simply not on form. This fallow period included the Aintree meeting, where I did have a great ride in the National on Bonanza Boy to finish in eighth place behind Little Polveir and Jimmy Frost, having his first ride in the race. Jimmy is a tall man for a jockey but a true horseman and a very good race-rider, and well deserved his victory.

Finally, on 13 April, Just Rose brought the losing streak to an end at Ludlow. I had now scored 190 winners, leaving me ten more to find to make my target of 200 before the end of the season. By 24 April I had crept up to 197 and the media circus started all over again, with members of the press continually on the phone asking when I thought I would ride my 200th winner. I told them that as there was no jump racing in England on either Tuesday or Wednesday that week, all I was certain of was that it wouldn't be either of those days. ITN rang to ask if I would mind if they followed me around the two tracks where I was riding on the Thursday, and offered me a helicopter to take me from the afternoon meeting at Hereford to the evening meeting at

Towcester. I agreed, thinking they were wasting their time as it was unlikely I would make the total that day.

My instincts seemed to be right: all four rides I had at Hereford got beaten, and in the first I had ridden a horse of Martin's only to see Charlie Brooks's Hello Steve go on to win. Second was as close as I got all afternoon. So it was a dejected party of me plus camera crew that flew to Towcester, where they thought I had three rides. I had forgotten to tell them that I had picked up a spare ride for Michael Robinson on 10–1 shot Gay Moore. Old Kilpatrick obliged for me in the first, and Canford Palm galloped through heavy ground up Towcester's steep hill to win the novice chase. The TV crew, under the impression that I wasn't riding again till the last, retired to the bar, from where they heard the commentator saying: 'Peter Scudamore in the fading light has only one fence to jump to become the first National Hunt jockey ever to ride two hundred winners in a season!' They just made it; and, apparently to show that fate deals out either alls or nothings, I finished the evening with a fourth winner on Market Forces.

The family were there to see the winners and take part in the racecourse celebrations, but we didn't make a great fuss about it. Two mementoes, however, do stick in my mind: before the Whitbread Gold Cup at Sandown Steve Cauthen presented me with a set of tumblers on behalf of the Flat jockeys; and I was sent a newspaper cutting from Australia which read: 'Milestone for Hoop: British jump jockey Peter Scudamore became the first jump rider ever to ride 200 winners in a season.'

It was still only 27 April, and the next target was Martin's 200th seasonal winner. He was now on 183, and I made a special point of driving down to his yard early the morning after reaching my own landmark to school horses in preparation for the final assault on the magical figure. My Cup Of Tea added one to the total at Taunton that evening, and by 17 May an across-the-card treble at Worcester and Newton Abbot had brought the tally up to 196. The pressure was now really on Martin; there weren't many chances left. If we had finished the season on or just over 150 winners we would have been delighted; but now we were so close to the 200 that not to make it would be excruciating. As Fred Winter had said to me in the past, 'No matter how many winners you have, you'll never be satisfied with the total.'

So it was off to Huntingdon next day for Chester and me for

*End of a long haul – Hazy Sunset provides my 221st and final winner of the 1988–9 season at Stratford on 3 June 1989* (BERNARD PARKIN) *(Right) Scu and The Shoe. With the legendary American rider Bill Shoemaker, who rode more winners than any other jockey in history, at Cheltenham on 11 June 1989. I rode in three match races against him as part of his farewell world tour* (LES HURLEY)

some serious work at the evening meeting. I had two horses to ride for Martin, neither of them very genuine. The first of these, Dusty Diplomacy, got up only in the very last stride, and the judge called for a photograph – then for an enlarged print. This was going to be very close. Nine times out of ten when you are involved in a photo-finish you have a pretty good idea of the result before it is announced, but you can get it wrong when one horse is finishing fast. As Chester walked beside me towards the winner's enclosure I told him I was fairly sure we had won; at the time the result of this photograph seemed the most important of my riding career. I went to weigh in still not knowing the official result, and while changing and altering my weight-cloth and saddle for the next race I missed the loudspeaker announcement. Only when I weighed out for the next did I finally learn that I had won – and that there was a Stewards' Inquiry. Fortunately the placings remained unaltered.

The next ride was Melendez, who as a four-year-old had won several times for the yard but who now was often reluctant to start. The best method of getting him going was to have him moving as the tapes went up. This evening he was in a mulish mood and already hesitating while walking round at the start. On the Starter's call I had the horse walking calmly towards the tape – then one horse turned, so the field could not go. Melendez was happy to stop. On the second attempt we missed the break as

Melendez planted himself while Martin's orders 'Get a good start' rang in my ears. Luckily the rest of them did not go off too fast, and by the second hurdle I was back in contention. After virtually riding a finish for the two circuits needed to complete the three miles of the race, an exhausted jockey on a fresh Melendez scraped home by half a length.

One hundred and ninety-eight; surely we were going to do it now! Attention turned to Stratford's delightful course by the Avon. The early summer meetings at this excellently run track bring in a lot of racegoers, and I feel sure that holding more spring and autumn meetings like this, with (one hopes) good weather and well watered ground to attract competitive fields, could be a way of increasing the appeal of National Hunt racing. Reg Lomas, the groundsman at Stratford, does an outstanding job: the course is always in good condition, with beautifully maintained fences and hurdles, and he will always give trainers who enquire an accurate forecast of the going – a courtesy which is not forthcoming from all tracks.

This evening my mind was on rather shorter-term concerns, however, namely the prospects for Mighty Prince in the first, ridden by Jonathon, and my ride in the second, Anti Matter. Jonathon played his part well and won without fuss, leaving me with the responsibility of putting up the magic number. Like so many of the Pond House horses, Anti Matter started odds-on favourite, but the race still had to be run and won. Many of the 152 winners Martin had given me so far this season were steering jobs, but much can go wrong to prevent the best-prepared horse winning: leathers or reins can break; plates can twist; you can be blocked, hampered, brought down. As I cantered to the start all these potential hazards were in my mind – and then the race was delayed as 66–1 outsider Truism lost his jockey and galloped several times round the track, unsettling the other horses and winding up the jockeys' nerves. But it must have been much worse for Martin, up in the stands, waiting.

As we finally lined up a horse to my side lashed out, missing Anti Matter by inches. All that meticulous planning to reach this milestone could have been wiped out in a split second. Then came the easy part: Anti Matter and I made headway three out and drew clear to win by five lengths. Martin had become the first National Hunt trainer ever to have trained 200 winners in a single season – and there were to be another eight before the jumping finally ended for us both at Stratford, where I rode Hazy Sunset to victory for Charlie Brooks, taking my own seasonal total to 221.

Martin's achievement in this season far surpassed my own. Two-thirds of my winners had come from his yard, and although I had a large input into the schooling, much of the reason they jumped so well lay in the fact that they were so fit. Every member of the Pond House team had got us there: David Pipe senior with his lawyers's and bookmaker's brain; Carol with her accounting and business expertise and the support without which Martin could not have survived; Chester, an unusual assistant trainer, dealing inimitably with the people more than the horses; Jonathon, Dennis and all the staff who kept the yard running with their shared dedication to the horses.

The old school National Hunt fraternity still found it hard to accept that a man who did not fit into their mould could attain such heights by virtue simply of flair, dedication and hard work. Despite all the unfounded allegations, all the malicious rumours, Martin would forge ahead to even greater success, leaving others behind him floundering until they could put their jealousy to one side and recognize the value of his methods.

*Chapter Twelve*

# BRANCHING OUT

—▸◂—

In midsummer 1989 I returned from the States, where I had gone to ride at Belmont Park, for three unusual engagements.

The first of these was at Headingley, where I had been invited to join the Radio Three ball-by-ball cricket commentary team for the test match against Australia; the third was actually to play cricket, under the captaincy of Imran Khan, in a six-a-side celebrity charity match; and in between I was going to ride in a challenge match at Cheltenham with the great American jockey Bill Shoemaker.

At Headingley I had the privilege of sitting in the commentary box while Brian Johnston and his colleagues delivered their prognostications on the day's play to come, then recorded with him a slot to be broadcast at lunchtime called 'A View from the Boundary'. We discussed my love of cricket, instilled into me at an early age by my father, who used to be a member of Worcester Cricket Club; and how I had played as a child at home and very badly at school, before joining the Jockeys' XI under the captaincy of David Nicholson. I related John Buckingham's story of a match in which he was umpiring while perched on a shooting stick, having an injured leg at the time, when David Nicholson was bowling. When John turned down an appeal for lbw, the Duke marched back by him, said 'Bollocks!' and kicked the shooting stick from underneath him.

My own tale of heroism was of batting for the Jockeys' XI in Barbados, when after several unfortunate defeats I hit the winning four against the Hotel XI using one of the two shots in my repertoire: 'the sweep' (the other one is 'the block'). We spoke too about the team I now play for, the Bunbury XI, which consists of sport, stage, music and screen personalities and which gives me the chance to play on some wonderful grounds – Trent Bridge, for example, and Canterbury, where Colin Cowdrey once saw my leg-spin bowling and described it as 'interesting little tweakers'. I

*The Twiston-Davies string in full flight at Grange Hill*
(*TANA WILLIS-JOHNSON*)

also follow the fortunes of Worcester and when I can I go to watch at the invitation of Mark Scott and Neale Radford, two of the players; their ground has an idyllic setting and is a welcome haven amid the rigours of a jockey's life.

On Sunday 11 June 1989 – a strange time to be in action at Prestbury Park – I went to Cheltenham to ride in three races on the Flat against Bill Shoemaker, who was making a farewell world tour. At fifty-seven years of age, 'the Shoe' had won more races than any other jockey in racing history: 8,802 over his long career, including all the US Triple Crown Races – the Kentucky Derby four times, the Preakness Stakes twice and the Belmont Stakes five times. It was a great honour to be asked to ride with him.

I was provided with horses by Martin Pipe's yard, Bill by Nigel Tinkler's. The undulations of Cheltenham must have been very strange for him, as must cantering to post without the outrider escort – especially on the strong hurdlers that we were riding, for he was a tiny man and had to carry three stone of lead to do the ten stone seven pounds weight for the challenge, whereas all I had was my five-pound saddle.

We rode three heats; in the first I rode Temple Reef to make all for the six furlongs, and was very worried when the Shoe put in a spirited challenge because I thought his Flat-race finishing technique would make my less subtle jumping style look weak and ungainly. But Temple Reef battled on gamely to win half a length. The second heat I won cleverly by a neck, and in the last I gave Celcius too much to do, allowing my opponent to prevail by a narrow margin. During the after-race presentations, made by the Princess Royal, the MC, Richard Pitman, asked tongue in cheek over the public address system whether the last race was crooked; I replied, 'It shows you how straight proper racing is and how bad I would be at stopping horses from winning!'

Then it was back to the cricket field for the six-a-side match in aid of the Save the Rain Forest fund. Each side contained a member of the Pakistan team; mine was captained by their captain, Imran Khan. Along with us were Johnny Gold, keen racing man and owner of Tramp nightclub; Errol Brown of pop group Hot Chocolate; the actor Dennis Waterman; and Mark Austin, the sports reader on ITN News. We were comprehensively thrashed by every side we played. For the last game I was promoted to opening the batting with Imran. The rules of the six-a-side game state that when you have scored twenty-five runs you must retire. When Imran had scored twenty-four and I one, he came down the wicket and said to me,

'I am now going to score six, and will have to retire. You start scoring.'

I replied, 'What the bloody hell do you think I've been trying to do stood here?!'

Later in the week at a team get-together in the restaurant at Tramp, Imran said to Dennis Waterman,

'The team played very, very badly the other day,' and Dennis replied,

'You can't ride horses, run a nightclub or act, so don't expect us to play cricket to your standard!'

It was during this summer that Nigel Twiston-Davies and I decided to go into business together, joining forces in the farm and forming a new Grange Hill Partnership. Farming was Nigel's first love, but it was not proving profitable at the time, and he needed to diversify to survive financially. Having had such success with Mrs Muck as a permit-holder, he now wanted to apply for a full trainer's licence, which would enable him to take in other people's horses to produce for racing, as well as running his own.

I too needed to be making plans for the future. A jump jockey's life is a precarious one, physically, professionally and financially. I did not want to find myself on the point of retirement and suddenly have to be scratching around for something to do. Partnership with Nigel seemed the ideal solution: I would continue my full-time career as a jockey, yet be closely involved in the training set-up. I also had an interest in the Peter Scudamore Bloodstock Company, run by my father from Herefordshire, which bred and dealt in store horses for National Hunt racing.

I financed my fifty per cent share in the business by selling the land I had bought in Herefordshire when I had sold the Condicote house. When we bought out the farm it consisted of 120 acres, a farmhouse (where Nigel and Cathy live), two cottages (in one of which Marilyn and I and the boys live) and various Cotswold stone buildings and cattle sheds. The first improvement we made, with help and advice from Martin Pipe – who was very pleased that I was establishing myself in business – was to put in a five-furlong all-weather gallop made from Fibresand, the surface used on the all-weather racetrack at Southwell. Later on, Nigel converted a cattle yard in the top acres above the farmhouse into a twenty-box yard.

Nigel already trained along very much the same lines as Martin, although the characters of the two establishments were, and remain, very different, and obviously both he and I were influenced a good deal by what I had seen at Pond House. I found that my experience in each yard helped me contribute to the other; Martin and I had always discussed the preparation of the horses, and just as I was able to feed these ideas back into Grange Hill, so my dealings with the horses there helped me to understand his problems better. My working relationship with Martin had never been of the kind which consists of the jockey simply taking orders from the trainer in the paddock: I had always been fully involved in working out how best to tackle the training of the horses from the time they arrived in the yard. In this way my time with Martin gave me an excellent basis from which to move into training myself.

The first horse I contributed to Grange Hill was an animal called Celtic Prince, known for a long time as Chester, after Chester Barnes. I acquired him at the Derby sales at Fairyhouse and brought him back home to be broken. To begin with, during the early stages of long-reining and lungeing, he was so docile and quiet that we thought he might have been broken before. Nigel's wife Cathy and my secretary, Fe Moore, an ex-event rider, were the first to sit on him, Nigel and I considering discretion to be the better part of valour. Then, one warm summer evening, as Chester was quietly walking round the paddock with Fe on his back and Marilyn leading, I – who stalwartly refused to have anything to do with young horses – was tempted to have a go. Fortunately I was called away by a phone call, for when I returned, helmet on head, all eager to be up, Chester started to bronc – and bronc and bronc. Fe went flying, and my helmet went flying back to the tackroom and stayed there.

Nigel and Cathy went on riding him for a while; after several mishaps this seemed increasingly to mean Cathy, and the morning visit to the toilet was making her very skinny, and Chester's behaviour was getting no better. So, in one of my brave moods in the Black Horse, I decided that I would sort this horse out. Next morning, Nigel legged me up on him – and as my bottom hit the saddle, I flew straight out again like a human cannonball. All this was being watched by Fe from the office window; when Cathy rang down to see how Nigel and I were getting on, Fe told her, 'If I were you I would run, or they'll be calling for you again; Scu is airborne!' On the assumption that brains will baffle brawn in the end, we decided to send Chester to my father's to continue his education. He returned still a nervous individual, but rideable, and went on to win several races.

What with all this activity the summer 'break' passed very quickly and soon the family and I were back down in the West Country preparing for another campaign at Pond House – for a year in which the bookies were offering me no price about winning my fifth consecutive championship.

It was just eight weeks since the 1988–9 season had drawn to a close at Market Rasen, but in those weeks decisions had been made, and the new term opened without some famous names – or with them, but in different roles. Mercy Rimell had decided to retire from training, and Simon Sherwood had hung up his boots in May, having won nine out of his ten rides on Desert Orchid, and opted to follow in his brother Oliver's footsteps by taking out a full training licence.

Martin and I teamed up to form the Pipe/Scudamore Racing Club, aimed at attracting the smaller punter into ownership. We started off by buying fifteen horses, in which we sold shares at £250 each. This was to be a thoroughly enjoyable venture; I made many friends among the members as well as benefiting enormously from the winners the club gave me.

Again I won the opening race of the season at Newton Abbot, this time on Hazy Sunset, the horse that had closed my account

*Centre stage with six former champion jump jockeys at the Champion Jockey's Ball at Cheltenham in November 1989. From left to right are Stan Mellor, John Francome, Graham Thorner, me (with photo of my 1988 Mackeson winner Pegwell Bay), Ron Barry, Jack Dowdeswell and Bob Davies (BERNARD PARKIN)*

with a winner the previous June, and rode two more winners at the same fixture. It was here, too, that Martin's father bought Skipping Tim for 5,500 guineas in the auction after his victory in the Torbryan selling handicap chase. This half-brother to Run And Skip, trained by Philip Hobbs, had sailed home twenty-five lengths ahead of Fils-de-Roi – with me a further twenty lengths back on Dusty Diplomacy.

The following day I was schooling a horse called Zamore when it reared over backwards with me. I jumped straight back on, not thinking I had done any damage; then I felt sick and dizzy, and noticed that my left knee wasn't working properly. I got off again straight away, knowing by now that it is of the utmost importance to get medical attention as soon as you know you are hurt, as speed in getting treatment can radically affect your recovery time. I had twisted the ligaments in my knee, and though I had to miss the following day's rides at Devon and Exeter (including two winners), with the knee strapped up I was able to ride on the second day of the meeting, where my spirits were given a lift by a win on Madame Ruby.

Next day there was the long drive to Market Rasen in Lincolnshire, to ride Hazy Sunset in a two-horse handicap chase – and the horse fell at the last! Luckily for me I was a very long way clear by then, and had managed to keep hold of the horse, so despite the inconvenience of a strapped knee I managed to remount and still win by thirty lengths.

At the end of the following week I made a swift trip to Saratoga in upstate New York, to be reunited with Jimmy Lorenzo, my mount at Belmont Park earlier that summer. This is the oldest racecourse in the USA, founded in 1863, and the atmosphere is that of a classic 'meet', far more traditional than the urban maelstrom of Belmont Park. Racing moves up here in the fall as the Flat season at Belmont closes down, and the mood is more relaxed; Saratoga is a spa town with a European air, where patrons breakfast on verandahs, and the meeting is something of an American equivalent to Royal Ascot. The racing is mixed jump and Flat, the big races being four Grade 1 events of which the Travers Stakes is the most famous. Sadly, Jimmy Lorenzo, running in a steeplechase, finished lame.

Back at Pond House, the early part of the season brought the extra worry of a cough among the horses. It was not affecting all of them; Martin, with his usual alertness to any change in the yard, had managed to catch it early and isolate the sufferers. He felt that the virus might have been acquired by one of the horses he had run on the Flat at the Chepstow Welsh Derby meeting; one of the dangers of having Flat runners during the summer is that the younger, more susceptible horses are exposed to any infection that is going.

Many of the horses, however, were feeling very well indeed. When Skipping Tim had been bought in, his jockey, David Hood, told me that the horse was unmanageable at home and a very awkward ride on the racecourse – in fact, Philip Hobbs had been glad to see the back of him. This rang true to me; I knew that Run And Skip had presented similar problems to his trainer John Spearing, who had found him difficult to school at home. But my confidence was magically boosted when David told Martin that if he could not find a jockey, he would ride the horse for him. Martin took his time with Skipping Tim, treating him as an individual and having him exercised by himself to keep him relaxed. Nevertheless I was a little apprehensive when the time came for his first schooling session over fences.

All new inmates are schooled at home before they run, and this morning I had both Skipping Tim and another new recruit, Boardmans Style, to deal with. Further improvements had been made to the schooling facilities by now, with two more fences added to the existing three. It is usual to school horses at home over obstacles smaller than those they will meet on the racecourse, so as not to un-nerve them; but one of our new fences was a near-racecourse-size open ditch, and the one being un-nerved this morning was me, schooling two tearaways over these obstacles.

My fears were unfounded; both horses schooled well, going quietly just once each up over the fences. The good work on Boardmans Style was, however, ruined the next day when he bolted before the start on his racecourse debut, doing a whole circuit with me completely unable to pull him up. Perhaps I shouldn't say that the work was quite wasted; at one point I aimed him at a steeplechase fence to try to stop him, and he jumped it nicely. When he finally pulled himself up he had to be withdrawn from the race – which was ironic, because at the previous meeting I had been fined fifty-five pounds for not parading a hard-pulling horse past the stands, even though I had been given permission to go down early. Skipping Tim's racecourse behaviour was somewhat better; he went on to record twenty-five wins, and became a favourite of mine. Philip Hobbs was a bit sore when he saw this troublemaker come good, but he did replace him with Joint Sovereignty to soften the blow, a classy horse that won him the Mackeson Gold Cup.

It was during this season that all-weather racing arrived, and Martin sent horses to both Southwell and Lingfield, the first two courses to install all-weather tracks, for trial races on the new surfaces. The first trial was at Southwell on Fibresand, jumping hurdles similar to doors on their side that knock down. To me this seemed an excellent surface to gallop on and jump off; it was not firm, and the horses did not slip. The drawbacks were that it would be very unforgiving to fall on, for both horse and rider, and for the jockey the friction of clothes against the sand and nylon fibres of which the surface is made up would prevent the body gliding over the top as happens on grass, presenting the possibility of quite severe skin abrasions. On turf, you are more likely to be injured on hard than on soft ground, but there are usually fewer runners on the faster ground, whereas on the all-weather you could have both fast ground and large fields, making falling a very unenticing prospect. Lingfield's Equitrack surface, consisting of oiled sand particles, seemed a faster surface to ride on, but had the same disadvantages in terms of potential injuries.

Despite these reservations, the innovation held out exciting opportunities for the sport in general: now there could be racing in all but the most exceptionally bad weather conditions.

In the trial at Lingfield, Martin gave Regal Ambition his first outing on a racecourse over hurdles. He won it easily, and turned out to be one of the best horses I have ever ridden over timber. His first victory in an official race was at Worcester, where he became my 1,138th winner, bringing me level with John Francome's career record. I was delighted to have matched his achievement, remembering that when John had passed Stan Mellor, the previous record-holder, he had said that he expected that I in turn would pass him. As yet, of course, I had not actually passed the record, and now I had the non-racing press following me around again, wanting to be there when I clocked up my next winner.

I was anxious to get the actual breaking of the record over and done with so that the media attention would fade away again; however, the next day held the prospect of only one ride, Bar Fly at Towcester, and he had no real chance. We led until three out, and, desperately wanting to get the business over and done with, I tried too hard going to the last, putting us both on the floor in a nasty fall. After the race one bright spark of a reporter asked me: 'Why did you fall off?'

The next meeting was Ascot, where I was riding Sabin Du Loir in the Racecall Hurdle, an event he had already won twice. But now he was reverting to hurdles for his first run of the season and although he started 6–5 on favourite he could only finish a well beaten fourth. In the last race of the day I was riding Espy for Charlie Brooks, and again ended up on the floor at the last through trying too hard. This was the horse's first ever run over fences and I should have allowed for his inexperience, but I was upsides the eventual winner at the last and asked him for a big jump – and he couldn't respond.

Again the press were baffled that I did not ride winners every day. 'Scudamore Is Still Stuck' and 'Scudamore's Agony At Ascot' were among the next morning's headlines, written by people who evidently didn't realize that falls and losers are just part of the game. In fact, my strike rate this season had been notably high: when on 12 October 1989 I topped the fifty mark again, beating my own previous year's record by twelve days, I had had just ninety-eight rides, so just over one in two of them had been winners.

Anyway, no one had to wait much longer: the next day, still at Ascot, Arden, trained by Charlie Brooks, jumped me into the history books. Colonel Sir Piers Bengough presented me with a bottle of champagne to mark the occasion, after which it was into the helicopter and up to Warwick to ride two for Martin later in the afternoon. All this produced was a second in the novice chase on Walnut Way, and another meeting with the floor in a handicap hurdle. Three falls in three days: that was a much more realistic encapsulation of National Hunt racing than the glory days that bring the press out like moths to the flame.

Martin and I very rarely fell out; however, there were two particular occasions when harsh words passed, both in this season. The first occurred after a novice chase at Wincanton, in which I was riding Walnut Way. The ground was slippery; one horse had slipped up on a bend, and I had let the mare drift around some of the turns so as to avoid her doing the same thing. She was also jumping left-handed with me, which lost more ground, and we were beaten seven lengths into second place. When I returned to the unsaddling enclosure, Martin said: 'You've gone.'

I didn't reply. I knew how hard he worked, and sometimes things got to him, but obviously the remark hurt. Fortunately, I won the last two races that day and four the next at Devon and Exeter, so I hadn't gone after all. And we laugh about it now.

The other flare-up was at Taunton, where I was riding Crofter's Nest for the Pipe/Scudamore Racing Club in a three-horse handicap hurdle. In the paddock, with various club members standing round, he told me to hold the horse up; but when I got down to post nobody wanted to make the running, so I led for a while in a slowly run race and was in second place and beaten when I fell at the last. Martin was livid, because the owners had heard him tell me how he wanted the horse ridden, and I had not done as he asked; but in less pressured moments, he would be the first to acknowledge that you can't always ride a race to suit yourself if the race is not run at a pace to suit your horse.

Making his seasonal reappearance at what was becoming one of our favourite tracks, Chepstow, Bonanza Boy warmed up for his attempt at a second Welsh National with a win in the Rehearsal Chase. On the same day Celtic Shot made his first racecourse appearance over fences; he had schooled boldly and well at Uplands, though I was conscious that he still tended to stand off too far sometimes. The race chosen for his steeplechase debut was an Arlington Premier Chase, which was not a novice chase but a race confined to horses that had not won over fences before the previous season; and in this event he was taking on last year's Arkle Chase winner, Waterloo Boy – a somewhat strange opponent against which to pit a horse on its chasing debut.

In fact, the reasoning behind Charlie Brooks's decision to enter the horse in a race of this standard was sound. The field was likely to be small, which would give Celtic Shot a good look at the fences; and such other runners as did participate were likely to be decent horses, thus minimizing the likelihood of fallers which might bring him down. Fields in this kind of race do tend to cut up: trainers with good novice chasers from the previous season are hoping they might have a future Gold Cup horse and therefore are reluctant to run them too much or on less than perfect ground, while trainers with new season chasers cannot see the point in starting them off in a race in which the likes of Waterloo Boy will be running, for if they win or finish close to a proven chaser who has no excuses that day, the handicapper will come down hard on them, which hampers them for future races.

Bearing out Charlie's arguments, there were just five runners, and I jumped Celtic Shot off in front, but on the outside; I did want him to have light at his fences, especially early on, to lessen the chances of his standing too far off. My orders had been above all else to make sure I got him round. Showing no signs of his inexperience, he jumped well until Waterloo Boy came by as we approached the third last. Keeping in mind my orders, I continued to play for safety over the last three fences, and he ran on up the finishing straight to be beaten by a neck. The connections were delighted; I was furious, as I hate finishing second, but swallowed my annoyance. I had done what was asked of me and the horse had come through well.

There are, too, cases where you learn more about a horse when it finishes second than you do when it wins; one such was a race at Cheltenham six days after Celtic Shot's chasing debut when I rode Regal Ambition into second place a short head behind Remittance Man and Richard Dunwoody. I had been beaten because although I made the running I did not stretch the field enough, and I now knew that my horse was capable of going a good gallop the whole way.

Milestones were by now in sight again. On 13 December Martin, Chester and I trooped off to Haydock Park where victories with Gold Service and Sabin Du Loir brought Martin up to the ninety-nine mark for the season, and a further victory on Baies, trained by Charlie Brooks, completed a personal treble for me. Not all the pleasure of this day lay in the winning itself; the performances of Baies and Sabin, both foot perfect on this good to soft ground over the daunting fences of Haydock, gave me a great deal of job satisfaction.

The following day brought more satisfaction, of several sorts. A first winner, King's Rank, marked Martin's fastest 100 winners – another record; a second, Celtic Shot's first victory over fences; and a third, on Miinnehoma, another winner for Martin and another treble for me.

My own 100th winner of the season was just round the corner, coming on 20 December at Bangor in the middle of a 71–1 treble on Miss Chalk, Redgrave Devil and Abbotts View. I had got to my 100 on exactly the same day as the previous year (bearing in mind that my first celebration, after Fu's Lady won on 15 December, turned out to be premature), but it had taken me only 242 rides to get there, forty-nine fewer than last year.

By this time Nigel's application for a licence had been approved and he was now a fully fledged trainer, presiding over, among others, Mrs Muck, Tipping Tim, Celtic Prince, Nougat Russe,

Regular Vulgan and Babil. Obviously, my riding commitments meant that at this stage I was making very little input into the yard, but there were occasions when I went to buy horses on behalf of our new owners. Mark Christoffi had asked us to buy a horse for him and pointed out that one he particularly liked was going to the sales in Newmarket. I went over to inspect it, trying to remember all that my father and Martin had taught me on my previous visits to sales in their company. I found that the situation takes on a completely different aspect when the decision is your own, and you are spending someone else's money.

Looking at the colt, I could not find much wrong with his conformation; most important of all, his tendons seemed fine. As is usual, I had studied the form of the horse and asked around about his character and ability, even though whenever you ask several people about a horse you get conflicting reports. Summing it all up for Mark, who was there at the sales, I said that I liked the horse and that we should go to 16,000 guineas for him. We went to the sale ring to wait for his lot number to be called in. As the bidding went up and up I began to hope that somebody else would have set a higher ceiling on him and I would not be faced with the responsibility of taking him home. But no one had, it seemed, and my heart was in my mouth as he was knocked down to Mark for 15,000 guineas. Babil was now to be trained at Grange Hill.

It's after you've bought the horse, naturally, that you hear all the bad things about it. 'Oh,' someone will say, 'you bought that animal, did you? I'm told the owner thinks it's more of a woman than a man.' But Babil at home came to play a very important part in the yard. He was a bit of a character; he did everything with his ears tightly pricked forward, and life was a game to him. He didn't want to lead the string; he would stop, squeal, grab branches from the hedges. When he was first taken on to the all-weather strip he would not stand on the strange terrain, and in his work he was lazy. Teaching him to jump over the baby logs was impossible, he wouldn't go near them; but eventually we got his confidence and he began to love jumping. He was fourth in his first race over hurdles at Uttoxeter.

On the day after my 100th winner, the Grange Hill yard had had its first treble – not of winners but of runners. It was difficult to find enough racing bridles for them. That afternoon at Towcester the first of our runners was Regular Vulgan in division one of the novice chase; as the form book says, 'whipped round at start, tailed off when fell first'. This was back down to earth with a vengeance. In division two it was Nougat Russe, whom I pulled up before two out. Then Babil, who was becoming more and more co-operative and now really enjoying his jumping, led in his race until the approach to the last, and finished second. A leading trainer chose to criticize my riding of Babil to Nigel, saying I should not have tried to make all, that I would do him no good because I was trying to make all his horses like Martin Pipe's. Perhaps he was right on this last point, for he was to learn in the future that a lot of our horses would be fit and run to the line.

Babil, indeed, went on to prove himself an excellent advertisement for the new yard. In the following spring he recorded a fifth win over hurdles with what was by now becoming a typical gutsy performance. He was in front with a mile to go and then looked beaten when Stratford Ponds landed in front of him at the second last; but Babil would not give in and, almost back upsides at the final flight, stayed on the more strongly up the run-in to prevail by a length at the line, and in so doing clipped almost three seconds off the track record for two and a half miles.

I very rarely had to resort to the stick to galvanize Babil into running; he would run for me, and the more I drove him along the more he would find. Sometimes it can be very hard to establish a rhythm with a less than genuine horse who throws his head back at you, making it difficult to push him out; but Babil, responding to every urging, made it easy. The fact that I had been involved in buying him, together with his determined character, made Babil one of my all-time favourites.

The three-day Christmas holiday put me in a good mood with a marvellous Chepstow meeting, at which Regal Ambition made all to win fifteen lengths unchallenged in the Philip Cornes novice hurdle and Bonanza Boy went on to win the Welsh National for the second year running. Then in the New Year I had a brief trip to France to ride Lady Joseph's All Jeff for Charlie Brooks at Cagnes-sur-mer, the coastal track to which the French steeplechasing fraternity decamps for the winter months. The ride was even briefer; we fell at the second fence. All Jeff stayed down in France to run in the Grand Prix de Nice, but I came straight back. I love racing abroad, but it feels a long way to go when things don't work out.

As the year gathered pace towards another Cheltenham Festival, Celtic Shot was being touted by some as a Gold Cup prospect. His first big test was to be in the Arlington Premier Chase at Cheltenham on 27 January, which faced me with the unenviable task of deciding whether to ride him or Sabin Du Loir. I felt that on the form book Celtic Shot should have been just the better of the two; and I also felt a certain loyalty to him from the Champion Hurdle. Brian Kilpatrick, Sabin's owner, was very understanding when I told him of my decision – which turned out to be the wrong one, for although I headed Sabin Du Loir between the third last and second last fences, he galloped on to beat me by two and a half lengths. Celtic Shot's Festival plans were now in tatters; the Gold Cup was no longer a realistic proposition and the connections were unsure whether to run him in the two-mile or the three-mile novice chase. It was decided to run him first at Ascot over the longer distance, but he fell there when well beaten.

Regal Ambition's Festival preparation, on the other hand, continued very encouragingly with an easy win at Leicester that left Danny Harrold twenty-five lengths behind. Mrs Pitman was so disappointed with her horse's performance that she complained about the Stewards' failure to order a dope test into Danny Harrold's poor running. But the Pipe camp felt that her horse had simply been beaten by a very talented individual.

Another Pipe horse limbering up for Cheltenham at this time was the mighty Chatam, whose previous race over hurdles had been a farcical two-horse contest at Prestbury Park. Martin and I knew that our opponent, Beech Road, liked to run his races from behind, and thought that the only way to beat him was to make sure that he had to make the pace in front. When we were called under Starter's orders, therefore, I moved to the gate as if I were going to go on, but as the tapes went up I whipped Chatam in behind Beech Road and tracked him through much of the race – but in the end he was still too good for the big horse.

Chatam was then switched to fences, and though falling on his first appearance at Chepstow when going very well, he went on to win next time out very easily in a novice chase at his favourite course, Newbury. On the same day, Fu's Lady beat the 9–4 favourite Norton's Coin in a two-and-a-half-mile handicap chase.

On the first day of the 1990 Festival, Celtic Shot went off 4–1 favourite in the Arkle Chase, but finished a very disappointing sixth, and Fu's Lady fell with me when coming down the hill in the last. The closest I got to a winner that afternoon was second place on Nomadic Way in the Champion Hurdle; I had missed the Irish equivalent on him because the original running, on 4 February, was postponed because of bad weather at Fairyhouse, and when the race was run again on the tenth, I was riding Chatam and Fu's Lady at Newbury, so Brendan Powell got the ride – and won.

But on the Wednesday our banker of the meeting, Regal Ambition, won the Sun Alliance Novices' Hurdle in the style of a true champion, knocking seven and a half seconds off the course record, and convincing me that, with his size and scope, he had the potential to be the best horse I had ever ridden. He made most of the running (I had learnt from my mistake on that earlier run) and when challenged approaching the last quickened clear to win by twelve lengths.

He was to be our only Festival winner that year. In the Gold Cup I rode Bonanza Boy, but the good to firm ground was much too fast for him, and I watched from behind as the greatest upset in the history of the race occurred when Graham McCourt produced 100–1 outsider Norton's Coin with a perfect run to win three-quarters of a length from Toby Tobias, with the 11–10 on favourite Desert Orchid unable to catch either of them.

I was on Bonanza Boy again for the Grand National, but this year we finished a well beaten sixteenth. The little horse was never able to lay up with the pace and moreover was coming to dislike the Aintree fences. He doggedly jumped round, however, and I was awarded a plaque for having completed the Grand National course five times.

My only winner at the Aintree meeting this year was Sayparee, trained by Martin for Mr Eric Scarth. This victory I put down to the advice of Sayparee's breeder, the great Irish trainer Paddy Mullins, who told me to hold the horse up for as long as possible. The Aintree hurdle track is very fast and most jockeys, well aware of this, go a good gallop, so a lot of horses tend to tire up the deceptively long straight. If you hold a horse up here you can get into a lot of trouble on the sharp bends, but Sayparee was travelling very well throughout and I was able to hold him up longer than I would most horses and still avoid traffic problems.

Knowing that Martin would rather I did not get to the front than get there too soon, I had the confidence to wait until the final 100 yards before going on to win by a length.

Steve Smith Eccles had a winner at this meeting for Tim Thomson Jones on Fidway, a horse that had nearly landed me in an embarrassing position. I had ridden him in a hurdle at Sandown earlier in the spring when he finished sixth, jumping slowly early on but making good headway from two out and finishing strongly. On dismounting I said to the connections that I felt the horse had a lot of potential, and that as it was now March they should either put him away now for next season or, if they did run him again, make sure it was in a decent race so that if he won he would not be losing his maiden tag for an insignificant amount of prize money.

He came out again for a race at Nottingham on fast ground, in which I was riding Abbotts View, a horse on whom I had won three times for Charlie Brooks and who I knew, like his sire Monksfield, preferred soft going. Marilyn had come with me to Nottingham as we were going to the NEC that evening to see a David Bowie concert, and I remarked to her that I thought Abbotts View, my only mount of the day, might well be beaten by Fidway. My reasoning proved correct and Fidway won by seven lengths.

I thought no more about this incident until we had a phone call at home from Peter Smiles, Head of Security at the Jockey Club, asking to speak to Marilyn about the 'large bet' that a Sunday newspaper had told him she had had on Fidway at Nottingham. Marilyn told him the simple truth – that she had had just five pounds on Fidway, and that under the Rules of Racing she is perfectly entitled to bet, even though I am not. We spoke to our solicitor about the imputation and also to Monty Court, who put a small piece in the *Sporting Life* to help defuse the situation. Nothing further happened; but it just goes to show how a blameless incident can end up on a solicitor's desk and the front page of a Sunday newspaper if someone wants to make trouble.

With Aintree over, Martin's and my thoughts turned to how we might achieve the double century for a second time, but hopes of my own 200 were dealt a severe blow when Huntworth unseated me in the Golden Miller Chase at Cheltenham on 18 April, leaving his hind legs in a ditch and firing me over his head and on to the floor. I was very shaken by the fall and later X-rays revealed that I had broken a rib.

I was now faced with the problem of getting fit again not only to ride at Ayr in the Scottish Champion Hurdle and Scottish National in ten days' time, but also to go on to America to ride Regal Ambition, who had been sold to race in the States, in the $750,000 Dueling Grounds International Hurdle. My rib healed quickly, but the wrist was more of a problem; I did not have full movement in it and it was painful to pull on the reins. Even after treatment at the Lilleshall Rehabilitation Centre it was clear that I was in no condition to ride in either Scotland or America, so Jonathon Lower took my mounts. At Ayr he won the Champion Hurdle on Sayparee, but finished unplaced on Bonanza Boy in the Scottish National. Very sadly for Regal Ambition and his new connections, the horse broke down badly in the race and had to be retired from the sport.

Martin, in the meantime, had notched up his 196th winner of the season and was hoping to reach 200 on 7 May, with ten runners spread across the Bank Holiday meetings at Devon and Exeter, Fontwell, Haydock and Ludlow. This was eighteen days after my fall, and I went to ride work at Pond House that morning, with my racecourse comeback scheduled for Devon and Exeter in the afternoon. By now I was able to hold the reins comfortably, but when I turned my wrist to take a pull it was very sore. I thought I was being soft, and that I wouldn't notice it

*The prolific winner Hopscotch, on whom I won seven races in the 1990–1 season – including this one in the Food Brokers 'Finesse' Hurdle at Cheltenham in January 1991 (GERRY CRANHAM)*

in a race. However, my first ride that day, Ultra Violet, jumped very badly and turning into the straight ran out left-handed; I was unable to prevent him because my wrist was so weak. I knew that Martin would be cross and irritable so near the 200 mark, so instead of admitting that my wrist was hurting I went out to ride in the next, which I won on Gold Service. Now, with Martin in a better frame of mind, I was able to tell him that I was not happy with the state of my wrist and that I was going to give up the rest of the day's rides. Jimmy Frost replaced me on Don't Be Late, who, with Walk Of Life winning simultaneously at Fontwell, brought Martin up to his second successive double century. He went on adding to the total up to the end of the season, when his closing score stood at 224, surpassing his own record of the previous year.

I was at a loss to know why my wrist would not heal, and on advice from Jimmy Duggan sought a second opinion from Mary Bromiley, a physiotherapist from near Lambourn. Mary suspected that I had dislocated a bone within the wrist and suggested that I have it X-rayed again. She was quite right: I had turned a bone round, and as three weeks had passed since the original injury, there was a danger that the bone might have died due to lack of blood supply. If this had happened it could have serious implications for my riding career.

I went into Cheltenham hospital for surgery. The pain when I came round from the anaesthetic was the most intense I had ever suffered – a result, I was told, of the wrist swelling up under the plaster. After a few days the plaster came off; the surgeon informed me that the operation had gone well, and that although I would never regain complete mobility in that wrist, the bone was all right and the prognosis was not as gloomy as had originally been feared. With a lot of physiotherapy and more help from Mary Bromiley, and much to the surprise and delight of the surgeon, I got seventy-five per cent of the movement back in the wrist.

My riding season had obviously come to its end, and though I got no higher than 170 winners, they were enough to secure me the championship. With the knowledge of this, and of Martin's success, to add satisfaction to the relief of knowing that I would be fit to ride again next season, I went off to Barbados with the family for a holiday.

## Chapter Thirteen

# LONG HAUL

———◄►———

In autumn 1990, despite six championship titles under my belt, I came out to start the new season under pressure to reassert myself. Any jockey whose mounts have won for other riders while he has been laid off knows that he risks losing the rides altogether; and I had missed the last month of the previous season, giving other riders the chance to show their skills on horses I now wanted to reclaim.

It's important, too, when you want to show people that you are back in earnest, that you have retrieved your fitness; and it can take quite a time to get back into peak condition after a long lay-off. That summer, though I ran and swam regularly, and rode out once I had had some leather wrist supports made to help protect me from any further damage, I still felt that I needed some race-riding practice to put the final touches to my condition. I was therefore delighted when I got an invitation to go to Sweden to ride at Taby, a racecourse just outside Stockholm, as part of a promotion of racing at the World Equestrian Games.

I knew Taby from my earlier summer trips to Scandinavia: it is a left-handed track, the hurdle course with English-style obstacles and the steeplechase course a figure-of-eight with small continental-style fences. I rode one winner during the evening's event, but was pleased simply to be back riding in a race, after all the anxiety about my wrist injury. Later in the evening Marilyn and I joined the show-jumping fraternity for dinner – Nick Skelton, John and Michael Whitaker, and *chef d'équipe* Malcolm Wallace, who was commentating on the show-jumping events in the Games. We had a great evening, the latter part of which Nick and I spent winding each other up about our respective fitness and each other's sports, and next morning I awoke remembering with horror some of the things I think I said. But I can't have behaved too badly, as Nick still speaks to me if I see him at one of the major shows, or at Warwick racecourse where he goes to watch steeplechasing.

The real test came, of course, when National Hunt racing started in England again. Back at Newton Abbot for the first race of the season, I was standing in the paddock before mounting Walk Of Life when Chester Barnes, who seems to be oblivious to the factors affecting a jockey's career, pointed out to me and the horse's owners how well Mark Perrett had ridden it at the end of the last season. So I was even more pleased than I would normally have been to get up on the line and win by a head.

The first real success story of the 1990–1 season for me and Martin was Hopscotch, a tiny bay filly who had been owned and bred by the Queen and trained on the Flat by Willie Hastings-Bass before being sold to Martin at Ascot sales for 11,400 guineas. Racing under the banner of the Pipe/Scudamore Racing Club, she won nine races over hurdles this season, the first of which was an easy victory at Worcester. A further four were to be at Cheltenham. By Dominion, a favourite sire of Martin's, Hopscotch had never won on the Flat, but took to jumping from the first time we schooled her. She was a hard puller, and early on in her career you had to be careful when riding her not to let her over-jump.

One of Charlie Brooks's early season runners, Bokaro, was being prepared for the Sport of Kings Challenge at Belmont Park on 19 October. This was a very dry autumn and in search of good ground for his first run Charlie sent the horse to Perth – an 824-mile round trip from Lambourn. Although he did not jump very well, this former French hurdler, who had finished second at Auteuil in June, won by a length, opening Charlie's account for the season and confirming that he was in good enough shape to justify the long trip to the States in the middle of October.

I was lucky to be in good enough shape for the American trip myself. The day after the Perth race, I had a very bad fall at Taunton and thought I had broken my knee. But X-rays at Cheltenham hospital on the way home revealed nothing broken, and after physiotherapy from Mary Bromiley I was fit enough to ride at Cheltenham six days later, where four winners took my total to 32. Mary was becoming a lynchpin of this year's championship campaign.

So, on 18 October, I flew out to New York for the Belmont Park event with Richard Dunwoody and Hywel Davies. I had wanted to go out on Concorde on the Friday morning, to avoid missing the previous day's racing in England, but Lady Joseph, Bokaro's owner and a delightful person, was not happy with this in case there was a hold-up and I didn't get there on time. In her words, ' . . . in case a wheel falls off it; it has happened to me when I was trying to arrive on time!' Naturally I had to give way gracefully, but travelling out early meant missing winners for Martin on the Thursday.

On arrival in New York I was expecting to be picked up by Charlie, who was already over there supervising Bokaro's final preparations. When he failed to arrive, the three of us caught a taxi to a hotel near the racecourse, with Hywel keeping a close eye on our expenses. The next morning it was off to Belmont Park to go through the rigmarole of getting our New York riding licences. Richard and I passed our medicals but there was a problem with Hywel's inability to see very well out of one eye – a problem that I was convinced had more to do with his consumption of bourbon

**GET FIT SOON, PETER ~ FROM YOUR FRIENDS AT THE PARTY!**
Cheltenham Racecourse, Mackeson Night
10 November 90

*"Please don't bring any more ~ if I jack it up any higher he'll fall out and break the other one!"*

and ginger the previous night than with any long-term visual defect. After convincing a very confused nurse that anything he lacked in one eye he made up for with his excellent sight in the other, we were let through to the weighing room to change.

Hywel created quite an impression here. He smokes roll-ups, which in the weighing rooms around England he leaves part-smoked, balanced on the edge of the bench where he has changed, while he goes out to ride. (As I change next to him, I have to be very careful not to sit on them.) At Belmont, he had one South

American rider following him around picking up his fag-ends, thinking they were joints. The valet looking after Hywel was small in stature but large in vocal strength; when Hywel told him that he had won the Grand National for the Duchess of Westminster, a New York drawl could be heard over some distance proclaiming: 'I only know one fucken duchess, and when I get home she got my supper on the table!'

The race itself went like a dream. Bokaro made all to win well, finding the American fences much more to his liking than English hurdles. Hywel and Richard were unplaced behind me; Richard stayed on to ride in the Breeders' Cup Chase, which was won by Morley Street, while Hywel and I flew back to England that evening – a precipitate return that in my case proved fruitless, my ride at Kempton the next day being soundly beaten.

All the yards I was riding for were running well, and two winners for Nigel were particularly pleasing. We were now amassing a

*(Left) The Bernard Parkin cartoon sent by revellers at the Mackeson Gold Cup night party in November 1990 – which I was forced to miss following the fall from Black Humour at Market Rasen*
*(BERNARD PARKIN)*

*Colonel Sir Piers Bengough, Clerk of the Course at Ascot, seems to be deciding whether I'm wearing the prohibited jeans in the unsaddling enclosure: in fact he's checking progress on my broken leg a few weeks after the Black Humour fall*
*(GERRY CRANHAM)*

very exciting collection of horses at Grange Hill, and the first winner of the season epitomized this promising stamp of horse when Captain Dibble, who had previously won a bumper, put up an impressive performance to win at Worcester first time over hurdles. The second victory for the team was scored by Babil, who won comfortably over hurdles at Newbury.

With everyone on song, I was having a wonderful run. Celtic Shot made a very good seasonal reappearance to win at Wetherby on Saturday 3 November; on the following Monday Skipping Tim gave me my fiftieth winner; and on the Tuesday Sabin Du Loir produced the type of form which made me believe him to be one of the best steeplechasers I had ever sat on when beating Desert Orchid at Devon and Exeter. At the end of that week, with Nigel wanting me to go to Cheltenham to ride Celtic Prince on the first day of the Mackeson meeting, I went to Market Rasen to ride Massingham and Black Humour for Charlie. All week I had been worrying about whether to ride Wingspan or Fu's Lady for Martin in the Mackeson. I needn't have bothered.

The day at Market Rasen started well, with a lucky win on Massingham: Mark Dwyer had a nasty fall on Otterburn House when just in the lead, allowing me to go on to a six-length victory. As a result of Mark's injury I replaced him on Invasion in the novice chase and thus recorded one of the most remarkable wins of my career when the horse fell three out but did not actually roll over; I was able to stay aboard while he scrambled up and catch the horse that had gone ahead of me on the line.

My next ride was Black Humour in a handicap hurdle. I had first seen this horse two years earlier on a visit to Timmie Hyde's stud in Ireland with Charlie Brooks to look at another prospect for the yard, and I liked him very much. Since then he had been very impressive when winning a novice hurdle with me at Uttoxeter, though his jumping was sometimes not of the best. I considered him an exceptionally good horse, possibly even a prospect for the Champion Hurdle, and on this day he started 5–4 on favourite. But he was never travelling well and when I asked him to stand off at the fifth hurdle he put down and rolled over, trapping my leg underneath.

At first I didn't think any serious damage had been done; it was only when I went to stand up that I realized that something was badly wrong. My leg felt as if it had been shattered. Remembering the difficulty of getting my boot off the last time I broke my leg, I quickly removed it before the pain hit me, shouting across to the ambulance crew what I had done as they arrived. Their fast, efficient work spared me from any more pain. They brought out gas and air for me to breathe in, put a splint on my leg and took me carefully on a stretcher to the ambulance room. I pleaded with the doctor to get me taken to see John Webb, the orthopaedic surgeon in Nottingham, so that he could deal with my leg, but to no avail; I was taken off to Lincoln County Hospital where X-rays confirmed that I had suffered a straightforward break of the fibula and tibia. This news was a relief as I had feared something much worse. Then at last I was transferred to Nottingham where John Webb was waiting for me, dressed in a dinner jacket.

'My wife is not very pleased with you,' he told me. 'You're going to make me late.'

Having inspected the X-rays, he then said, 'I can put you in plaster for sixteen weeks or I can operate on you and perhaps have you back riding in ten.'

As he knew, in my position it was vital that I was back in action as soon as possible. I was therefore delighted to wake from the operation the next morning to find twenty stitches down my shin where a surgical plate had been inserted to speed up the healing process. Within a very short time John Webb had me moving my ankle, impressing on me the need to prevent any unnecessary swelling and therefore to keep the leg up wherever possible.

After a week I was discharged from hospital to begin the long haul back to fitness. There was plenty to do. One new departure was working with the BBC race commentary team, sitting next to Richard Pitman to analyse the day's sport. This was a wonderful opportunity for me to begin to understand the problems faced by the television commentators, and I thoroughly enjoyed it, though as a novice I made the inevitable mistakes. On one occasion I was talking about the horses circling at the start and was supposed to be keeping to a numerical sequence of runners. Diverted on to an interesting point by a horse appearing on camera I started to talk about it – out of sequence – and heard a voice in my headphones say, 'What's that idiot talking about now?'

I was getting plenty of other media work through a company called Chasing Promotions, which Marilyn runs. The idea of the company, which acts as an agency for jockeys to represent them in promotional work, came up one day when Steve Smith Eccles and I were sitting outside the weighing room at Bangor, talking about the times when we were asked to speak or appear at events. We believed that a lot of opportunities for jockeys to do this sort of work were getting wasted; there were many occasions on which Steve or I could not do a job that was offered to us, and if there were an agency system in operation, that agency would be able to find someone else suitable who was available. This kind of work is a godsend for injured jockeys; opening betting shops, talking in racecourse hospitality units, occasional television work – it all earns you a few pounds and stops you going mad with boredom while you can't actually ride, and the clients get a good professional jockey who might very well not be available when in full work.

Financially, lay-offs can be a big worry, though injured jockeys do now have the support of the Professional Riders' Insurance Scheme, funded by racehorse owners, which makes payments to jockeys when they cannot work through injury. I also had a private insurance scheme which helped a little. Nevertheless, being out of action for a considerable period means a substantial loss in earning power, which just adds to the general impatience to get going again. As I had no plaster on my leg, I was able to start doing some fitness work within a week of leaving hospital. I swam every day, and also joined the local gymnasium and did a weight-training course. And when I had time, there was the yard at Grange Hill to keep me in touch.

As it was my left leg that I had broken I was able to get about thanks to my sponsors, Peugeot, who lent me an automatic car. At times, even in this so-called 'resting' period, my schedule got very tight. In early December I went to the Horsewriters' Derby Awards Luncheon in London before flying to Dublin on the evening of the same day to launch the *Irish Racing Annual* and then catching the first plane back to Heathrow the following morning to don my morning suit for a 10.00 a.m. prompt appointment at Buckingham Palace to receive my MBE. I was terrified that I was not going to get back to England in time for the ceremony, and kept wondering whether anyone else had ever failed to arrive on time to be presented with an honour.

At least I knew which entrance to go to, which would save a minute or two, as I had been there before at the invitation of the Princess Royal, for drinks before going on to a dinner held by the

Worshipful Company of Farriers at the London Guildhall. On that earlier occasion I had also been extremely nervous about arriving on time and had ordered a taxi prematurely, which meant asking the taxi driver to do a detour to avoid arriving too early; he was getting very suspicious of our request to go to the Palace and when he eventually pulled into the courtyard he told us that it was the first time he had been there, and that he had thought we were hoaxers. After walking along a long, red-carpeted corridor, Marilyn and I were shown into the apartment where the Princess Royal and several of her friends were having drinks. Exactly on time we went down to the black state cars that were taking the party on to the dinner. As they drew out on to the roundabout we were met by motorbike outriders who stopped the traffic to allow us a clear passage; we went straight through red lights and over road junctions and arrived at the Guildhall spot on time. After the usual formal ceremonies we sat down to dinner and the conversation got round to cooking. I asked the Princess if she had a microwave, and she said no, she had a cook.

Once more I made it to the Palace on time, accompanied by Marilyn and the boys, though on this occasion it was something of a rush. When I went up to collect the MBE, still on my crutches, the Queen asked me how Hopscotch was.

The Friday and Saturday of that week were the days of the December Cheltenham meeting, and the commentator and columnist Jim McGrath ('Hotspur' of the *Daily Telegraph*) came to stay overnight. During Friday night there was a terrific snowstorm that not only wiped out the racing at Cheltenham but also closed all the local roads as well as bringing down many power lines. By Saturday evening we still had no electricity. However, Saturday night was also the occasion of Raymond Mould's fiftieth birthday party at Guiting Grange, a mile away from us, and as Raymond and Jenny had an electricity generator and a party laid on that none of their friends could get to, they very kindly invited our household across. The only way to get there was on foot, so off we all hiked in the arctic conditions, with Captain (Nigel) Scott in the lead and me hobbling along holding everyone up. Eventually we arrived to the wonderful welcome of light and warmth at Guiting Grange, and Jim was royally entertained.

The next morning the weather had still not relented and the

roads were no clearer. Jim was due to catch a plane on Tuesday morning to take his family to Hong Kong, and as he lay in the bath in one of the majestically decorated en suite bathrooms of the Grange he wondered how he was to explain to his wife the hardships he was enduring – especially as the south-east of England, where he lived, had had no snow. Luckily by mid-Monday the roads were passable again.

On the following Wednesday my hectic social diary showed yet another appointment at Buckingham Palace, this time an invitation to a special party laid on for the birthday decades of certain members of the royal family: the Princess Royal's fortieth, Prince Andrew's thirtieth and Princess Margaret's sixtieth. As Marilyn and I entered the ballroom and were announced to the Queen, she turned to Prince Philip and said, 'Oh look, he's back again.'

My leg was mending well, with regular checks by John Webb to monitor progress, and nine weeks after the accident I was given the go-ahead to start riding out again, with a plastic support round the leg. This support was moulded from the front of the knee down to the bottom end of the shin-bone, and at the back ran down to below the heel. This made it impossible to ride in, because when I did manage to get a boot on – an over-sized one – the rigid plastic restricted any movement in my ankle, so I adapted it by chopping off the heel part. I couldn't get jodhpurs on, so I wore loose trousers with leather chaps over them.

I started riding out for Martin again on 16 January 1991. To begin with I felt little twinges of pain in the leg, but all the fitness work had paid off and overall I felt happy with my condition. To start with, though, I was inevitably slightly wary of the leg, and I also felt out of touch and lacking in confidence with the horses. Riding at my old length of leather I found the plastic support uncomfortable, so I had to ride considerably shorter than I was used to; after a while I felt a lot happier with this length and wished I had pulled my leathers up a few holes earlier in my career. With hindsight I could see that one of the reasons why I had broken the leg was that I was sitting too deep into the horse, so that when he rolled over my leg was trapped, whereas if I had been riding shorter I would have been on top rather than wrapped round him and would probably have been thrown clear. Once I got used to riding shorter I felt I went with the horse better when jumping, and I fell off less often.

After a few schooling sessions, I spoke to the Jockey Club Chief Medical Officer, Dr Michael Allen, and arranged to see him on Tuesday 22 January. I didn't expect to be passed fit to ride straight away, and it was with a mixture of delight and apprehension that I received the news that I could begin race-riding again at Cheltenham at the end of the week. As I wandered out into Portman Square I leafed through my diary, wondering where my first winner would come from, and then remembered that there was racing at Newton Abbot on Thursday and that Martin had good runners there. So I ran – as best I could, still going a bit short – back to Dr Allen to ask him if he would pass me fit for Thursday. He agreed. In the back of my mind, even though the doctor had assured me that my left leg was now as strong as my right again, there lurked a lingering doubt; but I knew that would only be exorcised when I started racing again.

Thanks to the skill of the surgeon, ten weeks after snapping my leg in two places I rode Outside Edge to win for Martin. I also missed a winner, though: I could have ridden Tree Poppy for Charlie Brooks, but having schooled her the morning before I thought I would be stupid to give her her first ride over fences on the day of my comeback.

On the day Black Humour fell on me, I was seventeen winners in front of Richard Dunwoody; when I returned, I was twenty adrift of his total of seventy-four. It seemed that I had only an outside chance of being champion jockey this year; but while I knew that I was going to be deposed at some stage, I wasn't going to sit back and just let it happen. Throughout the rest of the season I was going to have to be more choosy about the rides I took, and to go on riding with the plastic support under a pair of enlarged boots. John Webb had assured me that I was unlikely to break my leg in the same place again, and that even if I did he could perform another operation, the only problem being that every time he opened up the leg there would be the risk of infection.

The winning streak continued on the Friday, with a victory on Fu's Lady in the two-mile handicap chase at Wincanton, so I went to Cheltenham feeling confident and won the first race on little Hopscotch. This was followed by a second victory on Celtic

Shot, who felt really wonderful, jumping very well and making all to beat a class field, with Toby Tobias second and Norton's Coin third. This impressive win prompted the bookies to make him 9–2 ante-post favourite for the Gold Cup, and I felt that on this form he could do it.

The pleasure of these achievements was, however, wiped out when Rusch de Farges fell heavily with me at the ditch later in the afternoon. I escaped unhurt, but the horse broke its neck and died instantly.

A treble at Leicester the following Tuesday with Primatice and two very good horses, Captain Dibble and Granville Again, made me feel that I was still in with a chance of holding on to the title. Richard was still riding winners too, but the race was back on in earnest, and if only I could remain sound, if only the weather was kind and if only I chose the right meetings and the right horses, I might still be champion jockey in June.

The three 'if onlys' were to confront me many times over the remaining months of the season. Two of the potential problems, the weather and the choice of track, presented themselves together on the Saturday following Celtic Shot's win at Cheltenham. Racing was abandoned at Chepstow, where I had looked to have a good chance of riding two or three winners, and I had to decide whether to go to Wetherby to ride Sabin Du Loir, for whom Martin had booked Graham McCourt, or Sandown to ride Voyage Sans Retour, for whom he had not yet engaged a jockey. I plumped for Sandown.

As soon as you make a choice like this you wish you had taken the other option. You see all the problems with the horse you have chosen, and all the dangers to the other one seem to diminish. On this Saturday I was very lucky: I had led into the straight, but Voyage hung left and was in third place approaching the last, with no chance, when the new leader Deep Sensation, who was cruising, fell; this left my old mate Fidway in front, a position he no longer relished for long, and when he hesitated up the long hill I pushed Voyage out and he ran on to win three-quarters of a length. Meanwhile, Sabin Du Loir had fallen at Wetherby.

The weather continued to play havoc with the fixture list, and between 2 and 16 February the only racing that could take place was on the all-weather tracks at Southwell and Lingfield – though there was a turf meeting in Ireland which I went across for, finishing second in the Irish Champion Hurdle on Nomadic Way. The all-weather circuit has created its own specialist trainers and jockeys, and it was only when the trainers for whom I rode started running their horses here when the weather prohibited turf racing that I began to ride on the new surfaces. At Southwell on 11 February Vigano became my first winner on an all-weather track; but, over-jumping at the first, he pitched on landing, sending a jolt up my left leg – the one I had broken in November.

After dismounting in the winner's enclosure I could barely walk back to weigh in. I didn't have a ride in the next race and thought that the pain would wear off, as sometimes happens. When I went out for my next ride, cantering to post was very uncomfortable; I couldn't put much pressure on my left foot in the stirrup iron, so my right leg was having to do all the work of keeping my balance. My mount, Tom Clapton, made all and won, but I was no more than a passenger. It is very dangerous to ride in this kind of condition as you are not in proper control of your horse, and I gave up my next ride to Graham McCourt, who won easily on Tim Soldier. When you are fighting to catch up in a championship race, having to give up winning rides really preys on your mind; what if you lost the title by one? But the more you worry about your misfortune, the more stress you load on yourself, and this affects your decisions and your riding performance. I used to try to avoid getting into this cycle of stress by concentrating hard on the immediate objective: to get fully fit again as soon as possible.

I went straight back to Mary Bromiley, who confirmed that I had jolted the ankle joint; although it was very painful, with treatment it would not take long to mend. I was in action again the following day at Lingfield, riding one winner before giving up the remainder of my rides. I just had to keep trying to ride until I could bear the pressure on the ankle. I was very irritated to hear people saying that I had come back too quickly and was being greedy; or, on the other hand, that I was not really trying as I did not like racing on the all-weather surface. Again, the only thing to do was to shut these carping comments out and concentrate on fitness and racing. The frost and snow were, after all, giving me a breathing space in which to recover; and I had had the chance to sample racing on the new surfaces. My brief experience on the all-weather tracks showed me that some horses needed a run to get used to the faster going, and also to accustom themselves to the hurdles, which knock down very easily.

Turf racing resumed on Saturday 16 February at Windsor – for me, with a winner for Charlie Brooks on Espy. With less than a month to go before the Festival, there were some important Cheltenham trials coming up, notably two at Warwick that Wednesday, for Rolling Ball and Run For Free. Rolling Ball had come over from France two years previously and had been very impressive in a novice hurdle at Haydock before injuring a tendon in his next run. After a year's absence on account of this injury, he won at Bangor with Jonathon on board before being defeated in a handicap hurdle, and it was decided to switch him to steeplechasing. Having won over the French style of hurdles, he was not daunted by English fences and quickly adapted to jumping them well at home. Although he was a three-miler, he was quick enough in schooling to win over two miles. Today, over the longer distance, would be his first racecourse outing over the stiffer obstacles.

I wanted to avoid anyone taking him on early in the race; I knew that if I could settle him in front he would get the trip, and the fences would make him concentrate and take his mind off pulling. There were, however, several other front-running types in the race, one of which was the favourite Tildarg, ridden by Jamie Osborne. In situations like this there is no point in two horses taking each other on, because if they go too fast in the early stages both risk being beaten through tiring too soon. On this particular day, neither Jamie nor I wanted to give way, so we both jumped off to make it; but after a couple of fences Jamie saw that his horse was not so quick through the air as mine, and sat in behind me. Once this happened Rolling Ball settled in between his fences; but every time he saw a fence coming up he quickened into it. In fact, he found them very easy and became complacent, not choosing a stride until near the fence, which made it difficult for me to work out where he wanted to pick up. But despite this rather disconcertingly cavalier jumping, he put up a faultless round and won easily, putting himself in many people's eyes at the head of the list for the three-mile novice chase at Cheltenham. I had my doubts; the combination of this complacency with his lack of experience didn't inspire real confidence. Run For Free, however, sailed home in an effortless trial for the Sun Alliance Hurdle, convincing me that he was this year's Cheltenham banker.

*One of my great favourites: Bonanza Boy at Ascot in February 1989*

*One of the most satisfying moments of my career - passing the post on Captain Dibble after winning the William Hill Scottish National at Ayr in April 1992.*

*A lovely horse at the peak of his form – Rushing Wild easily winning the Anthony Mildmay, Peter Cazalet Memorial Chase at Sandown Park in January 1993. He later ran second to Jodami in the Gold Cup but was tragically killed in the Irish Grand National (TREVOR JONES)*

*Schooling a young hurdler with Martin Pipe* (GERRY CRANHAM)

*Olympian flies over the last flight to win the Sunderlands Imperial Cup at Sandown Park in March 1993. He was my final winner on the course, and carried just ten stone – note the size of the saddle* (GERRY CRANHAM)

*Richard Dunwoody may have taken over the championship in the 1992-3 season but I still got one over on him every now and then: Martin Pipe's good four-year-old Viardot pings the last before beating Richard and odds-on favourite Home Counties in the Ripley Hurdle at Sandown Park in February 1993* (GERRY CRANHAM)

*Granville Again provides one of Martin Pipe's greatest training achievements when jumping the last to win the Champion Hurdle in March 1993* (GERRY CRANHAM)

*One of the most promising young horses I've ridden for a good while, Young Hustler takes the last from Superior Finish to win the Sun Alliance Novices' Chase at the 1993 Cheltenham Festival (GERRY CRANHAM)*

*Michael and proud Dad after reaching the frame in the local gymkhana*

*Thomas - a future contender for his Dad's record?*

*Unwinding at Mucky Cottage*

At the Kempton meeting towards the end of the week I had a trial of my own to face: my first ride on Black Humour since he broke my leg. I had already had to confront the psychological barrier of riding at Market Rasen; however much I tried to shut it out of my mind, I still had to jump the hurdle where Black Humour came down on me, and if the stride was in doubt approaching the obstacle I tended to go short, and was relieved when I found myself galloping away from it. There was the same mental block with Black Humour; never again would I trust him one hundred per cent to stand off a hurdle when I asked him to. I was doubly relieved when he jumped well and won.

Granville Again, full brother to Morley Street, also won at this meeting in a race that taught me things about the horse that were to be useful later on. We missed the break, and through the early part of the race were further down the field than either I or Martin would have liked, but he was in the lead by the second last and won well.

That day ended with one of the saddest moments in my whole racing life, when Mucky, ridden by Carl Llewellyn, broke her near fore cannon bone when racing round the final bend. After a successful operation to save her by pinning the bone she seemed well on the road to recovery; but then infection suddenly set in and she had to be put down.

The death of any horse is a terrible blow to those who are close to it – the owner, the trainer, people in the yard, and above all the lad or lass who looks after it at home. As a jockey riding a lot of different horses, I was usually less close to any one of them than the lads and lasses, and with many other horses to ride it was easier to come to terms with a loss. But I always felt, if a horse I was riding died or suffered a fatal injury, that I had let down whoever looked after that horse, because I had been entrusted with its care during the race and had failed to bring it back safely. The public do not see the genuine emotion felt by a jockey when a horse has died. Whenever I could I tried to keep a stable lass away from her horse if it had become seriously injured on the racecourse. I know, too, that some trainers and handlers, particularly women, never forgave me, or felt a long-standing hostility towards me, because I had been on a horse when it died.

Mrs Muck's death was different from any other, and left a particular void. She had put Grange Hill on the map; and she had been so brave, honest and kind, qualities that had won her many followers. Through her we had all had so much fun, not just in winning but in the way she raced.

Normally I would take a day off racing before Cheltenham, to avoid the risk of a niggling injury denying me participation in the biggest and best three days of the season. This year, with the pressure of the struggle for the championship, I felt that I could not afford this luxury, and on the Monday went to Plumpton, not one of my favourite courses, to ride four for Martin, who was doing all he could to help me retain my title. A fall on First Legion in the opener very nearly proved me wrong in departing from my normal rule; the horse rolled over me and I was lucky to escape without being hurt.

I always felt Plumpton was an idiots' course. It is a left-handed oblong track, nine furlongs round, built on the side of a hill and favouring speed rather than stamina. Jockeys kicked for home five fences from the line, so racing down the hill they had no time to find their stride and would as a result be taking uncalculated risks. My theory for surviving steeplechasing was that you took calculated risks, deciding when and where to push your horse; but at Plumpton I had to abandon that theory, unless I was on a superior horse, and just guess at strides down the hill. At least I had a winner in Leading Role to make the calculated risk of coming here at all worth while.

I arrived at the first day of the Festival just five winners behind Richard, and pleased to be there; even a blank day on the Tuesday did not seem a disaster. I was slightly unfortunate on Granville Again in the first race, which did not go my way at all; after holding him up on the inside I was hampered coming up the hill when a horse fell in front of me on the flat, leaving me a lot of ground to make up from the top of the hill, and then I was squeezed for room on the home turn and unable to make any further progress. We finished second, four lengths behind the heavily backed Destriero.

There were no such excuses later in the afternoon when Run For Free and I came home a neck behind Mark Perrett and Kings Curate. Mark had given his horse a tremendous ride, being off the bridle for much of the race and forcing a challenge at the last hurdle; up the run-in I looked like getting the better of the duel until Run For Free's habit of hanging left cost him the race when he ducked across the track where the running rail ended. In doing this he lost ground that made the difference between winning and losing.

We raced Run For Free in a special bit that was designed to prevent or at least mitigate his habit of hanging. This bit consisted of a metal tube which ran through the mouth in the same way as an ordinary bit, but contained a metal bar six inches longer than the tube, at the ends of which the round bit-rings on to which the reins connect were fixed. The theory behind this is that a horse will hang when it gets the bit fixed on one side of its mouth, enabling it to lean on that end of the bit. The long bar to which the reins were attached, sliding through the tube in the horse's mouth, would prevent the horse being able to fix on one side of the bit in that way.

An older theory of how to stop a horse hanging is to turn its head in the direction it is leaning: if I had done this with Run For Free I would have gone round in ever-decreasing circles.

My recent return from injury made the next day's victory on

*Racing's a serious business* (GEORGE SELWYN)

the front-running Rolling Ball one of the moments in my career I most savoured. His second performance over English fences was spectacular, and he soon had the twenty-runner field strung out behind him. His impetuous attitude led him into one real blunder on the first circuit, but confounding my fears he then started to concentrate on the job and kept on up the hill to win.

Chatam's victory on the Thursday in the Cathcart Chase made me leading rider of the meeting; but the day was overcast somewhat by an unhappy ride on Celtic Shot in the Gold Cup, for which he started favourite. There had been rumours before the race that all was not well with the horse and that he had abnormally high levels of muscle enzymes, which indicates damage to muscle fibres which causes the enzymes to leak through the cell walls into the bloodstream. In the race, I was never happy with the way he was travelling; I had intended to ride him near the front, but I did not want to be on the outside of Desert Orchid, who habitually jumped right-handed and thus might push me wide, as he would no doubt be up there near the pace. Celtic Shot failed to hold his position; whether it was because we went down the inside I do not know. We did make up ground on the outside to take the lead at the top of the hill, but approaching the third last he made a bad mistake and weakened to finish seventh behind Garrison Savannah.

Whether his poor performance was a result of my riding or his muscle problems is impossible to say. He had, while I had been injured, run bad races that were attributed to the muscle damage; and when I chose to ride him again at Aintree in the Martell Chase, instead of Aquilifer, much the same thing happened. Again he started favourite, and again he failed to deliver the goods. In fact, he ran abysmally, jumping as though his back was not right; on reflection I should have pulled him up, but it was only a five-runner race which he should have won easily, and he did not feel tired.

Aquilifer stormed home with Richard on board, and as we pulled up Richard had the decency to say he felt sorry for me; but this did not prevent me from being relieved of the duties of riding Celtic Shot. On dismounting I reported that the horse was not himself, but heard from other sources that David Horton and Charlie Brooks had blamed me for the bad running, believing that I had not made enough effort on him, and also attributing the Gold Cup failure to my going down the inside. I later learned

that the horse had indeed pulled muscles in his back, and thought
that once this had been discovered I would be reunited with him
– especially as I had twice turned down rides on Brian
Kilpatrick's horses, Sabin Du Loir and Aquilifer, to ride him.

In between Cheltenham and Aintree I had been edging
towards Richard's score, and Bonanza Boy's twenty-length
victory on bottomless ground in the Ansells National at Uttoxeter
put me within two of his total. But at Newbury the following
weekend I acquired another painful injury that held up my
progress, when Chatam unseated me at the thirteenth fence. I
landed very hard on my left buttock, and not realizing that I had
done anything more than get another bruise I went on riding for
the rest of the afternoon. Having showered after the last, I felt
my body stiffening up so decided once again to call in on Mary
Bromiley on my way home. She diagnosed a haemotoma – a
blood clot – on my bottom, and after laser treatment on the
Saturday and Sunday I felt fit enough to ride in the coming
week.

On my way to Sandown on the Tuesday I rode out at Nicky
Henderson's, where the BBC were filming. In doing so I must
have irritated the blood clot as it started to bleed again, and by
the time I got to the racecourse I was feeling sick and drowsy,
with a tingling feeling in my buttock. There was to be no riding
for me that day – in fact, despite several more attempts, no riding
until 2 April, by which time I had missed many winners for
Martin over the bank holiday weekend and Richard had moved
four ahead of me on 101.

I went down to Martin's on the Monday thinking I could ride
but was unable to raise my left leg due to the tightness in my
buttock, and though I could get on I could not lean forward to
canter. I got down again and had another go the next morning,
when I found that by using a longer leather I was able to canter
and somewhat uncertainly declared myself fit to ride. In my first
race at Chepstow that afternoon I finished second riding
Riverside Boy in this old-fashioned style, but I took some stick in
the weighing room as I was looking more like Fred Archer than a
modern jump jockey. I managed to silence my critics with a
double on High Knowl and Bradmore's Chum.

I recovered from this latest injury only just in time for
Liverpool, but although the poor running of Celtic Shot made
me wonder whether I need have bothered, the Friday brought

better luck with victories on Granville Again and Trefelyn Cone
– and the latter marked my 100th winner of the season. But the
Grand National itself, again with Bonanza Boy, brought us only a
fifth place.

There were rumours at this time, published in two newspapers,
that this was to be my last season riding. This annoyed me, as I
had no intention of retiring yet, and had to quash the stories
firmly as they were putting added pressure on me and causing
friction with connections of some horses I was riding. In fact,
what with the injuries, the travelling, and the constant anxiety
about whether I would make the top of the table this year, I was
beginning to feel a bit worn out.

My schedule took me to Perth on Tuesday and Wednesday
23rd and 24th April, Ludlow and Wincanton on Thursday 25th
and Taunton on Friday 26th. The travelling was rewarded with
three winners by the Thursday, and then I finally moved in
front of Richard with a treble at the Taunton meeting. To me
personally this was a real achievement and I felt quite emotional
about the third victory. But it was Richard's misfortune that
sealed the championship for me and put an end to his chances.
At the Thursday evening meeting at Wincanton he had won a
two-mile handicap chase on Came Down which was followed by
a Stewards' Inquiry on an objection that he had hampered the
runner-up. The objection was overruled, but the owner of the
second horse, Colonel Whitbread, appealed and at the
subsequent inquiry Richard received a five-day ban, to run from
16 May to 22 May. This effectively put an end to his hopes of
the title.

Not, of course, that he just threw in the towel. Although this
must have been a very difficult period for him, he did get help
from outsiders to try to keep the challenge going: for example, he
was offered the use of a helicopter to take him round the tracks,
thus increasing the number of horses he could ride. And
occasionally jockeys were giving up rides to him: John White, for
example, Nicky Henderson's second jockey, got off Over And
Above to allow Richard a winner on the evening of my treble at
Taunton. But I too was winning, with another treble at Ascot on
30 April that put me four ahead. The backing of Martin Pipe and
his helicopter seemed to be making some people think I had an
unfair advantage.

All was in fact not well at Pond House. For a while now there had been someone dogging Martin and the yard, asking questions in the area and interviewing people who might have a grudge against him. It became apparent that someone was conducting some kind of hostile investigation into Martin's training operation. At first I had the impression that this was another campaign against Martin based on jealousy and gossip, and that whoever was behind it wanted to prove that blood doping and steroid use were practised in the yard. I could not really believe that a serious television programme could be made on the basis of malicious rumour. Later Martin told me that the investigator was a freelance journalist working for *The Cook Report* – an investigative television programme fronted by Roger Cook that conducts its own inquiries into criminal misdeeds. It became apparent that the programme was out to try to show that Martin's successes were achieved at the expense of his horses' welfare.

Martin was having to devote a lot of his time to defending himself against this assault. A sombre mood descended over the yard as it became known that the programme was being prepared, but for a long time I felt that the programme-makers would see sense once they had done their research and call the whole thing off. When it seemed that it was in fact going ahead, I felt that a great injustice was being done; this was trial by television, with Martin declared guilty even before the programme was screened.

Much discussion and argument in the house centred on whether Martin should appear on the programme or not. I felt that he should, but he was so incensed by the injustice of what was happening that he did not want to. Eventually he decided that he would, in order not to give the Cook team the chance of a 'door-stepping' scene of the kind that tends to give the impression of guilt. The interview was to be recorded on a Sunday, and I drove down to give Martin what little support I could. Martin had gathered a team around him which included Fran Morrison, a former television reporter, Lindsay Moffat, a solicitor, and a man called John Stoneborough who had previously worked with Roger Cook.

The morale of the Pond House team, which included Barry Simpson, who runs the Racing Club, Carol and me, was high as the final outlines of the questions to be put were passed between the solicitors of the two sides. We knew there was nothing to be frightened of; though their research had gone on over a long period they had been ill-advised and had little knowledge of racing. When we entered the lounge, where the interview was to take place, I shook hands with Roger Cook because he seemed a perfectly decent man and I felt sorry for him as someone whose research team had not done their homework properly: if they had, he would not have needed to be there.

The atmosphere in the room was tense as Cook followed a line of questioning that was trying to prove that Martin was running horses that were unfit to race. At times one or another of the Pond House team chuckled at the questions and Martin's replies that embarrassed his interrogator. For example, Cook had a go at Martin for winning small races, and asked, 'Perhaps you should try winning one of the really big ones; you've not won a Gold Cup or at Aintree, have you?'

Martin's reply was: 'I was leading trainer at Cheltenham and at Aintree this year.'

Martin knows his business inside out; he photographs and has reports written on every horse as it enters and leaves the yard. Every possible detail is logged. The only time he showed any uncertainty was when Roger Cook asked him about the number of horses that returned to the yard from previous seasons, saying, 'You don't have any horses in training now that you had in 1986, do you?' Martin did not have the figures in front of him to dispute the proposition. At the end of the interview, Roger Cook seemed upset and made a hasty exit.

The programme went out eight days later, while I was travelling home from racing at Devon and Exeter. It was horrible to feel that at that very moment an assassination job was being done on a friend's working methods and personal character. When I eventually saw the programme I felt upset by it, disturbed by the use of innuendo and half-truth in 'evidence' against Martin. It seemed to me that to anyone not knowing the real facts the yard could come across in a bad light.

Fortunately, those who knew more about Martin, and those who refused to be browbeaten by a loaded presentation, rallied round, and Martin received much support from fellow racing professionals. But of the many letters and articles that appeared in print, the one I liked best was not from an 'insider'. It appeared in the *Somerset County Gazette* of 10 May 1991:

Dear Sir

I write with reference to the Cook Report on ITV on Monday, the programme about Martin Pipe, the National Hunt racing trainer.

I wish to state that I have no connection with, nor knowledge of, the racing industry. I am in a unique position in that NO outsider sees Martin Pipe's horses for so long, and so often. You see, I drive the Hemyock to Taunton shuttle bus, which passes within yards of Pond House (Martin Pipe's stable). I pass there 12 to 14 times a day, and I see all of his horses on the road. I am within a yard of these beautiful animals, and their work-riders.

The evidence for the smear campaign against Martin Pipe was weak and ludicrous, to put it mildly. The evidence of my own eyes, day, day out, is that the animals were in supreme condition and the boys and girls that ride them are obviously content and happy.

It seems to me that if one comes from London, or Liverpool, or one of these so-called 'in places', genius is acknowledged – but here in beautiful Somerset or Devon, to be successful, kind and modest – which is what the whole of the West Country know Martin Pipe to be – then it's the hatchet job, the smears, the innuendo, the lies. I hope I echo the sentiments of all good people here in the West Country.

I send Mr Pipe, his family, his staff, his jockeys and, yes, his horses, my respect and my admiration.

Peter Peake

The programme did highlight one problem that needs to be addressed, namely the running of horses on hard ground. But what I learnt most from it was to question any investigative report that I saw on television and to be suspicious of the programme-makers' motives; are they concerned with telling the truth, or with getting high viewing figures?

The transmission of the programme was by no means the end

of the affair; Martin was informed that the *Cook Report* was intending to look into developments since it went out. We were told that they were going to highlight an incident at Huntingdon on 10 May when a horse had unfortunately broken down, reported thus by Mick Connaughton of the *Sporting Life*: 'Nottage broke down on his near fore approaching the final flight, and Peter Scudamore was left the unenviable task of driving out an injured horse.' We were informed that the equine vet John Williams, who had appeared on the original *Cook Report* programme, was going to identify the moment the horse broke down.

Memory can be a funny thing, but I was sure that the injury had not occurred until a stride or two before the winning post, when it was too late to pull up before the line had been passed. I studied the film with Martin and it is clear that the horse did indeed not break down until the point I identified. The incident emphasized, though, that we were the ones under the microscope, and were assumed to be blameworthy whenever a horse was injured.

I was not to finish the season without further injury to myself. I fell on Tri Folene on her first run over fences at Taunton, banging the wrist that had been operated on the previous season hard into the ground. I carried on to the end of the season before the discomfort persuaded me to get it examined by the surgeon who had performed the original operation, and his X-rays showed that I had a hairline fracture along the outside wrist bone. I had been very fortunate to have kept riding for the final days of the season.

The numbers were there again, after all our struggles: my seventh title with 141 winners and Martin's third consecutive trainers' title with a record 230 winners. Particularly satisfying was the healthy figure of nineteen winners for the thriving new Grange Hill Partnership. But I was not sorry to see this season end. It had been a long, hard slog of relentless travelling and repeated injury, crowned with the unwarranted intrusion of ill-informed 'investigators'. The scars will remain.

## Chapter Fourteen

# CLASS ACTS

—————————►◄•————————

By August 1991 I was fit and refreshed after the troubles of the previous year and ready to go again. My riding arrangements were going to be a bit different this year, as I had had a call from Charlie Brooks to say that Graham Bradley was now to be first jockey at Uplands. He said this decision had been made because of my increasing lack of availability to him, which to an extent I understood; but on the other hand, the reason I had been unavailable for quite a lot of the previous season was that I had broken my leg coming off one of his horses.

In fact this change dovetailed quite well with developments at home. The Grange Hill yard was now big enough to be considered a second string to Pond House, and Nigel and I decided that I would share the rides with Carl Llewellyn, whom we both thought an excellent rider who was just missing out on the big winners.

The outlook for Martin's stable was also exciting. Our early season star this year was to be The Blue Boy, another in the sequence of horses illustrating Martin's knack for selecting three-year-olds off the Flat and after extensive schooling turning them into multiple winners not only on the little country tracks but at Cheltenham level – horses such as Melendez, Liadett and Hopscotch. This year, too, there was a real Gold Cup hope in Carvill's Hill, sent over from Ireland for Martin to train. At least if I was not going to be riding for Charlie any more there would be no division of loyalties with the programme of Celtic Shot.

In August I was invited to France to ride at Clairefontaine, the jumping equivalent of nearby Deauville, renowned for its sixteen days of Flat racing in August. Surrounded by Normandy-style buildings adorned with brightly coloured flowerbeds and hanging baskets, Clairefontaine is one of the most attractive jumping courses I have ever visited. The track is flat, the late summer ground well watered, and the numerous obstacles are a smaller version of the typical French fences, coming at you quickly as the route twists and turns, placing a premium on quick, accurate jumping. This is not a provincial course like Senonnes, where I had had such an enjoyable time earlier this summer; the facilities for the public are quite superb, and the weighing room the equal of any to be found in Great Britain.

I was here to ride Silver Word for Philippe Lamotte d'Argy and won a race on him, enjoying his fast and precise jumping; I returned later in the month to ride him in his victory in the Grand Steeplechase de Deauville. Silver Word was an exceptionally good exponent of the art of French steeplechasing and gave me an appetite for it; but though I was in fact asked to go back on several more occasions, my commitments to my home yards prevented me from doing so. I did have one further ride on Silver Word, at Auteuil, but the softer ground, bigger fences and galloping track did not suit him so well, and he failed to get the trip.

It had become a great ambition for Martin to train all the winners on a day's racecard, a feat no trainer – or, indeed, jockey – had ever achieved. The idea of preparing runners for a clean sweep through the card had been under consideration for some time, and in Devon this August we were going to make an attempt. It sounds as if it shouldn't be that difficult at a small meeting with moderate horses, but I knew perfectly well that even under such conditions it can often be hard enough to ride one winner, let alone six.

My rides were Nordic's Delight, Arabian Sultan, Refute, Takemethere, The Blue Boy and Ever Smile. The first five came home as planned and the atmosphere in the crowd at the Devon course was electric as I went for the big six. Unfortunately, it was not to be; but even though we were a bit deflated at the actual moment, our disappointment soon evaporated into delight – to have five winners out of six runners and take all six home safe and sound is, after all, quite a feat for one day's racing. Some people said to me that it must have been gutting to lose the last race, but in fact I think it would have been worse to have lost the first one and then won the other five. At least as we came up the final straight of the final race we were still in with a chance of that little piece of history.

Martin and I were not the only ones to be amassing multiple

winners at a single meeting that autumn. On Saturday 5 October Peter Niven rode five winners at Kelso, and on the same day Nigel had his first four-timer as a trainer when Tipping Tim, Gulsha, Captain Dibble and Grange Brake all won at Uttoxeter. As for me, I had gone to ride at Chepstow in the Timeform Handicap Hurdle, where I fell at the third last and the horse rolled on top of me. As usual, I didn't realize that any damage had been done and went out to ride in the next on Martin's Miss Bobby Bennett. I did notice then, however, that my shoulder was very sore and I was unable to lift my right arm very high. Luckily, I did not have any more rides booked until Thursday of the following week, but even then, although I continued to ride some winners, the soreness in my shoulder was getting worse rather than better. On returning from a meeting at Devon and Exeter I went to see a specialist who confirmed after taking some X-rays that I had two small cracks in the collar-bone. He told me to take nine days off, but when I told him I had done it nine days ago he said I might as well go on riding.

Then, in a three-mile novice chase at Towcester, I was brought down at the first and fell on my shoulder, giving it a severe jolt. I felt the bone move and thought I had broken it

*My second Hennessy. Chatam flies the last on his way to victory in the 1991 running* (GERRY CRANHAM)

again, so I cancelled all my rides for the next day and went off once more to see Mary Bromiley. I was feeling really fed up at the prospect of missing the next three weeks' racing at a vital point of the season, with the big autumn races coming up. But the diagnosis was not so bad as I had feared. Mary told me that I could not possibly have broken the bone because I had too much movement in the arm for that to be the case; further X-rays showed that the earlier break had calcified and my latest fall had shifted the callus. Though this was painful for a time, thankfully it did not stop me riding for more than a day, and I was soon able to ring Martin and tell him I would be back aboard his runners. This was, in fact, the last serious injury I was to receive race-riding.

If that injury had been more serious I would have missed a great treble when Sabin Du Loir won three early autumn Pattern races. First, at Wincanton, he broke the track record for two miles five furlongs when beating Desert Orchid. Then at Devon and Exeter on 5 November he gave a faultless display of galloping and jumping to beat Waterloo Boy, to whom he was giving six pounds, in the Grade 2 Plymouth Gin Holden Chase – in the process taking his career winnings to date over £200,000. And finally in this brilliant run he took on Desert Orchid again at Huntingdon. The crowds who had flocked into the little course to see Dessie witnessed a great race, but Sabin came out on top once more to win by four lengths.

Sabin, though he made the occasional mistake, was on his day as good a horse as you could ever wish to ride. His career total of wins was now twenty and the duel with Desert Orchid was 4–1 in Sabin's favour, but this wonderful horse never won the championship race his courage and ability deserved.

This was the first season in which I had a number of top-class horses available for me to ride at one time. The next to reappear was Granville Again, who opened his Champion Hurdle campaign with an effortless win in the Sport of Kings Hurdle at Leopardstown. This victory also marked the start of his pursuit of the $100,000 bonus on offer to the horse who could win all three European legs of the Sport of Kings Challenge series, one of the American legs of which Bokaro had won the previous year. In the next leg at Cheltenham Granville beat Tyrone Bridge three-quarters of a length, arriving at the last going very easily but not doing much in front when I shook him up. Every time I rode this very talented horse I learnt something new and different about his quirks. He finally won the bonus at Chepstow with a much more impressive victory, again over Tyrone Bridge. This time I rode him with more confidence and kept him on the bridle longer; he is one of those horses who travels better while you are sitting still on him.

Carvill's Hill and Chatam were our two chasing giants, in both stature and ability. Neither had been free of jumping problems; it was Chatam who had given me that painful buttock injury when unseating me at Newbury the previous spring, but since then he had had an intensive schooling programme and in November 1991 we were back at Newbury for the Hennessy Gold Cup.

When I walked into the paddock to get my riding instructions and leg-up from Martin, he was as usual studying the other runners and noting details about the opposition on his racecard – what extras the horse was carrying, whether it looked fit, even down to how it was plated. This was Chatam's first run of the season, but we knew he was fit: he was only one kilo heavier than when he won at Cheltenham in March.

Big though he is, Chatam is a bit of a coward until he gets warmed up, and in the parade ring he was slightly on edge, throwing his head forward and pulling the reins out of my hands. Down at the start, I lined up towards the inside; Newbury is a left-handed track and, like Run For Free, Chatam has a habit of jumping left-handed. If you ride this type of horse down the wing of the fence they very often keep straighter. We set off at a good gallop; I double-checked the pace that had been set by watching the horses in front of me, knowing their form and ability. The pace was not troubling Chatam and he was travelling well enough, but with him I was always aware that he could make a blunder at any stage of the race. After we had gone about a mile, Mark Pitman, on the joint favourite Garrison Savannah, began to talk to me, saying he was not going well and was making mistakes. Sometimes I would talk during a race, but on this occasion I was concentrating too hard to reply.

As I turned down the back straight I asked Chatam to quicken up and kept him jumping out of my hand; by the time we turned for home I was beginning to look for a run down the inside of Bruce Dowling – whom I had put through the wing when he had tried to come up my inside on this very course a couple of years back. Today the gap appeared and Chatam took the lead at the third last. I knew now that if he stood up we would win.

Martin told me afterwards that as he and Chester were watching the race together, Chester was screaming as Chatam landed over the third last, 'He's won! He's won!' and Martin replied,

'He'd won when we'd schooled him earlier in the week.'

He also won at the line.

Chatam did run once more that season, again at his favourite track, Newbury, but his racing career has since been hampered by a problem with splints on his forelegs – bony growths that can be painful to the horse and make him lame.

Our other giant, Carvill's Hill, had come to us with an illustrious but troubled history. He had been trained in Ireland by Jim Dreaper, but there had been problems keeping him sound, and eventually Paul Green, the majority owner, decided to send him to Martin to see if he could sort him out.

There was great excitement when Carvill's arrived in the yard, and I went with Martin to check him over. Mary Bromiley, as talented with horses as with humans, examined him and found the source of the back problem to be located in the sacro-iliac joint on the left side of his pelvis. After giving the horse an injection into the joint to enable him to use the muscles on that side without pain, she then constructed a treatment programme to build up the muscles on the near-side quarter, which had wasted as a result of the injury. The programme included elements such as the fitting of a heavy shoe on the near hind that would make the muscles on that side work harder, and trotting exercise in circles in the indoor school.

This special programme was carried on at the same time as normal exercise. I had the unenviable task of riding this huge horse in his first canter up the all-weather track – I say 'unenviable' because Martin is always very tense in such circumstances in case anything goes wrong, in other words, in case I fall off. Again, when we came to give the horse his first jump over a fence I was worried about him getting loose. I had seen him jump in Ireland and fall at Gowran Park on his last run. While still trying to compensate for the pelvic injury, Carvill's tended to jump left-handed – a trait I was familiar with in Run For Free and Chatam. But when schooling him I found that he was able to stand off his fences or fiddle them, and he seemed happy jumping, so I had a lot of confidence in him when we came out for our first race of the season in the Rehearsal Chase at Chepstow.

I was lucky to get as far as the starting gate for the big race. Riding The Leggett earlier that day, I was unseated at the stands bend when the horse jinked suddenly and ran out. I was very pleased to get up off the floor in one piece. Martin was not totally happy that Carvill's was really fit for this first run, and he had a good-class field to beat – including two other Pond House runners, Aquilifer and Bonanza Boy. I had intended to drop him in a little bit over the first few fences, but his long stride soon

*Run For Free usually made one blunder in a race. In this novices' chase at Newton Abbot in February 1992, he waited until the second last to produce his corker – but we survived and won (GERRY CRANHAM)*

took him to the front, where, despite a challenge from Martin Foster on Aquilifer, he jumped well to win by ten lengths.

Having more than one runner from his own yard in a race puts a trainer in a difficult position because people will tend to accuse him of favouring one horse over another. Sometimes there is no choice, however; if the race conditions suit more than one horse, they should both have their chance, and such was the case on this day with all three of the Pond House runners. There are those, too, who will suggest that a jockey will not try to beat another runner from the same yard, whereas in fact nothing could be further from the truth: it is considered a feather in the jockey's cap if he can do so. The same applies when a jockey takes an outside ride; far from not being sufficiently competitive against a horse from his 'home' yard, he is more likely to want to beat it to justify his own choice. I have heard punters saying that so-and-so let another horse win because he was riding against his own stable: this is complete nonsense.

Some outsiders thought that I had a clash of interests now that I was riding for both Martin and Nigel, but it just doesn't work like that. I wanted to prove my worth to both yards and whenever I was opposing a horse belonging to the other stable, I wanted to beat it.

Not for one minute do I believe that racing is whiter than white; however, the stories about jockeys stopping horses from winning for financial gain are grossly exaggerated. Never once was I approached by anyone who wanted me to stop a horse; maybe it did happen before my time, but my father told me that it only ever once happened to him, so that is just one approach in over thirty years of riding between us. In my eyes this makes racing a straight sport. In any case, I would have thought it virtually impossible to get away with stopping a horse in modern jump racing, with connections, Stewards and everyone else having access to films of the race from all angles taken from points all round the racecourse.

Jockeys do ride bad races: they come from too far behind, get boxed in, get a bad start – and all these errors can be misconstrued as deliberately not trying. In fact, I think the biggest problem with consistency of form is fitness: many trainers run their horses when they are not fully fit, and it is completely unfair to the horse for a jockey to push it hard in these circumstances. And it is impossible to police the fitness of runners, because horses can show marked improvement in form for many reasons – the going, their well-being, the jockey's riding tactics and so on. The present handicap system does, however, worry me, as it is not conducive to getting horses to do their best, and horses seem to be handicapped on the basis not only of ability but also of who trains them. I have seen horses leave Martin's yard and drop down the weights a stone within a very short time.

Wherever I travel, in this country or abroad, someone will say to me that racing is crooked; but I have seen very little evidence of it.

The next big test for Carvill's Hill was the Coral Welsh National, which he won by twenty lengths. Many newspapers reported this as an 'awesome display'; but riding him it did not really feel like that. He set off in front at a tremendous pace down the very long run to the first fence; with him again I liked to keep a constant contact with his head, which is easier at the beginning of a race when he is fresh and taking a good hold of the bridle. With this contact established on a short rein I was able to hold him into his fences. I could feel when he was going to make a mistake a long way from the fence: approaching on the wrong stride, he was unable to adjust it and so ran into the bottom of the fence and hopped over. He did this with me on the first circuit, and then coming past the stands well clear he dropped the bridle. I think he thought he only had one circuit to do. At the time I wasn't sure of this, though, and was hoping that we were not now going to get beaten through having gone off so fast. Along the back straight I sat still on him, which allowed the pursuing pack to close up, but as he ran round the long final turn into the straight with five fences to jump he picked up again and, despite being a little awkward at the last, galloped relentlessly to the line.

With Carvill's Hill's next outing scheduled for the Irish Gold Cup at Leopardstown in February, Martin relaunched another stable star on 3 January when Miinnehoma, a good novice hurdler two seasons previously, ran at Newton Abbot. By now the pressures of the season were beginning to get to Martin. His burning desire to do well, and the frustrations that go with not being able to work a miracle with every single horse that comes into the yard, put him under immense stress. Very few people have the appetite for work that he does. Late at night he can be seen still working in the office or leading a horse in from the horse-walker on his bicycle (he cycles everywhere round the yard). He has an excellent staff and works to an efficient, well-oiled system, but does not like to delegate and so all the decision-making ends up with him, with the constant pressure of phone call after phone call to be taken and made.

In particular, only Martin can decide where to run his horses, a matter on which the press at times find him hard to deal with. This is not intentional secretiveness on his part; it is just that he will not run horses in races that he does not consider suitable for them, and this means taking into account a string of variables that affect the horse's chances, including the state of the ground and what else is running. He will be making decisions on whether horses run or not right up to final declaration time – in the winter, 10.30 a.m. on the day before the race – and hates to be disturbed by the phone in the last half-hour before this deadline.

When the stress began to affect Martin he became more tense and dogmatic. He would leave me in no doubt about the importance of nothing going wrong with a horse and would tell me that it could not get beaten – a statement I hate to make, and don't much like to hear. Miinnehoma's victory at Newton Abbot therefore came as a relief rather than as a moment to savour. He jumped the fourth last rather slowly, and as Richard Dunwoody on Calabrese came by me and led to the second last I could see Martin's face in my mind's eye – but luckily the horse responded to my urgings and won. That evening Martin went away on a very necessary holiday.

At least all the work and pressures were bringing their rewards. Martin's 100th winner of the season came on 15 January and mine followed a fortnight later on Run For Free, who was having his first run over fences at Lingfield. I was no longer riding the outsiders that I had in the past, partly by choice; I felt I had a responsibility to the good horses in the yard to stay sound to ride them, especially given my injury record of the previous season. I still had the plate in my leg, though I no longer wore the plastic support, and even if you are not thinking about it the knowledge that it is there is in the back of your mind.

Also, riding for Martin had spoilt me; we listened to each other's opinions, he was direct in the orders he gave me, and he stood by me with owners. So many trainers I had ridden for lacked his thorough knowledge of racing and, unable to assess either horse or race accurately, could not give correct riding instructions. I was even becoming a little cynical, knowing sometimes when I got off a horse that if Martin had trained it I would probably have won. Moreover, I was no longer prepared to ride a no-hoper over the last three fences as if there were no tomorrow – something you must go on doing if you want outside rides.

An owner–trainer team for whom it was always a pleasure to ride was Jack Joseph and the Devon yard run by Jimmy Frost and his mother. I have a great admiration for Jimmy, a rider who has made the most of limited opportunities and who became a good friend of mine both in and out of the weighing room. Jack I first came across when riding Life Guard, trained by David Elsworth, to win for him at Wincanton. Jack is a permit-holder himself but also has horses with other yards, most of them with the Frosts. Jimmy rode the majority of his horses and I stepped in when he was not available.

Jack asked me to ride Combermere for him in the Charterhouse Mercantile Chase at Ascot because Jimmy could not do the weight. Much to his disgust, the race was taking place on the same day that he was going into hospital for a hip replacement operation, and he wouldn't be able to watch the race because he would be in the operating theatre. This was probably just as well, as if he had watched the race he would have needed his heart operated on too. Combermere was just starting his run going to the second last when Pendennis fell in front of him, necessitating a drastic swerve to avoid being brought down. This looked as if it had put paid to any chance we might have had, but the tenacious little horse got up in the last stride to win a short head. Usually I hated visiting people in hospital, but this made going to see Jack a lot easier; and as I entered the hospital and asked for directions to his room, the nurse told me that his first question on waking up had been 'What happened at Ascot?'

The next stop in Carvill's Hill's preparation for the Gold Cup was Leopardstown for the Hennessy Cognac Gold Cup, a race in which he had previously finished first and second. Whenever I was riding in Ireland I would try to fly out the night before in case fog caused any delay in taking off or landing, especially at this time of year. So, after racing at Chepstow on the Saturday, where Run For Free won his third race over fences, Martin, Carol, Maz and I caught a plane from Heathrow to Dublin. Not lacking Irish contacts, we were all able to stay with friends overnight and met up the following morning at the races. Here we were greeted with the news that Carvill's had not travelled very well and had banged his head on the top of the plane while loading, giving himself a nosebleed. The whole team was obviously very concerned, and Martin seriously considered not running the horse; but after a thorough inspection and confirmation from the vet that he was OK it was decided to go ahead.

I walked the track, remembering my error on Lastofthebrownies and taking particular note of the right route. I noticed that there was now a set of rails leading from the second last to the home turn and was surprised not to see a plaque pinned to them commemorating my awful mistake. The fences in Ireland vary more from course to course than they do in this country, but the Leopardstown fences were built in a similar style to those at Cheltenham. There are no water jumps; the ditches (called 'the regulation') are constructed differently on the take-off, with a lower ditch board, and the gorse fronting the fence fills more of the ditch. I do not believe that has much effect, but the lower board is, in my view, better; the high ditch boards at Cheltenham can sometimes catch a horse out if he leaves his hind legs behind.

*One of the finest finishes of the 1992 Cheltenham Festival. I have Miinnehoma half a length clear of Bradbury Star (Declan Murphy) at the last, and the margin at the line was the same* (GERRY CRANHAM)

The Irish jockeys were very helpful to me, and I tried to return the compliment when they rode in England. However, among themselves they seemed even more competitive and harder than we were, and you would often see some quite rough scrimmaging for position on the inside. The start was also different: in general, the horses were not brought to a standstill behind the starting gate before they were let go, and English jockeys were often caught out by this. It was not a bias towards the Irish by the Starter, simply that they always tended to let the field go more quickly.

I took a ride in the first race, a twenty-eight runner novice hurdle, which seemed rather a stupid thing to do with Carvill's Hill running later in the afternoon. As there is less racing in Ireland there are fewer opportunities for trainers to run their horses, so the fields tend to fill up more. It would be the exception rather than the rule to have a field of this size in England. I had been warned by Victor Bowens, his trainer, that Commercial Artist often ran into trouble in a race, which can happen with a horse that lacks a turn of foot, so, unusually for me, I chose to go down the middle, where I hoped to find a bit more room; if you can avoid gaps closing in front of you, you are more likely to be able to hold the position you want.

Leopardstown is a deceptive course, a lot stiffer to ride than it looks. The oval track is just under two miles round, with a long back straight that can tempt inexperienced jockeys into starting to race too soon: the final furlong has a rise to it that is very tiring for the horses. Commercial Artist seemed to be going nowhere when I turned towards the last hurdle upsides in front; then Mark Dwyer to my inside jumped into my horse's quarters, pushing his front across and knocking my stick out of my hand. But in a very tight finish I won by a short head from the second horse, with the third the same distance behind. After a Stewards' Inquiry I was allowed to keep the race.

In the chase I got the start wrong: the Starter let the field go from well behind the tape, and instead of getting Carvill's well up into the bridle I let go of his head and let him run. He flew the first two fences but made an almighty blunder at the third which would have had a smaller horse on the floor. From then on, however, I had him back on the bridle and his jumping was faultless; the going was faster than he supposedly liked it, but it often happens that the extra bounce horses get from good ground helps them to jump better. He came home to win by fifteen lengths, leaving us all very confident of his chances in the Gold Cup. Given reasonable luck, I felt sure he would win.

The Irish air must have done me good; at Fontwell the day after Leopardstown, I rode three winners. Then on the Thursday I had my second win that season on Fidway, Steve Smith Eccles, his regular pilot, being sidelined with a broken ankle. I had learnt how to ride Fidway both from the race on him when we were defeated and from watching him run with other jockeys on board, and had held him up to win at Sandown. In the Kingwell Hurdle at Wincanton he gave me a great ride which I remember particularly well. On the last turn, when the horses in front began to quicken, I took a pull at him, and after a few strides he drew confidence from this and ran back to the quarters of the leaders, enabling me to sit still on him before putting him in front halfway up the run-in. Earlier on in my career I might not have won this race, as in those days to get him on the bridle I would have given him a slap and a kick, which doesn't work with Fidway. Now I was riding with much more confidence – and riding to benefit the horse, not to please the watchers in the stands.

On 3 March I rode my 1,500th career winner, on the Pipe/Scudamore Racing Club's Slavi, beating Nigel's horse Gaelstrom into second place. A week later we were in the thick of the Cheltenham Festival once more.

All the publicity directed at the Pipe runners was focusing on Granville Again and Carvill's Hill, but Martin insisted that his banker for the meeting was Miinnehoma, owned by the comedian Freddie Starr. After the *Cook Report*, Freddie said that when he was staying with the Pipes the vet would take an armful of blood from him and put it into the horses: 'It didn't make them run any faster but they told great jokes!' For myself, I was not sure whether Miinnehoma or Run For Free was the better horse, but eventually plumped for Miinnehoma in the Sun Alliance Novices' Chase.

On the Tuesday everything went wrong. In the first I was well beaten. In the second, the Arkle Chase, I rode Tinryland for Nicky Henderson, who told me that the horse did not want to be in front for too long and that on his previous win at Kempton he had run freely with Jamie Osborne over the first few fences. Having seen from the form book that his last win had been over two miles four furlongs, I had originally planned to jump him off with the pace; but following my riding orders I set off steadily. The horse was always off the bridle and was soon in arrears, but he ran on well to finish second behind Jamie on Oliver Sherwood's Young Pokey.

When I came into the unsaddling enclosure none of the Henderson connections would speak to me. I felt a bit miffed at this as I had ridden according to the trainer's instructions, and even more miffed when I learnt that Mrs Henderson had told Nigel that I never rode novice chase winners anyway, implying that I did not give horses a ride. This is not the sort of gossip that one wants to have going round the racecourses.

In the Champion Hurdle Granville Again was bidding for his fifth win off the reel and going very well when we fell at the second last. Whether we would have won I will never know, but at the time I could not have been happier with the position we were in. The winner was Royal Gait, ridden by Graham McCourt and trained by James Fanshawe, who had been assistant trainer to David Nicholson when I was riding there. While I was delighted for him, I was a bit worried that my injury problems had come back to plague me: a horse from behind Granville had stood on my hand, and with my Gold Cup ride on Carvill's still to come the possibility that I might have broken it hardly bore thinking about.

Wednesday brought better fortunes, starting with being able to ride: the bones in my hand were not broken and ice packs had taken the swelling down. Then Martin's banker, Miinnehoma, won the Sun Alliance Novices' Chase by half a length from Bradbury Star. It was a good prelude to Gold Cup day.

I think it was a great relief to Martin, after all the pressure and the media preoccupation with Carvill's Hill, that the horse arrived sound at the track. He was to have seven rivals, among them Golden Freeze, who, so the papers said, was being run by Mrs Pitman to take on Carvill's in the early stages of the race. This didn't worry me as Martin Foster on Aquilifer had done just that at Chepstow, and I would have been quite content to sit in behind any horse that wanted to take us on.

As we circled at the start the pre-race nerves ebbed away, as they always do once the business is about to begin. It became obvious that Michael Bowlby on Golden Freeze was indeed going to take us on early in the race, and I set off on his outside, so that he could not trap me on the rails. As the tapes went up I let

Carvill's run to the first to try to dominate the race from the outset, and being just in front of Golden Freeze I tried to intimidate him by squeezing him up on the inside, the idea being that this would make Michael leave us alone in front. He was having none of this and held his ground to the first fence, which Carvill's got completely wrong, all but falling. That, I thought, should make him concentrate.

After this blunder I was perfectly happy to let Golden Freeze go on; but he reined back to try to sit upsides me again, then as soon as I went upsides him he raced along with me. As we turned the bend to face the second ditch up the hill I moved up Michael's inside to go to the front again, and as I did so he turned to me and said, 'Look, I didn't want to do this. I hope you win,' a remark I took as demonstrating the camaraderie and mutual respect among jump jockeys. I then concentrated on the rest of the race, and although his jumping down the hill was at times bad, as I headed out on the second circuit I thought Carvill's would win. But it was not to be; approaching the second last I was headed by Cool Ground, The Fellow and Docklands Express, and after jumping the final fence a tired horse Carvill's came home last of the five finishers.

I was disappointed; but the horse and I had done our best and in the circumstances of the day we were not good enough. (I was actually much more disappointed about Granville Again's fall in the Champion Hurdle; he, I felt, had been the really unlucky one.) Immediately after the race a Stewards' Inquiry was announced to look into Carvill's Hill's running. Martin and I attended but at the time could throw no real light on his poor performance. Later we discovered that he had both pulled muscles in his chest and incurred a tendon injury, and was likely to be off the course for some time; and his bad jumping probably had more to do with these problems than with any tactics employed by Golden Freeze's connections.

None the less, I felt very cross about those tactics. I bore no grudge against Michael Bowlby, who was just doing his job, but I did have a go at Mark Pitman the next day. He denied all knowledge of what riding tactics were to be used, and on the Saturday I apologized to him. In the past, having ridden for Mrs Pitman, I had respected her for her courage and her understanding of horses, but the 1992 Gold Cup and the events that followed it destroyed that respect. I even read in the newspapers that Michael Bowlby was taking legal advice over my reporting of the comment he made in the race, though I never heard anything about it. A few weeks later I spoke to him again, at Ascot, and said, 'We both know what you said, and life's too short to go around avoiding each other.' We have never mentioned the subject since.

To suggest that Golden Freeze was a genuine pacemaker was stretching both logic and common sense somewhat. It was also suggested that I had employed the same tactics on Beau Ranger in the 1987 King George VI Chase, and this was simply ludicrous. I didn't want to sit upsides Desert Orchid; I wanted to make the running, as did Cybrandian. That's why we all went off so fast. The Jockey Club Disciplinary Committee held an inquiry to determine whether Michael Bowlby had breached the Rules of Racing by not allowing Golden Freeze to run on his merits, and I was called to give evidence. Eventually it was decided that no breach had occurred.

The racing programme continued its annual progress, and some time before the Jockey Club announced the result of its deliberations we were all up at Aintree again for the Grand National meeting. I rode one winner here on Cyphrate and had a great ride in the National on Docklands Express to finish fourth behind Party Politics and Carl Llewellyn – not a bad win for a

*Thumbs up: Martin Pipe and I in the unsaddling enclosure at Stratford in May 1992 after Woodland Minstrel had become our 150th – and final – winner together that season* (BERNARD PARKIN)

jockey whom I had said couldn't ride big winners. Carl had in fact already won a big winner for Nigel when Tipping Tim took the Ritz Club Handicap Chase on Gold Cup day to give the Grange Hill yard its first Festival win – and in doing so gave us a huge amount of pleasure to mitigate the frustration and disappointment of that day.

Not that Aintree was free from controversy this year. In the past, the fences on the Mildmay course – normal steeplechase fences rather than the huge hawthorn and spruce obstacles on the National course – had been quite soft on the top, allowing horses to brush through the upper few inches. This year, however, they had been squared off through the top and widened at the base, causing a lot of falls for the novices and problems for other horses. The meeting was marred by protests from many angry trainers and jockeys, and later in the year the Aintree executive altered the fences to make them less harsh.

The following weekend I made my now familiar trip to Ayr for the Scottish Champion Hurdle and National. I felt under a certain amount of pressure riding Granville Again on the Friday, having been beaten on him in his last two Festival races at Cheltenham, but he put up a very impressive performance to win. That evening Hywel Davies and I, along with Nigel and Cathy, stayed with former jockey Sam Morshead at his house about an hour's drive away from the track, where he is Clerk of the Course. As a lot of people travel a fair distance to Ayr for the two-day meeting, Sam organized a party on the racecourse for the Friday night, at which I celebrated Granville's win and had to be driven back to Sam's house by Hywel.

The next morning I wasn't feeling too well, but was perked up by Captain Dibble, who put up a tremendous performance for a novice in the Scottish National. He had always been a kind and honest horse and, though never very fast at home, always stayed on well up the gallops. In his first run, in a bumper at Sandown, we had two runners, the second of which was a flying machine at home. It was this flying machine that led on the bend into the straight, but failed to take the home turn and threw his jockey while jumping the hedge at the far side of the turn. Meanwhile Captain Dibble came storming up the hill to win by six lengths. Dibble won the Scottish National in similar fashion, after which Nigel insisted that I should always have a drink before I rode for him.

This year for the first time Martin took some horses to run at the Punchestown Spring Festival Meeting. This was one of the best-run meetings you could ever wish to attend, with good-quality racing and a splendid Irish festival atmosphere, and to add to the enjoyment of being there we had two winners. It was a particular pleasure to win the John Harty Memorial Race on Aquilifer; John, who had died from motor neurone disease, had always been a staunch friend and had helped to get me launched as a jockey by arranging a job for me with Jim Bolger in Ireland back in the summer of 1979.

My other victory at Punchestown, on Milford Quay, was soured by the fact that Michael Cooney, owner of the third-placed Captain Brandy, objected to me for carrying the wrong weight. The problem arose because for some reason the Turf Club officials use a different racecard from that used by the valets and general public. In the latter, the horse was down to carry the correct weight of twelve stone, whereas in the officials' card he was down to carry only eleven stone ten pounds. On 10 June I went back to Ireland with James Rogers, Milford Quay's owner, and David Pipe senior, representing Martin (who was away on one of his well-earnt holidays), to put our case. Mr Pipe did not let the fact that this was his first trip in a plane put him off his stride, and presented a brilliant defence which I felt proved beyond doubt that we had carried the correct weight. However, the Turf Club felt otherwise and we lost the race, though we did at least keep the prize money. Back in England Milford Quay won again for us, at Warwick on the day when Martin reached his fourth consecutive double century with Flying Speed.

The season ended for me, as it usually did if I managed to get that far uninjured, at Stratford. Torrential rain led to the cancellation of the final steeplechases, but Martin and I went out on a high note with a double over hurdles.

During these last weeks of the season the metal plate in my leg had been causing me some discomfort, and after a visit to John Webb it was decided that it should come out. So once racing had finished I went into hospital for the removal operation, which went very well but left me with a temporarily weakened leg. I made the most of the three weeks' recuperation period by taking Maz to Portugal for a week, after which the whole family went down to Salcombe for a holiday together.

## Chapter Fifteen

# PULLING UP

———◄►◄———

In June 1992 I was thirty-four. From the very start of my career I had felt that thirty-five was quite old enough to be racing over fences, but now that day was approaching I did not feel ready to make the decision to quit. I was still enjoying my riding, and still keen to win the big races – especially the Gold Cup and the Grand National. On the other hand, I had always looked at race-riding as a calculated risk, and part of the calculation is knowing when to stop. Better to retire one ride too early than one ride too late. Or, as Steve Smith Eccles put it with characteristic bluntness, 'The only heroes are dead heroes.'

A jockey's life isn't so bad now; there have been vast improvements in safety and welfare since my father's time in the saddle, notably through the Jockeys' Association of Great Britain, a body dedicated to looking after the interests of both Flat and National Hunt jockeys throughout the country.

One area in which the Association has been very active is that of pension rights and insurance. It lobbied Parliament to lower the age at which jockeys could claim on the pension fund to which they have contributed, and now National Hunt riders may claim their pensions at thirty-five, Flat jockeys at forty-five. Each year, 0.06 per cent of prize money is put into the fund, and each jockey is given units according to the number of rides he or she has each season. In 1993 the value of these amounted to about £300,000, bringing the total value of the pension fund to £2.2 million. Some jockeys also take out personal insurance policies to cover them in case of injury.

There is also the Professional Riders' Insurance Scheme (PRIS), a fund to which owners contribute every time they pay for a jockey to ride; from this fund payments are made to a jockey, for a limited period of up to seventy-eight weeks, when he or she cannot ride in races because of injury. This scheme is often confused with the Injured Jockeys' Fund, a charitable organization set up to help jockeys past and present who are not entitled to claim under the PRIS and who are in need of help for an indefinite period – the Fund is still looking after people who were injured in the 1960s. It gains its income from donations, auctions, functions and the very popular Christmas cards and calendars produced and sold widely every year.

It is almost laughable to compare the provisions made to protect jockeys today, both physically and financially, with the situation in my father's day. When he started riding there were no body protectors and no proper helmets, only cork ones –

*One of the stalwarts of Grange Hill – the mare Gaelstrom nips over the last to land the Capital Ventures Hurdle at Cheltenham in November 1992*

marginally better than no protection at all, but they had no chinstraps and regularly came off in a fall; and it was still considered a little soft to school in one. Nor was there any limit to the number of horses in a race; he once went round Hereford in a novice chase with forty runners. He rode from 1950 to 1966 and was one of the last of the generation that included Fred Winter, Bryan Marshall and Dave Dick; his career overlapped with the next generation of Jeff King, David Mould, Josh Gifford, Stan Mellor and Terry Biddlecombe – the greats of the modern era of shorter stirrups, easier fences, limited fields and the Jockeys' Association.

My father took out two insurance policies to cover him should a fall prevent him from continuing his career as a jockey. He also had the good sense to put his earnings from racing into Prothither Farm, rather than spending them on fast cars and high life as so many sporting stars did. In the event this was just as well, because when the fall came that put an end to his riding career, neither insurer would pay up. The first one said that my father would be able to earn a living as a farmer, and so his livelihood had not been destroyed. The second took refuge in a technicality: the cheque for the premium arrived on the Tuesday morning with the 'agent' advising the Jockeys' Association on insurance, but the insurance company said that the adviser was not actually an agent, and as my father's fall occurred on the same Tuesday afternoon they denied that the money had in fact arrived when the claim arose.

Being lucky enough to ride a lot of winners throughout my career, I was encouraged by the Secretaries of the Jockeys' Association to accept the responsibility attached to being in a

*'Moonie' and I. Young Hustler winning the Postlip Chase at Cheltenham in October 1992*

prominent position as a jockey and to take a leading role in the affairs of the Association. For the last five years of my riding career I had the honour of being Joint President.

The Association has had its problems, mainly because, relying as it does on subscriptions from jockeys, it lacks the financial backing necessary to enable it to help its members in the ways it would like to. It also suffers from the apathy of those of its members who take improvements in their working conditions for granted and complain about the decisions taken by those who do bother to go to Association meetings. As so often, it is not the most prominent or the busiest who complain of having no time for such activities: Michael Caulfield, the present Secretary, told me that Lester Piggott, formerly President of the Association, rarely missed a Council meeting and always took a great interest in the proceedings.

Having seen and heard of the problems faced by my father and his contemporaries, I appreciate the advances made by the Association in safety standards and welfare. It is easy to forget that, for a jockey, life was once more difficult, and many of those riding today do not put enough effort into supporting the body that has fought for these improvements, and continues to represent their interests. There is so much more it could do, and would like to do, if it had the interest and the backing it needs: for example in re-training former jockeys for other professions.

Many of the improvements in the medical field came about through the work of the Jockey Club Chief Medical Officer, Dr Michael Allen, and a retrograde step made while I was riding was the dismissal – for what reason remains obscure – of his successor, Dr Rodney O'Donnell, in 1992. He made great progress in gaining the confidence of jockeys who were therefore coming to him with injuries to be treated instead of hiding them. A National Hunt jockey will ride as often as possible, and will take risks to do so. I have known jockeys ride with broken collarbones, cracked arms and cracked wrists because they did not trust the doctors to pass them fit to ride quickly enough. There is all the difference between ignoring an injury altogether and being kept in wraps for an excessively long period of recuperation, and as riders came to see that Rodney O'Donnell understood this, the incidence of jockeys riding while seriously unfit to do so was diminishing. All this hard-won trust was lost with his removal and his departure severely demoralized the profession.

Even if there was a thought in the back of my mind in August 1992 that this might just be my last season riding, the immediate prospects were too exciting for it to seem a very real possibility. Grange Hill was growing fast and playing a bigger part in my life; it had become a more professional set-up, with a routine that continues today. The stable is divided into two yards, about a quarter of a mile apart, one next to Mucky Cottage and one next to Nigel's farmhouse. The horses are fed at seven, and first lot pulls out at eight, with the strings from the two yards meeting up to go round the roads before doing their faster work on the all-weather gallop. Nigel, Cathy and Maz ride out at least two lots a day, and I join them when I can. Carl Llewellyn schools twice a week and has been joined by a conditional jockey, David Bridgwater, renowned for his determination.

The quality of horses was improving along with the organization of the business, and the best of them in autumn 1992 was Young Hustler, who after a successful season of hurdling showed himself to be a natural over fences the first time we schooled him. All the horses begin their jumping with tuition from Tommie Gretna, an international event trainer whose yard is just twenty minutes away from Grange Hill in the horsebox, and we regularly take horses over for him to loose school – that is, jump round an indoor arena with no rider aboard – and then afterwards go over some jumps in an outside manege with one of the jockeys up. Young Hustler (or 'Moonie', as he is known at home) went through this apprenticeship and was then schooled over the fences at home. He loved it.

Moonie is a bouncy little horse and loves to get on with his work; he likes to be in front when the string goes out for exercise. On his first run over fences at Stratford he was very keen cantering to post and I tried to calm him down and encourage him to have a bit of respect for his fences – but he would have none of it and bounded round exuberantly to finish second after tiring going to the penultimate fence. I was very pleased with him and felt sure he would win a race or two.

I had my usual great start to the season, with a superb pool of horses to ride for Martin – even with Carvill's Hill sidelined through injury – as well as Nigel's growing and improving stable. However, my nose was put out of joint as Nigel was getting more of the publicity than I, with five winners out of six runners at the early Perth two-day meeting. All the horses that won here had special significance for us. The first was Celtic Prince, 'Chester', the horse we couldn't break. Two more were owned by Jenny Mould, our neighbour at Guiting Grange – Emily's Star, whom she had bred herself, and Grange Brake, whom Nigel had bought at Doncaster because it kept neighing at him as he walked past its box. Sweet Duke had been bought by Paul Webber for the Peter Scudamore Bloodstock Company and was now owned by Andy Mavrou; and Petosku was another originally acquired by the Bloodstock Company, now owned by Fred Mills and his son Wayne. Great supporters of myself and Nigel, they had named the Petoski gelding after me, and their next purchase was dubbed Twist 'N' Scu.

Fred Mills, who likes a touch, tells the story of how when he was first married he had spent most of the money saved up for his honeymoon on the horses, and on the way to the wedding stopped off at a betting shop and had a treble with what was left over on three of Terry Biddlecombe's mounts. At the reception after the ceremony he told his wife that they couldn't go on their honeymoon because he had spent the money; then his best man appeared to tell him that Terry had won on all three – the honeymoon was on again.

On Saturday 26 September another good horse of Nigel's made its seasonal reappearance; this was Gaelstrom, who made the thirteenth winner from twenty-seven runners when winning a head in a mares-only novice hurdle at Stratford. For a filly having her second season over hurdles she did not win as easily as we hoped, but the distance was a little too short for her; also she had got very wound up before racing and through over-exuberance did not jump as well as she might have. I had been beaten on her at Worcester the previous season when really we should have won, but this turned out to be a blessing in disguise as it meant she remained a novice for the new season.

According to the morning racing papers, I had three certainties to ride at the Cheltenham October meeting, but here the luck deserted us for a while. Young Hustler's blood test showed a high white blood cell count, indicating the presence of a virus, and we were unable to run him; Dagaz, starting 5–4 favourite, broke down; and Gaelstrom over-jumped at the second last and fell when clear in the novice hurdle. Still, there was consolation for the yard when Tipping Tim won – even though I was on Tri Folene at the time. For me, this was the beginning of a fallow period, with not much luck and not many rides, that took the edge off my early season momentum and allowed Richard Dunwoody to catch me up and then overtake me in the jockeys' championship.

There was a cheerful interlude in October with one of the rare occasions when Flat and jump jockeys get together: a mixed race over hurdles, organized by Rodger Farrant. Michael Hills, Frankie Dettori, Kevin Darley, John Carroll and George Duffield rode against Brendan Powell, Richard Dunwoody, Graham McCourt, Carl Llewellyn and me. Some of the Flat boys had never ridden over hurdles before, and we went round the course hollering instructions across at them: I could hear Richard, who rode upsides Frankie for much of the way, telling him to stick his legs forward. They paid good attention to our guidance and Michael Hills went on to win easily, putting all us jump jockeys in our place.

At Cheltenham in November Tipping Tim won the Mackeson Gold Cup for Nigel and Valfinet put up a scintillating performance in the handicap hurdle which reminded me very much of Celtic Shot when he won the same race two years previously. The yard celebrated with the Cup in the Black Horse, but I was demoted to babysitting in preparation for the next day's racing – because this was to be Cheltenham's first Sunday meeting, and Morley Street versus Granville Again was to be the main event of the day. I know that Sunday racing is hard for the stable staff, but I do believe it is important for racing to take place on the days when the public can go and see it. This trial day was very well run and was organized to be a real family fun day out. My fun, however, ended when Morley Street beat me a length in a slowly run race. I saw no real excuses for Granville that day.

There was another disappointment in store for me at Chepstow, where I had had such good times, when I chose Miinnehoma in preference to Run For Free as my mount in the Rehearsal Chase. I had won on Run For Free at Haydock, beating Jodami, in his first race of the season, and the owners had expressed a wish that I should ride him whenever he ran, but in the Rehearsal Chase I chose the other as he had the better form. On the day it did not work out; Mark Perrett took the winning ride, and after going on to take the Welsh National on the horse replaced me for good. This brought thoughts of retirement closer to the surface of my mind again: if I was to bring on the horses through their novice stages and then not be able to ride them when they were producing their best, was it really worth the risk? I did not, and do not, blame Martin in any way; it is the owners who pay the bills and the owners who decide who rides their horses. I was paid no retainer to ride for Martin, so whatever decision I made I was not letting him down, and whoever he was asked to put up he was not letting me down (though he would always let me back on a horse when he could). This is one of the main reasons why he and I worked so well together.

The great thing about riding for a good yard is that sooner or later there are always winners to make you forget your troubles, and after this lean spell a treble on the rain-softened ground at Warwick really bucked me up. The first of these was Catch The Cross, an enigmatic horse that cannot be put in front until near the winning post. Riding horses like this over fences can be difficult: you don't want to move on them in the later stages of a race or they will stop trying for you, but on the other hand you need to keep up your momentum over the fences. Catch The Cross was cantering with me at the second last when I was trying to sit still and not hit the front too soon, and just to show me how well he was going he picked up out of my hands, nearly falling, but running on to win by four lengths. The second winner was also for Martin – Elite Reg, owned by Tony Lomas who backs his own judgement and claims horses in the after-race auctions, then sends them to Martin to improve. The third was Dakyns Boy, trained by Nigel, who went on to win his next two starts as well.

It was at Haydock the next day that I witnessed an incident that I believe affected my judgement in the Grand National. The second flight in the two-and-a-half-mile hurdle race was dolled off by mistake and the jockeys missed it out, believing that it was marked out thus because it was unsafe in some way. They were then all stopped after a circuit, grouped together and sent off again to complete the race, this time jumping the hurdle from which the dolls had now been removed. The race, and the result, were allowed to stand on the grounds that the dolling-off had been an accident.

How are jockeys to know why a fence has been dolled off, and what are they supposed to do if they see a fence or hurdle so marked, when approaching at speed? Earlier in the season a fence had been dolled off by mistake at Kelso and the race was declared void. Then at Wolverhampton I rode in a novice chase in which Brendan Powell fell and broke his leg on the first circuit, and the fence was dolled off because he was lying injured on the landing side. We pulled up and went back, and once Brendan was off on a stretcher the attendants removed the dolls – so off we went again, jumped the fence and completed the race. On returning to the weighing room I was informed that the race was void. No one seemed to know the rules on void races; it looked as though if you did not jump the fence the race would be declared void, but on one occasion a different interpretation seemed to be applied. This lack of consistency was a disaster waiting to happen.

The Christmas racing presented me with an awkward decision: should I ride Granville Again in the Christmas Hurdle at Kempton, or should I go to Chepstow for the Welsh National meeting, where Chatam, Run For Free and Miinnehoma were to run? In the end I came down for Granville Again; but we finished only third to Mighty Mogul, while I missed three winners at Chepstow.

In late February I went to Fairyhouse to do some work for Peugeot, who were entertaining at the racecourse, and picked up a spare ride in the novice hurdle. While I was riding round the parade ring on this horse Kieran O'Toole, a jockeys' agent, approached me to ask if I would ride a horse in the EBF Novice Chase Final later that afternoon; I was not particularly keen to do so, but after some persuading accepted the ride. My instructions from the trainer, Harry De Bromhead, were to make the running if I could, as he believed that nobody else would go on; he also said that the horse might jump the first fence slowly, having fallen in his previous race, and that I should let him do his own thing rather than get after him.

When I got down to post it became clear that several other horses were going to go on and set the pace, and we did indeed jump the first slowly; thereafter we were soon tailed off and finished last of five, fifteen lengths behind the winner, Flashing Steel. It was clear to me from the way the horse ran throughout that he had lost his confidence, and I should really have pulled up; but there were only five runners, which meant that just one faller could have meant fourth prize money for the connections I was riding for if I completed.

Far from appreciating this thought, when I came in the trainer was seething and reported me to the Stewards for 'not giving the horse a fair chance'. When both he and I confirmed his riding instructions the Stewards took no action; but I knew that the whole incident would look bad for Martin and his owners. When horses get beaten, it is easy to blame the jockey; either he was crooked or he didn't give the horse a ride, and I was beginning to get labelled as one who didn't give horses a ride. This is not a label you want to go on long with, however unjustified it is; and here was another reason for me to take a long hard look at my career.

My long-term enthusiasm was no more revived by a visit to the all-weather track at Southwell, with its new French-style hurdles, a week before the Cheltenham Festival. I had five rides, and I hated the new hurdles. The horses seemed to pay less respect to the hurdles the further they went. I left the course not wanting to go back.

I was, of course, looking forward to the Festival, though again I had those agonizing choices to make as to which horses to ride. I was making no real inroads into Richard's lead in the championship and didn't really expect to catch up. By now the feeling that this might be my last set of Festival rides was quite strong, and I was determined to make the most of them and to enjoy the meeting.

*The sweetest moment. Coming into the winner's enclosure with Granville Again after the 1993 Champion Hurdle (BERNARD PARKIN)*

Grange Hill becomes an overnight stop for many of our friends during the Cheltenham week. Steve Smith Eccles regularly stays with us, as do Paul and Fiona Webber with Nigel and Cathy. When first lot pulls out we are often joined by owners and friends who have come to watch the horses work before I make my early exit to the racecourse. Once there I sit and study the racing papers, looking at the day's form and the future runners, before spending up to an hour in the sauna if I need to do a low weight. Then at 11.45 I change and visit the hospitality tents and boxes, working for Chasing Promotions, and after that I go to the Pipe/Scudamore Racing Club hospitality chalet to have a chat with the members and discuss the day's and the next day's runners with Martin.

At least I had no decisions to make about my first ride in this meeting, Lemon's Mill being Martin's only runner in the race. Before this she had had only two runs over hurdles, the second of which, at Warwick, she had won. Now she gave the best run of her life to finish a game second to Montelado, ridden by Charlie Swan, who broke the track record in a most impressive performance. Lemon's Mill's owners were delighted with her result; it is a real pleasure to ride for owners who appreciate when a horse has run to the best of its ability, even if it hasn't won.

My next ride, by contrast, had involved a very difficult decision. It was the Champion Hurdle: should I ride Granville Again, who had not run since his defeat at Kempton, or Valfinet, who had gone from strength to strength since his early season Cheltenham win? Valfinet was a fabulous front runner and probably the most fluent jumper of a hurdle that I had ever ridden; his attitude to racing had impressed me immensely as soon as he arrived in England. He had run too freely in his early races, but had now learnt to pace himself properly. He was also owned by Alison and Frank Farrant, among the most loyal and friendly owners I have ridden for.

I think that had it not been for my recent record of choosing the wrong horses, and Martin's insistence on Granville's well-being, I might have gone for Valfinet. I had gone down to Pond Farm several times to ride work on Granville and, stupid as it sounds, my main worry was that he was working too well: I could hardly hold him, and I wondered whether racing had just become all too much for him. I had great admiration for Claire Richmond, who rode him in his work every morning; it was a big responsibility to hold him and to try to keep him settled every day.

Granville it was to be.

The weighing room at Cheltenham is normally a hive of activity, but minutes before the riders leave for the paddock for a big race it quietens down. Jockeys go through their habitual nervous routines, checking themselves in the mirror, turning their sticks over between their fingers as they sit on one of the tables in the middle of the room where the valets prepare the saddles. One or two have the annoying habit of thwacking the table with their stick, which always startled me, as I would usually be deep in thought.

As soon as I sat on Granville I was delighted to feel how relaxed he was, and as I undid his bottom plaits, out of habit and so that I would have a piece of mane to hold on to to help keep my hands down (and stop me falling off), I felt very confident. Today, I thought, he will win, a feeling I rarely had.

The horse was still relaxed when the starting gate went up; I took the middle outer route, and by the time I got to the top of the hill with three hurdles to jump he was still just lobbing along. I felt the temptation to give him a little touch down the shoulder with my stick, just to make sure the energy was still there for when we needed it, but decided that would be stupid: I had been trying to get him relaxed, so what would be the point in winding him up now? Going to the second last, Sod's Law decreed that I arrived on exactly the same stride as I had the year before; but this time we were nearer to the inside and when I asked him up – for a split second, in the only doubt of the whole race, I wondered if he would rise – he soared and I was able to put my hands down on him and cruise into the straight. When Mark Perrett on Royal Derbi joined me on my outside, Granville quickened to the line to win by a length. I was delighted – for myself, certainly, but most of all for Martin and Carol.

In the Ritz Club Chase I was on Cache Fleur – a difficult ride, because he is a slow horse that needs to be settled in to get him jumping and come with one long run, and to do this you are dependent on the others setting a good fast gallop. In this race it didn't happen and we finished fourth, with Paul Holley on Give Us A Buck riding a superb race to win a short head from Country Member. Then in the last race of the day I rode Cabochon for Jack Joseph and the Frosts (Jimmy was serving the last day of a suspension); sadly, though he started favourite he failed to get the trip and finished well down the field.

Nigel had four runners on the Wednesday and was very wound up. When in this mood he is like an unexploded bomb. Earlier in the season a horse due to start favourite had pricked its foot, and its lad rode the horse out early to see if it was sound. When they came back into the yard, Nigel asked the lad whether the horse was lame.

'He's a bit quiet,' said the lad.

Nigel exploded: 'I didn't ask you how the f— h— he was, I want to know if he's f— sound or not!'

Luckily he was (and won).

Having had a first Festival winner the previous season – Tipping Tim, who was going for the Gold Cup this year – and notched up fifty winners this season so far, it was important for the yard to maintain the momentum by having another winner here, and this pressure had been causing Nigel's tension level to rise for some time. On one occasion as the string rode out he turned to the staff and threatened to 'sack the whole lot of you if we don't have a winner at the Festival!'.

I was not riding for the yard in the first race, the Sun Alliance Novices' Hurdle, but instead for Martin on Lord Relic, who had been unbeaten in his last three races despite not being the best of jumpers. I set off in front over the first two hurdles, but was soon passed by Gaelstrom, who led until three out; then I got a run up her inside and took the lead again until landing over the last, when Gaelstrom battled her way back to beat me. It was an extremely courageous performance by the mare, but a disappointing one by Lord Relic, who had beaten her very easily when they had last met at Newbury. When asked what my feelings were when she came by me, I said truthfully that if I had to be beaten at all, I would rather it was by her than by any of the other seventeen runners; but once more I was irritated by the implication in the question that I did not try as hard against a runner from a stable I was involved with.

In the corresponding chase event I had to choose between Martin's Capability Brown and Nigel's Young Hustler. Capability Brown was undoubtedly a very good horse but preferred soft ground, and though he had won all four of his races over fences was not the greatest of jumpers. On his second run, at Haydock, he had practically been on the floor at the first before recovering to win; and at Chepstow a few days later he actually did fall three out in a nine-runner novice chase. Because he took a long time to fall, sticking a leg out to save himself, by the time I came off him he was at a standstill; I quickly grabbed the reins and, using my Pony Club games experience, was able to vault straight back on and get going again before the nearest pursuer had quite caught up to win by thirty lengths. It must have been very demoralizing for the other runners not to be able even to beat a faller.

Young Hustler – Moonie – was an altogether different proposition. Since his defeat at Stratford he had won on seven of

*My last winner at the Cheltenham Festival, March 1993. Olympian takes the last flight in the Coral Cup perfectly, and lands connections a £50,000 bonus for winning this race after taking the Imperial Cup four days earlier* (GEORGE SELWYN)

his twelve outings. These included the Great Yorkshire Handicap Chase at Doncaster and the Arlington Premier Chase Final at Newbury, but perhaps his best run was at Worcester, where he had been beaten half a length, at level weights, by The Illywhacker, who had finished third to The Fellow in the King George VI Chase at Kempton. With his excellent jumping, good form and ability to handle any ground he seemed clearly to have the better chance of the two.

Moonie still loved to bowl along in front, but with a stiff three miles ahead I was not over-anxious to make the running, especially as I knew we would go a good gallop anyway. I set off down the middle of the course, knowing that he always hung away from the direction of the track; by taking this route I would not have to pull him so sharply round the bends, which meant that he would not have the chance to lean away from me. As for my plans not to make the running, Moonie had other ideas and raced Capability Brown for the lead until my rejected mount unseated Adrian Maguire at the fourteenth, allowing Moonie to settle at last and come home three lengths clear of the rest of the field. He really is a most remarkable horse, and deserved all the accolades that were heaped on him. His achievements as a novice over fences were the greatest of any horse I have been associated with. The yard had two Festival winners, the staff kept their jobs and the Black Horse made a healthy profit: champagne and paracetamol for all.

My day was still far from over, and in the next race I rode what I considered to be my best chance of the meeting: Olympian, who was going for the £50,000 bonus on offer to the horse who could win both the Imperial Cup and the newly created Coral Cup Handicap Hurdle over two miles five furlongs. Olympian was an ideal horse for Martin: a well handicapped front runner, and an easy ride except for occasional hesitation at the start. At Sandown in the Imperial Cup – unusually for a competitive hurdle race – nothing wanted to go on, and the rest of the field lined up behind me, allowing me to walk in and get a good start. In the Coral Cup, practically every one of the twenty-one runners wanted to make it, and I could picture Martin's face as Olympian hesitated when the tapes went up. It was not until the second flight that I got to the front, but from there on I only had to steer him the right way, and he stayed on to win two and a half lengths and give me my third winner of the meeting.

I had a pleasant surprise in the fourth race of the day, the two-mile Queen Mother Champion Chase. I was riding Cyphrate, who had been impressive when winning a two-mile handicap at Ascot but had disappointed since. The real contenders seemed to be Katabatic and Waterloo Boy, old campaigners of many duels, and at the start I said to Declan Murphy, riding Deep Sensation, 'You and I will be fighting it out for third place.' I could hardly believe what was happening when Cyphrate cruised down the hill into the lead three out, then to be joined by Declan at the last and finally beaten three-quarters of a length by this artistic rider.

That second was my final placing of the meeting. I rode in the last race of the day – the only bumper in which professionals who have lost their claim can ride – and abandoned my long-held policy of not going down the inside in large fields at Cheltenham, getting 'murdered' several times as a result. I was also unplaced in the Triumph Hurdle on Her Honour – a filly who had had a somewhat notorious pre-Cheltenham campaign.

After becoming my 1,600th winner at Haydock, Her Honour was quoted as ante-post favourite for the Triumph, but then lost a bad race at Warwick on very sticky ground, where she started 5–1 on favourite. As she had run very freely with me over the first four hurdles, I sat still on her when I was headed approaching the third last to give her a breather and allow her to retrieve some energy to get her home; but though she did rally approaching the last she was beaten half a length. If I had kicked on instead of sitting quietly on her perhaps I would have won; but I believe there is an art to riding races from the front that consists of relaxing the horse and using those that challenge you to quicken up the pace. This is what I had tried to do with Her Honour, but when the others came up to me she did not take them on.

It was her next race, again ending in defeat, that was her most notorious, ending as it did in a positive dope test. Martin was not

*Maz puts one over the old man. On the day after the 1993 Cheltenham Festival, she poses with Bushfire Moon after winning the Timeform 'Friends of the Human Race' race on Comic Relief Day at Cheltenham. I went to Wolverhampton that afternoon but didn't ride a winner* (BERNARD PARKIN)

at Kempton that Friday, and as Chester gave me the leg-up in the parade ring I was pleased to notice how much more relaxed Her Honour was than she had been at Warwick. I thought the penny had dropped and that she had got the hang of how to race, so we decided to try different riding tactics, dropping her in rather than going to the front. I was still pleased with her as she cantered easily to post. But during the race she never picked the bridle up and jumped badly to finish sixth of the eleven runners.

I hadn't been hard on her once her chance had gone, and unsaddled to a barrage of abuse from some of the punters who had backed her as favourite. A routine blood test was taken from the mare and I reported to the Stewards' Inquiry that I had no explanation for her poor running. Every time I rode a horse for Martin, I wrote a report on the race; on this occasion I wrote that the running was too bad to be true. This turned out to be quite correct when a few weeks later the results of the dope test came through, showing the mare's blood to have contained ACP – a drug used to relax and calm animals, frequently used when clipping unruly horses.

Later on I was interviewed by Jockey Club Security and asked to give a statement on my recollections of the race, which I did. But I felt that the Jockey Club had handled the incident badly, especially in allowing the mare to run again at Taunton without informing the public that she had tested positive, and on the Channel Four Racing *Morning Line* programme I also expressed criticism of Roger Buffham, the Jockey Club's Head of Security, for suggesting that a stable lad was responsible for the doping.

This programme caused quite a stir in Portman Sqaure and David Pipe, Head of Public Relations for the Jockey Club (not to be confused with Martin's father), rang Andrew Franklin, producer of Channel Four Racing, to register his disapproval of remarks made by John McCririck, Jim McGrath, Lesley Graham and myself – he told Andrew that I didn't know what I was talking about. Andrew then demanded a meeting between all of those who had appeared on the programme, plus Roger Buffham and David Pipe, to address these allegations. The Jockey Club representatives did not emerge well from this meeting, at which they could produce no arguments to substantiate the accusations made against the racing team.

On leaving the meeting I had a discussion with Roger Buffham in the course of which he explained to me some of the difficulties involved in trying to catch dopers and his idea for deterring them, namely, to withdraw from the race any horse that the jockey or trainer is not happy with, giving the betting market time to re-form, so that it becomes pointless to dope a horse – a practice of which a crooked and/or illegal bookmaker is likely to be the main beneficiary. But it has to be said that I had not the slightest suspicion before the race that Her Honour had been got at; indeed, I was more pleased with her calmness than otherwise as I took her changed demeanour to indicate an improved mental attitude on her part. He also pointed out that the Jockey Club had set up a 'hotline' so that people who suspected illegal activity could make immediate contact; and, more gloomily, that doping was very difficult to prove.

In the end, then, the Triumph Hurdle, the race that should have been the climax to Her Honour's season, was more of a footnote to a not very felicitous episode. My remaining Cheltenham choices fared little better. In the BonusPrint Stayers' Hurdle I chose John Fairbrother's horse Sweet Glow over Martin's other three runners and Nigel's horse Sweet Duke, only to see Pragada and Mark Perrett finish in front of us, second to Shuil Ar Aghaidh. And in the Gold Cup, my last ride at the meeting, I chose Chatam over Rushing Wild – no longer having the option of Run For Free – only for the big horse to run an appalling race after blundering at the first.

I couldn't even ride a winner at Wolverhampton on the Friday, and on the same day Maz outshone me with a winner in a Flat race in the Comic Relief Red Nose Day for charity, riding a horse trained by Nigel.

Immediately after Cheltenham I felt that I could go on riding for another season, just picking and choosing my mounts, but on the Monday I was beaten on Woody Will, one of Oliver Sherwood's horses, in a novice chase at Uttoxeter. I knew that my heart was no longer in it. I enjoyed the big meetings, but no longer relished chasing round the smaller tracks on moderate horses. Bluntly, I realized that riding a winner at Uttoxeter was just not the most important thing in the world. I knew I could earn a living out of the saddle – after all, I had been taking care to prepare for the day when this would happen: I was already writing for a newspaper, and had the chance to write for the *Daily Mail;* there was the offer of a television job with the BBC; and there was the partnership with Nigel in the farm and the stable. I knew that it was very nearly time to get out, while I was still on top.

But there was still the National to come – one of the few remaining races I really wanted to win. As it turned out, this Grand National was to be a race I would remember more than any other. I had several choices of ride from Martin's yard: Bonanza Boy, Chatam, Riverside Boy, Roc De Prince – but I chose Captain Dibble from Nigel's stable on the basis of his second place at Sandown ahead of Rushing Wild.

The usual preliminaries over – the nervous paddock chatter, the long walk to the course and the parade – we were at last circling at the start. After what seemed an abnormally long wait we were finally called into line. The alteration of Becher's two years ago, making that feared obstacle much easier to jump on the inside, meant that more jockeys wanted to start on the inside and that in turn meant that there was very little room to be found in the line-up and the horses pushed closer and closer to the gate. Twice I took up position next to John White on Esha Ness – we had to disperse and come in a second time because of animal rights protestors on the course, though we did not know the reason as we could not see them. As we came in again the horse on the other side of me was Sure Metal, which I considered had no chance of jumping round, so I said to the jockey, Seamus O'Neill, 'Get that thing out of here, we don't want to be tracking you,' at which John White burst out laughing.

'I'll remember this National,' he said, 'for you trying to kick poor Seamus out of the starting gate!'

I looked towards the Starter and urged my horse forward as his hand pulled the lever down, so that he would be moving as soon as the tape had gone up. This time the tape did not rise properly, and I ducked under it; as Dibble got into his stride I heard the call of 'false start'. Soon we were back replaying the battle for position behind the tape. The next time we got a really good break and hurtled towards the first up with the leaders; Dibble jumped the fence well balanced, as I thought he would. At the third, the big ditch, he ran right up to the boards and cleared it effortlessly. This race was becoming a real thrill as we headed towards the next major test, Becher's; then he was over this with barely a nod. We met with a bit of interference as the leaders swung across me to take their line over the Canal Turn, and by now I was able to assess the horses I had around me. I couldn't see Chatam, and wondered if he had fallen early on. I wanted to avoid any fallers in front, so I picked the clearest route towards the inside that I could see as we turned back to the racecourse proper and jumped what would be the penultimate and the last fences next time round.

Approaching the Chair I shook Dibble up to maintain my position when all of a sudden the horses in front of me veered about and slowed down. I could see one or two big dolls in front of the Chair, but this was a fence we had not jumped yet so there couldn't be anyone lying injured on the landing side. I could only think that it was some practical joker, or perhaps there were some animal rights protestors lying on the other side of the fence. I was totally confused as to what to do; the fact that the dolls were not

*One of racing's most embarrassing days. Officials try to flag down the field after one circuit of the 1993 Grand National. My mount Captain*

*Dibble is at the point of the curve of the running rail, and I have just spotted Martin Pipe waving me to stop*
*(DAVID HASTINGS)*
*(Left) 'What happens now?' I wait with Captain Dibble's trainer Nigel Twiston-Davies as the powers that be try to decide whether or not to re-run the 1993 National (TREVOR JONES)*

properly laid out decided me and I went on to jump the fence along with those in front (Dibble even kicked the bollard on the way past and still jumped superbly). On landing I saw Martin waving me down; there must, I supposed, have been some trouble further down the course. I pulled up. Then someone said it was a false start. My first reaction was that someone was taking the mickey; then I looked across and saw a group of horses and jockeys who hadn't started. Of this bunch, I couldn't tell who had the biggest grin on his face, Jamie or Chatam.

Complete confusion reigned as I dismounted and waited for some announcement. At the time the whole incident was so ridiculous it was almost funny: I could hear the commentary continuing to follow those runners that had not pulled up after the first circuit. The Black Horse at Naunton came to the rescue when Edward Bowen Jones, whose wife Victoria looks after Dibble, came out to bring a group of us tea laced with whisky as we stood around discussing what the outcome might be. Eventually the remainder of the field came in to be told what I by then knew: that the race was void. John White, who 'won', now had something else to remember this year's Grand National by . . .

I returned to a weighing room resigned to the fact that there would be no Grand National this year. As to whose fault it was, there were a number of factors, but surely the greatest share of the blame must rest with those responsible for ensuring an adequate recall procedure. There was much dispute after the race as to whether the recall man raised his flag or not, a point that seems irrelevant, because whether he did or not, the jockeys did not see him. The buck stops firmly on the desk of the Jockey Club: they ran racing and were in charge of discipline.

Back home I looked ahead at the coming months and thought: I will retire when the season ends. Then I thought again. There is an old adage in racing, 'When you think about pulling up, pull up. Don't jump one more fence.' So I went to discuss my decision with the Pipe family. Martin and Carol were very understanding (David Pipe senior thought I should have given up long ago). Now I had my future to consider, and the sooner I got myself organized the better; and I had a book to write . . .

THE

# SCUDAMORE RECORD

————▸◂◂◂—————

*Compiled by Sean Magee*

———➤◄———

Peter Scudamore is the most successful jockey in the history of National Hunt racing, so it is appropriate to include in his autobiography the basic facts of his riding record, notably:

*His career total of 1,678 winners in Britain is the highest ever achieved by a jump jockey. (Add together the originally published end-of-term statistics for his fifteen winning seasons and you get 1,677 winners, but that is without taking into account the chocolate biscuit. Torymore Green won a novices' chase at Nottingham in March 1987, with Peter Scudamore second on April Prince. Then Torymore Green failed the dope test – a chocolate biscuit containing a prohibited substance had found its way into his feed – and during the close season the race was awarded to the Scudamore horse.)

*Peter Scudamore was champion jockey a record eight times (including the title shared with John Francome in 1981–2). Previous best was Gerry Wilson with seven titles (1932–3 to 1940–1). John Francome also took seven, including the shared one.

*Scu's total of 221 winners in the 1988–9 season is the highest ever achieved by a jump jockey. No other National Hunt rider has ever exceeded 200 – the previous record winning total was Jonjo O'Neill's 149 in 1977–8.

———➤◄———

The fifteen seasons during which Peter Scudamore rode winners break down as fo*f*llows:

### 1978–9

9 wins (from 81 rides; strike rate 11 per cent)
First winner: Rolyat in Amateur Riders' Handicap Hurdle at
Devon and Exeter, 31 August 1978.

### 1979–80

34 wins (193 rides; 18 per cent; ninth in jockeys' table)

### 1980–1

91 wins (570 rides; 16 per cent; second in table to John
Francome)
Won Tote Pattern Handicap Chase (Sugarally)

### 1981–2

120 wins (623 rides; 19 per cent; shared championship with
John Francome)

### 1982–3

93 wins (694 rides; 13 per cent; second to John Francome)
Won Aintree Chase (Artifice), Scottish Champion Hurdle
(Royal Vulcan)

### 1983–4

98 wins (644 rides; 15 per cent; third behind John Francome
and Jonjo O'Neill)
Won Scottish Champion Hurdle (Rushmoor), Tia Maria
Handicap Hurdle (Bajan Sunshine)

### 1984–5

50 wins (508 rides; 10 per cent; fifth)
Won Aintree Hurdle (Bajan Sunshine)

### 1985–6

91 wins (537 rides; 17 per cent; champion for second time –
first outright championship)
Won H & T Walker Gold Cup (Very Promising), Welsh National
(Run And Skip), Anth'ony Mildmay, Peter Cazalet Memorial
Chase (Run And Skip), Embassy Premier Chase Final
(Very Promising), Gainsborough Chase (Burrough Hill Lad),
Daily Express Triumph Hurdle (Solar Cloud), Ritz Club
National Hunt Chase (Charter Party)

## 1986–7

124 wins (578 rides; 21 per cent; champion for third time)
Won Christmas Hurdle (Nohalmdun), Queen Mother Champion
Chase (Pearlyman), Cathcart Chase (Half Free), William Hill
Scottish National (Little Polveir)

## 1987–8

132 wins (557 rides; 24 per cent; champion for fourth time)
Won Mecca Bookmakers Handicap Hurdle (Celtic Shot),
Champion Hurdle (Celtic Shot)

## 1988–9

221 wins (663 rides; 33 per cent; champion for fifth time)
Won Mackeson Gold Cup (Pegwell Bay), Hennessy Cognac
Gold Cup (Strands of Gold), Welsh National (Bonanza Boy),
Racing Post Chase (Bonanza Boy), Imperial Cup
(Travel Mystery), Grand Annual Chase (Pukka Major),
Welsh Champion Hurdle (Celtic Shot)

## 1989–90

170 wins (523 rides; 33 per cent; champion for sixth time)
Won Welsh National (Bonanza Boy), Sun Alliance Novices'
Hurdle (Regal Ambition)

## 1990–1

141 wins (422 rides; 33 per cent; champion for seventh time)
Won Sun Alliance Novices' Chase (Rolling Ball), Cathcart Chase
(Chatam), Ansells National (Bonanza Boy)

## 1991–2

175 wins (513 rides; 34 per cent; champion for eighth time)
Won Hennessy Cognac Gold Cup (Chatam), Welsh National
(Carvill's Hill), Sun Alliance Novices' Chase (Miinnehoma),
Scottish Champion Hurdle (Granville Again), Scottish National
(Captain Dibble)

## 1992–3

129 wins (419 rides; 31 per cent; second to Richard Dunwoody)
Won Anthony Mildmay, Peter Cazalet Memorial Chase (Rushing
Wild), Imperial Cup (Olympian), Champion Hurdle
(Granville Again), Sun Alliance Novices' Chase (Young Hustler),
Coral Cup (Olympian)
Final winner: Sweet Duke in Alpine Meadow Handicap Hurdle
at Ascot, 7 April 1993.

————

Of the 1,678 winners, 688 were in steeplechases and 990 in hurdle races, of which 6 (all in the 1990–91 season) were on all-weather surfaces.

————

Peter Scudamore's overall career strike rate of wins to rides is 22 per cent.

————

Only three jump jockeys have amassed career totals of over 1,000 winners:

Peter Scudamore 1,678 (1978–93)
John Francome 1,138 (1970–85)
Stan Mellor 1,035 (1954–72)

————

Peter Scudamore's first winner for trainer Martin Pipe was Hieronymous in the Oyster Novices' Hurdle at Haydock Park on 2 March 1985. By the end of his career he had clocked up 792 successes for the Pipe yard:

| | |
|---|---|
| 1984–5 | 2 |
| 1985–6 | 8 |
| 1986–7 | 42 |
| 1987–8 | 89 |
| 1988–9 | 158 |
| 1989–90 | 122 |
| 1990–1 | 116 |
| 1991–2 | 150 |
| 1992–3 | 105 |
| Total | 792 |

Those 792 winners represent 47 per cent of the career total of 1,678. His strike rate on rides for Pipe overall was 37 per cent, and during the phenomenal 1988–9 season 44 per cent, when the 158 Pipe-trained horses provided 71 per cent of Scudamore's total of 221 winners.

Of the 792 Pipe winners, 353 (45 per cent) started odds-on favourite.

———◦▸◂◦———

The shortest-priced winner Peter Scudamore rode in Britain was Sweet Glow, 10–1 on favourite to beat one opponent in a handicap hurdle at Newton Abbot on 15 May 1991. His longest-priced winner was 40–1 chance Solar Cloud in the Daily Express Triumph Hurdle at Cheltenham on 13 March 1986.

———◦▸◂◦———

Peter Scudamore rode 100 or more winners on four racecourses:

Newton Abbot 127
Worcester 114
Devon and Exeter [Exeter] 111
Chepstow 100

———◦▸◂◦———

Among Scu's many wins overseas were the Guinness Galway Hurdle at Galway on Rushmoor in 1986, the Temple Gwathmey Chase at Belmont Park, New York, on Jimmy Lorenzo in 1989, the Queen Mother Supreme Hurdle at Belmont Park on Bokaro in 1990, and the Hennessy Cognac Gold Cup at Leopardstown, Dublin, on Carvill's Hill in 1992.

———◦▸◂◦———

# The Winners

The following pages list all Peter Scudamore's winners in Great Britain. The letter H after the date indicates a hurdle race, C a steeplechase. In the 1990–1 season, A after the date indicates a hurdle race on an all–weather surface.

During the course of Peter Scudamore's career Liverpool racecourse officially became Aintree, and Devon and Exeter changed its name to Exeter. For ease of reference the names have not been altered in these lists.

## 1978–9: TOTAL WINNERS 9

| Date | Course | Horse | Trainer | SP |
|---|---|---|---|---|
| 31 Aug H | Devon & Exeter | ROLYAT | G. Balding | 11–4 |
| 15 Sep H | Newton Abbot | ROLYAT | G. Balding | 5–4F |
| 14 Nov C | Ludlow | MAJESTIC TOUCH | F. Yardley | 13–8 |
| 25 Nov C | Wolverhampton | JOHN BOY | D. Edmunds | 7–4F |
| 4 Dec C | Folkestone | CANDLEWICK GREEN | F. Yardley | 13–2 |
| 7 Mar C | Worcester | JACKO | D. Nicholson | 9–1 |
| 31 Mar C | Liverpool | MAC'S CHARIOT | D. Nicholson | 10–1 |
| 2 Apr C | Newbury | JACKO | D. Nicholson | 7–2 |
| 28 May C | Hereford | TURO | D. Nicholson | 9–4 |

## 1979–80: TOTAL WINNERS 34

| Date | Course | Horse | Trainer | SP |
|---|---|---|---|---|
| 25 Aug H | Hereford | LOW PROFILE | F. Yardley | 10–11F |
| 4 Sep H | Newton Abbot | MAGIC NOTE | W. Williams | 5–1 |
| 8 Sep C | Hereford | BECK 'N CALL | M. Scudamore | 20–1 |
| 13 Sep H | Newton Abbot | MAGIC NOTE | W. Williams | 11–4 |
| 3 Oct C | Ludlow | BECK 'N CALL | M. Scudamore | 5–1 |
| 3 Nov H | Worcester | OAKPRIME | D. Nicholson | 33–1 |
| 8 Nov C | Uttoxeter | SEA LANE | Earl Jones | 5–1 |
| 12 Nov C | Fontwell Park | BIRSHELL | G. Balding | 100–30 |
| 17 Nov H | Warwick | OAKPRIME | D. Nicholson | 10–1 |
| 19 Nov C | Leicester | REGAL COMMAND | D. Nicholson | 11–10F |
| 21 Nov C | Worcester | SEA LANE | Earl Jones | 2–1JF |
| 21 Nov C | Worcester | BIRSHELL | G. Balding | 11–10F |
| 24 Nov C | Wolverhampton | SOLIDITY | D. Nicholson | 8–1 |

| | | | | |
|---|---|---|---|---|
| 26 Nov C | Wolverhampton | EASTERN CITIZEN | D. Nicholson | 7–1 |
| 26 Nov H | Wolverhampton | OAKPRIME | D. Nicholson | 9–4F |
| 4 Dec H | Newton Abbot | POLLY TOODLE | E. Swaffield | 8–1 |
| 4 Dec C | Newton Abbot | RIB LAW | J. Wright | 14–1 |
| 6 Dec H | Taunton | RAG TIME BAND | G. Balding | 33–1 |
| 10 Dec C | Nottingham | FLITGROVE | D. Nicholson | 10–1 |
| 12 Dec C | Worcester | GAMBLING PRINCE | Mrs G. Jones | 6–4F |
| 13 Dec C | Uttoxeter | PRINCELY CALL | Mrs G. Jones | 14–1 |
| 17 Dec C | Leicester | JACKO | D. Nicholson | 4–1 |
| 17 Dec C | Leicester | LASOBANY | W. Stephenson | 10–1 |
| 26 Dec C | Wolverhampton | GAMBLING PRINCE | Mrs G. Jones | 8–11F |
| 29 Dec H | Leicester | POLAR EXPRESS | D. Nicholson | 16–1 |
| 5 Jan C | Sandown Park | GAMBLING PRINCE | Mrs G. Jones | evensF |
| 7 Jan C | Leicester | JACKO | D. Nicholson | 5–2F |
| 8 Jan H | Leicester | BURROUGH HILL LAD | J. Harris | 9–4F |
| 8 Jan C | Leicester | LASOBANY | W. Stephenson | 7–1 |
| 11 Jan H | Ascot | SWASHBUCKLING | F. Rimell | 8–1 |
| 12 Jan H | Warwick | PIRATE SON | F. Rimell | 7–2 |
| 21 Jan C | Fontwell Park | ABO | N. Callaghan | 15–8F |
| 22 Jan H | Worcester | MELALEUCA | F. Rimell | 4–5F |
| 24 Jan C | Huntingdon | SALAD | D. Nicholson | 9–4F |

### 1980–1: TOTAL WINNERS 91

| | | | | |
|---|---|---|---|---|
| 9 Aug H | Worcester | CRITICAL TIMES | W. Stephenson | 16–1 |
| 9 Aug H | Worcester | BOARDMANS SPECIAL | W. Stephenson | 2–1 |
| 16 Aug C | Market Rasen | ORANGE TAG | P. Allingham | 9–2 |
| 16 Aug H | Market Rasen | JOTA | W. Wharton | 5–2F |
| 18 Aug H | Worcester | KIBCOY | W. Stephenson | 9–2 |
| 20 Aug C | Devon & Exeter | VIRGIN SLAVE | J. Wright | 7–4 |
| 27 Aug H | Fontwell Park | MATRA HUL | P. Allingham | 11–4F |
| 13 Sep C | Worcester | SMART BUCK | D. Nicholson | 14–1 |
| 1 Oct H | Ludlow | CRITICAL TIMES | D. Nicholson | 5–2 |
| 8 Oct C | Cheltenham | MANBULLOO | D. Nicholson | 14–1 |
| 10 Oct C | Worcester | LUCKY CALL | D. Nicholson | 16–1 |
| 11 Oct H | Uttoxeter | BOYNE HILL | D. Nicholson | 85–40F |
| 18 Oct C | Kempton Park | AINGERS GREEN | D. Nicholson | 4–1 |
| 18 Oct H | Kempton Park | BROADSWORD | D. Nicholson | 7–1 |
| 24 Oct C | Ludlow | LENEY DUAL | D. Nicholson | 4–1 |
| 24 Oct H | Ludlow | HAZELDEAN | D. Nicholson | 5–2 |
| 30 Oct H | Wincanton | FENNY BOY | J. Thorne | 7–1 |
| 31 Oct C | Sandown Park | TEN POINTER | D. Nicholson | 6–1 |
| 4 Nov C | Hereford | RIB LAW | J. Wright | 8–1 |
| 10 Nov H | Nottingham | CHAMPERS CLUB | D. Weeden | 14–1 |
| 10 Nov H | Nottingham | BROADSWORD | D. Nicholson | 7–2 |
| 13 Nov C | Wolverhampton | POLAR EXPRESS | D. Nicholson | 20–1 |
| 17 Nov C | Leicester | TEN POINTER | D. Nicholson | 7–4F |
| 17 Nov H | Leicester | SAILOR'S RETURN | D. Nicholson | 4–1 |
| 18 Nov C | Leicester | COLLARS AND CUFFS | D. Nicholson | 11–8F |
| 21 Nov H | Newbury | HAZELDEAN | D. Nicholson | 9–4 |
| 24 Nov C | Windsor | LENEY DUAL | D. Nicholson | 9–2 |
| 26 Nov H | Ludlow | SAILOR'S RETURN | D. Nicholson | 6–4JF |

| 26 Nov H | Ludlow | CHINA GOD | W. D. Francis | 20–1 |
|---|---|---|---|---|
| 29 Nov H | Sandown Park | BROADSWORD | D. Nicholson | 11–4F |
| 2 Dec C | Newton Abbot | RAPALLO | M. Scudamore | 4–1 |
| 10 Dec C | Worcester | BRIDGE ASH | J. Johnson | 5–1 |
| 10 Dec C | Worcester | MOIFAST | D. Nicholson | 9–2 |
| 12 Dec C | Devon & Exeter | RIB LAW | J. Wright | 5–1 |
| 13 Dec C | Nottingham | RIZZIO | D. Nicholson | 4–1 |
| 16 Dec H | Ludlow | CHINA GOD | W. D. Francis | 11–1 |
| 17 Dec H | Warwick | FATA MORGANA | D. Weeden | 9–4F |
| 20 Dec H | Chepstow | BROADSWORD | D. Nicholson | 15–8F |
| 26 Dec C | Wolverhampton | BRIDGE ASH | J. Johnson | 5–2F |
| 26 Dec H | Wolverhampton | ASCENCIA | P. Bailey | 9–4 |
| 27 Dec H | Wolverhampton | GREAT DEVELOPER | D. Nicholson | 7–2 |
| 31 Dec C | Cheltenham | TEN POINTER | D. Nicholson | 15–8F |
| 3 Jan H | Newbury | NEW LYRIC | D. Nicholson | 20–1 |
| 5 Jan H | Nottingham | MERCILESS KING | D. Nicholson | 14–1 |
| 5 Jan C | Nottingham | SOMETHING–IN–HAND | P. Felgate | 4–1 |
| 8 Jan H | Lingfield Park | ENTEBBE | F. Yardley | 9–1 |
| 8 Jan H | Lingfield Park | GREAT DEVELOPER | D. Nicholson | 15–8F |
| 10 Jan C | Sandown Park | OAKPRIME | D. Nicholson | 5–1 |
| 10 Jan H | Sandown Park | BROADSWORD | D. Nicholson | 4–7F |
| 12 Jan H | Wolverhampton | SEA CARGO | J. Johnson | 100–30F |
| 17 Jan H | Ascot | SIR GORDON | D. Nicholson | 7–2 |
| 19 Jan H | Fontwell Park | TOMPION | Mrs D. Oughton | 6–1 |
| 20 Jan C | Worcester | SLIPPERY DICK | D. Nicholson | 9–4F |
| 20 Jan C | Worcester | SAILOR'S RETURN | D. Nicholson | 15–2 |
| 23 Jan C | Kempton Park | SHERMOON | D. Nicholson | 7–1 |
| 24 Jan H | Haydock Park | SIR GORDON | D. Nicholson | 4–5F |
| 28 Jan C | Wolverhampton | BRIDGE ASH | J. Johnson | 7–2 |
| 2 Feb H | Leicester | SAILOR'S RETURN | D. Nicholson | 14–1 |
| 3 Feb H | Leicester | BEE STING | P. Cundell | 2–1 |
| 7 Feb C | Stratford | GREENWAYS | A. Jarvis | 7–2 |
| 7 Feb H | Stratford | DANHAGEN | A. Jarvis | 5–6F |
| 9 Feb H | Fontwell Park | GREAT DEVELOPER | D. Nicholson | 5–1 |
| 10 Feb C | Carlisle | MR ORYX | F. Yardley | 10–1 |
| 13 Feb H | Newbury | BROADSWORD | D. Nicholson | 8–13F |
| 13 Feb C | Newbury | SUGARALLY | G. Fairbairn | 8–1 |
| 18 Feb H | Worcester | BEE STING | P. Cundell | 10–11F |
| 21 Feb C | Nottingham | JACK MADNESS | J. Gifford | 6–1 |
| 28 Feb C | Kempton Park | SUGARALLY | G. Fairbairn | 9–2 |
| 2 Mar C | Doncaster | HIGHWAY PATT | D. Nicholson | 7–4 |
| 2 Mar H | Doncaster | CHINA GOD | W. D. Francis | 12–1 |
| 5 Mar C | Ludlow | PRINCE OF PLEASURE | M. Tate | 13–2 |
| 5 Mar H | Ludlow | STRATHDEARN | W. D. Francis | 5–2F |
| 6 Mar C | Newbury | LENEY DUAL | D. Nicholson | 5–2F |
| 7 Mar H | Hereford | FRED PILLINER | M. Scudamore | 5–2F |
| 7 Mar C | Hereford | PRINCELY CALL | Mrs G. Jones | 5–1 |
| 13 Mar H | Sandown Park | TOMPION | Mrs D. Oughton | 5–2JF |
| 14 Mar H | Doncaster | KILLER SHARK | G. Pritchard–Gordon | 4–5F |
| 23 Mar C | Wolverhampton | CHEERS | J. Edwards | 9–2 |
| 24 Mar C | Nottingham | HIGHWAY PATT | D. Nicholson | 11–4 |
| 3 Apr H | Liverpool | BROADSWORD | D. Nicholson | 6–5F |

| | | | | |
|---|---|---|---|---|
| 8 Apr C | Ascot | SPRING CHANCELLOR | W. A. Stephenson | 33–1 |
| 9 Apr H | Worcester | GENEROUS BID | J. Wright | 9–2 |
| 9 Apr H | Worcester | ROYAL WREN | J. Wright | 6–1 |
| 10 Apr H | Ayr | NELLIES LAD | W. A. Stephenson | 7–2JF |
| 15 Apr H | Ludlow | VAGABOND III | P. Ransom | 20–1 |
| 18 Apr C | Towcester | LUCKY CALL | D. Nicholson | 4–1 |
| 20 Apr H | Chepstow | PASSING PARADE | M. O'Toole | 5–2 |
| 20 Apr C | Chepstow | BAWNOGUES | M. Tate | evensF |
| 21 Apr C | Uttoxeter | TANORA | M. Tate | 4–1 |
| 30 Apr C | Hereford | MR FASTBAC | F. Yardley | 7–1 |
| 30 May C | Stratford | RAPALLO | M. Scudamore | 5–1F |

**1981–2: TOTAL WINNERS 120**

| | | | | |
|---|---|---|---|---|
| 1 Aug H | Market Rasen | CAN–DO–MORE | N. Callaghan | 11–8F |
| 3 Aug C | Newton Abbot | PRAIRIE MASTER | R. Peacock | 5–4F |
| 8 Aug H | Worcester | CAN–DO–MORE | N. Callaghan | 4–9F |
| 17 Aug H | Worcester | CAN–DO–MORE | N. Callaghan | 5–4F |
| 17 Aug C | Worcester | TANORA | M. Tate | 7–2 |
| 31 Aug H | Huntingdon | ARNALDO | N. Callaghan | evensF |
| 2 Sep H | Worcester | ARNALDO | N. Callaghan | 4–9F |
| 2 Sep C | Worcester | TANORA | M. Tate | 1–2F |
| 9 Sep H | Fontwell Park | ROTINGO | Mrs D. Oughton | 5–2 |
| 17 Sep H | Uttoxeter | HARVESTER SOLAR | R. Hartop | 7–2 |
| 19 Sep H | Warwick | FREIGHT FORWARDER | A. Pitt | 4–1 |
| 25 Sep H | Fakenham | CELIA'S HALO | W. Holden | 15–8F |
| 30 Sep H | Ludlow | SUJONO | M. Scudamore | 9–4F |
| 3 Oct C | Chepstow | CONNA VALLEY | D. Nicholson | 2–1F |
| 10 Oct C | Uttoxeter | CONNA VALLEY | D. Nicholson | 4–6F |
| 10 Oct C | Uttoxeter | FLAMENCO DANCER | R. Perkins | 11–4 |
| 14 Oct H | Plumpton | CHUMMYS BEST | D. Nicholson | 12–1 |
| 15 Oct C | Taunton | RICHMEDE | M. Stephens | 5–1 |
| 19 Oct H | Fontwell Park | ARNALDO | N. Callaghan | 100–30F |
| 22 Oct C | Newbury | LENEY DUAL | D. Nicholson | 7–2 |
| 23 Oct C | Ludlow | CONNA VALLEY | D. Nicholson | 13–8F |
| 24 Oct H | Stratford | SIR GORDON | D. Nicholson | 7–2F |
| 28 Oct H | Ascot | GOLDSPUN | D. Nicholson | 5–1 |
| 28 Oct C | Ascot | CAPTAIN JOHN | A. Goodwill | 7–2 |
| 29 Oct C | Wincanton | SHERMOON | D. Nicholson | 3–1F |
| 31 Oct H | Worcester | BROADHEATH | D. Nicholson | 12–1 |
| 31 Oct C | Worcester | SPARTAN CLOWN | D. Nicholson | 12–1 |
| 31 Oct H | Worcester | KINTBURY | D. Nicholson | 9–2 |
| 2 Nov C | Lingfield Park | TOMPION | Mrs D. Oughton | 9–2 |
| 4 Nov H | Newbury | JUNGLE JIM | D. Nicholson | evensF |
| 5 Nov C | Uttoxeter | LUCKY CALL | D. Nicholson | 5–2F |
| 9 Nov H | Nottingham | MAD MOMENTS | G. Blum | 4–1 |
| 9 Nov H | Nottingham | GOLDSPUN | D. Nicholson | 11–8 |
| 11 Nov C | Newbury | POLAR EXPRESS | D. Nicholson | 11–4F |
| 12 Nov H | Stratford | WARNER FOR SPORT | M. Tate | 7–4F |
| 12 Nov C | Stratford | CONNA VALLEY | D. Nicholson | 3–1 |
| 16 Nov C | Wolverhampton | BAWNOGUES | M. Tate | 13–2 |
| 21 Nov C | Ascot | LENEY DUAL | D. Nicholson | 9–2 |

| | | | | |
|---|---|---|---|---|
| 21 Nov H | Ascot | KINTBURY | D. Nicholson | 11–2 |
| 21 Nov H | Ascot | GOLDSPUN | D. Nicholson | evensF |
| 26 Nov H | Wincanton | MERCILESS KING | D. Nicholson | 9–1 |
| 27 Nov H | Leicester | ROYAL VULCAN | N. Callaghan | 1–5F |
| 27 Nov C | Leicester | CRITICAL TIMES | D. Nicholson | 100–30 |
| 5 Dec H | Kempton Park | ROYAL VULCAN | N. Callaghan | 4–6F |
| 7 Dec H | Nottingham | SALTHOUSE | N. Callaghan | 2–1F |
| 6 Jan C | Towcester | MR ORYX | F. Yardley | 7–2 |
| 21 Jan C | Lingfield Park | SULIMNOS | C. House | 12–1 |
| 21 Jan H | Lingfield Park | BUCKWHEAT CAKE | I. Balding | 12–1 |
| 22 Jan H | Kempton Park | RIZZIO | D. Nicholson | 10–1 |
| 22 Jan H | Kempton Park | LULAV | D. Nicholson | 2–1F |
| 25 Jan H | Leicester | ON A CLOUD | D. Nicholson | 11–8F |
| 27 Jan H | Wolverhampton | PALATINATE | D. Nicholson | 6–1 |
| 28 Jan C | Huntingdon | SPIN AGAIN | D. Morley | 2–1 |
| 29 Jan C | Doncaster | CONNA VALLEY | D. Nicholson | 7–1 |
| 30 Jan H | Cheltenham | BROADSWORD | D. Nicholson | 11–2 |
| 2 Feb H | Leicester | STORMY SPRING | D. Nicholson | 8–1 |
| 2 Feb C | Leicester | SAILOR'S RETURN | D. Nicholson | 7–4F |
| 4 Feb C | Towcester | FALKLAND PALACE | D. Morley | 9–4F |
| 4 Feb C | Towcester | NORTON PLACE | D. Nicholson | 6–1 |
| 8 Feb H | Wolverhampton | STOWELL GROVE | D. Nicholson | 5–2F |
| 8 Feb H | Wolverhampton | AVOGEM | Mrs M. Rimell | 5–2F |
| 10 Feb C | Ascot | SAILOR'S RETURN | D. Nicholson | 4–1 |
| 11 Feb C | Huntingdon | CONNA VALLEY | D. Nicholson | 3–1 |
| 12 Feb H | Newbury | LULAV | D. Nicholson | 9–2 |
| 12 Feb H | Newbury | RIZZIO | D. Nicholson | 4–1 |
| 15 Feb C | Nottingham | KALKASHANNDI | D. Morley | 4–1F |
| 15 Feb H | Nottingham | BROADSWORD | D. Nicholson | 4–6F |
| 15 Feb C | Nottingham | SALDATORE | D. Morley | 6–1 |
| 16 Feb H | Towcester | MY BOY JACK | D. Nicholson | 3–1 |
| 17 Feb C | Worcester | BANNORAN | D. Nicholson | 7–2 |
| 17 Feb H | Worcester | SEA CARGO | J. Johnson | 12–1 |
| 19 Feb C | Fakenham | TRAGUS | D. Morley | 9–4 |
| 20 Feb C | Nottingham | SAILOR'S RETURN | D. Nicholson | 4–1 |
| 20 Feb C | Nottingham | SALDATORE | D. Morley | 4–1 |
| 20 Feb H | Nottingham | RAY CHARLES | D. Nicholson | 4–6F |
| 23 Feb H | Huntingdon | MERCILESS KING | D. Nicholson | 7–1 |
| 25 Feb H | Warwick | MY BOY JACK | D. Nicholson | 2–1 |
| 26 Feb H | Kempton Park | LEANDER BLUE | D. Nicholson | 9–2 |
| 1 Mar H | Doncaster | PELARO | A. Jarvis | 4–1 |
| 1 Mar H | Doncaster | WARNER FOR SPORT | M. Tate | 3–1F |
| 2 Mar C | Plumpton | MOUNT TEMPLE | D. Morley | 12–1 |
| 2 Mar H | Plumpton | SPANISH BAY | M. Masson | 4–1 |
| 3 Mar H | Worcester | STEEL TRADER | D. Nicholson | 11–4F |
| 3 Mar C | Worcester | BANNORAN | D. Nicholson | 11–4F |
| 5 Mar C | Newbury | BORDER INCIDENT | R. Head | 9–4 |
| 6 Mar C | Hereford | CLASSIFIED | N. Henderson | 7–4F |
| 8 Mar C | Windsor | JACKO | D. Nicholson | 100–30F |
| 9 Mar H | Folkestone | SIR GIVENCHY | W. Musson | 7–2 |
| 9 Mar C | Folkestone | TRAGUS | D. Morley | 5–2 |
| 9 Mar H | Folkestone | LEFT BANK | D. Morley | 9–4F |

| 11 Mar C | Wincanton | KILVE | J. Thorne | evensF |
|---|---|---|---|---|
| 20 Mar H | Uttoxeter | RAY CHARLES | D. Nicholson | 8–13F |
| 20 Mar C | Uttoxeter | JACKO | D. Nicholson | 11–8F |
| 22 Mar H | Wolverhampton | STANDON ROCK | P. Kelleway | 8–11F |
| 22 Mar C | Wolverhampton | WELLFORT | M. Tate | 6–4F |
| 22 Mar H | Wolverhampton | KARMALI | Mrs M. Rimell | 5–2 |
| 24 Mar C | Worcester | BRIDGE ASH | J. Johnson | 11–10F |
| 26 Mar H | Newbury | THE FOODBROKER | D. Kent | 13–2 |
| 27 Mar C | Bangor-on-Dee | NO HURRY | Mrs M. Rimell | 4–9F |
| 30 Mar H | Wolverhampton | CELTIC BREW | Mrs M. Rimell | 4–6F |
| 30 Mar C | Wolverhampton | BRAVE JACK | Mrs M. Rimell | 10–11F |
| 30 Mar H | Wolverhampton | EASTERN LINE | Mrs M. Rimell | 5–4F |
| 31 Mar C | Huntingdon | POLAR EXPRESS | D. Nicholson | 7–2 |
| 2 Apr C | Liverpool | SILENT VALLEY | I. Jordon | 16–1 |
| 5 Apr C | Fontwell Park | FALKLAND PALACE | D. Morley | 15–8 |
| 6 Apr C | Hereford | BRAVE JACK | Mrs M. Rimell | 5–4 |
| 7 Apr H | Ascot | GAYE CHANCE | Mrs M. Rimell | 7–4F |
| 7 Apr C | Ascot | NEW LYRIC | D. Nicholson | 13–2 |
| 8 Apr C | Worcester | JACKO | D. Nicholson | 15–8F |
| 12 Apr C | Chepstow | CELTIC ISLE | Mrs M. Rimell | 11–8F |
| 12 Apr H | Chepstow | GAYE BRIEF | Mrs M. Rimell | evensF |
| 12 Apr H | Chepstow | EASTERN LINE | Mrs M. Rimell | 6–4F |
| 12 Apr C | Chepstow | MIDNIGHT SONG | T. Forster | 6–4 |
| 13 Apr H | Chepstow | BORN TO REASON | Mrs M. Rimell | 5–1 |
| 21 Apr H | Cheltenham | AVOGEM | Mrs M. Rimell | 7–1 |
| 22 Apr H | Cheltenham | EASTERN LINE | Mrs M. Rimell | 7–4F |
| 22 Apr C | Cheltenham | MASTERSON | Mrs M. Rimell | 6–1 |
| 23 Apr C | Market Rasen | TARTAN HEATH | M. Scudamore | 4–5F |
| 23 Apr H | Market Rasen | KING'S PICCOLO | W. Musson | 7–1 |
| 24 Apr C | Bangor-on-Dee | BRAVE JACK | Mrs M. Rimell | 4–9F |

### 1982–3: TOTAL WINNERS 93

| 21 Aug H | Hereford | HALLEL | D. Nicholson | 5–4F |
|---|---|---|---|---|
| 30 Aug H | Plumpton | LOGAN | M. Masson | 10–11F |
| 30 Aug C | Plumpton | GOLD CHIEF | K. Bailey | 11–8F |
| 31 Aug C | Southwell | GRAND TRIANON | G. Cunard | 7–2 |
| 1 Sep H | Worcester | HALLEL | D. Nicholson | 7–2 |
| 2 Sep H | Uttoxeter | TINKER'S TRIP | D. Nicholson | 4–9F |
| 8 Sep C | Fontwell Park | GLISSANDO | B. Wise | 7–1 |
| 8 Sep H | Fontwell Park | LOGAN | M. Masson | 15–8 |
| 18 Sep C | Warwick | PURPLE HAZE | D. Morley | 2–5F |
| 20 Sep H | Plumpton | LOGAN | M. Masson | 8–11F |
| 23 Sep C | Uttoxeter | BOSH SHOT | C. Vernon Miller | 5–1 |
| 24 Sep H | Fakenham | SOLARIUM | W. Musson | 15–8F |
| 2 Oct H | Chepstow | MR FOODBROKER | P. Haynes | 7–4F |
| 6 Oct C | Cheltenham | ROINEVAL | M. Tate | 3–1 |
| 8 Oct H | Worcester | CAPTAIN DYNAMO | D. Nicholson | 9–2 |
| 9 Oct C | Uttoxeter | THE REVEREND OWEN | D. Nicholson | 11–4 |
| 16 Oct C | Kempton Park | BROADHEATH | D. Nicholson | 7–4JF |
| 22 Oct H | Ludlow | CONNAUGHT RIVER | D. Nicholson | evensF |
| 23 Oct H | Newbury | BALANCHINE | D. Nicholson | 5–2JF |

| | | | | |
|---|---|---|---|---|
| 23 Oct C | Newbury | CELTIC ISLE | Mrs M. Rimell | 7–4F |
| 23 Oct C | Newbury | LENEY DUAL | D. Nicholson | 3–1 |
| 29 Oct H | Devon & Exeter | BEAU RANGER | J. Thorne | 7–4F |
| 30 Oct H | Worcester | FUNKY ANGEL | P. Felgate | 6–1 |
| 30 Oct H | Worcester | CAPTAIN DYNAMO | D. Nicholson | 9–4 |
| 1 Nov C | Lingfield Park | BROADLEAS | D. Nicholson | 2–5F |
| 2 Nov H | Fontwell Park | BRAUNSTON BROOK | D. Oughton | 11–8JF |
| 3 Nov H | Newbury | GAINSAY | D. Nicholson | 4–1 |
| 5 Nov H | Sandown Park | NOON GUN | D. Morley | 6–1 |
| 6 Nov C | Sandown Park | ARTIFICE | J. Thorne | 8–11F |
| 6 Nov C | Sandown Park | LENEY DUAL | D. Nicholson | 4–1 |
| 6 Nov H | Sandown Park | CONNAUGHT RIVER | D. Nicholson | 7–4F |
| 6 Nov H | Sandown Park | CAPTAIN DYNAMO | D. Nicholson | 4–6F |
| 8 Nov H | Nottingham | GAINSAY | D. Nicholson | 7–4 |
| 10 Nov C | Newbury | OAKPRIME | D. Nicholson | 13–8F |
| 11 Nov H | Wincanton | SUNDIAL | D. Nicholson | 3–1F |
| 16 Nov C | Nottingham | KALKASHANNDI | D. Morley | 20–1 |
| 16 Nov H | Nottingham | MEMBER'S RELISH | D. Nicholson | 8–1 |
| 17 Nov H | Worcester | GOLDSPUN | D. Nicholson | 2–11F |
| 18 Nov C | Kempton Park | BANNORAN | D. Nicholson | 11–4 |
| 19 Nov C | Ascot | ROINEVAL | M. Tate | 5–2 |
| 20 Nov H | Ascot | CONNAUGHT RIVER | D. Nicholson | 4–5F |
| 24 Nov H | Ludlow | SUNDIAL | D. Nicholson | 7–4F |
| 25 Nov H | Wincanton | WILD GEESE | J. Thorne | 11–4JF |
| 26 Nov H | Newbury | PRIMROLLA | D. Nicholson | 5–4F |
| 29 Nov C | Folkestone | LEFT BANK | D. Morley | 5–1 |
| 3 Dec H | Sandown Park | FITZHERBERT | L. Kennard | 2–1F |
| 4 Dec H | Sandown Park | GAINSAY | D. Nicholson | 3–1F |
| 7 Dec H | Hereford | AN–GO–LOOK | M. Scudamore | 9–1 |
| 9 Dec H | Uttoxeter | CHAMPERS CLUB | D. Weeden | 11–2 |
| 10 Dec C | Cheltenham | STORMY SPRING | D. Nicholson | 7–4 |
| 16 Dec C | Haydock Park | CLOUNAMON | D. Nicholson | 9–4F |
| 17 Dec C | Doncaster | SWARM | P. Harris | 9–1 |
| 22 Dec C | Lingfield Park | MR GUMBOOTS | D. Nicholson | evensF |
| 27 Dec H | Kempton Park | GAMBIR | D. Nicholson | 4–1 |
| 1 Jan C | Newbury | LEANDER BLUE | D. Nicholson | 9–1 |
| 1 Jan H | Newbury | AMBIANCE | P. Bailey | 7–4 |
| 5 Jan H | Hereford | NOTRE CHEVAL | D. Nicholson | 11–4JF |
| 11 Jan H | Leicester | NOTRE CHEVAL | D. Nicholson | 3–1JF |
| 15 Jan H | Ascot | GAMBIR | D. Nicholson | 6–4F |
| 18 Jan H | Worcester | FITZHERBERT | L. Kennard | 11–4 |
| 22 Jan H | Haydock Park | CHARTER PARTY | D. Nicholson | 5–2 |
| 28 Jan H | Doncaster | COMEDIAN | D. Nicholson | 7–4F |
| 3 Feb C | Towcester | SAM SMITH | D. Nicholson | 5–1 |
| 25 Feb C | Kempton Park | ACARINE | P. Harris | 13–8F |
| 26 Feb C | Kempton Park | KATHIES LAD | A. Jarvis | 13–8F |
| 2 Mar C | Wetherby | ABERSING | D. Todd | 13–2 |
| 5 Mar C | Newbury | LEANDER BLUE | D. Nicholson | 8–1 |
| 5 Mar C | Newbury | KATHIES LAD | A. Jarvis | 5–4F |
| 7 Mar C | Windsor | JACKO | D. Nicholson | 10–1 |
| 7 Mar H | Windsor | CORDUROY | D. Nicholson | 25–1 |
| 9 Mar C | Bangor–on–Dee | MOUNT OLIVER | M. Scudamore | 15–8 |

| | | | | |
|---|---|---|---|---|
| 18 Mar H | Lingfield Park | AVERNUS | T. Forster | 5–1 |
| 21 Mar C | Wolverhampton | CONNA VALLEY | D. Nicholson | 12–1 |
| 22 Mar C | Nottingham | JACKO | D. Nicholson | 9–2 |
| 25 Mar H | Newbury | JUNGLE JIM | D. Nicholson | 4–5F |
| 28 Mar C | Wolverhampton | GALLEON BEACH | J. Edwards | 8–11F |
| 30 Mar C | Ludlow | SAILORS RETURN | D. Nicholson | 2–1F |
| 30 Mar H | Ludlow | BOLD IMAGE | B. Preece | 16–1 |
| 30 Mar H | Ludlow | BEN EWEN | D. Nicholson | 7–2 |
| 4 Apr H | Chepstow | NOTRE CHEVAL | D. Nicholson | 5–1 |
| 5 Apr H | Chepstow | SOMAY | D. Nicholson | 5–2 |
| 5 Apr C | Chepstow | CHINGOLO | Mrs S. Davenport | 12–1 |
| 5 Apr H | Chepstow | BOLD IMAGE | B. Preece | 7–2 |
| 5 Apr C | Chepstow | RO'S OWEN | R. Head | 9–4 |
| 9 Apr C | Liverpool | ARTIFICE | J. Thorne | 9–1 |
| 11 Apr C | Fontwell Park | SIR PLUS | D. Morley | evensF |
| 15 Apr C | Ayr | BURNT OAK | D. Nicholson | 11–10F |
| 15 Apr H | Ayr | ROYAL VULCAN | N. Callaghan | 7–2 |
| 26 Apr C | Perth | CUMBERLAND BASIN | J. Edwards | 11–4 |
| 29 Apr H | Taunton | RETSEL | S. Woodman | 11–2 |
| 12 May C | Uttoxeter | LESELUC | G. Balding | 11–2 |
| 18 May C | Perth | CUMBERLAND BASIN | J. Edwards | 11–10F |
| 27 May H | Towcester | CAPTAIN OATES | M. Hinchliffe | 5–2 |

### 1983–4: TOTAL WINNERS 98

| | | | | |
|---|---|---|---|---|
| 1 Aug C | Market Rasen | OPARAU | P. Felgate | 15–8F |
| 6 Aug H | Worcester | SINGING FOOL | A. Pitt | 5–1 |
| 10 Aug H | Fontwell Park | RETSEL | S. Woodman | 4–1JF |
| 13 Aug H | Bangor–on–Dee | FUNKY ANGEL | P. Felgate | 9–4F |
| 13 Aug C | Bangor–on–Dee | OPARAU | P. Felgate | 11–8F |
| 18 Aug H | Devon & Exeter | LE BEAU* | J. Thorne | 5–2 |
| 20 Aug C | Hereford | CHRYSIPPOS | M. Scudamore | 7–4 |
| 29 Aug C | Huntingdon | RAMBLIX | G. Cunard | 3–1 |
| 3 Sep C | Stratford | ST ALEZAN | M. Tate | 7–1 |
| 7 Sep H | Bangor–on–Dee | WHATTON MARINA | P. Felgate | 4–6F |
| 7 Sep C | Bangor–on–Dee | OPARAU | P. Felgate | 9–4 |
| 7 Sep H | Bangor–on–Dee | FUNKY ANGEL | P. Felgate | 12–1 |
| 9 Sep H | Newton Abbot | PRINCELY LAD | M. Tate | 2–1JF |
| 17 Sep C | Bangor–on–Dee | ST ALEZAN | M. Tate | 9–4 |
| 21 Sep C | Fontwell Park | HOT TOMATO | W. Clay | 2–1F |
| 21 Sep H | Fontwell Park | RETSEL | S. Woodman | 3–1 |
| 22 Sep H | Uttoxeter | FUNKY ANGEL | P. Felgate | 7–2 |
| 23 Sep C | Worcester | WINTERLAND | J. Thorne | 5–2 |
| 28 Sep C | Ludlow | GIN N' LIME | C. Vernon Miller | 5–1 |
| 29 Sep C | Ludlow | DOCTOR FITZ | M. Tate | 11–8F |
| 30 Sep C | Wincanton | WINTERLAND | J. Thorne | 4–6F |
| 4 Oct C | Devon & Exeter | ARTIFICE | J. Thorne | 6–4F |
| 5 Oct C | Cheltenham | ST ALEZAN | M. Tate | 7–2 |
| 6 Oct C | Cheltenham | DON SABREUR | D. Pearman | 15–2 |
| 8 Oct C | Worcester | PREMIER CHARLIE | P. Harris | 11–1 |
| 21 Oct H | Newbury | CONNAUGHT RIVER | D. Nicholson | 12–1 |
| 22 Oct C | Stratford | CAPTAIN DYNAMO | D. Nicholson | 6–1 |

| 26 Oct C | Cheltenham | ST ALEZAN | M. Tate | 8–11F |
|---|---|---|---|---|
| 28 Oct C | Devon & Exeter | THE COUNTY STONE | J. Thorne | 9–2 |
| 2 Nov C | Newbury | CAPTAIN DYNAMO | D. Nicholson | 5–4JF |
| 2 Nov H | Newbury | CONNAUGHT RIVER | D. Nicholson | 6–4 |
| 5 Nov C | Sandown Park | LUCKY CALL | D. Nicholson | 13–8F |
| 7 Nov C | Nottingham | COMEDIAN | D. Nicholson | 11–10F |
| 8 Nov H | Hereford | ONLY FOR LOVE | D. Nicholson | 7–4F |
| 9 Nov C | Newbury | BURNT OAK | D. Nicholson | 4–1 |
| 9 Nov C | Newbury | VOICE OF PROGRESS | D. Nicholson | 11–2 |
| 12 Nov H | Cheltenham | PALATINATE | D. Nicholson | 5–1 |
| 14 Nov C | Wolverhampton | COMEDIAN | D. Nicholson | 6–5F |
| 14 Nov C | Wolverhampton | FURY BOY | D. Nicholson | 11–10 |
| 16 Nov C | Worcester | VOICE OF PROGRESS | D. Nicholson | 4–7F |
| 17 Nov C | Kempton Park | BROADHEATH | D. Nicholson | 5–6F |
| 19 Nov C | Ascot | WALNUT WONDER | R. Hickman | 9–2 |
| 19 Nov C | Ascot | INTEGRATION | E. Retter | 13–8 |
| 21 Nov H | Leicester | STEEL KID | D. Nicholson | 2–5F |
| 26 Nov C | Newbury | VOICE OF PROGRESS | D. Nicholson | 8–11F |
| 26 Nov C | Newbury | WALNUT WONDER | R. Hickman | 2–1 |
| 28 Nov H | Wolverhampton | HAYAKAZE | D. Nicholson | 8–1 |
| 29 Nov C | Huntingdon | LANDING BOARD | P. Harris | 6–1 |
| 30 Nov C | Doncaster | COMEDIAN | D. Nicholson | 8–13F |
| 1 Dec C | Warwick | GAMBIR | D. Nicholson | 5–2F |
| 1 Dec C | Warwick | SAILOR'S RETURN | D. Nicholson | 11–2 |
| 2 Dec C | Sandown Park | BROADHEATH | D. Nicholson | 6–4 |
| 15 Dec H | Haydock Park | TECHNICAL MERIT | Mrs K. Coulman | 8–1 |
| 22 Dec C | Hereford | NATIVE BREAK | Mrs W. Sykes | 12–1 |
| 27 Dec C | Kempton Park | DUKE OF MILAN | N. Gaselee | 9–4 |
| 27 Dec C | Kempton Park | JUGADOR | P. Haynes | 6–1 |
| 28 Dec H | Warwick | CITY LINK EXPRESS | D. Wilson | 20–1 |
| 30 Dec C | Newbury | BURNT OAK | D. Nicholson | 7–4F |
| 31 Dec C | Newbury | THE COUNTY STONE | J. Thorne | 9–4 |
| 2 Jan C | Cheltenham | VOICE OF PROGRESS | D. Nicholson | 1–8F |
| 2 Jan C | Cheltenham | TOM'S LITTLE AL | W. Williams | 9–1 |
| 2 Jan H | Cheltenham | GLEN ROAD | J. Thorne | 9–2 |
| 7 Jan C | Haydock Park | GAMBIR | D. Nicholson | 8–11F |
| 9 Jan H | Chepstow | ONLY FOR LOVE | D. Nicholson | 8–1 |
| 16 Jan C | Wolverhampton | STOWELL GROVE | D. Nicholson | 7–2 |
| 19 Jan C | Lingfield Park | SOMMELIER | R. Gow | 5–2F |
| 30 Jan C | Leicester | FRED PILLINER | M. Scudamore | 2–1F |
| 6 Feb H | Wolverhampton | ANOTHER PAL | D. Nicholson | 4–1 |
| 10 Feb C | Newbury | CAPTAIN DYNAMO | D. Nicholson | 7–2 |
| 15 Feb C | Worcester | CHARTER PARTY | D. Nicholson | 7–4F |
| 17 Feb H | Sandown Park | BAJAN SUNSHINE | M. Tate | 7–2 |
| 18 Feb C | Nottingham | BRONWYN | Mrs S. Davenport | 20–1 |
| 18 Feb H | Nottingham | HOORAH HENRY | D. Nicholson | 7–2 |
| 23 Feb H | Wincanton | IL PONTEVECCHIO | D. Murray Smith | 5–1 |
| 3 Mar H | Haydock Park | EASTERN LINE | D. Nicholson | evensF |
| 5 Mar H | Windsor | IL PONTEVECCHIO | D. Murray Smith | 2–1 |
| 6 Mar H | Warwick | MISTY DALE | J. Edwards | 12–1 |
| 10 Mar C | Sandown Park | CHARTER PARTY | D. Nicholson | 4–6F |
| 16 Mar C | Wolverhampton | BRONWYN | Mrs S. Davenport | 3–1 |

| | | | | |
|---|---|---|---|---|
| 19 Mar H | Wolverhampton | HAYAKAZE | D. Nicholson | 11–1 |
| 21 Mar H | Worcester | FEELS RIGHT | D. Nicholson | 6–1 |
| 22 Mar C | Towcester | LULAV | D. Nicholson | 9–4 |
| 24 Mar C | Newbury | CHARTER PARTY | D. Nicholson | 4–6F |
| 27 Mar C | Sandown Park | GAMBIR | D. Nicholson | 2–1 |
| 30 Mar C | Liverpool | TARQOGAN'S CHOICE | J. Edwards | 11–1 |
| 4 Apr C | Ascot | TOM'S LITTLE AL | W. Williams | 4–1 |
| 4 Apr H | Ascot | RUSHMOOR | R. Peacock | 16–1 |
| 11 Apr C | Cheltenham | GAMBIR | D. Nicholson | evensF |
| 12 Apr H | Cheltenham | COMMONTY | C. Bell | 12–1 |
| 13 Apr H | Ayr | RUSHMOOR | R. Peacock | 3–1JF |
| 7 May H | Haydock Park | BAJAN SUNSHINE | M. Tate | 6–1 |
| 18 May C | Stratford | ROUSPETER | D. Nicholson | 6–1 |
| 22 May H | Newton Abbot | RUBERCOLA | M. Scudamore | 5–1 |
| 28 May C | Hereford | ROUSPETER | D. Nicholson | 2–7F |
| 28 May C | Hereford | NATIVE BREAK | Mrs D. Sykes | 9–4F |
| 30 May C | Worcester | LULAV | D. Nicholson | 15–8 |
| 1 Jun C | Stratford | ROUSPETER | D. Nicholson | 20–21F |
| 2 Jun H | Stratford | EASTER LEE | D. Elsworth | 9–2F |

\* = dead heat.

## 1984–5: TOTAL WINNERS 50

| | | | | |
|---|---|---|---|---|
| 16 Aug C | Newton Abbot | PRINCELY LAD | M. Tate | 11–8F |
| 25 Aug C | Market Rasen | MARSHAL NIGHT | R. Woodhouse | 7–1 |
| 1 Sep H | Hereford | BURLEY HILL LAD | R. Woodhouse | 2–1 |
| 14 Sep C | Newton Abbot | PRINCELY LAD | M. Tate | 11–4 |
| 21 Sep C | Huntingdon | BEN EWEN | D. Nicholson | 4–7F |
| 3 Oct H | Ludlow | MARINERS DREAM | R. Hollinshead | 6–1 |
| 4 Oct H | Ludlow | HIGHLAND GOLD | D. McCain | 6–1 |
| 6 Oct C | Chepstow | BROADHEATH | D. Nicholson | 8–1 |
| 6 Oct H | Chepstow | STATESMANSHIP | R. Hannon | 14–1 |
| 13 Oct C | Uttoxeter | PALATINATE | D. Nicholson | 11–8JF |
| 18 Oct H | Wincanton | MARINERS DREAM | R. Hollinshead | 2–1 |
| 26 Oct H | Newbury | STATESMANSHIP | R. Hannon | 4–1 |
| 2 Nov C | Sandown Park | MASTER TERCEL | J. Spearing | 5–2 |
| 6 Nov H | Fontwell Park | IT'S TOUGH | S. Woodman | 2–1F |
| 9 Nov H | Cheltenham | STATESMANSHIP | R. Hannon | 6–1 |
| 13 Nov C | Hereford | JO COLOMBO | Mrs D. Sykes | 7–1 |
| 13 Nov C | Hereford | ONLY FOR LOVE | D. Nicholson | 9–4F |
| 23 Nov H | Newbury | AGAINST THE GRAIN | D. Nicholson | 5–4F |
| 26 Nov H | Wolverhampton | BOSSANOVA BOY | P. Makin | 7–1 |
| 27 Nov C | Huntingdon | LEANDER BLUE | D. Nicholson | 7–4 |
| 1 Dec C | Chepstow | TOM'S LITTLE AL | W. Williams | evensF |
| 12 Dec C | Haydock Park | VERY PROMISING | D. Nicholson | 8–11F |
| 12 Dec H | Haydock Park | TRIPLE JUMP | G. Thorner | 12–1 |
| 19 Dec C | Worcester | CHARTER PARTY | D. Nicholson | 11–2 |
| 26 Dec C | Kempton Park | GAINSAY | D. Nicholson | 7–2 |
| 29 Dec H | Newbury | ACE OF SPIES | L. Kennard | 8–11F |
| 29 Jan H | Leicester | DIXTON HOUSE | M. Scudamore | 2–5F |
| 30 Jan C | Hereford | FRED PILLINER | M. Scudamore | 11–2 |
| 8 Feb C | Newbury | CHARTER PARTY | D. Nicholson | 7–2 |
| 1 Mar C | Newbury | VERY PROMISING | D. Nicholson | 3–1 |

| | | | | |
|---|---|---|---|---|
| 2 Mar H | Haydock Park | HIERONYMOUS | M. Pipe | 5–1 |
| 7 Mar C | Wincanton | BROADHEATH | D. Nicholson | 4–1JF |
| 9 Mar H | Chepstow | ACE OF SPIES | L. Kennard | 8–15F |
| 15 Mar C | Wolverhampton | FURZEN HILL | J. King | 6–1 |
| 16 Mar C | Chepstow | CORBIERE | Mrs J. Pitman | 7–4F |
| 20 Mar H | Worcester | MAUJENDOR | M. Tate | 7–1 |
| 23 Mar C | Newbury | CHARTER PARTY | D. Nicholson | 3–1 |
| 27 Mar C | Huntingdon | MACOLIVER | Mrs J. Pitman | 7–1 |
| 30 Mar H | Liverpool | BAJAN SUNSHINE | M. Tate | 11–1 |
| 3 Apr H | Ascot | BAJAN SUNSHINE | M. Tate | 4–1 |
| 9 Apr H | Chepstow | MAUJENDOR | M. Tate | 4–5F |
| 10 Apr C | Cheltenham | CONNAUGHT RIVER* | D. Nicholson | 6–1 |
| 20 Apr H | Stratford | FRENCH UNION | D. Nicholson | 5–1 |
| 26 Apr H | Bangor-on-Dee | FRENCH UNION | D. Nicholson | 5–2F |
| 26 Apr C | Bangor-on-Dee | RUBERCOLA | M. Scudamore | 11–4 |
| 4 May C | Worcester | STOWELL GROVE | D. Nicholson | 12–1 |
| 6 May H | Ludlow | GOLDEN RAIDER | M. Pipe | 7–2 |
| 10 May H | Stratford | BRIMSTONE LADY | W. Musson | 4–5F |
| 16 May C | Ludlow | AN-GO-LOOK | M. Scudamore | 100–30 |
| 18 May H | Newcastle | BRIMSTONE LADY | W. Musson | 5–2 |

\* = dead heat

## 1985–6: TOTAL WINNERS 91

| | | | | |
|---|---|---|---|---|
| 26 Aug H | Newton Abbot | AMBIANCE | L. Kennard | 3–1 |
| 28 Aug H | Newton Abbot | AMBIANCE | L. Kennard | 5–4F |
| 4 Sep C | Southwell | OLIVER ANTHONY | N. Gaselee | 6–4F |
| 16 Sep C | Southwell | OLIVER ANTHONY | N. Gaselee | 6–4F |
| 23 Sep H | Plumpton | DERBY DAY | D. Wilson | 9–2 |
| 24 Sep C | Sedgefield | POLLY'S PAL | S. Payne | 5–1 |
| 2 Oct H | Ludlow | LITTLE SLOOP | D. Nicholson | 11–8F |
| 3 Oct C | Ludlow | MICK'S RITUAL | P. Felgate | 5–1 |
| 17 Oct C | Wincanton | COMEDIAN | D. Nicholson | 8–11F |
| 17 Oct H | Wincanton | LITTLE SLOOP | D. Nicholson | 4–6F |
| 19 Oct C | Stratford | HENRY KISSINGER | D. Gandolfo | 4–6F |
| 19 Oct H | Stratford | DERBY DAY | D. Wilson | 15–1 |
| 23 Oct H | Cheltenham | INCHGOWER | W. Wightman | 5–2F |
| 25 Oct C | Newbury | TOM'S LITTLE AL | W. Williams | 7–4 |
| 26 Oct H | Worcester | DERBY DAY | D. Wilson | 8–13F |
| 2 Nov C | Chepstow | VERY PROMISING | D. Nicholson | 5–2 |
| 2 Nov C | Chepstow | TICKITE BOO | D. Nicholson | 3–1 |
| 2 Nov C | Chepstow | FRENCH UNION | D. Nicholson | 2–1F |
| 2 Nov H | Chepstow | COTTAGE RUN | D. Nicholson | 9–1 |
| 13 Nov C | Newbury | FRENCH UNION | D. Nicholson | 7–4JF |
| 16 Nov C | Ascot | VERY PROMISING | D. Nicholson | 6–1 |
| 20 Nov C | Worcester | GAMBIR | D. Nicholson | 11–2 |
| 23 Nov H | Newbury | TICKITE BOO | D. Nicholson | evensF |
| 28 Nov C | Warwick | DEEP IMPRESSION | N. Gaselee | 4–1 |
| 29 Nov H | Sandown Park | YABIS | J. Edwards | 9–1 |
| 30 Nov H | Chepstow | PLAYSCHOOL | D. Barons | 11–1 |
| 4 Dec H | Worcester | KOFFI | D. Nicholson | 11–8F |
| 4 Dec H | Worcester | SOLAR CLOUD | D. Nicholson | 13–8F |
| 6 Dec C | Cheltenham | RUN AND SKIP | J. Spearing | 6–4F |

| | | | | |
|---|---|---|---|---|
| 7 Dec H | Lingfield Park | THAT'S YOUR LOT | J. Francome | 7–4F |
| 13 Dec C | Warwick | DEEP IMPRESSION | N. Gaselee | 10–11F |
| 21 Dec C | Chepstow | RUN AND SKIP | J. Spearing | 13–1 |
| 26 Dec C | Kempton Park | BOLANDS CROSS | N. Gaselee | 11–8F |
| 26 Dec H | Kempton Park | YABIS | J. Edwards | 7–1 |
| 26 Dec C | Kempton Park | CHARTER PARTY | D. Nicholson | 2–1F |
| 27 Dec H | Kempton Park | ARBITRAGE | G. Thorner | 6–1 |
| 1 Jan H | Cheltenham | TANGOGNAT | R. Simpson | 3–1 |
| 2 Jan H | Cheltenham | MRS MUCK | N. Twiston–Davies | 14–1 |
| 4 Jan C | Sandown Park | RUN AND SKIP | J. Spearing | 7–2 |
| 9 Jan C | Wincanton | THE COUNTY STONE | J. Thorne | 5–2F |
| 11 Jan H | Ascot | TICKITE BOO | D. Nicholson | 5–2JF |
| 11 Jan C | Ascot | VERY PROMISING | D. Nicholson | 5–4F |
| 15 Jan H | Windsor | PRIVATE VIEWS | N. Gaselee | 11–4 |
| 17 Jan C | Kempton Park | BOLANDS CROSS | N. Gaselee | evensF |
| 17 Jan H | Kempton Park | SOLAR CLOUD | D. Nicholson | 6–4F |
| 24 Jan C | Doncaster | VOICE OF PROGRESS | D. Nicholson | 15–2 |
| 25 Jan H | Cheltenham | TANGOGNAT | R. Simpson | 7–4F |
| 29 Jan C | Windsor | MEMBERSON | P. Dufosee | 5–2F |
| 29 Jan H | Windsor | YOUNG NICHOLAS | N. Henderson | 8–1 |
| 1 Feb C | Sandown Park | BURROUGH HILL LAD | Mrs J. Pitman | 100–30 |
| 3 Feb C | Wolverhampton | STEARSBY | Mrs J. Pitman | evensF |
| 3 Feb C | Wolverhampton | KING BA BA | R. Gow | 2–1F |
| 5 Feb C | Ascot | BOLANDS CROSS | N. Gaselee | 2–1F |
| 7 Mar H | Carlisle | MOODY GIRL | R. Hollinshead | 5–1 |
| 8 Mar C | Chepstow | ROLL–A–JOINT | G. Thorner | 9–4 |
| 8 Mar C | Chepstow | ETON ROUGE | Mrs M. Rimell | 2–1F |
| 13 Mar H | Cheltenham | SOLAR CLOUD | D. Nicholson | 40–1 |
| 13 Mar C | Cheltenham | CHARTER PARTY | D. Nicholson | 12–1 |
| 15 Mar H | Chepstow | SHEER STEEL | P. Cundell | 20–1 |
| 15 Mar C | Chepstow | ETON ROUGE | Mrs M. Rimell | 2–1 |
| 15 Mar C | Chepstow | KING JO | Mrs M. Rimell | 5–2 |
| 15 Mar H | Chepstow | CELTIC FLEET | J. Spearing | 10–11F |
| 19 Mar C | Worcester | MEISTER | J. Old | 9–1 |
| 20 Mar C | Towcester | VELESO | J. King | 7–1 |
| 22 Mar H | Newbury | CROONING BERRY | W. Musson | 15–2 |
| 25 Mar C | Sandown Park | I HAVENTALIGHT | F. Winter | 15–8F |
| 26 Mar H | Huntingdon | TARCONEY | P. Cundell | 9–4F |
| 27 Mar H | Ludlow | TREGEIROG | R. Francis | 9–2 |
| 27 Mar H | Ludlow | ROYAL CEDAR | Mrs M. Rimell | 6–4F |
| 29 Mar C | Southwell | GAINSAY | Mrs J. Pitman | 2–1JF |
| 9 Apr H | Ascot | GAYE BRIEF | Mrs M. Rimell | 4–1 |
| 11 Apr C | Towcester | CIMA | J. Old | 11–8F |
| 12 Apr H | Ascot | MRS MUCK | N. Twiston–Davies | 8–1 |
| 16 Apr C | Cheltenham | CHARTER PARTY | D. Nicholson | 11–4F |
| 17 Apr H | Cheltenham | GALLANT BUCK | D. Elsworth | 6–1 |
| 19 Apr H | Stratford | SPORTING MARINER | M. Pipe | 4–7F |
| 21 Apr H | Carlisle | BLUE SPARKIE | J. Old | 11–2 |
| 22 Apr H | Nottingham | GRUNDY LANE | M. Pipe | 5–4F |
| 2 May H | Taunton | COURTLANDS GIRL | W. Fisher | 11–4JF |

| 3 May C | Worcester | SILVER WIND | Mrs M. Rimell | 11–4 |
| 5 May H | Ludlow | SPORTING MARINER | M. Pipe | 1–4F |
| 9 May H | Newton Abbot | SPORTING MARINER | M. Pipe | 4–7F |
| 17 May H | Newcastle | MRS MUCK | N. Twiston–Davies | 11–4F |
| 17 May C | Newcastle | SILENT VALLEY | I. Jordon | 5–1 |
| 23 May C | Towcester | OLIVER ANTHONY | N. Gaselee | 9–2 |
| 26 May H | Hereford | HIT THE HEIGHTS | M. Pipe | 7–2 |
| 26 May H | Hereford | BELLEKINO | R. Frost | 7–4F |
| 26 May H | Hereford | BANDELERO | M. Pipe | 2–1F |
| 27 May H | Uttoxeter | ROYAL SHOE | M. Pipe | 7–2 |
| 30 May C | Stratford | LOCHRUN | Mrs J. Pitman | 5–1 |
| 30 May H | Stratford | FATHER MAC | M. Pipe | 6–1JF |

### 1986–7: TOTAL WINNERS 124

| 6 Aug H | Devon & Exeter | ERIC'S WISH | B. Preece | 2–1F |
| 13 Aug H | Fontwell Park | DERBY DAY | D. Wilson | 6–5F |
| 16 Aug H | Bangor-on–Dee | DISCOVER GOLD | K. Bridgwater | 7–1 |
| 16 Aug H | Bangor-on–Dee | TARQOGAN'S BEST | R. Peacock | 11–8F |
| 20 Aug H | Devon & Exeter | MELENDEZ | M. Pipe | evensF |
| 22 Aug H | Bangor-on–Dee | TARQOGAN'S BEST | R. Peacock | 8–13F |
| 25 Aug C | Huntingdon | IKOYI SUNSET | Mrs N. Macauley | 9–4 |
| 26 Aug H | Newton Abbot | TAMANA DANCER | M. Pipe | 2–1F |
| 2 Sep H | Devon & Exeter | MELENDEZ | M. Pipe | 4–7F |
| 5 Sep H | Hereford | SEDGEWELL LADY | M. Pipe | evensF |
| 15 Sep C | Southwell | BALUCHI | B. Preece | 7–4F |
| 17 Sep H | Devon & Exeter | MELENDEZ | M. Pipe | 8–13F |
| 20 Sep H | Warwick | TAMINO | F. Winter | 7–4F |
| 20 Sep H | Warwick | PRASINA MATIA | N. Gaselee | 9–2 |
| 22 Sep H | Plumpton | FIB | N. Henderson | 7–4 |
| 1 Oct H | Ludlow | ADAMSTOWN | M. Pipe | 5–4F |
| 1 Oct C | Ludlow | BALUCHI | B. Preece | 4–5F |
| 2 Oct H | Fontwell Park | PRASINA MATIA | N. Gaselee | 4–5F |
| 3 Oct H | Hereford | RUSHMOOR | R. Peacock | 2–9F |
| 6 Oct C | Southwell | BALUCHI | B. Preece | 1–2F |
| 8 Oct H | Cheltenham | KAMADEE | F. Winter | 4–7F |
| 9 Oct H | Cheltenham | MELENDEZ | M. Pipe | 8–11F |
| 10 Oct C | Worcester | ISHKOMANN | J. Spearing | 4–6F |
| 16 Oct H | Wincanton | ADAMSTOWN | M. Pipe | 4–9F |
| 18 Oct H | Bangor-on–Dee | ADAMSTOWN | M. Pipe | 2–5F |
| 22 Oct H | Cheltenham | MELENDEZ | M. Pipe | 4–6F |
| 24 Oct C | Newbury | I HAVENTALIGHT* | F. Winter | 2–1 |
| 30 Oct C | Wincanton | ULAN BATOR | F. Winter | 10–11F |
| 30 Oct C | Wincanton | HALF FREE | F. Winter | 8–11F |
| 1 Nov H | Chepstow | POWERLESS | F. Winter | 5–2F |
| 5 Nov C | Newbury | MALYA MAL | F. Winter | 3–1 |
| 5 Nov C | Newbury | ULAN BATOR | F. Winter | evensF |
| 8 Nov H | Cheltenham | MELENDEZ | M. Pipe | 5–2 |
| 10 Nov H | Plumpton | DIMENSION | Mrs N. Smith | 9–2 |
| 11 Nov H | Devon & Exeter | KEYBOARD KING | D. Wilson | 6–1 |
| 11 Nov C | Devon & Exeter | ADMIRAL'S CUP | F. Winter | 11–4 |
| 11 Nov C | Devon & Exeter | CONQUERING | F. Winter | 11–4F |

| | | | | |
|---|---|---|---|---|
| 15 Nov C | Ascot | BOLANDS CROSS | N. Gaselee | 4–1 |
| 17 Nov H | Leicester | POWERLESS | F. Winter | 9–2 |
| 25 Nov H | Huntingdon | NIPPY CHIPPY | N. Callaghan | 2–1F |
| 26 Nov H | Plumpton | LONGGHURST | M. Pipe | 9–4F |
| 29 Nov C | Chepstow | CYBRANDIAN | M. H. Easterby | 11–10F |
| 1 Dec C | Nottingham | LOCHRUN | Mrs J. Pitman | evensF |
| 2 Dec C | Hereford | LARRY–O | F. Winter | 6–4F |
| 5 Dec C | Cheltenham | I HAVENTALIGHT | F. Winter | 6–4F |
| 6 Dec H | Lingfield Park | MARETH LINE | M. Pipe | 9–4F |
| 6 Dec C | Lingfield Park | BOLANDS CROSS | N. Gaselee | 6–5F |
| 8 Dec H | Bangor–on–Dee | REDGRAVE ARTIST | M. Pipe | 4–5F |
| 10 Dec H | Haydock Park | MOU–DAFA | M. Pipe | 15–8 |
| 10 Dec C | Haydock Park | TARQOGAN'S BEST | R. Peacock | 5–1 |
| 11 Dec C | Haydock Park | CORBIERE | Mrs J. Pitman | 9–2 |
| 13 Dec H | Ascot | NOHALMDUN | M. H. Easterby | 13–8 |
| 13 Dec H | Ascot | OUT OF THE GLOOM | R. Hollinshead | 4–1 |
| 15 Dec C | Leicester | WICKED UNCLE | F. Winter | 4–1 |
| 17 Dec C | Worcester | RIBOBELLE | M. Pipe | 7–4F |
| 18 Dec H | Hereford | CAPULET | C. James | 13–8 |
| 18 Dec C | Hereford | MALYA MAL | F. Winter | 15–8 |
| 20 Dec H | Chepstow | HIGH KNOWL | M. Pipe | 4–5F |
| 22 Dec C | Towcester | IVOR ANTHONY | I. Balding | 4–1 |
| 26 Dec H | Kempton Park | YABIS | J. Edwards | 7–2JF |
| 27 Dec H | Kempton Park | NOHALMDUN | M. H. Easterby | 15–8F |
| 30 Dec C | Worcester | BROWN TRIX | F. Winter | 11–10F |
| 1 Jan H | Cheltenham | HIGH KNOWL | M. Pipe | 4–7F |
| 3 Jan H | Newbury | HARRY'S BAR | F. Winter | 7–2 |
| 6 Jan C | Folkestone | LARRY–O | F. Winter | 4–1 |
| 10 Jan C | Sandown Park | LOCHRUN | Mrs J. Pitman | 7–1 |
| 24 Jan C | Kempton Park | WOLLOW WILL | F. Winter | 11–4 |
| 26 Jan H | Leicester | SMITH'S GAMBLE | Mrs J. Pitman | 7–4F |
| 27 Jan C | Chepstow | GOLD BEARER | F. Winter | 6–4F |
| 27 Jan H | Chepstow | ADMIRALS ALL | F. Winter | 10–1 |
| 4 Feb H | Windsor | QUICKSTEP | M. Pipe | 7–1 |
| 9 Feb H | Fontwell Park | QUICKSTEP | M. Pipe | 7–4F |
| 14 Feb C | Newbury | PEARLYMAN | J. Edwards | 3–1JF |
| 16 Feb H | Nottingham | CANFORD PALM | F. Winter | 7–2 |
| 21 Feb C | Windsor | BAJAN SUNSHINE | F. Winter | 5–2F |
| 21 Feb H | Windsor | REDGRAVE ARTIST | M. Pipe | 8–1 |
| 23 Feb H | Fontwell Park | CORPORAL CLINGER | M. Pipe | 8–11F |
| 25 Feb H | Warwick | KESCAST | M. Pipe | 5–2F |
| 26 Feb H | Wincanton | HYPNOSIS | D. Elsworth | 25–1 |
| 26 Feb C | Wincanton | LIFE GUARD | D. Elsworth | 9–2 |
| 27 Feb H | Kempton Park | GALLANT BUCK | D. Elsworth | 5–2JF |
| 2 Mar C | Leicester | PAN ARCTIC | T. Bill | 9–4 |
| 3 Mar H | Nottingham | CROIX DE GUERRE | Mrs J. Pitman | 21–20F |
| 3 Mar C | Nottingham | APRIL PRINCE** | F. Winter | 11–1 |
| 9 Mar H | Windsor | FOLK DANCE | G. Balding | 7–4F |
| 13 Mar H | Sandown Park | CANFORD PALM | F. Winter | 3–1 |
| 13 Mar H | Sandown Park | BAIES | F. Winter | 11–2 |
| 18 Mar C | Cheltenham | PEARLYMAN | J. Edwards | 13–8F |
| 19 Mar C | Cheltenham | HALF FREE | F. Winter | 5–4F |

| | | | | |
|---|---|---|---|---|
| 21 Mar H | Chepstow | DON'T RING ME | M. Pipe | 100–30 |
| 23 Mar H | Wolverhampton | DON'T RING ME | M. Pipe | 8–13F |
| 26 Mar C | Towcester | TOUR DE FORCE | P. Makin | 6–1 |
| 28 Mar H | Newbury | HIGH PERFORMANCE | F. Winter | 4–1 |
| 31 Mar C | Sandown Park | HAZY SUNSET | F. Winter | 8–1 |
| 1 Apr H | Huntingdon | GREAT GANDER | J. Spearing | 9–4 |
| 2 Apr H | Liverpool | CONVINCED | M. Pipe | 100–30F |
| 8 Apr H | Ascot | MRS MUCK | N. Twiston–Davies | 9–4F |
| 10 Apr C | Ayr | BALLY–GO | J. FitzGerald | 7–2 |
| 11 Apr C | Ayr | LITTLE POLVEIR | J. Edwards | 12–1 |
| 15 Apr H | Ascot | CANFORD PALM | F. Winter | 100–30F |
| 18 Apr C | Towcester | GOLD BEARER | F. Winter | evensF |
| 18 Apr H | Towcester | ADMIRALS ALL | F. Winter | 11–8F |
| 21 Apr H | Chepstow | MOUNTAIN CRASH | J. Edwards | 13–8F |
| 21 Apr H | Chepstow | NITIDA | M. Pipe | 11–2 |
| 27 Apr H | Southwell | UP COOKE | M. Pipe | 8–15F |
| 30 Apr H | Wincanton | CHIEF PAL | N. Gaselee | 4–5F |
| 2 May C | Uttoxeter | DEEP AND EVEN | F. Winter | 11–4 |
| 2 May C | Worcester | MOU–DAFA | M. Pipe | 7–4 |
| 7 May H | Newton Abbot | NASKRACKER | M. Pipe | evensF |
| 7 May H | Newton Abbot | RIBOBELLE | M. Pipe | 4–1 |
| 8 May H | Newton Abbot | JOIST | M. Pipe | 3–1 |
| 8 May H | Newton Abbot | GUYMYSON | M. Pipe | 3–1 |
| 9 May H | Hereford | LEVANTINE ROSE | M. Pipe | 2–1JF |
| 14 May H | Ludlow | RAHIIB | M. Pipe | 5–2 |
| 15 May H | Taunton | PURPLE PRINCE | M. Pipe | 8–11F |
| 16 May H | Bangor–on–Dee | SPECIAL VENTURE | O. O'Neill | 13–8F |
| 19 May H | Newton Abbot | UP COOKE | M. Pipe | 4–6F |
| 21 May C | Stratford | SEDGEWELL LAD | M. Pipe | 7–2 |
| 22 May H | Towcester | NASKRACKER | M. Pipe | 8–11F |
| 23 May C | Warwick | ADMIRAL'S CUP | F. Winter | 8–13F |
| 23 May H | Warwick | PRASINA MATIA | N. Gaselee | 1–4F |
| 25 May H | Cartmel | NITIDA | M. Pipe | 2–5F |
| 25 May H | Cartmel | GUYMYSON | M. Pipe | 2–1 |
| 25 May C | Cartmel | MOU–DAFA | M. Pipe | 2–5F |

\* dead heat

\*\* April Prince finished second in the race, but the first past the post, Torymore Green, was subsequently disqualified after failing the drugs test.

### 1987–8: TOTAL WINNERS 132

| | | | | |
|---|---|---|---|---|
| 1 Aug C | Newton Abbot | RAHIIB | M. Pipe | 5–4JF |
| 1 Aug H | Newton Abbot | BRADMORE'S SONG | M. Pipe | 5–1 |
| 3 Aug H | Newton Abbot | DUSTY DIPLOMACY | M. Pipe | 7–2 |
| 3 Aug H | Newton Abbot | MY CUP OF TEA | M. Pipe | 2–1JF |
| 5 Aug H | Devon & Exeter | COME ON GRACIE | M. Pipe | 11–4F |
| 6 Aug II | Devon & Exeter | SAFFAN | M. Pipe | 4–7F |
| 13 Aug H | Newton Abbot | GUYMYSON | M. Pipe | 100–30 |
| 13 Aug C | Newton Abbot | RAHIIB | M. Pipe | 8–13F |
| 13 Aug H | Newton Abbot | PRINCESS SEMELE | M. Pipe | 11–10F |
| 13 Aug H | Newton Abbot | MY CUP OF TEA | M. Pipe | 4–5F |
| 14 Aug H | Devon & Exeter | KEECAGEE | M. Pipe | 4–6F |

| 14 Aug H | Devon & Exeter | SAFFAN | M. Pipe | 1–3F |
|---|---|---|---|---|
| 14 Aug C | Devon & Exeter | MEMBER'S ONLY | M. Pipe | 4–9F |
| 24 Aug H | Hereford | REPETITIVE | M. Pipe | 85–40F |
| 25 Aug H | Devon & Exeter | SAFFAN | M. Pipe | 2–7F |
| 25 Aug H | Devon & Exeter | REPETITIVE | M. Pipe | 5–1 |
| 29 Aug H | Hereford | BEDROCK | M. Pipe | 9–4 |
| 31 Aug C | Newton Abbot | PARCELSTOWN | D. Gandolfo | 5–4 |
| 3 Sep H | Worcester | REPETITIVE | M. Pipe | 5–6F |
| 3 Sep H | Worcester | PRINCESS SEMELE | M. Pipe | 11–8F |
| 10 Sep H | Newton Abbot | BRADMORE'S SONG | M. Pipe | 11–8F |
| 11 Sep H | Newton Abbot | ARASTOU | J. Francome | 11–2 |
| 12 Sep C | Worcester | TARQOGAN'S BEST | R. Peacock | 7–2 |
| 16 Sep H | Devon & Exeter | COME ON GRACIE | M. Pipe | 3–1 |
| 19 Sep H | Warwick | SAFFAN | M. Pipe | 6–4F |
| 23 Sep H | Devon & Exeter | COME ON GRACIE | M. Pipe | 6–1 |
| 1 Oct H | Taunton | SMILING BEAR | M. Pipe | 4–6F |
| 6 Oct C | Devon & Exeter | GRATIFICATION | F. Winter | 3–1F |
| 6 Oct H | Devon & Exeter | SLAVE KING | Mrs N. Sharpe | 14–1 |
| 8 Oct C | Cheltenham | MRS MUCK | N. Twiston–Davies | 11–4JF |
| 9 Oct C | Worcester | PUCKS PLACE | N. Gaselee | 9–2 |
| 15 Oct H | Wincanton | RAINBOW LADY | M. Pipe | 3–1F |
| 16 Oct H | Market Rasen | BRADMORE'S SONG | M. Pipe | 11–10F |
| 16 Oct H | Market Rasen | HE IS GREADY | R. O'Leary | 3–1 |
| 23 Oct H | Newbury | CELTIC CHIEF | Mrs M. Rimell | 7–2 |
| 23 Oct H | Newbury | SEA ISLAND | M. Pipe | 2–1F |
| 30 Oct H | Devon & Exeter | PEARLY GLEN | F. Winter | 14–1 |
| 31 Oct C | Sandown Park | TARCONEY | P. Cundell | 100–30 |
| 31 Oct H | Sandown Park | CELTIC SHOT | F. Winter | 3–1 |
| 4 Nov H | Newbury | CELTIC CHIEF | Mrs M. Rimell | 8–15F |
| 6 Nov C | Bangor–on–Dee | BALUCHI | B. Preece | 6–4F |
| 7 Nov C | Chepstow | UP COOKE | M. Pipe | 14–1 |
| 7 Nov H | Chepstow | PAT'S JESTER | R. Allan | 4–1F |
| 9 Nov H | Wolverhampton | BICKERSTAFFE | M. Pipe | 2–1F |
| 12 Nov C | Wincanton | BOLANDS CROSS | N. Gaselee | 10–11F |
| 13 Nov C | Cheltenham | PEARLYMAN | J. Edwards | 7–4F |
| 14 Nov H | Cheltenham | CELTIC SHOT | F. Winter | 9–4F |
| 16 Nov H | Wolverhampton | PANIENKA | M. Pipe | 9–2 |
| 18 Nov H | Worcester | OBSERVER CORPS | Mrs W. Sykes | 3–1F |
| 19 Nov H | Taunton | LEADING ROLE | M. Pipe | 11–8F |
| 19 Nov H | Taunton | CATS EYES | M. Pipe | 4–6F |
| 19 Nov H | Taunton | NASKRACKER | M. Pipe | 9–1 |
| 20 Nov H | Ascot | SABIN DU LOIR | M. Pipe | 5–2 |
| 23 Nov H | Leicester | ONE TO MARK | M. Pipe | 11–2 |
| 23 Nov H | Leicester | LEADING ROLE | M. Pipe | 30–100F |
| 23 Nov H | Leicester | HOPE DIAMOND | N. Gaselee | 8–11F |
| 24 Nov H | Wolverhampton | ANOTHER SEEKER | F. Winter | 7–1 |
| 25 Nov H | Haydock Park | CHARLIE DICKINS | R. Hollinshead | 13–2 |
| 25 Nov C | Haydock Park | BEAU RANGER | M. Pipe | 6–4F |
| 26 Nov H | Wincanton | WOLFHANGAR | F. Winter | 5–1 |
| 28 Nov H | Newbury | CELTIC CHIEF | Mrs M. Rimell | 8–11F |
| 30 Nov C | Nottingham | DEEP AND EVEN | F. Winter | 4–1 |
| 1 Dec C | Newton Abbot | QUICKSTEP | M. Pipe | 9–4 |

| | | | | |
|---|---|---|---|---|
| 4 Dec H | Sandown Park | DEEP TREASURE | F. Winter | 13–8F |
| 5 Dec H | Sandown Park | CELTIC SHOT | F. Winter | 6–4F |
| 7 Dec H | Worcester | SEA ISLAND | M. Pipe | 10–11F |
| 14 Dec C | Warwick | BRIGHT INTERVALS | F. Winter | 5–4F |
| 29 Dec H | Stratford | BELDALE STAR | M. Pipe | 1–8F |
| 1 Jan H | Windsor | CELTIC SHOT | F. Winter | 5–2F |
| 12 Jan H | Newton Abbot | WINGSPAN | M. Pipe | 11–4 |
| 12 Jan H | Newton Abbot | SPORTING MARINER | M. Pipe | 2–5F |
| 18 Jan C | Fontwell Park | CATS EYES | M. Pipe | 100–30 |
| 19 Jan C | Worcester | MITHRAS | B. Preece | 100–30 |
| 29 Jan C | Doncaster | BAIES | F. Winter | 7–2 |
| 29 Jan H | Doncaster | DRUMLIN HILL | F. Winter | 15–2 |
| 10 Feb C | Ascot | BARNBROOK AGAIN | D. Elsworth | 1–5F |
| 15 Feb H | Nottingham | AMBASSADOR | M. Pipe | 3–1JF |
| 17 Feb C | Folkestone | MITHRAS | B. Preece | 3–1 |
| 18 Feb H | Leicester | TABAREEK | M. Pipe | evensF |
| 12 Mar C | Chepstow | ARDESEE | D. Wintle | 4–1F |
| 12 Mar C | Chepstow | CATS EYES | M. Pipe | 5–6F |
| 15 Mar H | Cheltenham | CELTIC SHOT | F. Winter | 7–1 |
| 18 Mar H | Wolverhampton | PARLEZVOUSFRANCAIS | M. Pipe | 7–4JF |
| 24 Mar H | Taunton | HARRISON | M. Pipe | 10–11F |
| 26 Mar H | Newbury | CHATAM | M. Pipe | 10–11F |
| 29 Mar C | Sandown Park | TARCONEY | P. Cundell | 12–1 |
| 2 Apr C | Plumpton | TOP GOLD | R. Hodges | 5–4F |
| 2 Apr H | Plumpton | PARLEZVOUSFRANCAIS | M. Pipe | 4–9F |
| 4 Apr H | Chepstow | SEA ISLAND | M. Pipe | 1–2F |
| 4 Apr H | Chepstow | FANDANGO BOY | M. Pipe | 11–4 |
| 6 Apr H | Ascot | CONVINCED | M. Pipe | 11–2 |
| 12 Apr H | Fontwell Park | BELDALE STAR | M. Pipe | 11–8F |
| 14 Apr H | Taunton | GUYMYSON | M. Pipe | 5–4F |
| 16 Apr C | Bangor–on–Dee | BAIES | F. Winter | 11–8F |
| 16 Apr H | Stratford | TABAREEK | M. Pipe | 11–2 |
| 19 Apr H | Devon & Exeter | PARLEZVOUSFRANCAIS | M. Pipe | 8–11F |
| 19 Apr H | Devon & Exeter | NAYSHAN | M. Pipe | 3–1 |
| 20 Apr C | Cheltenham | TEN OF SPADES | Mrs M. Rimell | 11–8F |
| 20 Apr C | Cheltenham | BEAU RANGER | M. Pipe | 11–10F |
| 28 Apr H | Wincanton | COURTLANDS GIRL | W. Fisher | 8–1 |
| 30 Apr H | Market Rasen | PARLEZVOUSFRANCAIS | M. Pipe | 1–2F |
| 30 Apr H | Market Rasen | TABAREEK | M. Pipe | 1–2F |
| 2 May H | Ludlow | AMBASSADOR | M. Pipe | 6–4F |
| 2 May C | Ludlow | MOU–DAFA | M. Pipe | 9–4F |
| 5 May C | Newton Abbot | TORSIDE | M. Pipe | 7–4F |
| 5 May H | Newton Abbot | FANDANGO BOY | M. Pipe | 6–1 |
| 7 May H | Hereford | AMBASSADOR | M. Pipe | 5–4F |
| 7 May C | Market Rasen | MOU–DAFA | M. Pipe | 2–5F |
| 10 May H | Towcester | PHAROAH'S LAEN | M. Pipe | 7–2F |
| 10 May C | Towcester | WHISKEY EYES | M. Pipe | 4–6F |
| 11 May H | Wincanton | MENDIP STAR | M. Pipe | 8–15F |
| 12 May H | Ludlow | BURNING | M. Pipe | 4–7F |
| 13 May H | Taunton | GHAWWAS | M. Pipe | 13–8 |
| 13 May H | Taunton | ALWAYS SPECIAL | M. Pipe | 4–9F |
| 13 May C | Taunton | DOCK BRIEF | M. Pipe | 15–8F |

| 14 May H | Warwick | FANDANGO BOY | M. Pipe | 8–1 |
|---|---|---|---|---|
| 16 May H | Southwell | BURNING | M. Pipe | 4–9F |
| 17 May H | Towcester | JOARA | M. Pipe | 9–4 |
| 17 May C | Towcester | MOU–DAFA | M. Pipe | 8–13F |
| 18 May H | Newton Abbot | MY CUP OF TEA | M. Pipe | 3–1JF |
| 18 May H | Newton Abbot | JUST CHEEKY | M. Pipe | 11–10F |
| 20 May C | Fontwell Park | SHENLEY'S LADY | M. Pipe | 15–8 |
| 20 May H | Fontwell Park | RULING DYNASTY | R. O'Sullivan | 5–2 |
| 24 May C | Ludlow | QUICKSTEP | M. Pipe | 7–2 |
| 25 May H | Cartmel | LAHARNA GIRL | M. Pipe | 4–7F |
| 26 May H | Taunton | JUST CHEEKY | M. Pipe | 8–15F |
| 26 May H | Taunton | GUYMYSON | M. Pipe | 9–4F |
| 28 May H | Hexham | RUTHS LOVE | M. Pipe | 5–1 |
| 28 May H | Hexham | ELEGANT ISLE | M. Pipe | 1–2F |
| 30 May H | Cartmel | BURNING | M. Pipe | 2–9F |
| 31 May H | Uttoxeter | JOARA | M. Pipe | 7–1 |
| 31 May C | Uttoxeter | CELTIC FLEET | J. Spearing | 9–2 |

**1988–9: TOTAL WINNERS 221**

| 30 Jul C | Newton Abbot | RAHIIB | M. Pipe | 10–11F |
|---|---|---|---|---|
| 1 Aug H | Newton Abbot | BENISA RYDER | M. Pipe | 4–1 |
| 3 Aug C | Devon & Exeter | BIG PADDY TOM | M. Pipe | 4–5F |
| 3 Aug H | Devon & Exeter | CELCIUS | M. Pipe | 7–4F |
| 4 Aug H | Devon & Exeter | STAR OF KUWAIT | M. Pipe | 8–11F |
| 6 Aug C | Southwell | MY CUP OF TEA | M. Pipe | 4–6F |
| 10 Aug H | Fontwell Park | RULING DYNASTY | R. O'Sullivan | evensF |
| 11 Aug H | Newton Abbot | MAINTOWN | M. Pipe | 7–2 |
| 11 Aug C | Newton Abbot | BIG PADDY TOM | M. Pipe | 2–7F |
| 11 Aug H | Newton Abbot | HI–HANNAH | M. Pipe | 8–13F |
| 11 Aug C | Newton Abbot | AFRICAN STAR | M. Pipe | 13–8F |
| 12 Aug H | Devon & Exeter | BRILLIANT FUTURE | M. Pipe | 1–2F |
| 12 Aug H | Devon & Exeter | CELCIUS | M. Pipe | 4–7F |
| 12 Aug H | Devon & Exeter | PERTEMPS NETWORK | M. Pipe | 1–3F |
| 15 Aug C | Worcester | MY CUP OF TEA | M. Pipe | 4–9F |
| 24 Aug H | Devon & Exeter | PERTEMPS NETWORK | M. Pipe | 4–6F |
| 24 Aug H | Devon & Exeter | LIADETT | M. Pipe | 8–11F |
| 24 Aug C | Devon & Exeter | CHALK PIT | C. Brooks | 13–8JF |
| 26 Aug H | Bangor–on–Dee | HI–HANNAH | M. Pipe | 10–11F |
| 29 Aug H | Newton Abbot | AFFORD | M. Pipe | 11–10F |
| 29 Aug C | Newton Abbot | AFRICAN STAR | M. Pipe | 1–2F |
| 29 Aug C | Newton Abbot | MY CUP OF TEA | M. Pipe | 8–11F |
| 31 Aug H | Newton Abbot | PERTEMPS NETWORK | M. Pipe | 8–11F |
| 2 Sep C | Hereford | CHALK PIT | C. Brooks | 2–1 |
| 3 Sep H | Stratford | BRILLIANT FUTURE | M. Pipe | 6–4F |
| 7 Sep H | Fontwell Park | THAT THERE | M. Pipe | 11–8F |
| 7 Sep H | Fontwell Park | LIADETT | M. Pipe | 4–7F |
| 8 Sep H | Newton Abbot | CHIROPODIST | M. Pipe | 13–8F |
| 8 Sep C | Newton Abbot | AFRICAN STAR | M. Pipe | 1–5F |
| 8 Sep C | Newton Abbot | MY CUP OF TEA | M. Pipe | 5–2 |
| 9 Sep H | Newton Abbot | DICK'S FOLLY | M. Pipe | 8–15F |
| 17 Sep H | Warwick | HIGH KNOWL | M. Pipe | 4–9F |

| 21 Sep C | Devon & Exeter | INSULAR | I. Balding | 2–5F |
| 26 Sep H | Fontwell Park | CELCIUS | M. Pipe | 3–1 |
| 26 Sep H | Fontwell Park | HI–HANNAH | M. Pipe | 2–1F |
| 28 Sep H | Ludlow | CHIROPODIST | M. Pipe | evensF |
| 5 Oct C | Cheltenham | MY CUP OF TEA | M. Pipe | 11–4 |
| 5 Oct H | Cheltenham | LIADETT | M. Pipe | 9–4 |
| 6 Oct C | Cheltenham | CHALK PIT | C. Brooks | 5–4F |
| 7 Oct H | Worcester | CELCIUS | M. Pipe | 2–1F |
| 8 Oct H | Worcester | PARLEZVOUSFRANCAIS | M. Pipe | 1–7F |
| 11 Oct H | Newton Abbot | CHIROPODIST | M. Pipe | 11–4 |
| 11 Oct C | Newton Abbot | TARQOGAN'S BEST | M. Pipe | 85–40F |
| 12 Oct H | Plumpton | SAYFAR'S LAD | M. Pipe | 8–11F |
| 13 Oct H | Wincanton | AFFORD | M. Pipe | 4–6F |
| 19 Oct H | Cheltenham | LIADETT | M. Pipe | 11–10 |
| 19 Oct C | Cheltenham | MY CUP OF TEA | M. Pipe | 7–4F |
| 22 Oct H | Stratford | ESPY | C. Brooks | 8–15F |
| 24 Oct C | Fakenham | WOLFHANGAR | C. Brooks | 11–10F |
| 27 Oct C | Wincanton | PHAROAH'S LAEN | M. Pipe | 7–2F |
| 28 Oct H | Devon & Exeter | THAT THERE | M. Pipe | evensF |
| 29 Oct H | Ascot | AFFORD | M. Pipe | 2–1JF |
| 29 Oct C | Ascot | BAJAN SUNSHINE | C. Brooks | 15–8JF |
| 3 Nov C | Kempton Park | CANFORD PALM | M. Pipe | 2–1 |
| 4 Nov H | Bangor–on–Dee | AFFORD | M. Pipe | 2–7F |
| 5 Nov H | Chepstow | BRUTON STREET | C. Brooks | 5–1 |
| 8 Nov H | Devon & Exeter | SAYFAR'S LAD | M. Pipe | 10–11F |
| 8 Nov H | Devon & Exeter | FIDDLERS THREE | T. Forster | 6–4F |
| 8 Nov H | Devon & Exeter | THAT THERE | M. Pipe | 4–7F |
| 9 Nov C | Newbury | DONALD DAVIES | N. Twiston–Davies | 5–1 |
| 9 Nov C | Newbury | WOLFHANGAR | C. Brooks | 11–8F |
| 9 Nov C | Newbury | SPRINGHOLM | D. Nicholson | 5–6F |
| 11 Nov H | Market Rasen | LAVROSKY | M. Pipe | 6–4JF |
| 11 Nov H | Market Rasen | BLUE RAINBOW | M. Pipe | 9–4 |
| 12 Nov C | Cheltenham | PEGWELL BAY | T. Forster | 6–1 |
| 12 Nov C | Cheltenham | RUN AND SKIP | J. Spearing | 4–1 |
| 12 Nov H | Cheltenham | LIADETT | M. Pipe | 8–11F |
| 14 Nov C | Wolverhampton | SWING TO STEEL | M. Pipe | 6–4 |
| 16 Nov H | Kempton Park | PENALTY DOUBLE | C. Brooks | 4–1 |
| 16 Nov H | Kempton Park | ADMIRALS ALL | C. Brooks | 3–1 |
| 17 Nov H | Taunton | BLUE RAINBOW . | M. Pipe | 4–9F |
| 17 Nov C | Taunton | GOLDEN GLITTER | M. Pipe | 4–1JF |
| 18 Nov H | Ascot | MAN ON THE LINE | R. Akehurst | 7–2 |
| 18 Nov H | Ascot | SABIN DU LOIR | M. Pipe | 1–2F |
| 21 Nov H | Leicester | CELTIC SHOT | C. Brooks | 1–6F |
| 23 Nov H | Haydock Park | JABRUT | M. Pipe | 9–4JF |
| 23 Nov C | Haydock Park | TARQOGAN'S BEST | M. Pipe | evensF |
| 23 Nov C | Haydock Park | BEAU RANGER | M. Pipe | 13–8F |
| 24 Nov H | Haydock Park | ENEMY ACTION | M. Pipe | 8–11F |
| 24 Nov C | Haydock Park | RUN AND SKIP | J. Spearing | 4–5F |
| 25 Nov C | Newbury | PHAROAH'S LAEN | M. Pipe | 8–15F |
| 25 Nov C | Newbury | BARNBROOK AGAIN | D. Elsworth | 1–3F |
| 26 Nov C | Newbury | STRANDS OF GOLD | M. Pipe | 10–1 |
| 29 Nov C | Newton Abbot | BONANZA BOY | M. Pipe | 8–11F |

| 30 Nov H | Hereford | GO WEST | M. Pipe | 13–8F |
|---|---|---|---|---|
| 30 Nov H | Hereford | SUNWOOD | M. Pipe | 100–30F |
| 30 Nov H | Hereford | SONDRIO | M. Pipe | 5–4F |
| 2 Dec H | Sandown Park | MAN ON THE LINE | R. Akehurst | 4–7F |
| 7 Dec C | Huntingdon | FU'S LADY | M. Pipe | 4–6F |
| 7 Dec H | Huntingdon | ESPY | C. Brooks | 13–8F |
| 8 Dec H | Taunton | SUNWOOD | M. Pipe | 6–5F |
| 9 Dec H | Cheltenham | ENEMY ACTION | M. Pipe | evensF |
| 12 Dec C | Warwick | DEEP MOMENT | Mrs M. Rimell | 15–8F |
| 14 Dec H | Haydock Park | SONDRIO | M. Pipe | 1–2F |
| 14 Dec C | Haydock Park | RUSCH DE FARGES | M. Pipe | 16–1 |
| 14 Dec C | Haydock Park | PHAROAH'S LAEN | M. Pipe | 4–9F |
| 15 Dec C | Haydock Park | STEPASIDE LORD | M. Pipe | evensF |
| 15 Dec H | Haydock Park | VOYAGE SANS RETOUR | M. Pipe | 1–2F |
| 15 Dec C | Haydock Park | FU'S LADY | M. Pipe | evensF |
| 20 Dec H | Ludlow | SAYFAR'S LAD | M. Pipe | 4–6F |
| 20 Dec C | Ludlow | SWING TO STEEL | M. Pipe | 11–10F |
| 20 Dec C | Ludlow | CROWECROPPER | B. Preece | 13–8F |
| 26 Dec H | Newton Abbot | SAYFAR'S LAD | M. Pipe | 4–6F |
| 26 Dec C | Newton Abbot | SABIN DU LOIR | M. Pipe | 1–2F |
| 27 Dec H | Chepstow | ENEMY ACTION | M. Pipe | 8–15F |
| 27 Dec C | Chepstow | BONANZA BOY | M. Pipe | 9–4F |
| 27 Dec C | Chepstow | FU'S LADY | M. Pipe | 5–6F |
| 27 Dec C | Chepstow | ELEGANT ISLE | M. Pipe | 9–4 |
| 29 Dec C | Taunton | MARETH LINE | M. Pipe | 11–8F |
| 29 Dec H | Taunton | DELKUSHA | M. Pipe | 7–4F |
| 30 Dec C | Newbury | BAIES | C. Brooks | 10–11F |
| 31 Dec C | Newbury | BATTLE KING | C. Brooks | 7–2 |
| 5 Jan C | Lingfield Park | JUVEN LIGHT | R. Akehurst | 4–5F |
| 5 Jan H | Lingfield Park | HONEST WORD | M. Pipe | 3–1 |
| 6 Jan C | Haydock Park | SILVER ACE | M. Pipe | 13–8 |
| 7 Jan H | Haydock Park | ROLLING BALL | M. Pipe | 4–11F |
| 7 Jan C | Haydock Park | MARETH LINE | M. Pipe | 2–7F |
| 7 Jan H | Haydock Park | STOCKSIGN | B. Key | 2–1 |
| 9 Jan C | Wolverhampton | ELEGANT ISLE | M. Pipe | 5–6F |
| 9 Jan H | Wolverhampton | BATTALION | C. Brooks | 6–5F |
| 9 Jan H | Wolverhampton | BALUCHI | B. Preece | 3–1F |
| 10 Jan C | Newton Abbot | OUT OF THE GLOOM | M. Pipe | 4–11F |
| 10 Jan C | Newton Abbot | RUSCH DE FARGES | M. Pipe | 4–7F |
| 10 Jan H | Newton Abbot | MIGHT MOVE | M. Pipe | 11–8F |
| 11 Jan C | Plumpton | ROSCOE HARVEY | C. Brooks | 15–8F |
| 13 Jan C | Ascot | SABIN DU LOIR | M. Pipe | 6–5F |
| 14 Jan H | Ascot | PERTEMPS NETWORK | M. Pipe | 8–11F |
| 14 Jan H | Ascot | SONDRIO | M. Pipe | 2–7F |
| 17 Jan H | Worcester | FETCHAM PARK | M. Pipe | 2–1JF |
| 17 Jan C | Worcester | CELTIC FLIGHT | Mrs M. Rimell | 5–1 |
| 18 Jan H | Ludlow | KINGS RANK | M. Pipe | 2–5F |
| 19 Jan C | Lingfield Park | JUVEN LIGHT | R. Akehurst | 1–3F |
| 19 Jan H | Lingfield Park | HONEST WORD | M. Pipe | 8–15F |
| 20 Jan H | Kempton Park | BATTALION | C. Brooks | 5–2F |
| 21 Jan H | Haydock Park | OUT OF THE GLOOM | M. Pipe | 3–1 |
| 21 Jan C | Haydock Park | BRUTON STREET | C. Brooks | 7–4 |

| | | | | |
|---|---|---|---|---|
| 24 Jan C | Chepstow | CANFORD PALM | C. Brooks | 5–2F |
| 24 Jan H | Chepstow | ELVERCONE | A. J. Wilson | 4–1 |
| 25 Jan C | Wolverhampton | BALUCHI | B. Preece | 2–1 |
| 25 Jan H | Wolverhampton | PROTECTION | A. Turnell | 5–2 |
| 26 Jan H | Taunton | LE CYGNE | M. Pipe | 15–8F |
| 27 Jan C | Wincanton | PUKKA MAJOR | T. Thomson Jones | 11–2 |
| 31 Jan H | Leicester | TEL–ECHO | M. Pipe | 11–10F |
| 31 Jan C | Leicester | BALUCHI | B. Preece | 5–6F |
| 31 Jan H | Leicester | CELCIUS | M. Pipe | 4–1 |
| 1 Feb C | Hereford | ADMIRALS ALL | C. Brooks | evensF |
| 2 Feb C | Lingfield Park | WINGSPAN | M. Pipe | 11–10F |
| 6 Feb H | Fontwell Park | DELKUSHA | M. Pipe | 11–8F |
| 6 Feb H | Fontwell Park | BATTALION | C. Brooks | 10–11F |
| 7 Feb H | Warwick | ANTI MATTER | M. Pipe | evensF |
| 7 Feb H | Warwick | PERTEMPS NETWORK | M. Pipe | 6–4 |
| 8 Feb C | Ascot | SABIN DU LOIR | M. Pipe | 1–2F |
| 10 Feb C | Newbury | JUVEN LIGHT | R. Akehurst | 4–7F |
| 11 Feb C | Newbury | ADMIRALS ALL | C. Brooks | 15–8F |
| 13 Feb H | Nottingham | THE GAELCHARN | C. Brooks | 7–4F |
| 14 Feb C | Newton Abbot | WINGSPAN | M. Pipe | 8–15F |
| 14 Feb C | Newton Abbot | LET HIM BY | M. Pipe | 7–4F |
| 14 Feb H | Newton Abbot | AVIONNE | M. Pipe | 4–9F |
| 15 Feb C | Worcester | BALUCHI | B. Preece | 15–8F |
| 15 Feb H | Worcester | SAYFAR'S LAD | M. Pipe | 4–6F |
| 16 Feb H | Leicester | AU BON | M. Pipe | 11–8F |
| 18 Feb C | Nottingham | PHOENIX GOLD | J. FitzGerald | 15–8F |
| 20 Feb C | Fontwell Park | LET HIM BY | M. Pipe | 2–1 |
| 22 Feb H | Warwick | SAYFAR'S LAD | M. Pipe | 9–4 |
| 22 Feb C | Warwick | PHAROAH'S LAEN | M. Pipe | 7–2 |
| 22 Feb H | Warwick | TRAVEL MYSTERY | M. Pipe | 6–4F |
| 23 Feb H | Folkestone | GO WEST | M. Pipe | 6–4F |
| 25 Feb C | Kempton Park | BONANZA BOY | M. Pipe | 5–1 |
| 28 Feb H | Nottingham | LE CYGNE | M. Pipe | 4–5F |
| 1 Mar C | Worcester | BEAU RANGER | M. Pipe | 40–85F |
| 2 Mar H | Lingfield Park | KUMAKAS NEPHEW | M. Pipe | 4–1 |
| 4 Mar C | Newbury | ADMIRALS ALL | C. Brooks | evensF |
| 4 Mar H | Newbury | PERTEMPS NETWORK | M. Pipe | 4–5F |
| 4 Mar C | Hereford | SILVER ACE | M. Pipe | 1–2F |
| 4 Mar H | Hereford | GO WEST | M. Pipe | 11–10F |
| 11 Mar H | Chepstow | FETCHAM PARK | M. Pipe | 8–15F |
| 11 Mar H | Sandown Park | TRAVEL MYSTERY | M. Pipe | 3–1F |
| 14 Mar C | Cheltenham | PUKKA MAJOR | T. Thomson Jones | 4–1JF |
| 17 Mar H | Wolverhampton | LE CYGNE | M. Pipe | 4–7F |
| 17 Mar C | Wolverhampton | MITHRAS | B. Preece | 6–1 |
| 18 Mar C | Lingfield Park | SILVER ACE | M. Pipe | 6–4F |
| 22 Mar H | Worcester | TEMPLE REEF | M. Pipe | 3–1 |
| 22 Mar C | Worcester | FANDANGO BOY | M. Pipe | 11–10F |
| 22 Mar H | Worcester | CELCIUS | M. Pipe | 4–7F |
| 23 Mar H | Taunton | ANTI MATTER | M. Pipe | 8–11F |
| 27 Mar H | Chepstow | CELTIC SHOT | C. Brooks | 1–7F |
| 27 Mar H | Chepstow | GO WEST | M. Pipe | 1–7F |
| 27 Mar H | Chepstow | HILARION | J. Edwards | w.o. |

| 28 Mar H | Chepstow | OLD KILPATRICK | M. Pipe | 4–11F |
|---|---|---|---|---|
| 29 Mar H | Worcester | ELVERCONE | A. J. Wilson | 9–4JF |
| 13 Apr H | Ludlow | JUST ROSE | M. Pipe | 12–1 |
| 15 Apr H | Bangor-on-Dee | AU BON | M. Pipe | 8–11F |
| 15 Apr C | Bangor-on-Dee | WINGSPAN | M. Pipe | 2–1 |
| 18 Apr H | Devon & Exeter | OLD KILPATRICK | M. Pipe | 6–4F |
| 20 Apr H | Cheltenham | VOYAGE SANS RETOUR | M. Pipe | 9–4 |
| 22 Apr H | Uttoxeter | HIGH BID | M. Pipe | 5–4F |
| 24 Apr H | Southwell | AVIONNE | M. Pipe | 15–8 |
| 27 Apr H | Towcester | OLD KILPATRICK | M. Pipe | 13–8F |
| 27 Apr C | Towcester | CANFORD PALM | C. Brooks | 4–1 |
| 27 Apr C | Towcester | GAY MOORE | M. Robinson | 10–1 |
| 27 Apr H | Towcester | MARKET FORCES | N. Gaselee | 7–2 |
| 28 Apr C | Taunton | MY CUP OF TEA | M. Pipe | 4–6F |
| 5 May H | Newton Abbot | ANTI MATTER | M. Pipe | 4–7F |
| 6 May H | Warwick | RAAHIN | R. Akehurst | 15–8F |
| 9 May H | Chepstow | AU BON | M. Pipe | 11–10F |
| 10 May H | Worcester | RASTANNORA | M. Pipe | 8–13F |
| 12 May H | Taunton | AIMEE JANE | M. Pipe | 4–7F |
| 13 May H | Warwick | FATU HIVA | M. Pipe | 7–2F |
| 13 May C | Warwick | DUDIE | R. Akehurst | 2–1 |
| 17 May C | Worcester | AL MISK | M. Pipe | 10–11F |
| 17 May H | Worcester | FATU HIVA | M. Pipe | evensF |
| 18 May H | Huntingdon | HANSEATIC | N. Tinkler | 2–1F |
| 18 May C | Huntingdon | DUSTY DIPLOMACY | M. Pipe | 7–4 |
| 18 May H | Huntingdon | MELENDEZ | M. Pipe | 11–2 |
| 19 May H | Stratford | ANTI MATTER | M. Pipe | 8–13F |
| 20 May H | Bangor-on-Dee | CHIC CAROLYN | M. Pipe | evensF |
| 20 May C | Bangor-on-Dee | MY CUP OF TEA | M. Pipe | 8–13F |
| 27 May C | Southwell | DUSTY DIPLOMACY | M. Pipe | 4–11F |
| 29 May H | Devon & Exeter | MIGHTY PRINCE | M. Pipe | 1–3F |
| 29 May H | Devon & Exeter | AVIONNE | M. Pipe | 1–2F |
| 3 Jun C | Stratford | HAZY SUNSET | C. Brooks | 5–2 |

### 1989–90: TOTAL WINNERS 170

| 29 Jul C | Newton Abbot | HAZY SUNSET | C. Brooks | 2–5F |
|---|---|---|---|---|
| 29 Jul H | Newton Abbot | OUT RUN | M. Pipe | 6–5F |
| 31 Jul C | Newton Abbot | MY CUP OF TEA | M. Pipe | 9–4 |
| 3 Aug H | Devon & Exeter | MADAME RUBY | M. Pipe | 2–1 |
| 4 Aug C | Market Rasen | HAZY SUNSET | C. Brooks | 1–5F |
| 5 Aug H | Worcester | GREEN'S FINE ART | M. Pipe | 10–11F |
| 5 Aug H | Worcester | HARD TO HOLD | D. Thom | 7–2 |
| 10 Aug C | Newton Abbot | WALNUT WAY | M. Pipe | 5–4F |
| 10 Aug H | Newton Abbot | SHADEUX | M. Pipe | 1–3F |
| 11 Aug H | Plumpton | LOVELY WONGA | D. Wilson | 4–1 |
| 19 Aug H | Hereford | ABDERA | M. Pipe | 5–1 |
| 23 Aug C | Fontwell Park | BOARDMANS STYLE | M. Pipe | 5–4F |
| 23 Aug H | Fontwell Park | SINGLE SHOOTER | R. O'Sullivan | 5–2 |
| 25 Aug H | Devon & Exeter | ZAMORE | M. Pipe | 1–3F |
| 26 Aug C | Hereford | BOARDMANS STYLE | M. Pipe | 2–5F |
| 28 Aug H | Newton Abbot | ROYAL WONDER | M. Pipe | 4–11F |

| | | | | |
|---|---|---|---|---|
| 29 Aug H | Newton Abbot | LEMHILL | M. Pipe | 1–6F |
| 29 Aug H | Newton Abbot | TOP CROWN | M. Pipe | 4–5F |
| 29 Aug C | Newton Abbot | SKIPPING TIM | M. Pipe | 4–11F |
| 30 Aug C | Newton Abbot | SWING TO STEEL | M. Pipe | 6–4 |
| 30 Aug C | Newton Abbot | WALNUT WAY | M. Pipe | 4–5F |
| 31 Aug H | Worcester | GLENCOE BOY | J. O'Shea | 13–8 |
| 31 Aug H | Worcester | POLLOCK | M. Pipe | 4–5F |
| 1 Sep C | Hereford | SKIPPING TIM | M. Pipe | 2–5F |
| 1 Sep C | Hereford | BOARDMANS STYLE | M. Pipe | 2–9F |
| 7 Sep C | Newton Abbot | RULING DYNASTY | M. Pipe | 8–15F |
| 8 Sep C | Newton Abbot | SWING TO STEEL | M. Pipe | 5–4JF |
| 8 Sep H | Newton Abbot | MILFORD QUAY | M. Pipe | 8–15F |
| 8 Sep H | Newton Abbot | ZULU | M. Pipe | 2–7F |
| 13 Sep H | Devon & Exeter | ZAMORE | M. Pipe | 1–4F |
| 13 Sep C | Devon & Exeter | LATTIN GENERAL | C. Brooks | 5–4 |
| 16 Sep H | Warwick | AMAREDO | M. Pipe | 8–13F |
| 16 Sep H | Warwick | MILFORD QUAY | M. Pipe | 6–4F |
| 18 Sep C | Plumpton | REIN DE TOUT | M. Pipe | 2–5F |
| 18 Sep C | Plumpton | RULING DYNASTY | M. Pipe | 1–3F |
| 20 Sep C | Devon & Exeter | SKIPPING TIM | M. Pipe | 6–4JF |
| 23 Sep C | Market Rasen | HAZY SUNSET | C. Brooks | 11–4 |
| 28 Sep H | Taunton | POLLOCK | M. Pipe | 4–11F |
| 28 Sep H | Taunton | LONELY REEF | M. Pipe | 1–3F |
| 2 Oct C | Fontwell Park | REIN DE TOUT | M. Pipe | 10–11F |
| 2 Oct H | Fontwell Park | ROYAL WONDER | M. Pipe | 4–6F |
| 3 Oct H | Devon & Exeter | LOVELY WONGA | D. Wilson | 6–1 |
| 3 Oct H | Devon & Exeter | LONELY REEF | M. Pipe | 2–7F |
| 3 Oct C | Devon & Exeter | REIN DE TOUT | M. Pipe | 6–4F |
| 5 Oct H | Cheltenham | MILFORD QUAY | M. Pipe | evensF |
| 5 Oct C | Cheltenham | SKIPPING TIM | M. Pipe | 1–4F |
| 7 Oct C | Worcester | ASSAGLAWI | Miss H. Knight | 4–9F |
| 10 Oct C | Newton Abbot | HAZY SUNSET | C. Brooks | 6–5F |
| 11 Oct H | Plumpton | BLAKE'S PROGRESS | M. Pipe | 5–4F |
| 12 Oct H | Wincanton | IN–KEEPING | M. Pipe | 11–10F |
| 14 Oct H | Ayr | ARDEN | C. Brooks | 11–8F |
| 19 Oct C | Taunton | SAN OVAC | C. Brooks | 6–5F |
| 20 Oct H | Ludlow | WONDERINE | M. Pipe | 1–4F |
| 21 Oct H | Kempton Park | ROCHALLOR | M. Pipe | 11–8F |
| 24 Oct C | Plumpton | SAN OVAC | C. Brooks | 10–11F |
| 26 Oct C | Wincanton | BAJAN SUNSHINE | C. Brooks | 9–4 |
| 26 Oct H | Wincanton | WALK OF LIFE | M. Pipe | 11–8F |
| 27 Oct H | Devon & Exeter | MADAME RUBY | M. Pipe | 11–10F |
| 27 Oct H | Devon & Exeter | WONDERINE | M. Pipe | 4–5F |
| 27 Oct H | Devon & Exeter | GALWEX LADY | M. Pipe | 11–10F |
| 27 Oct H | Devon & Exeter | RULING DYNASTY | M. Pipe | 6–4F |
| 31 Oct C | Nottingham | MAINTOWN | M. Pipe | 7–4 |
| 31 Oct H | Nottingham | ROYAL WONDER | M. Pipe | 4–7F |
| 31 Oct C | Nottingham | ASSAGLAWI | Miss H. Knight | 2–5F |
| 1 Nov C | Newbury | BAJAN SUNSHINE | C. Brooks | 3–1 |
| 2 Nov H | Kempton Park | IN–KEEPING | M. Pipe | 4–1 |
| 4 Nov C | Chepstow | STAR'S DELIGHT | M. Pipe | 4–7F |
| 4 Nov C | Chepstow | WALNUT WAY | M. Pipe | 4–11F |

| | | | | |
|---|---|---|---|---|
| 6 Nov H | Plumpton | TRI FOLENE | M. Pipe | 2–1F |
| 7 Nov H | Devon & Exeter | MONARU | M. Pipe | 4–6F |
| 7 Nov C | Devon & Exeter | HUNTWORTH | M. Pipe | 4–6F |
| 8 Nov C | Newbury | SOLIDASAROCK | R. Akehurst | 10–11F |
| 9 Nov H | Uttoxeter | WONDERINE | M. Pipe | 6–4F |
| 10 Nov C | Cheltenham | STAR'S DELIGHT | M. Pipe | 1–2F |
| 14 Nov H | Worcester | REGAL AMBITION | M. Pipe | 4–5F |
| 18 Nov H | Ascot | ARDEN | C. Brooks | 5–6F |
| 22 Nov H | Haydock Park | TRI FOLENE | M. Pipe | 11–8F |
| 22 Nov C | Haydock Park | STAR'S DELIGHT | M. Pipe | 11–8F |
| 23 Nov H | Haydock Park | ROYAL WONDER | M. Pipe | 5–4F |
| 24 Nov H | Leicester | MONARU | M. Pipe | 8–15F |
| 27 Nov C | Nottingham | WOLFHANGAR | C. Brooks | 7–4JF |
| 27 Nov C | Nottingham | ESPY | C. Brooks | 1–4F |
| 28 Nov C | Newton Abbot | REDGRAVE DEVIL | M. Pipe | 5–4F |
| 29 Nov C | Hereford | FLAXEN KING | M. Pipe | 8–11F |
| 2 Dec C | Chepstow | BONANZA BOY | M. Pipe | 4–1 |
| 5 Dec H | Fontwell Park | MIINNEHOMA | M. Pipe | evensF |
| 7 Dec H | Uttoxeter | GALWEX LADY | M. Pipe | 2–5F |
| 7 Dec C | Uttoxeter | ESPY | C. Brooks | 4–7F |
| 8 Dec H | Cheltenham | ROYAL WONDER | M. Pipe | 85–40 |
| 8 Dec H | Cheltenham | VAGOG | M. Pipe | 9–4F |
| 9 Dec H | Cheltenham | RUN FOR FREE | M. Pipe | 9–4JF |
| 12 Dec C | Plumpton | BREAK OUT | C. Brooks | 6–4F |
| 13 Dec H | Haydock Park | GOLD SERVICE | M. Pipe | 11–8F |
| 13 Dec C | Haydock Park | SABIN DU LOIR | M. Pipe | 7–4F |
| 13 Dec C | Haydock Park | BAIES | C. Brooks | 20–1 |
| 14 Dec H | Haydock Park | KINGS RANK | M. Pipe | 9–4F |
| 14 Dec C | Haydock Park | CELTIC SHOT | C. Brooks | 2–5F |
| 14 Dec H | Haydock Park | MIINNEHOMA | M. Pipe | 4–9F |
| 20 Dec H | Bangor–on–Dee | MISS CHALK | M. Pipe | 5–2F |
| 20 Dec C | Bangor–on–Dee | REDGRAVE DEVIL | M. Pipe | 11–4F |
| 20 Dec H | Bangor–on–Dee | ABBOTTS VIEW | C. Brooks | 9–2F |
| 22 Dec H | Uttoxeter | BLACK HUMOUR | C. Brooks | 13–8F |
| 22 Dec C | Uttoxeter | SIRE NANTAIS | M. Pipe | 4–5F |
| 23 Dec H | Chepstow | REGAL AMBITION | M. Pipe | 10–11F |
| 23 Dec C | Chepstow | BONANZA BOY | M. Pipe | 15–8F |
| 23 Dec C | Chepstow | THE LEGGETT | M. Pipe | 9–4F |
| 26 Dec C | Kempton Park | CELTIC SHOT | C. Brooks | 30–100F |
| 27 Dec H | Wolverhampton | NINJA* | D. Nicholson | 20–1 |
| 28 Dec C | Taunton | THE LEGGETT | M. Pipe | 1–2F |
| 30 Dec H | Newbury | MIINNEHOMA | M. Pipe | 8–11F |
| 30 Dec H | Newbury | BABIL | N. Twiston–Davies | 8–1 |
| 1 Jan H | Devon & Exeter | LUCKY VERDICT | M. Pipe | 5–2 |
| 5 Jan C | Haydock Park | SABIN DU LOIR | M. Pipe | 2–7F |
| 5 Jan C | Haydock Park | STAR'S DELIGHT | M. Pipe | 1–4F |
| 6 Jan C | Sandown Park | CELTIC SHOT | C. Brooks | 2–5F |
| 8 Jan C | Chepstow | BLUE RAINBOW | M. Pipe | 9–4F |
| 8 Jan H | Chepstow | LUCKY VERDICT | M. Pipe | 4–6F |
| 8 Jan C | Chepstow | NORTH LANE | M. Pipe | 8–1 |
| 9 Jan H | Newton Abbot | SHADEUX | M. Pipe | 5–4 |
| 9 Jan H | Newton Abbot | MRS MUCK | N. Twiston–Davies | 15–2 |

| | | | | |
|---|---|---|---|---|
| 12 Jan H | Ascot | SAYYURE | N. Tinkler | 7–4 |
| 13 Jan C | Ascot | ESPY | C. Brooks | 5–1 |
| 13 Jan H | Ascot | AMBASSADOR | M. Pipe | 14–1 |
| 16 Jan C | Worcester | CLASSEY BOY | G. Ham | 9–2 |
| 18 Jan H | Newton Abbot | SILVER KING | M. Pipe | 2–5F |
| 20 Jan C | Haydock Park | HARLEY STREET MAN | M. Pipe | 2–1 |
| 20 Jan H | Haydock Park | CYPHRATE | M. Pipe | 2–5F |
| 23 Jan H | Chepstow | HARRY LIME | M. Pipe | 6–4F |
| 30 Jan H | Leicester | REGAL AMBITION | M. Pipe | 4–6F |
| 5 Feb H | Wolverhampton | STONE FLAKE | P. Kelleway | 9–2 |
| 8 Feb H | Wincanton | TREFELYN CONE | M. Pipe | 6–4JF |
| 9 Feb H | Newbury | SILVER KING | M. Pipe | 5–6F |
| 10 Feb C | Newbury | CHATAM | M. Pipe | 100–30 |
| 10 Feb C | Newbury | FU'S LADY | M. Pipe | 4–1 |
| 12 Feb H | Nottingham | RE–RELEASE | M. Pipe | 13–8F |
| 17 Feb C | Chepstow | WINGSPAN | M. Pipe | 5–1 |
| 19 Feb H | Wolverhampton | BATTALION | C. Brooks | 9–2 |
| 21 Feb H | Warwick | RUN FOR FREE | M. Pipe | 5–2 |
| 24 Feb H | Stratford | MISS CHALK | M. Pipe | 3–1 |
| 24 Feb C | Stratford | THE LEGGETT | M. Pipe | evensF |
| 2 Mar H | Haydock Park | BITTER BUCK | C. Brooks | 4–6F |
| 2 Mar H | Haydock Park | MILFORD QUAY | M. Pipe | 3–1 |
| 2 Mar C | Haydock Park | THE LEGGETT | M. Pipe | evensF |
| 3 Mar H | Newbury | MIINNEHOMA | M. Pipe | evensF |
| 3 Mar H | Hereford | ROYAL DERBI | N. Callaghan | 4–9F |
| 7 Mar H | Bangor–on–Dee | WILL JAMES | M. Pipe | 8–1 |
| 9 Mar H | Sandown Park | ABBOTTS VIEW | C. Brooks | 7–1 |
| 9 Mar H | Sandown Park | BATTALION | C. Brooks | 2–1F |
| 14 Mar H | Cheltenham | REGAL AMBITION | M. Pipe | 3–1F |
| 16 Mar H | Wolverhampton | DELTIC | M. Pipe | 3–1 |
| 16 Mar H | Wolverhampton | MY YOUNG MAN | C. Brooks | 8–11F |
| 17 Mar C | Uttoxeter | ESPY | C. Brooks | evensF |
| 19 Mar C | Wolverhampton | WINGSPAN | M. Pipe | 11–10F |
| 21 Mar H | Worcester | WALK OF LIFE | M. Pipe | 6–4F |
| 22 Mar H | Devon & Exeter | PERISTYLE | M. Pipe | 2–5F |
| 23 Mar H | Ludlow | DELTIC | M. Pipe | 1–2F |
| 27 Mar C | Sandown Park | THE LEGGETT | M. Pipe | 6–5F |
| 27 Mar C | Sandown Park | ALL JEFF | C. Brooks | 4–6F |
| 29 Mar H | Taunton | SUNSET COURT | C. Brooks | 8–15F |
| 29 Mar C | Taunton | DAWN PRINCE | M. Pipe | 2–1 |
| 31 Mar H | Ascot | BABIL | N. Twiston–Davies | 2–1 |
| 6 Apr H | Liverpool | SAYPAREE | M. Pipe | 10–1 |
| 11 Apr H | Ascot | AMBASSADOR | M. Pipe | 5–1 |
| 12 Apr H | Taunton | OTI | M. Pipe | evensF |
| 12 Apr H | Taunton | RASTANNORA | M. Pipe | 2–1 |
| 14 Apr C | Newton Abbot | MIGHTY PRINCE | M. Pipe | 4–1 |
| 14 Apr C | Newton Abbot | WITH GODS HELP | C. Brooks | 7–1 |
| 14 Apr C | Newton Abbot | CROWECROPPER | B. Preece | 9–4F |
| 16 Apr C | Newton Abbot | WINGSPAN | M. Pipe | 1–2F |
| 7 May H | Devon & Exeter | GOLD SERVICE | M. Pipe | 5–6F |

*Ninja was awarded the race after Sartorius, first past the post, failed the dope test.

**1990–1: TOTAL WINNERS 141**

| | | | | |
|---|---|---|---|---|
| 4 Aug C | Newton Abbot | WALK OF LIFE | M. Pipe | 7–4 |
| 4 Aug H | Newton Abbot | PHARAOH BLUE | M. Pipe | 10–11F |
| 8 Aug C | Devon & Exeter | CUT ABOVE AVERAGE | M. Pipe | 4–7F |
| 9 Aug H | Devon & Exeter | MAJESTIC RUN | M. Pipe | 4–9F |
| 9 Aug C | Devon & Exeter | BOARDMANS STYLE | M. Pipe | 2–1 |
| 9 Aug H | Devon & Exeter | ULTRA VIOLET | M. Pipe | 4–7F |
| 11 Aug H | Worcester | PHARAOH BLUE | M. Pipe | 4–9F |
| 11 Aug H | Worcester | HOPSCOTCH | M. Pipe | 11–10F |
| 14 Aug C | Devon & Exeter | BOARDMANS STYLE | M. Pipe | 2–13F |
| 24 Aug H | Devon & Exeter | PHARAOH BLUE | M. Pipe | 2–5F |
| 24 Aug H | Devon & Exeter | SOUTH SANDS | M. Pipe | 4–6F |
| 27 Aug H | Newton Abbot | HOPSCOTCH | M. Pipe | 4–11F |
| 27 Aug H | Newton Abbot | PHARAOH BLUE | M. Pipe | 4–6F |
| 29 Aug H | Newton Abbot | SOUTH SANDS | M. Pipe | 5–4F |
| 1 Sep H | Hereford | TACTOUKA | M. Pipe | 4–6F |
| 1 Sep H | Hereford | PHARAOH BLUE | M. Pipe | 11–10F |
| 5 Sep H | Fontwell Park | RULING DYNASTY | M. Usher | 100–30 |
| 6 Sep C | Newton Abbot | TARQOGAN'S BEST | M. Pipe | 7–2 |
| 6 Sep H | Newton Abbot | ULTRA VIOLET | M. Pipe | 9–2 |
| 7 Sep C | Newton Abbot | SKIPPING TIM | M. Pipe | 8–11F |
| 12 Sep H | Devon & Exeter | SQUADRON | M. Pipe | 4–9F |
| 12 Sep H | Devon & Exeter | HOPSCOTCH | M. Pipe | 4–7F |
| 15 Sep C | Worcester | SKIPPING TIM | M. Pipe | 6–4F |
| 19 Sep C | Devon & Exeter | DAWN PRINCE | M. Pipe | 9–4 |
| 20 Sep H | Uttoxeter | NEW DUDS | M. Pipe | 11–10 |
| 20 Sep H | Uttoxeter | PHARAOH BLUE | M. Pipe | 2–1 |
| 22 Sep C | Worcester | ASSAGLAWI | Miss H. Knight | evensF |
| 26 Sep H | Perth | BOKARO | C. Brooks | 11–10F |
| 2 Oct H | Cheltenham | NEW DUDS | M. Pipe | 1–3F |
| 3 Oct H | Cheltenham | HOPSCOTCH | M. Pipe | 8–11F |
| 4 Oct C | Cheltenham | WINGSPAN | M. Pipe | 7–4JF |
| 4 Oct H | Cheltenham | KALSHAN | M. Pipe | 13–8F |
| 6 Oct C | Worcester | ASSAGLAWI | Miss H. Knight | 10–11F |
| 6 Oct H | Worcester | CAPTAIN DIBBLE | N. Twiston–Davies | 8–1 |
| 9 Oct H | Newton Abbot | CHANAKEE | M. Pipe | 5–4F |
| 9 Oct C | Newton Abbot | WINGSPAN | M. Pipe | 4–9F |
| 9 Oct H | Newton Abbot | SQUADRON | M. Pipe | 4–5F |
| 13 Oct H | Warwick | KALSHAN | M. Pipe | 2–7F |
| 17 Oct H | Cheltenham | HOPSCOTCH | M. Pipe | 1–5F |
| 17 Oct C | Cheltenham | SKIPPING TIM | M. Pipe | 5–4F |
| 24 Oct H | Ascot | PORTO HELI | M. Pipe | 100–30 |
| 24 Oct C | Ascot | FU'S LADY | M. Pipe | 6–1 |
| 26 Oct C | Newbury | ESPY | C. Brooks | 11–8 |
| 31 Oct H | Newbury | BABIL | N. Twiston–Davies | 1–2F |
| 1 Nov H | Stratford | SQUADRON | M. Pipe | 3–1F |
| 2 Nov C | Bangor–on–Dee | OKEETEE | C. Brooks | 7–4F |
| 2 Nov H | Bangor–on–Dee | SALINE | M. Pipe | 9–2 |
| 3 Nov C | Wetherby | CELTIC SHOT | C. Brooks | 7–4F |
| 3 Nov H | Wetherby | BATTALION | C. Brooks | 11–8F |
| 5 Nov C | Wolverhampton | SKIPPING TIM | M. Pipe | 2–13F |

| 6 Nov C | Devon & Exeter | SABIN DU LOIR | M. Pipe | 7–2 |
|---|---|---|---|---|
| 6 Nov H | Devon & Exeter | MISS EUROLINK | M. Pipe | 7–1 |
| 9 Nov H | Market Rasen | MASSINGHAM | M. Pipe | 7–2 |
| 9 Nov C | Market Rasen | INVASION | J. Glover | 2–5 |
| 24 Jan C | Newton Abbot | OUTSIDE EDGE | M. Pipe | 6–5F |
| 25 Jan C | Wincanton | FU'S LADY | M. Pipe | 11–2 |
| 26 Jan H | Cheltenham | HOPSCOTCH | M. Pipe | 8–11F |
| 26 Jan C | Cheltenham | CELTIC SHOT | C. Brooks | 11–4 |
| 29 Jan H | Leicester | PRIMATICE | M. Pipe | 1–2F |
| 29 Jan H | Leicester | CAPTAIN DIBBLE | N. Twiston–Davies | 13–8 |
| 29 Jan H | Leicester | GRANVILLE AGAIN | M. Pipe | 2–9F |
| 30 Jan H | Nottingham | TIM SOLDIER | M. Pipe | 11–8F |
| 30 Jan H | Nottingham | RHODES | R. Akehurst | 5–1 |
| 1 Feb H | Bangor–on–Dee | LEADING ROLE | M. Pipe | 8–11F |
| 2 Feb H | Sandown Park | VOYAGE SANS RETOUR | M. Pipe | 8–1 |
| 11 Feb A | Southwell | VIGANO | M. Pipe | 4–5F |
| 11 Feb A | Southwell | TOM CLAPTON | M. Pipe | 4–6F |
| 12 Feb A | Lingfield Park | VIKING FLAGSHIP | M. Pipe | 2–7F |
| 14 Feb A | Lingfield Park | TOM CLAPTON | M. Pipe | 8–15F |
| 16 Feb C | Windsor | ESPY | C. Brooks | 10–11F |
| 18 Feb H | Fontwell Park | FORTLIMON | M. Pipe | 9–2 |
| 20 Feb H | Warwick | RUN FOR FREE | M. Pipe | 6–5F |
| 20 Feb C | Warwick | ROLLING BALL | M. Pipe | 7–2 |
| 21 Feb H | Wincanton | WELSH BARD | C. Brooks | 11–1 |
| 22 Feb H | Kempton Park | RIVERSIDE BOY | M. Pipe | 11–8F |
| 22 Feb H | Kempton Park | BLACK HUMOUR | C. Brooks | 9–4 |
| 23 Feb H | Kempton Park | GRANVILLE AGAIN | M. Pipe | 11–4 |
| 27 Feb C | Worcester | SABIN DU LOIR | M. Pipe | 4–6F |
| 28 Feb C | Ludlow | LAUDERDALE LAD | J. King | 4–6F |
| 2 Mar H | Haydock Park | NEW DUDS | M. Pipe | evensF |
| 4 Mar H | Windsor | BIENNIAL | M. Pipe | 100–30 |
| 6 Mar A | Southwell | JANE CRAIG | N. Twiston–Davies | 11–8F |
| 7 Mar H | Wincanton | TOM CLAPTON | M. Pipe | 4–5F |
| 7 Mar H | Wincanton | PARSON'S THORNS | C. Brooks | 6–5F |
| 8 Mar H | Sandown Park | RIVERSIDE BOY | M. Pipe | 5–4F |
| 9 Mar C | Chepstow | THE LEGGETT | M. Pipe | 3–1 |
| 11 Mar H | Plumpton | LEADING ROLE | M. Pipe | 13–8 |
| 13 Mar C | Cheltenham | ROLLING BALL | M. Pipe | 7–2 |
| 14 Mar C | Cheltenham | CHATAM | M. Pipe | 3–1 |
| 15 Mar H | Wolverhampton | TODA | M. Pipe | 6–4F |
| 15 Mar C | Wolverhampton | HIGH KNOWL | M. Pipe | 2–1F |
| 16 Mar H | Uttoxeter | TAPAGEUR | M. Pipe | 6–1 |
| 16 Mar C | Uttoxeter | BONANZA BOY | M. Pipe | 15–8F |
| 18 Mar C | Wolverhampton | THE LEGGETT | M. Pipe | 9–4F |
| 19 Mar C | Fontwell Park | ROYAL GREEK | M. Pipe | 2–1F |
| 21 Mar H | Devon & Exeter | GULSHA | N. Twiston–Davies | 11–10F |
| 22 Mar C | Newbury | AQUILIFER | M. Pipe | 11–10F |
| 2 Apr C | Chepstow | HIGH KNOWL | M. Pipe | 11–8 |
| 2 Apr H | Chepstow | BRADMORE'S CHUM | M. Pipe | 7–2 |
| 5 Apr H | Liverpool | TREFELYN CONE | M. Pipe | 9–1 |
| 5 Apr H | Liverpool | GRANVILLE AGAIN | M. Pipe | 5–4F |
| 12 Apr H | Wincanton | TAMARPOUR | M. Pipe | 7–1 |

| | | | | |
|---|---|---|---|---|
| 12 Apr C | Wincanton | ANTI MATTER | M. Pipe | 11–8F |
| 16 Apr H | Fontwell Park | EUROLINK THE LAD | M. Pipe | 11–10F |
| 17 Apr C | Cheltenham | ANTI MATTER | M. Pipe | 6–5F |
| 18 Apr H | Cheltenham | HOPSCOTCH | M. Pipe | 7–4 |
| 23 Apr H | Perth | SMOOTH STYLE | C. Brooks | 7–4F |
| 25 Apr H | Ludlow | TAKEMETHERE | M. Pipe | evensF |
| 25 Apr H | Wincanton | BALASANI | M. Pipe | 8–11F |
| 26 Apr A | Southwell | COLOUR SCHEME | M. Pipe | 4–5F |
| 26 Apr H | Taunton | EUROLINK THE LAD | M. Pipe | 8–11F |
| 26 Apr H | Taunton | OLNICETTO | M. Pipe | 9–1 |
| 26 Apr H | Taunton | MYFOR | M. Pipe | evensF |
| 30 Apr H | Ascot | VAGOG | M. Pipe | 5–1 |
| 30 Apr C | Ascot | FU'S LADY | M. Pipe | 5–2 |
| 30 Apr H | Ascot | EUROLINK THE LAD | M. Pipe | 9–4 |
| 2 May H | Newton Abbot | TAPAGEUR | M. Pipe | 8–15F |
| 2 May H | Newton Abbot | TAMARPOUR | M. Pipe | 2–9F |
| 4 May H | Uttoxeter | SWEET GLOW | M. Pipe | 6–4F |
| 4 May H | Uttoxeter | NORDIC DELIGHT | M. Pipe | 11–2 |
| 6 May H | Haydock Park | SWEET N' TWENTY | M. Pipe | 5–2F |
| 6 May H | Haydock Park | LEADING ROLE | M. Pipe | 8–15F |
| 7 May H | Chepstow | SQUIRE JIM | N. Twiston–Davies | 11–2 |
| 8 May H | Worcester | KENFIRE | M. Pipe | 4–7F |
| 9 May H | Huntingdon | NOTTAGE | M. Pipe | 6–4F |
| 9 May H | Uttoxeter | TOM CLAPTON | M. Pipe | 4–5F |
| 9 May H | Uttoxeter | TAMARPOUR | M. Pipe | 4–5F |
| 10 May C | Taunton | SHANNAGARY | R. Hodges | 4–1 |
| 11 May C | Warwick | ANTI MATTER | M. Pipe | 8–11F |
| 14 May H | Towcester | TAPAGEUR | M. Pipe | 5–2F |
| 15 May C | Hereford | TRI FOLENE | M. Pipe | 4–7F |
| 15 May H | Newton Abbot | SWEET GLOW | M. Pipe | 1–10F |
| 18 May C | Bangor–on–Dee | TRI FOLENE | M. Pipe | 4–9F |
| 18 May H | Warwick | AFFORD | M. Pipe | 7–4F |
| 18 May H | Warwick | TOM CLAPTON | M. Pipe | 9–4JF |
| 22 May H | Worcester | KENFIRE | M. Pipe | 2–1F |
| 22 May H | Worcester | TAPAGEUR | M. Pipe | 1–2F |
| 25 May H | Cartmel | SWEET N' TWENTY | M. Pipe | 1–3F |
| 27 May H | Hereford | TODA | M. Pipe | 11–10F |
| 27 May H | Hereford | SWEET GLOW | M. Pipe | 8–11F |
| 28 May H | Uttoxeter | MELENDEZ | M. Pipe | 12–1 |

## 1991–2: TOTAL WINNERS 175

| | | | | |
|---|---|---|---|---|
| 2 Aug H | Newton Abbot | THE BLUE BOY | M. Pipe | 4–7F |
| 7 Aug H | Devon & Exeter | EVER SMILE | M. Pipe | 8–11F |
| 7 Aug H | Devon & Exeter | STAGE PLAYER | R. Simpson | 8–15F |
| 7 Aug C | Devon & Exeter | REFUTE | M. Pipe | 3–1 |
| 8 Aug C | Uttoxeter | TAPAGEUR | M. Pipe | 8–13F |
| 8 Aug H | Uttoxeter | FLY THE WIND | M. Pipe | 9–4F |
| 10 Aug H | Worcester | NORDIC DELIGHT | M. Pipe | 9–4F |
| 10 Aug H | Worcester | ARABIAN SULTAN | M. Pipe | 5–1 |
| 10 Aug H | Worcester | PRIMITIVE SINGER | M. Pipe | 4–5F |
| 12 Aug H | Worcester | CIXI | M. Pipe | 10–11F |

| | | | | |
|---|---|---|---|---|
| 15 Aug H | Newton Abbot | TIMID | M. Pipe | 5–2 |
| 15 Aug H | Newton Abbot | THE BLUE BOY | M. Pipe | 1–3F |
| 17 Aug H | Bangor–on–Dee | EVER SMILE | M. Pipe | 1–4F |
| 23 Aug H | Devon & Exeter | NORDIC DELIGHT | M. Pipe | 4–9F |
| 23 Aug H | Devon & Exeter | ARABIAN SULTAN | M. Pipe | 2–9F |
| 23 Aug C | Devon & Exeter | REFUTE | M. Pipe | 2–5F |
| 23 Aug C | Devon & Exeter | TAKEMETHERE | M. Pipe | 4–11F |
| 23 Aug H | Devon & Exeter | THE BLUE BOY | M. Pipe | 2–15F |
| 26 Aug C | Newton Abbot | SAGART AROON | M. Pipe | 4–5F |
| 26 Aug H | Newton Abbot | FLY THE WIND | M. Pipe | 10–11F |
| 5 Sep H | Newton Abbot | FLY THE WIND | M. Pipe | 8–13F |
| 7 Sep H | Stratford | TIMID | M. Pipe | 8–13F |
| 11 Sep H | Devon & Exeter | BANNISTER | M. Pipe | 4–6F |
| 11 Sep H | Devon & Exeter | THE BLUE BOY | M. Pipe | 1–7F |
| 18 Sep H | Devon & Exeter | CIXI | M. Pipe | 4–9F |
| 26 Sep H | Taunton | BANNISTER | M. Pipe | 2–9F |
| 28 Sep H | Stratford | MISS BOBBY BENNETT | M. Pipe | 11–4 |
| 1 Oct H | Devon & Exeter | THE BLUE BOY | M. Pipe | 2–9F |
| 1 Oct H | Devon & Exeter | ARABIAN SULTAN | M. Pipe | 2–7F |
| 2 Oct H | Cheltenham | FUNAMBULIEN | M. Pipe | 2–1F |
| 3 Oct H | Cheltenham | PLATINUM ROYALE | M. Pipe | 5–2F |
| 5 Oct H | Chepstow | MISS BOBBY BENNETT | M. Pipe | 4–6F |
| 10 Oct H | Wincanton | PADDY TEE | M. Pipe | 11–4F |
| 10 Oct H | Wincanton | TOMAHAWK | R. Holder | 7–4F |
| 12 Oct H | Worcester | SWEET DUKE | N. Twiston–Davies | 6–4F |
| 15 Oct H | Devon & Exeter | PASSED PAWN | M. Pipe | 2–5F |
| 15 Oct H | Devon & Exeter | BANNISTER | M. Pipe | 1–2F |
| 15 Oct H | Devon & Exeter | TIMID | M. Pipe | 4–6F |
| 16 Oct H | Cheltenham | SWEET GLOW | M. Pipe | 3–1 |
| 16 Oct H | Cheltenham | ARABIAN SULTAN | M. Pipe | 5–4F |
| 23 Oct H | Ascot | THE BLUE BOY | M. Pipe | 8–11F |
| 24 Oct C | Wincanton | SABIN DU LOIR | M. Pipe | 8–11F |
| 25 Oct H | Devon & Exeter | AMADORA | M. Pipe | 2–5F |
| 25 Oct H | Devon & Exeter | RING OF FORTUNE | M. Pipe | 4–7F |
| 25 Oct H | Devon & Exeter | FLYING FERRET | M. Pipe | 3–1 |
| 30 Oct H | Fontwell Park | PASSED PAWN | M. Pipe | 11–8F |
| 31 Oct H | Kempton Park | ARABIAN SULTAN | M. Pipe | 30–100F |
| 1 Nov H | Bangor–on–Dee | PETOSKU | N. Twiston–Davies | 9–4 |
| 2 Nov H | Chepstow | TOMAHAWK | R. Holder | 5–4 |
| 2 Nov H | Sandown Park | THE BLUE BOY | M. Pipe | 8–15F |
| 5 Nov C | Devon & Exeter | SABIN DU LOIR | M. Pipe | 5–4F |
| 5 Nov H | Devon & Exeter | DERISBAY | M. Pipe | 7–2 |
| 6 Nov H | Newbury | KAYFAAT | M. Pipe | 15–8F |
| 7 Nov H | Uttoxeter | GRANGE BRAKE | N. Twiston–Davies | 7–4 |
| 11 Nov C | Wolverhampton | CATCH THE CROSS | M. Pipe | 5–6F |
| 13 Nov H | Worcester | YOUNG HUSTLER | N. Twiston–Davies | 6–1 |
| 13 Nov H | Worcester | SWEET DUKE | N. Twiston–Davies | 4–7F |
| 13 Nov C | Worcester | CAPTAIN DIBBLE | N. Twiston–Davies | 4–6F |
| 13 Nov C | Worcester | PAMBER PRIORY | T. Thomson Jones | 5–1 |
| 21 Nov H | Wincanton | YOUNG HUSTLER | N. Twiston–Davies | 7–2 |
| 21 Nov H | Wincanton | WOODURATHER | M. Pipe | 9–2 |
| 22 Nov H | Leicester | PASSED PAWN | M. Pipe | 1–3F |

| | | | | |
|---|---|---|---|---|
| 22 Nov H | Newbury | PRIMITIVE SINGER | M. Pipe | 5–1 |
| 23 Nov C | Newbury | CHATAM | M. Pipe | 10–1 |
| 25 Nov H | Wolverhampton | PASSED PAWN | M. Pipe | 8–13F |
| 26 Nov C | Huntingdon | SABIN DU LOIR | M. Pipe | 4–7F |
| 28 Nov C | Warwick | CUSHINSTOWN | M. Pipe | 11–4 |
| 28 Nov H | Warwick | STAGE PLAYER | M. Pipe | 15–8F |
| 29 Nov H | Sandown Park | ARABIAN SULTAN | M. Pipe | 7–4F |
| 30 Nov C | Chepstow | ROLLING BALL | M. Pipe | 1–3F |
| 30 Nov C | Chepstow | CARVILL'S HILL | M. Pipe | 7–4F |
| 30 Nov H | Chepstow | CAPABILITY BROWN | M. Pipe | 9–4F |
| 3 Dec C | Leicester | CATCH THE CROSS | M. Pipe | 4–11F |
| 5 Dec H | Taunton | WOODURATHER | M. Pipe | 6–5F |
| 6 Dec H | Cheltenham | GRANVILLE AGAIN | M. Pipe | 4–9F |
| 6 Dec C | Cheltenham | FU'S LADY | M. Pipe | 5–4 |
| 16 Dec H | Newton Abbot | WOODURATHER | M. Pipe | 7–1 |
| 21 Dec H | Chepstow | GRANVILLE AGAIN | M. Pipe | 4–11F |
| 21 Dec C | Chepstow | CARVILL'S HILL | M. Pipe | 9–4F |
| 21 Dec C | Chepstow | CYPHRATE | M. Pipe | 11–4 |
| 28 Dec C | Newbury | CHATAM | M. Pipe | 1–2F |
| 31 Jan H | Cheltenham | SWEET GLOW | M. Pipe | 2–1F |
| 1 Jan H | Devon & Exeter | FLORET | M. Pipe | 6–4F |
| 1 Jan H | Devon & Exeter | BIGHAYIR | M. Pipe | 11–8F |
| 3 Jan C | Newton Abbot | MIINNEHOMA | M. Pipe | 6–5F |
| 6 Jan H | Wolverhampton | HALKOPOUS | M. Tompkins | 4–5F |
| 10 Jan H | Ascot | MONTEBEL | N. Twiston–Davies | 2–1 |
| 10 Jan H | Ascot | SWEET GLOW | M. Pipe | 7–4F |
| 14 Jan C | Folkestone | AMBASSADOR | M. Pipe | 4–1 |
| 15 Jan H | Ludlow | YOUNG HUSTLER | N. Twiston–Davies | 15–2 |
| 16 Jan H | Taunton | PRINCESS MOODYSHOE | M. Pipe | 8–15F |
| 17 Jan C | Kempton Park | CACHE FLEUR | M. Pipe | 5–1 |
| 18 Jan H | Haydock Park | GRANVILLE AGAIN | M. Pipe | 1–2F |
| 20 Jan C | Leicester | THE ILLYWHACKER | Mrs J. Pitman | 8–13F |
| 21 Jan H | Chepstow | BEEBOB | M. Pipe | 2–5F |
| 21 Jan C | Chepstow | MIINNEHOMA | M. Pipe | 3–1 |
| 23 Jan H | Newton Abbot | BARRY WINDOW | M. Pipe | 7–4JF |
| 29 Jan H | Windsor | HALKOPOUS | M. Tompkins | 4–9F |
| 31 Jan C | Lingfield Park | LIADETT | M. Pipe | 13–8 |
| 31 Jan C | Lingfield Park | RUN FOR FREE | M. Pipe | 1–2F |
| 1 Feb H | Sandown Park | MONTEBEL | N. Twiston–Davies | 7–1 |
| 1 Feb H | Sandown Park | FIDWAY | T. Thomson Jones | 9–2 |
| 3 Feb H | Fontwell Park | WOODURATHER | M. Pipe | 2–1JF |
| 5 Feb C | Ascot | COMBERMERE | R. Frost | 11–4 |
| 6 Feb C | Wincanton | CACHE FLEUR | M. Pipe | 7–4F |
| 6 Feb C | Wincanton | STAR'S DELIGHT | M. Pipe | 2–13F |
| 7 Feb H | Bangor–on–Dee | TOM CLAPTON | M. Pipe | 13–8F |
| 8 Feb C | Newbury | NORMAN CONQUEROR | T. Thomson Jones | 3–1 |
| 10 Feb H | Hereford | PRINCESS MOODYSHOE | M. Pipe | 2–1F |
| 11 Feb C | Newton Abbot | RUN FOR FREE | M. Pipe | 2–5F |
| 11 Feb H | Newton Abbot | SLAVI | M. Pipe | 11–8F |
| 13 Feb H | Leicester | TERAO | M. Pipe | 7–2 |
| 13 Feb H | Leicester | GOLD MEDAL | M. Pipe | 5–4F |
| 13 Feb C | Leicester | MILFORD QUAY | M. Pipe | 4–7F |

| 15 Feb C | Chepstow | RUN FOR FREE | M. Pipe | 11–8F |
|---|---|---|---|---|
| 17 Feb H | Fontwell Park | TOM CLAPTON | M. Pipe | 4–11F |
| 17 Feb H | Fontwell Park | HONEST WORD | M. Pipe | 5–4F |
| 17 Feb C | Fontwell Park | LIADETT | M. Pipe | 1–6F |
| 20 Feb H | Wincanton | FIDWAY | T. Thomson Jones | 11–4 |
| 20 Feb H | Wincanton | VAL D'AUTHIE | M. Pipe | 13–2 |
| 26 Feb C | Worcester | STAR'S DELIGHT | M. Pipe | 2–1 |
| 28 Feb C | Haydock Park | RUN FOR FREE | M. Pipe | 4–5F |
| 28 Feb H | Haydock Park | VALFINET | M. Pipe | 4–5F |
| 29 Feb H | Haydock Park | SNOWY LANE | M. Pipe | 8–1 |
| 2 Mar H | Windsor | VAL D'AUTHIE | M. Pipe | 9–2 |
| 3 Mar H | Warwick | SLAVI | M. Pipe | 13–8F |
| 5 Mar C | Wincanton | KILHALLON CASTLE | N. Twiston–Davies | 1–3F |
| 5 Mar H | Wincanton | GOLD MEDAL | M. Pipe | 4–7F |
| 6 Mar H | Market Rasen | BEAUCHAMP FIZZ | M. Pipe | 2–5F |
| 7 Mar C | Chepstow | RIVERSIDE BOY | M. Pipe | 2–7F |
| 9 Mar H | Taunton | SPRING TO GLORY | M. Pipe | 1–2F |
| 9 Mar H | Taunton | FLYING SPEED | M. Pipe | 8–11F |
| 9 Mar H | Taunton | POLLOCK | M. Pipe | 9–2 |
| 11 Mar C | Cheltenham | MIINNEHOMA | M. Pipe | 7–2 |
| 14 Mar H | Uttoxeter | TERAO | M. Pipe | 85–40 |
| 14 Mar C | Uttoxeter | RE–RELEASE | M. Pipe | 9–2 |
| 17 Mar H | Fontwell Park | NOBLE INSIGHT | M. Pipe | 10–11F |
| 18 Mar H | Worcester | RING OF FORTUNE | M. Pipe | 8–11F |
| 18 Mar H | Worcester | POLLOCK | M. Pipe | 13–8F |
| 19 Mar H | Devon & Exeter | GOLD MEDAL | M. Pipe | 1–2F |
| 19 Mar H | Devon & Exeter | DORMERS DELIGHT | M. Pipe | 6–4F |
| 20 Mar H | Newbury | FAIR CROSSING | C. Brooks | 5–2F |
| 28 Mar H | Ascot | PRAGADA | M. Pipe | 5–1 |
| 2 Apr C | Liverpool | CYPHRATE | M. Pipe | 8–1 |
| 10 Apr H | Ayr | GRANVILLE AGAIN | M. Pipe | 4–7F |
| 11 Apr C | Ayr | CAPTAIN DIBBLE | N. Twiston–Davies | 9–1 |
| 14 Apr H | Fontwell Park | DIAMOND CUT | M. Pipe | evensF |
| 21 Apr H | Chepstow | SPRING TO IT | M. Pipe | 4–1 |
| 21 Apr C | Chepstow | CYPHRATE | M. Pipe | evens |
| 21 Apr C | Chepstow | CACHE FLEUR | M. Pipe | 17–2 |
| 24 Apr H | Taunton | FLORET | M. Pipe | 9–4F |
| 24 Apr H | Taunton | GRAND FRERE | M. Pipe | 40–85F |
| 25 Apr H | Market Rasen | PRINCESS MOODYSHOE | M. Pipe | 1–3F |
| 25 Apr C | Market Rasen | CATCH THE CROSS | M. Pipe | 4–6F |
| 25 Apr H | Market Rasen | MICK'S TYCOON | M. Pipe | 2–1JF |
| 1 May H | Newton Abbot | GRAND FRERE | M. Pipe | 11–10F |
| 2 May C | Uttoxeter | PHAROAH'S LAEN | M. Pipe | 6–1 |
| 4 May H | Devon & Exeter | VALFINET | M. Pipe | 5–2 |
| 5 May H | Chepstow | GOLD MEDAL | M. Pipe | 4–5F |
| 7 May H | Uttoxeter | BIGHAYIR | M. Pipe | 4–11F |
| 9 May H | Bangor–on–Dee | DIAMOND CUT | M. Pipe | 13–8F |
| 9 May H | Warwick | FLYING SPEED | M. Pipe | 11–4F |
| 9 May C | Warwick | MILFORD QUAY | M. Pipe | 5–2F |
| 9 May C | Warwick | SKIPPING TIM | M. Pipe | 8–11F |
| 12 May H | Newton Abbot | GRAND FRERE | M. Pipe | 4–11F |
| 13 May H | Newton Abbot | GALWAY STAR | M. Pipe | 4–1 |

311

| | | | | |
|---|---|---|---|---|
| 13 May H | Newton Abbot | FLYING SPEED | M. Pipe | 1–3F |
| 16 May H | Warwick | DIAMOND CUT | M. Pipe | 4–5F |
| 22 May H | Towcester | NOBLE INSIGHT | M. Pipe | 9–4JF |
| 25 May H | Uttoxeter | NOBLE INSIGHT | M. Pipe | 8–11F |
| 25 May H | Uttoxeter | DIAMOND CUT | M. Pipe | 1–4F |
| 25 May H | Uttoxeter | SPRING TO IT | M. Pipe | 7–4F |
| 29 May H | Stratford | GALWAY STAR | M. Pipe | 85–40F |
| 30 May H | Stratford | BIGHAYIR | M. Pipe | 8–11F |
| 30 May H | Stratford | WOODLAND MINSTREL | M. Pipe | 2–1F |

## 1992–3: TOTAL WINNERS 129

| | | | | |
|---|---|---|---|---|
| 1 Aug H | Newton Abbot | TOM CLAPTON | M. Pipe | 2–9F |
| 1 Aug H | Newton Abbot | MOHANA | M. Pipe | 4–5F |
| 3 Aug H | Newton Abbot | GALWAY STAR | M. Pipe | 4–5F |
| 3 Aug H | Newton Abbot | PASSED PAWN | M. Pipe | 5–2F |
| 5 Aug H | Devon & Exeter | GOLD MEDAL | M. Pipe | 1–7F |
| 13 Aug H | Newton Abbot | SLAVI | M. Pipe | 7–4JF |
| 13 Aug C | Newton Abbot | SKIPPING TIM | M. Pipe | 5–4JF |
| 13 Aug H | Newton Abbot | MOHANA | M. Pipe | 2–9F |
| 22 Aug H | Hereford | HIGHLAND SPIRIT | M. Pipe | 3–1 |
| 29 Aug C | Hereford | FAITHFUL STAR | M. Pipe | 11–8F |
| 29 Aug H | Hereford | PARIS OF TROY | N. Twiston–Davies | 8–11F |
| 31 Aug H | Newton Abbot | MOHANA | M. Pipe | 2–17F |
| 31 Aug H | Newton Abbot | SLAVI | M. Pipe | 2–9F |
| 31 Aug C | Newton Abbot | SKIPPING TIM | M. Pipe | 10–11F |
| 31 Aug C | Newton Abbot | GALWAY STAR | M. Pipe | 2–7F |
| 2 Sep H | Newton Abbot | GRAND FRERE | M. Pipe | 10–11F |
| 2 Sep H | Newton Abbot | MYVERYGOODFRIEND | M. Pipe | 5–4F |
| 9 Sep H | Devon & Exeter | THE BLACK MONK | M. Pipe | 13–8F |
| 12 Sep H | Bangor–on–Dee | MOHANA | M. Pipe | 2–9F |
| 12 Sep H | Bangor–on–Dee | YOUNG HUSTLER | N. Twiston–Davies | 1–2F |
| 16 Sep H | Devon & Exeter | THE BLACK MONK | M. Pipe | 2–13F |
| 24 Sep H | Taunton | HIGHLAND SPIRIT | M. Pipe | 4–9F |
| 24 Sep H | Taunton | GRAND FRERE | M. Pipe | 7–4F |
| 26 Sep H | Stratford | GAELSTROM | N. Twiston–Davies | evensF |
| 30 Sep H | Cheltenham | MOHANA | M. Pipe | 10–11F |
| 30 Sep H | Cheltenham | DAGAZ | N. Twiston–Davies | 100–30F |
| 30 Sep C | Cheltenham | TRI FOLENE | M. Pipe | 5–2F |
| 1 Oct C | Cheltenham | YOUNG HUSTLER | N. Twiston–Davies | evensF |
| 3 Oct H | Chepstow | SWEET DUKE | N. Twiston–Davies | 40–85F |
| 3 Oct H | Chepstow | GAELSTROM | N. Twiston–Davies | 4–7F |
| 13 Oct C | Devon & Exeter | FAITHFUL STAR | M. Pipe | 8–11F |
| 16 Oct H | Ludlow | HIGHLAND SPIRIT | M. Pipe | 4–6F |
| 3 Nov H | Devon & Exeter | GRAND HAWK | M. Pipe | evensF |
| 3 Nov H | Devon & Exeter | HIGHLAND SPIRIT | M. Pipe | 5–4F |
| 5 Nov H | Uttoxeter | GAELSTROM | N. Twiston–Davies | 2–1 |
| 13 Nov H | Cheltenham | GAELSTROM | N. Twiston–Davies | 13–8 |
| 14 Nov H | Cheltenham | VALFINET | M. Pipe | 7–2F |
| 14 Nov H | Cheltenham | MOHANA | M. Pipe | 6–4 |
| 15 Nov C | Cheltenham | SKIPPING TIM | M. Pipe | 3–5F* |
| 17 Nov H | Warwick | GOLD MEDAL | M. Pipe | 1–2F |

| 18 Nov C | Haydock Park | RUN FOR FREE | M. Pipe | 11–8F |
|---|---|---|---|---|
| 20 Nov H | Leicester | THE BLACK MONK | M. Pipe | 8–15F |
| 20 Nov H | Leicester | GRAND HAWK | M. Pipe | 1–3F |
| 21 Nov H | Ascot | BE MY HABITAT | Miss L. Siddall | 25–1 |
| 26 Nov H | Taunton | JUST | M. Pipe | 7–1 |
| 5 Dec C | Chepstow | MILFORD QUAY | M. Pipe | 2–7F |
| 5 Dec H | Chepstow | THE BLACK MONK | M. Pipe | 1–3F |
| 7 Dec H | Warwick | ELITE REG | M. Pipe | 5–1 |
| 7 Dec C | Warwick | CATCH THE CROSS | M. Pipe | 11–2 |
| 7 Dec C | Warwick | DAKYNS BOY | N. Twiston–Davies | 11–4 |
| 10 Dec H | Haydock Park | HER HONOUR | M. Pipe | 4–11F |
| 10 Dec H | Haydock Park | BIGHAYIR | M. Pipe | 1–2F |
| 11 Dec H | Cheltenham | HAWTHORN BLAZE | M. Pipe | 10–11F |
| 11 Dec H | Cheltenham | SWEET DUKE | N. Twiston–Davies | 7–2JF |
| 15 Dec H | Folkestone | MICK'S TYCOON | M. Pipe | 8–11F |
| 16 Dec H | Devon & Exeter | THE BLACK MONK | M. Pipe | 1–3F |
| 17 Dec C | Towcester | DAKYNS BOY | N. Twiston–Davies | 11–8F |
| 18 Dec H | Uttoxeter | LORD RELIC | M. Pipe | 6–1 |
| 18 Dec H | Uttoxeter | FLYING SPEED | M. Pipe | 2–1F |
| 19 Dec C | Ascot | CYPHRATE | M. Pipe | 9–2 |
| 26 Dec C | Kempton Park | DAKYNS BOY | N. Twiston–Davies | 9–2 |
| 26 Dec H | Kempton Park | NOBLE INSIGHT | M. Pipe | 25–1 |
| 1 Jan H | Devon & Exeter | ROBINGO | M. Pipe | 1–4F |
| 1 Jan C | Devon & Exeter | OBIE'S TRAIN | M. Pipe | 7–4F |
| 2 Jan H | Newbury | LORD RELIC | M. Pipe | 15–8F |
| 4 Jan H | Newbury | HAWTHORN BLAZE | M. Pipe | 13–8F |
| 4 Jan C | Newbury | YOUNG HUSTLER | N. Twiston–Davies | 7–2 |
| 7 Jan C | Worcester | GAY RUFFIAN | M. Pipe | 8–11F |
| 7 Jan C | Worcester | CAPABILITY BROWN | M. Pipe | 13–8F |
| 9 Jan C | Sandown Park | RUSHING WILD | M. Pipe | evensF |
| 9 Jan H | Sandown Park | SAUSALITO BOY | N. Twiston–Davies | 11–2F |
| 14 Jan C | Wincanton | YOUNG HUSTLER | N. Twiston–Davies | 13–8F |
| 14 Jan H | Wincanton | BEAUTIFUL DREAM | R. Baker | 10–1 |
| 14 Jan C | Wincanton | SABIN DU LOIR | M. Pipe | 85–40 |
| 15 Jan H | Ascot | BE MY HABITAT | Miss L. Siddall | 11–2 |
| 16 Jan H | Ascot | GRAND HAWK | M. Pipe | 11–4 |
| 19 Jan H | Folkestone | COOL CLOWN | M. Pipe | 8–13F |
| 19 Jan H | Folkestone | BOOGIE BOPPER | M. Pipe | 9–2 |
| 16 Jan C | Ludlow | GAY RUFFIAN | M. Pipe | 8–13F |
| 21 Jan H | Taunton | LAND OF THE FREE | M. Pipe | 40–95F |
| 21 Jan H | Taunton | VALFINET | M. Pipe | 1–2F |
| 21 Jan C | Taunton | RIVERSIDE BOY | M. Pipe | 9–4F |
| 23 Jan C | Haydock Park | CAPABILITY BROWN | M. Pipe | 2–5F |
| 21 Jan H | Haydock Park | PRAGADA | M. Pipe | 13–2 |
| 25 Jan H | Leicester | AS DU TREFLE | M. Pipe | 4–6F |
| 26 Jan H | Chepstow | ROBINGO | M. Pipe | 1–8F |
| 26 Jan C | Chepstow | CAPABILITY BROWN | M. Pipe | 8–15F |
| 27 Jan H | Wolverhampton | VIARDOT | M. Pipe | 1–6F |
| 27 Jan H | Wolverhampton | GROVE SERENDIPITY | M. Pipe | 7–4F |
| 29 Jan C | Uttoxeter | GAY RUFFIAN | M. Pipe | 2–5F |
| 3 Feb H | Leicester | TUDOR DA SAMBA | M. Pipe | evensF |
| 3 Feb H | Leicester | ROBINGO | M. Pipe | 3–1 |

343

| | | | | |
|---|---|---|---|---|
| 4 Feb H | Towcester | COOL CLOWN | M. Pipe | 11–8F |
| 5 Feb H | Lingfield Park | DAMIER BLANC | M. Pipe | 2–9F |
| 5 Feb C | Lingfield Park | HAWTHORN BLAZE | M. Pipe | 1–8F |
| 5 Feb C | Lingfield Park | BIG BEN DUN | J. Upson | 5–4F |
| 6 Feb H | Sandown Park | VIARDOT | M. Pipe | 11–4 |
| 8 Feb C | Fontwell Park | DAGOBERTIN | M. Pipe | 4–5F |
| 10 Feb H | Ascot | SWEET GLOW | M. Pipe | 4–6F |
| 10 Feb C | Ascot | CAPABILITY BROWN | M. Pipe | 11–8 |
| 15 Feb H | Hereford | MISS EQUILLA | M. Pipe | 5–2F |
| 18 Feb H | Leicester | FAITHFUL STAR | M. Pipe | 4–6F |
| 18 Feb C | Leicester | HAWTHORN BLAZE | M. Pipe | 8–13F |
| 20 Feb C | Chepstow | MILFORD QUAY | M. Pipe | 13–8 |
| 22 Feb C | Fontwell Park | SKIPPING TIM | M. Pipe | 6–4F |
| 25 Feb H | Wincanton | VALFINET | M. Pipe | 4–5F |
| 25 Feb H | Wincanton | ZAMIRAH | N. Twiston–Davies | 4–1JF |
| 27 Feb H | Haydock Park | AS DU TREFLE | M. Pipe | 5–4F |
| 26 Feb H | Kempton Park | GRAND HAWK | M. Pipe | 5–6F |
| 2 Mar C | Taunton | CLAXTON GREENE | M. Pipe | 11–8 |
| 2 Mar H | Worcester | PHARLY STORY | M. Pipe | 5–1 |
| 4 Mar H | Warwick | LEMON'S MILL | M. Pipe | evens |
| 5 Mar H | Fontwell Park | ON THE SAUCE | M. Pipe | 7–2 |
| 5 Mar C | Fontwell Park | SKIPPING TIM | M. Pipe | 8–15F |
| 6 Mar H | Newbury | ZAMIRAH | N. Twiston–Davies | 2–1 |
| 8 Mar H | Wolverhampton | GROVE SERENDIPITY | M. Pipe | 11–4 |
| 11 Mar C | Wincanton | SARAVILLE | M. Pipe | 7–4F |
| 13 Mar H | Sandown Park | OLYMPIAN | M. Pipe | 6–4F |
| 15 Mar H | Taunton | LAND OF THE FREE | M. Pipe | 5–6F |
| 15 Mar H | Taunton | HIGHLAND SPIRIT | M. Pipe | 13–8 |
| 16 Mar H | Cheltenham | GRANVILLE AGAIN | M. Pipe | 13–2 |
| 17 Mar C | Cheltenham | YOUNG HUSTLER | N. Twiston–Davies | 9–4 |
| 17 Mar H | Cheltenham | OLYMPIAN | M. Pipe | 4–1JF |
| 20 Mar H | Chepstow | PHARLY STORY | M. Pipe | 1–4F |
| 23 Mar C | Hereford | SKIPPING TIM | M. Pipe | 4–9F |
| 24 Mar H | Devon & Exeter | TUDOR DA SAMBA | M. Pipe | 3–1 |
| 31 Mar C | Worcester | SARAVILLE | M. Pipe | 3–1 |
| 3 Mar H | Liverpool | LEMON'S MILL | M. Pipe | 1–2F |
| 7 Apr H | Ascot | SWEET DUKE | N. Twiston–Davies | 5–2F |

* 15 November at Cheltenham was the first National Hunt meeting on a Sunday: price quoted is off–course Tote dividend.

# INDEX